PENGUIN BOOKS

The Water Dancer

'Coates's rhapsodic prose spins a soaring, scorching, supernatural tale of the imagination that sets this history alight and turns it into an original work of art' Bernardine Evaristo, author of *Girl, Woman, Other*

'Urgent, ambitious, flecked with forms of wonder-working . . . This book is quite literally about the power of stories . . . Coates writes as if he's thrown his readers into a carriage and is hurtling them through the woods . . . Tonally [*The Water Dancer*] resembles Stephen King as much as it does Toni Morrison, Colson Whitehead and the touchstone African-American science-fiction writer Octavia Butler' *The New York Times*

'Ambitious, powerful, beautifully executed . . . Slavery, Coates seems to be pointing out, isn't just about the past, it is about the present as well; not only about America, but about everywhere such inequalities exist' Helon Habila, *Guardian*

'A work of both staggering imagination and rich historical significance . . . Timeless and instantly canon-worthy' *Rolling Stone*

'An electrifying, inventive novel. [Coates] loses none of his mastery for conveying complex ideas and blending a deep knowledge of American history with scintillating wordsmanship . . . His craft shows on every page. A haunting adventure story told through the tough lens of history' *Boston Globe*

Ta-Nehisi Coates is a national correspondent for the *Atlantic* and the author of the number one *New York Times* bestseller *Between the World and Me*, winner of the National Book Award, and of the acclaimed essay collection *We Were Eight Years in Power*. A MacArthur Fellow, Coates has received the National Magazine Award, the Hillman Prize for Opinion and Analysis Journalism and the George Polk Award for his *Atlantic* cover story 'The Case for Reparations'. He lives in New York with his wife and son.

The Water Dancer

· A NOVEL ·

TA-NEHISI COATES

PENGUIN BOOKS

PENGUIN BOOKS

UK | USA | Canada | Ireland | Australia
India | New Zealand | South Africa

Penguin Books is part of the Penguin Random House group of companies
whose addresses can be found at global.penguinrandomhouse.com.

First published in the United States of America by One World 2019
First published in Great Britain by Hamish Hamilton 2019
Published in Penguin Books 2020
001

Printed and bound in Great Britain by Clays Ltd, Elcograf S.p.A.

A CIP catalogue record for this book is available from the British Library

ISBN: 978–0–241–98251–8

www.greenpenguin.co.uk

MIX
Paper from
responsible sources
FSC® C018179

Penguin Random House is committed to a
sustainable future for our business, our readers
and our planet. This book is made from Forest
Stewardship Council® certified paper.

For Chana

I.

My part has been to tell the story of the slave.
The story of the master never wanted for nar-
rators.

FREDERICK DOUGLASS

· I ·

A ND I COULD ONLY have seen her there on the stone bridge, a dancer wreathed in ghostly blue, because that was the way they would have taken her back when I was young, back when the Virginia earth was still red as brick and red with life, and though there were other bridges spanning the river Goose, they would have bound her and brought her across this one, because this was the bridge that fed into the turnpike that twisted its way through the green hills and down the valley before bending in one direction, and that direction was south.

I had always avoided that bridge, for it was stained with the remembrance of the mothers, uncles, and cousins gone Natchez-way. But knowing now the awesome power of memory, how it can open a blue door from one world to another, how it can move us from mountains to meadows, from green woods to fields caked in snow, knowing now that memory can fold the land like cloth, and knowing, too, how I had pushed my memory of her into the "down there" of my mind, how I forgot, but did not forget, I know now that this story, this Conduction, had to begin there on

3

that fantastic bridge between the land of the living and the land of the lost.

And she was patting juba on the bridge, an earthen jar on her head, a great mist rising from the river below nipping at her bare heels, which pounded the cobblestones, causing her necklace of shells to shake. The earthen jar did not move; it seemed almost a part of her, so that no matter her high knees, no matter her dips and bends, her splaying arms, the jar stayed fixed on her head like a crown. And seeing this incredible feat, I knew that the woman patting juba, wreathed in ghostly blue, was my mother.

No one else saw her—not Maynard, who was then in the back of the new Millennium chaise, not the fancy girl who held him rapt with her wiles, and, most strange, not the horse, though I had been told that horses had a nose for things that stray out from other worlds and stumble into ours. No, only I saw her from the driver's seat of the chaise, and she was just as they'd described her, just as they'd said she'd been in the olden days when she would leap into a circle of all my people—Aunt Emma, Young P, Honas, and Uncle John—and they would clap, pound their chests, and slap their knees, urging her on in double time, and she would stomp the dirt floor hard, as if crushing a crawling thing under her heel, and bend at the hips and bow, then twist and wind her bent knees in union with her hands, the earthen jar still on her head. My mother was the best dancer at Lockless, that is what they told me, and I remembered this because she'd gifted me with none of it, but more I remembered because it was dancing that brought her to the attention of my father, and thus had brought me to be. And more than that, I remembered because I remembered everything— everything, it seemed, except her.

It was autumn now, the season when the races came south. That afternoon Maynard had scored on a long-shot thoroughbred, and thought this might, at last, win the esteem of Virginia Quality he sought. But when he made the circuit around the great town square, leaning back, way back in the chaise and grinning large,

4

the men of society turned their backs to him and puffed on their cigars. There were no salutes. He was what he would always be—Maynard the Goof, Maynard the Lame, Maynard the Fool, the rotten apple who'd fallen many miles from the tree. He fumed and had me drive to the old house at the edge of our town, Starfall, where he purchased himself a night with a fancy, and had the bright notion to bring her back to the big house at Lockless, and, most fatefully, in a sudden bout of shame, insisted on leaving the back way out of town, down Dumb Silk Road, until it connected to that old turnpike, which led us back to the bank of the river Goose.

A cold steady rain fell as I drove, the water dripping down from the brim of my hat, puddling on my trousers. I could hear Maynard in the back, with all his games, putting his carnal boasts upon the fancy. I was pushing the horse as hard as I could, because all I wanted was to be home and free of Maynard's voice, though I could never, in this life, be free of him. Maynard who held my chain. Maynard, my brother who was made my master. And I was trying all I could to not hear, searching for distraction—memories of corn-shucking or young games of blind man's bluff. What I remember is how those distractions never came, but instead there was a sudden silence, erasing not just Maynard's voice, but all the small sounds of the world around. And now, peering into the pigeonhole of my mind, what I found were remembrances of the lost—men holding strong on watch-night, and women taking their last tour of the apple orchards, spinsters remanding their own gardens to others, old codgers cursing the great house of Lockless. Legions of the lost, brought across that baleful bridge, legions embodied in my dancing mother.

I yanked at the reins but it was too late. We barreled right through and what happened next shook forever my sense of a cosmic order. But I was there and saw it happen, and have since seen a great many things that expose the ends of our knowledge and how much more lies beyond it.

The road beneath the wheels disappeared, and the whole of the bridge fell away, and for a moment I felt myself floating on, or maybe in, the blue light. And it was warm there, and I remember that brief warmth because just as suddenly as I floated out, I was in the water, under the water, and even as I tell you this now, I feel myself back there again, in the icy bite of that river Goose, the water rushing into me, and that particular burning agony that comes only to the drowning.

There is no sensation like drowning, because the feeling is not merely the agony, but a bewilderment at so alien a circumstance. The mind believes that there should be air, since there is always air to be had, and the urge to breathe is such a matter of instinct that it requires a kind of focus to belay the order. Had I leapt from the bridge myself, I could have accounted for my new situation. Had I even fallen over the side, I would have understood, if only because this would have been imaginable. But it was as though I had been shoved out of a window right into the depths of the river. There was no warning. I kept trying to breathe. I remember crying out for breath and more I remember the agony of the answer, the agony of water rushing into me, and how I answered that agony by heaving, which only invited more water.

But somehow I steadied my thoughts, somehow I came to understand that all my thrashing could only but hasten my demise. And with that accomplished, I noted that there was light in one direction and darkness in another and deduced that the dark was the depths and the light was not. I whipped my legs behind me, and stretched out my arms toward the light, pulling the water until, at last, coughing, retching, I surfaced.

And when I came up, breaking through dark water and into the diorama of the world—storm clouds hung by unseen thread, a red sun pinned low against them, and beneath that sun, hills dusted with grass—I looked back at the stone bridge, which must have been, my God, a half mile away.

The bridge seemed to be almost racing away from me, because

the current pulled me along and when I angled myself to swim toward the shore it was that current still, or perhaps some unseen eddy beneath, pulling me downriver. There was no sign of the woman whose time Maynard had so thoughtlessly purchased. But whatever thoughts I had on her behalf were broken by Maynard making himself known, as he had so often, with hue and cry, determined to go out of this world in the selfsame manner that he'd passed through it. He was close by, pulled by the same current. He thrashed in the current, yelled, treaded a bit, and then disappeared under, only to reappear again seconds later, yelling, half treading, thrashing.

"Help me, Hi!"

There I was, my own life dangling over the black pit, and now being called to save another. I had, on many occasions, tried to teach Maynard to swim, and he took to this instruction as he took to all instruction, careless and remiss at the labor, then sore and bigoted when this negligence bore no fruit. I can now say that slavery murdered him, that slavery made a child of him, and now, dropped into a world where slavery held no sway, Maynard was dead the minute he touched water. I had always been his protection. It was I, only by good humor, and debasement, who had kept Charles Lee from shooting him; and it was I, with special appeal to our father, who'd kept him countless times from wrath; and it was I who clothed him every morning; and I who put him to bed every night; and it was I who now was tired, in both body and soul; and it was I, out there, wrestling against the pull of the current, against the fantastic events that had deposited me there, and now wrestling with the demand that I, once again, save another, when I could not even conjure the energy to save myself.

"Help me!" he yelled again, and then he cried out, "Please!" He said it like the child he always was, begging. And I noted, however uncharitably, even there in the Goose facing my own death, that I had never before recalled him speaking in a manner that reflected the true nature of our positions.

"Please!"

"I can't," I yelled over the water. "We are under the ox!"

With that admission of imminent death, memories of my life descended on me unbidden, and now the same blue light I'd seen on the bridge returned and enveloped me again. I thought back to Lockless, and all my loved ones, and right there in the middle of the misty river I saw Thena, on wash day, an old woman heaving the large pots of steaming water and, with the last of her powers, threshing the dripping garments until they were damp and her hands were raw. And I saw Sophia in her gloves and bonnet, like a woman of mastery, because that is what her task required of her, and I watched, as I had so many times before, as she hiked the bell of her dress to her ankles and walked down a back-path to see the man who held her chained. I felt my limbs submit, and the mystery and confusion of the events that had deposited me into the depths nagged me no longer, and this time, when I went under, there was no burning, no straining for breath. I felt weightless, so that even as I sank into the river, I felt myself rising into something else. The water fell away from me and I was alone in a warm blue pocket with the river outside and around me. And I knew then that I was, at last, going to my reward.

My mind journeyed further back still, to those who'd been carried out of this Virginia, out Natchez-way, and I wondered how many of them might well have gone farther still, far enough to greet me in that next world I now approached. And I saw my aunt Emma, who worked the kitchen all those years, walking past with a tray of ginger cookies for all the assembled Walkers, though none for her or any of her kin. Perhaps my mother would be there, and then, at the speed of thought, I saw her flittering, before my eyes, water dancing in the ring. And thinking of all of this, of all the stories, I was at peace, and pleased even, to rise into the darkness, to fall into the light. There was peace in that blue light, more peace than sleep itself, and more than that, there was freedom, and I knew that the elders had not lied, that there really was a home-place of our own, a life beyond the Task, where every moment is as daybreak over mountains. And so great was this freedom that I became aware of a nagging weight that I had always taken as unchangeable, a weight that now proposed to follow me into the forever. I turned, and in my wake, I saw the weight, and the weight was my brother, howling, thrashing, screaming, pleading for his life.

All my life, I had been subject to his whims. I was his right arm and thus had no arm of my own. But that was all over now. Because I was rising, rising out of that world of the Quality and the Tasked. My last sight of Maynard was of him thrashing in the water and grappling after what he could no longer hold, until he began to blur before me, like light rippling on a wave, and his cries diminished beneath the loud nothing all around me. And then he was gone. I would like to say that I mourned right then, or took some manner of note. But I did not. I was headed to my ending. He was headed to his.

The apparitions now steadied before me, and I focused on my mother, who was no longer dancing, but instead kneeling before a boy. And she put her hand upon the boy's cheek, and she kissed him on his head, and she placed the shell necklace in his hand, and closed his hand around the thing, and then she stood, with both hands over her mouth, and she turned and walked off into the distance and the boy stood there watching, and then cried after her, and then followed after her, and then ran after her, and then fell as he ran, and lay there crying into his arms, and then stood again and turned, this time toward me, and walking over, he opened his hand and offered the necklace, and I saw, at long last, my reward.

· 2 ·

ALL MY LIFE I had wanted to get out. I was unoriginal in this—all the Tasked felt the same. But, separate from them, separate from all of Lockless, I possessed the means.

I was a strange child. I talked before I walked, though I never talked much, because more than anything, I watched and remembered. I would hear others speak, but I did not so much hear them as see them, their words taking form before me as pictures, chains of colors, lines, textures, and shapes that I could store inside of me. And it was my gift to, at a moment's beckoning, retrieve the images and translate them back into the exact words with which they had been conjured.

By the time I was five, I could, having only heard it once, holler out a work song, its calls and responses, and to that add my own improvisations, all to the wide-eyed delight of my elders. I had individual names for individual beasts, marked by where I had seen them, the time of day, and what the animal was doing, so that one deer was Grass in Spring and another Broken Oak Branch, and so it was with the pack of dogs that the older ones so often warned me of, but they were not a pack to me, but each singular, singular even if I never saw them again, singular as any lady or gentleman whom I never saw again, for I remembered them too.

And there was never a need to tell me any story twice, because if you told me that Hank Powers cried for three hours when his daughter was born, I remembered, and if you told me that Lucille Simms made a new dress out of her mother's work clothes for Christmas, I remembered, and if you spoke of that time Johnny Blackwell pulled a knife on his brother, I remembered, and if you told me all the ancestors of Horace Collins, and where in Elm County they were born, I remembered, and if Jane Jackson recited all her generations, her mother, her mother's mother, and every mother stretching all the way to the edge of the Atlantic, I remembered. So it was natural that I recall, even in the maw of the Goose, even after the bridge fell away and I stared down my own doom, that this was not my first pilgrimage to the blue door.

It had happened before. It had happened when I was nine years old, the day after my mother was taken and sold. I awoke that cold winter morning knowing she was gone as a fact. But I had no pictures, no memory, of any goodbye, indeed no pictures of her at all. Instead I recalled my mother in the secondhand, so that I was sure that she had been taken, in the same way that I was sure that there were lions in Africa, though I had never seen one. I searched for a fully fleshed memory, and found only scraps. Screams. Pleading—someone pleading with me. The strong smell of horses. And in the haze of it all, an image flickering in and out of focus: a long trough of water. I was terrified, not simply because I had lost my mother, but because I was a boy who remembered all his yesterdays in the crispest colors, and textures so rich I could drink them. And there I was, awakening with a start to nothing but ephemera, shadows, and screams.

I must get out. This also came to me as a feeling more than a thought. There was an ache, a breach, a stripping of me that I knew I had been helpless to prevent. My mother was gone and I must follow. So that winter morning, I put on my osnaburg shirt and pants, then slipped my arms into my black coat and tied up my brogans. I walked out onto the Street, the common area between two long rows of gabled log cabins where those of us who tasked in the tobacco field made our homes. An icy wind cut up the dusty ground between the quarters and slashed at my face. It was a Sunday, two weeks after Holiday, in the small hours just before sunrise. In the moonlight, I could see smoke rising up in white puffs out of the cabin chimneys, and behind the cabins, trees black and bare, swaying drunkenly in the whistling wind. Were it summer, the Street would have, even at that hour, been alive with garden trade—cabbages and carrots dug up, chicken eggs collected to be bartered, or even taken up to the main house and sold. Lem and the older boys would have been out there, with fishing poles on their shoulders, smiling, waving to me and yelling, "Come on, Hi!" as they headed for the Goose. I would have seen Arabella there with her brother Jack, sleepy-eyed but soon to be plucking marbles in a dirt ring they'd drawn up between two cabins. And Thena, the meanest woman on the Street, might have been sweeping her front yard, beating out an old rug, or rolling her eyes and sucking her teeth at someone's foolishness. But it was winter in Virginia, and all in possession of good sense were huddled inside by the fires. So when I walked outside, there was no one on the Street, no one peering out the door of their quarters, no one to grab my arm, swat my bottom twice, and yell, "Hi, this cold bout to be the death of you! And where is your momma, boy?"

I walked up the winding path and into the dark woods. I stopped just out of view of Boss Harlan's cabin. Was he part of this? He was the enforcer of Lockless, a low white who meted out "correction" when it was deemed appropriate. Boss Harlan was the physical hand of slavery, presiding over the fields while his wife, Desi, ruled the house. But when I sorted through the scraps of memory, I did not find Boss Harlan among them. I could see the water trough. I could smell the horses. I had to get to the stables. I was certain that something I could not name awaited me there, something crucial about my mother, some secret path, perhaps, that would send me to her. Walking into those woods with the winter wind cutting through me, I heard again the seemingly aimless voices, now multiplying around me—and in my mind turned again to a vision: the trough of water.

And then I was running, moving as fast as my short legs could carry me. I had to get to the stables. My whole world seemed to hinge upon it. I approached the white wooden doors and pushed up the bolt lock until the doors sprang open and knocked me to the dirt. Rising quickly and rushing inside, I found the elements of my morning vision scattered there before me—horses and the long trough of water. I came close to each of the horses and looked them in the eyes. The horses only stared stupidly back. I walked over to the trough of water and stared down into the inky blackness. The voices returned. Someone pleading with me. And now visions formed in the blackness of the water. I saw the Tasked who'd once lived down on the Street but were now lost to me. A blue mist began rising up out of the inky darkness, illuminated from within by some source. I felt the light pulling me, pulling me into the trough. And then I looked around me and saw the stable fading away, as sure as the bridge did all those years later, and I thought that this was it, the meaning of the dream: a secret path that would deliver me from Lockless to reunite me with my mother. But when the blue light cleared, I saw not my mother but a wooden gabled ceiling, which I recognized as the ceiling of the cabin I had departed only minutes before.

I was on the floor, on my back. I tried to stand, but my arms and legs felt weighted and chained. I managed to rise up and stumble over to the rope bed I shared with my mother. The sharp smell of her was still in our room, on our bed, and I tried to follow that scent down the alleys of my mind, but while all the twists and turns that marked my short life were clear before me, my mother appeared only as fog and smoke. I tried to recall her face, and when it did not come, I thought of her arms, her hands, but there was only smoke, and when I searched to remember her corrections, her affections, I found only smoke. She'd gone from that warm quilt of memory to the cold library of fact.

I slept. And when I awoke, late that same afternoon, I awoke full in the knowledge that I was alone. I have now seen a great many children in the same place I found myself in that day, orphans, feeling themselves abandoned and left open before all the elements of the world, and I have seen how some explode in tantrum while others walk in an almost stupor, how some cry for days and others move with an uncanny focus, addressing only the moment before them. Some part of them has died, and like surgeons, they know that amputation must be immediate. So that was me, that Sunday afternoon, when I rose, still in those same brogans and osnaburg, and wandered out again, this time finding my way to the storehouse where I would collect the weekly peck of corn and pound of pork deeded to my family. I brought them back to my home, but I did not stay. Instead, I retrieved my marbles, my only possession besides the sack of victuals and the clothes I was wearing, and walked back out until I reached the last building on the Street, a large cabin set back from the others. Thena's home.

The Street was a communal place but Thena kept to herself, never joining in on the gossip, small talk, or singing. She worked the tobacco and then she went home. Her habit was to scowl at us children for playing our rowdy games within earshot or sometimes to emerge almost whimsically from her cabin, wild-eyed, swinging her broom at us. For anyone else, this would have brought conflict of some sort or the other. But I had heard that Thena had not always been this way, that in another life, one lived right here on the Street, she was a mother not just to five children of her own but to all the children of the Street.

That was another age, one I did not remember. But I knew that her children were gone. What was I thinking facing her door, holding my sack of pork and cornmeal? Surely there were others who would have taken me in, others who actually enjoyed the company of children. But there was just one on the Street who I knew understood the suffering that was just then compounding in me. Even when she swung her broom at us, I sensed the depth of that loss, her pain, a rage that she, unlike the rest of us, refused to secret away, and I found that rage to be true and correct. She was not the meanest woman at Lockless, but the most honest.

I knocked on the door and, receiving no answer and now feeling the cold, I pushed my way in. I left the ration just inside the door, then climbed the ladder to the loft, where I laid myself, looking down, waiting for her to return. She walked in a few minutes later, looked up, and gave me her familiar scowl. But then she walked over to the fireplace, started it up, and pulled a pan down from the mantel above, and within minutes the familiar smell of pork and ash-cake filled the cabin. She looked up at me once more and said, "You got to come down if you want to eat."

I lived with Thena for a year and a half before I got to the precise root of her rage. On a warm summer night I was awakened from the small pallet I maintained up in the loft of the cabin by loud moaning. It was Thena, talking in her sleep. "It's fine, John. It's fine." And she spoke this with such clarity that when I first heard it, I thought she was speaking to someone present. But when I looked down from the loft, I saw that she was still sleeping. I had already gotten into the habit of leaving Thena to her ghosts, but the more she spoke, the more it seemed to me that this time she was in distress. I climbed down to rouse her. As I got closer, I heard her still moaning and talking: "It's fine, fine, I told you. Fine, John." I reached out and pulled on her shoulder, shaking it until she awoke with a start.

She looked up at me, and then around the dark cabin, uncertain of where she was. Then her eyes narrowed and focused again on me. I had for the past year and a half been mostly immune to Thena's rages. Indeed, much to the relief of the Street, the rages had diminished, as though maybe my presence had begun to heal an old wound. This was incorrect and I knew it as soon as I saw her focusing on me.

"Hell you doing here!" she said. "Little rugrat, get the hell out of here! Get the hell out!" I scrambled outside and saw that it was almost dawn. The yellow spray of sun would soon be peeking over the trees. I walked back to the old cabin I'd shared with my mother and sat on the steps, until it was time for the Task.

I was eleven by then. I was a small boy for my age, but no exception was made, and I was put to work like a man. I daubed and chinked the cabins. I hoed the fields in summer and hung leaves like all the rest in the fall. I trapped and fished. I tended the garden, even after my mother was gone. But on a hot day like the one that was coming, I was sent with the other children to bring water to the tasking folk in the fields. So all that day I took my place in a relay of children that extended from the well near the main house of the estate down and out to the tobacco fields. When the bell rang and everyone repaired for supper, I did not return to Thena's. Instead I took up a safe vantage point in the woods and watched. The Street was by then lively but my eye was on Thena's cabin. Every twenty minutes or so, I saw her walk out and look both ways as though expecting a guest and then walk back inside. When I finally came back to the cabin, it was late and I found her sitting on a chair by the bed. I knew by the two empty bowls sitting on the mantel that she had not yet eaten.

We had supper, and just as it was time to retire, she turned to me and said in a cracked whisper, "John—Big John—was my husband. He died. Fever. I think you should know that. I think you should understand some things bout me, bout you, bout this place."

She paused here and looked into the fireplace, where the last of the cooking embers were dying.

"I try not to fret it much. Death is as natural as anything, more natural than this place. But the death that come out of *this* death, out of my Big John, wasn't nothing natural about that. It was murder."

The din and racket of the Street had died down and there was only now the low and rhythmic whining of the insects of the night. Our door was open to allow for an easy July breeze. Thena pulled her pipe from over the fireplace, lit it, and began to puff.

"Big John was the driver. You know what that mean, don't you?"

"Mean he was boss of the fields down here."

"Yes, he was," she said. "Was chosen to superintend all the tobacco teams. Big John wasn't no driver 'cause he was the meanest like Harlan. He was a driver because he was the wisest—wiser than any of them whites, and their whole lives depended on him. Them fields, they ain't just fields, Hi. They the heart of the thing. You been around. You seen this place and all its fancy things, you know what they have."

I did. Lockless was massive, thousands of acres carved out of the mountains. I loved to steal away time from the fields to explore these acres, and what I'd found were orchards flush with golden peaches, wheat fields waving in the summer wind, cornstalks crowned with yellow silken hope, a dairy, an iron-works, a carpentry house, an ice-house, gardens filled with lilacs and lilies of the valley, all of it engineered in exact geometry, in resplendent symmetry, the math of which I was too young to comprehend.

"Nice, ain't it?" Thena said. "But all of it start with what's right down here in the fields, and with what's right here in this pipe. Master of it all was my man Big John. Weren't nobody who knew more about the ways and knacks of the golden leaf than my man. He could tell you the best way to dig out the horn-worms, which leaves you s'pose to sucker and which you might like to leave be. So that gave him a kind of a favor with the whites. Was how I got this big house here.

"And we was good about it. Gave our extra helping of victuals to those who did not have. It was John who insisted on it."

She stopped to puff again on her pipe. I watched as lightning bugs drifted in, glowing yellow against the shadows.

"I loved that man, but he died, and after that, it all went bad. First terrible harvest I remember came after John was gone. Then there was another. Then another. Folks'll tell you even John couldn't have saved us. It was the land, cursing these whites for what they done to it, for how they done stripped it down. Still some red Virginia left, but soon it all gon be Virginia sand. And they know it. So it's been hell since John been gone. Hell on me. Hell on you.

"I think of your aunt Emma. I think of your momma. I am remembered to them both—Rose and Emma. Why, they were a pair. Loved each other. Loved to dance. I am remembered to them, I say. And though it hurt sometime, you cannot forget, Hi. You cannot forget."

I looked on dumbly as she spoke, as the full weight of having already forgotten now came upon me.

"I know I will not forget my babies," Thena said. "They took all five of 'em down to the racetrack, and put 'em in a lot with the rest, and sold 'em, sure as they sell these hogsheads of tobacco."

Now Thena bowed her head, and brought her hands to her brow. When she looked back up at me, I saw the tears streaking down her cheek.

"When it happened, I spent most of my time cursing John, for it was my figuring that if John had lived, my babies would still be here with me. It was not just his particular knowledge, it was my sense that John would have done what I could not find the courage to do—he would have stopped them.

"You know how I am. You done heard how they talk about me but you also know something is broken in old Thena, and when I seen you up in that loft, I had a feeling that same something was broken in you. And you had chosen me, for whatever your young reasoning, you had picked me out."

She stood now and began her nightly routine of putting her home in order. I climbed up into the loft.

"Hi," she called out. I looked back to see her watching me.

"Yes, ma'am," I said.

"I can't be your mother. I can't be Rose. She was a beautiful woman, with the kindest heart. I liked her and I do not like many anymore. She did not gossip and she kept to herself. I can't be what she was to you. But you have chosen me, I understand that. I want you to know that I understand."

I stayed up late that night peering up at the rafters, thinking on Thena's words. *A beautiful woman, the kindest heart, did not gossip, kept to herself.* I added this to the memories of her I'd collected from the people on the Street. Thena could not know how much I needed those small jigsaws of my mother, which together, over the years, I forged into a portrait of the woman who lived in dreams, like Big John, but only as smoke.

And what of my father? What of the master of Lockless? I knew very early who he was, for my mother had made no secret of the fact, nor did he. From time to time, I would see him on horseback making his tour of the property, and when his eyes met mine he would pause and tip his hat to me. I knew he had sold my mother, for Thena never ceased to remind me of the fact. But I was a boy, seeing in him what boys can't help but see in their fathers—a mold in which their own manhood might be cast. And more, I was just then beginning to understand the great valley separating the Quality and the Tasked—that the Tasked, hunched low in the fields, carrying the tobacco from hillock to hogshead, led backbreaking lives and that the Quality who lived in the house high above, the seat of Lockless, did not. And knowing this, it was natural that I look to my father, for in him, I saw an emblem of another life—one of splendor and regale. And I knew I had a brother up there, a boy who luxuriated while I labored, and I wondered what right he had to his life of idle pursuit, and what law deeded me to the Task. I needed only some method to elevate my standing, to place me at some post where I might show my own quality. This was my feeling that Sunday when my father made his fateful appearance on the Street.

Thena was in a better mood than normal, sitting out on the stoop, not scowling or running off any of the younger children when they scampered past. I was in back of the quarter, between the fields and the Street, calling out a song:

> Oh Lord, trouble so hard
> Oh Lord, trouble so hard
> Nobody know my troubles but my God
> Nobody know nothing but my God

I went on for verse after verse, taking the song from trouble to labor to trouble to hope to trouble to freedom. When I sang the call, I changed my voice to the sound of the lead man in the field, bold and exaggerated. When I sang the response, I took on the voices of the people around me, mimicking them one by one. They were delighted, these elders, and their delight grew as the song extended, verse after verse, till I'd had a chance to mimic them all. But that day, I was not watching the elders. I was watching the white man seated atop the Tennessee Pacer, his hat pulled low, who rode up smiling his approval at my performance. It was my father. He removed his hat, and took a handkerchief from his pocket and mopped his brow. Then he put the hat back on, and reached into his pocket, pulled out something, and flicked it toward me, and I, never taking my eye off of him, caught it with one hand. I stood there for a long moment, locking eyes with him. I could feel a tension behind me: the elders, now afraid that my impudence might bring Harlan's wrath. But my father just kept smiling, then nodded at me and rode off.

The tension eased and I went back to Thena's cabin, climbed up to my loft space. I pulled from my pocket the coin my father flipped to me just before he'd ridden off, and I saw that it was copper, with rough uneven edges and a picture of a white man on the front, and on the back there was a goat. Up in that loft, I fingered the rough edges, feeling that I had found my method, my token, my ticket out of the fields and off the Street.

And it happened that next day, after our supper. I peered down from the loft to see Desi and Boss Harlan talking to Thena in low tones. I was afraid for her. I had never seen Desi or Harlan wrathy, but the stories I'd heard were enough. It was said that Boss Harlan once shot a man for using the wrong hoe and Desi once beat a girl in the dairy with a carriage whip. I looked down and saw Thena looking at the floor, nodding occasionally. When Desi and Harlan left, Thena called me down.

In silence she walked me out onto the fields, where no one would eavesdrop. It was now late in the evening. I felt the stiff air of summer releasing into the night. I was all anticipation, feeling I knew what was coming, and when I heard the night sounds of nature all around us like a chorus, I believed they were singing to a grand future.

"Hiram, I know how much you see. And I know that even though we all have to handle the brutal ways of this world, you have handled them better than some of your elders. But it's bout to get more brutal," she said.

"Yes, ma'am."

"White folks come down to say your days in the fields is over, that you going up top. But they ain't your family, Hiram, I want you to see that. You cannot forget yourself up there, and we cannot forget each other. They calling us up, now, you hear? *Us*. That trick of yours, and I seen it, we all seen it, it got me too. I am to come up and tend to you, and you might think you have saved me

21

from something, but what you have really done is put me right under their eye.

"We have our own world down here—our own ways of being and talking and laughing, even if you don't see me doing much of neither. But I got a choice down here. And it ain't great, but it is ours. Up there, with them right over you . . . well, it's different.

"You gon have to watch yourself, son. Be careful. Remember like I told you. They ain't your family, boy. I am more your mother standing right here now than that white man on that horse is your father."

She was trying to tell me, trying to warn me of what was coming. But my gift was memory, not wisdom. And the next day when Roscoe, my father's jowly, affable butler, came for us, I had to work hard to hide away all my excitement. We walked up from the tobacco fields, past the field-hands, their songs ringing out:

> When you get to heaven, say you remember me
> Remember me and my fallen soul
> Remember my poor and fallen soul

And then we were past the wheat fields and crossing the green lawn, and through the flower garden, until I saw, elevated on a small hill, the big house of Lockless shining like the sun itself. When we were closer, I took in the stone columns, the portico, and the fanlight over the entrance. It was all so magnificent. This house, I felt with a sudden shiver, belonged to me. It was mine by blood. I was correct, but not in the sense I thought.

Roscoe glanced back at me, grimacing I think, seeing that shine in my eyes. "We go this way," he said. He led us away from the door, to the base of the small hill on which the house stood, and at that base, I saw the entryway to a tunnel. As we walked through, other tasking folk emerged from side rooms to greet Thena and Roscoe as they streamed past into smaller adjoining tunnels. We were in a warren, an underworld beneath the great house.

We stopped in front of one of the side rooms and it was clear that here was my place. There was a bed, a table, a washbasin, a vase, and a cloth. There was no loft. There was no under-space. There was no window. Roscoe lingered at the door with me by his side as Thena put down her bag of things. She didn't take her eyes off of me and I could feel her words repeating in that stare—*They ain't your family*. But after a moment her stare broke and all she said was, "Might as well take him up." Roscoe put his hand on my shoulder and led me back into the Warrens and up a set of stairs, until we faced a wall. Roscoe touched something I did not see and the wall slid away and we walked out from the darkness into a wide room flooded with light and filled with books.

I stood in the doorway, my senses overwhelmed: the flooding light in the room, the smell of turpentine, the gold and blue Persian rugs, the shine of the wood floors beneath them, but the books were what held my eyes. I had seen books before—there were always one or two of us down on the Street who could read and who kept old journals or songbooks in their cabins—but never so many, shelves from floor to ceiling on every wall. I did my best not to stare. I knew what happened to coloreds who were too curious about the world beyond Virginia.

Diverting my eyes from the books, I saw my father, dressed down to his waistcoat and shirtsleeves, seated in one corner of the room, watching me and watching Roscoe. Turning my head, I saw in the other corner a boy, older than me, and white. By some trick of the blood, I knew at once that this was my brother. My father waved his hand lightly, effortlessly, and I saw that Roscoe recognized in this motion that he must take his leave. And so he turned, as though executing a military maneuver, and disappeared back behind the sliding wall. And I was there alone with my father, Howell Walker, and with my brother, and they both regarded me in curious silence. I reached into my pocket and found the copper coin and fingered its rough and uneven edges.

· 3 ·

M Y ASSIGNMENT CAME DOWN from my father to Desi to
Thena to me—make myself useful. So each day I would
rise before the sun, as did all the Tasked, and walk about the house,
fitting in where I could—raising the kitchen fires for Ella, the head
cook, fetching the milk from the dairy, retrieving the trays after
breakfast—or labor outside with Roscoe, washing and grooming
the horses, or in the apple orchard with Pete, grafting saplings.
There was always work to be done, for while the needs of the
house had not diminished, the numbers of the Tasked had, and
that was my first inkling that even here in the house the Tasked
could be sent Natchez-way. I worked energetically, more still
when, from time to time, I would catch my father glancing my
way with a thin sidelong smile. He'd found a use for me.

It was autumn of my thirteenth year, four months after I took
up residence in the main house. My father had called for a social to
celebrate the season. All day a kind of private fatigue blanketed
those who tasked in the house. Early that morning I brought the

24

eggs up to Ella, whose large and welcoming smile I'd come to regard as a natural portion of the morning. But nature was beside itself this day, so that when I came upon Ella with my wicker basket of eggs, she only shook her head and motioned for me to put the eggs on the table where Pete stood picking through a bushel of apples.

Ella sidled next to Pete, cracked and separated six eggs, and then beat the whites. She spoke just above a whisper and would not give full vent to her feelings. "They don't think about nothing and nobody," Ella said. "It's wrong, Pete. And you know it's wrong."

"It's all right, Ella," he said. "It's worse things to be wrathy about."

"Ain't wrathy. Just want some consideration. Is that too much? Was supposed to be small supper tonight. How it spread out to the whole county?"

"You know what it is," Pete said. "You know what is going on with them."

"No, I don't," Ella said. "Hi, get me that rolling pin. And get that fire going, will you?"

"You got eyes, you know. It ain't like it was. The gold leaf ain't what it was. All the old families gone west. Tennessee. Baton Rouge. Natchez. Them kinda places. Ain't too many left. And those that's still here feel a tightness between them. They holding on. Small supper bigger to them now. Don't none of 'em know who moving out next. This goodbye might be they last."

Now Ella laughed quietly to herself but it felt boisterous and mocking, wide enough that I wanted to join her though there was nothing funny going on. "Hi, that thing there, baby," she said, motioning to the shelves. When she called me baby, I got warm inside. I left the fire and took the dough cutter off the shelf and brought it over. Ella was still laughing to herself. She looked up and gave that large and welcoming smile.

Then the smile shrank and she looked dead at me, looked

through me almost, and then turned to Pete, "I don't care nothing for they feelings. This boy here know more about goodbye than all of them put together. And he ain't nothing but a boy."

All that day there was the same tension among the Tasked as I'd seen in Ella. But neither my father nor Desi knew or cared, and that evening when the carriages and chaises began arriving, all of us were smiles and pleasantries. I was assigned to the waitstaff. By then I had learned how to wash and groom myself until I shined, how to hold the silver tray in my left hand and serve with my right, how to disappear into the corners, emerging to scrape away bread and then fading again back into the shadows. When dinner adjourned, we cleared away the dishes and stood in the cherry-red drawing room and waited at attention while the guests all settled into the room's deep chairs and divans.

I looked across the room, meeting eyes with the three others charged with attending to whatever need struck our guests. Then I watched the guests themselves, trying to anticipate whatever need might strike them. I took note of Maynard's tutor, Mr. Fields, a young man, overly serious with deep-set eyes, drawn back in his chair. It was hard to stay in the moment. I found myself admiring the women's fashion—their white bonnets, their pink fans, their side-curls, the baby's breath and daisies in their hair. There was less to see in the men, who wore all black. But still I thought them beautiful, for there was distinction in how they walked, grace in their smallest movements, as when they opened the bay doors and repaired out back, leaned into one of the Tasked to light their cigars, and spoke of gentlemanly things. I imagined myself among them, settled into a chair or whispering into a lady's ear.

They played seventeen hands of cards. They drank eight demijohns of cider. They ate lady-cake until they could barely stand. Then, just past midnight, a woman with her bonnet on backward began cackling hysterically. One of the men in black began berating his wife. Another nodded off in the corner. The Tasked on the waitstaff grew tense, a subtle tension I was sure the guests could not detect. My father sat staring at the fire and Mr. Fields sat back in his chair, looking bored. The woman stopped cackling and pulled down her bonnet, revealing a broken mask of streaked face-paint.

The woman was one of the Caulleys—Alice Caulley—a family, many years ago, split in two. Half had gone off to Kentucky while half remained. I remember her because the Caulleys who left took along those who tasked for them and among that number was Pete's sister, Maddie. I never met her. But he spoke of her often, and whenever news of her filtered up from Kentucky through the grapevine of tasking folks who moved between the Caulley branches—news that she was alive and whole, united with the remnants of family that traveled with her—his face would light up and remain as such for the rest of the week.

"Give us a song!" Alice snapped, and when no one answered, she walked over to Cassius, one of the men in waiting, and slapped him. Now she yelled again, "Sing, damn you!"

It always happened like this—that is what I had been told. Bored whites were barbarian whites. While they played at aristocrats, we were their well-appointed and stoic attendants. But when they tired of dignity, the bottom fell out. New games were anointed and we were but pieces on the board. It was terrifying. There was no limit to what they might do at this end of the tether, nor what my father would allow them to do.

The slap roused him. My father stood up and looked around nervously.

"Come now, Alice. We have something better than any Negro song," he said, and turned to me, and though he did not say another word I knew what he wanted.

I scanned the room and caught sight of a deck of oversized cards stacked on one of the small coffee tables. I recognized the cards as the kind Maynard used in his reading lessons. On one side the cards were all the same—a map of the known world. On the other side they each featured an acrobat contorted into the shape of a different letter, with a short rhyme underneath. I had overheard Maynard reading from these cards with his tutor. I had with sideways glances, and a few minutes of study here and there, memorized them, for no other reason than the fact of enjoying the silly rhymes on each side. Now I retrieved the cards from the table and turned toward Alice Caulley.

"Mrs. Caulley, would you shuffle, ma'am?"

She leaned over unsteadily, took the cards from me, and shuffled them in her hands. And then I asked if she would be so kind as to let me inspect them. Having done this, I handed them back to her and asked that she place them each on the table, face-down in any order. I watched her hands until the small coffee table was covered with maps in miniature.

"And what now, boy?" she asked warily.

I asked that she pick up a card and show it to anyone she pleased, except me. When she'd done this, she turned back to me with raised eyebrows. I said, "With the rest he'll agree, and assist them with a letter 'E.'"

Now her eyebrows retreated some toward their natural position as skepticism turned to pique. "Again," she said, and then picked another card, showed it to more people now. I said, "Here he is, twisted and twined, to make an 'S' if you do not mind."

And then the pique turned to a slight smile. I felt the tension in the room slack a bit. She picked another, showed it, and I said, "He's forced to train hard, less the letter 'C' be marred."

Now Alice Caulley laughed, and when I looked over, I saw my father smiling thin and small, and though the others who tasked like me that evening were still standing at attention, I felt the fear flowing out of their stoic faces. Alice Caulley kept reaching for the cards, flipping faster now. But I matched her speed. "Here's a letter 'V' to view. You'll find its shape just like new." . . . "With his hands in the air, a letter 'H' he does declare."

By the time the deck was done, they were all laughing and now applauding. The man in the corner was no longer snoring but looked up, trying to understand the sudden commotion. When the applause died down, Alice Caulley, her smile carrying the edge of menace, looked to me and said, "And what else, boy?"

I stared at her for a moment, longer than any tasking man should, and nodded. I was only twelve, but I was fully confident of what came next, a trick I had long practiced down in the Street. Having the guests in my confidence, I requested that they line up against the drawing room wall. I went first to Edward Mackley, who wore his blond curls pinned back like a woman, asking him to tell me the first moment he knew he loved his wife. And then I asked Armatine Caulley, Alice's cousin, her favorite place in all the world, and then I went to Morris Beacham, and asked him to tell me about the first time he'd hunted pheasant. I went down the line like this until I held a clutch of stories in my head, so many that no one else could remember who had said what and what the particular details were. Only Mr. Fields, Maynard's gruff tutor, declined. But when I went back down the line, repeating back to each of the speakers their own stories, in every detail, but with drama and embellishment, I saw the tutor pull up to the edge of his seat, and his eyes were aglow like all the others', aglow like those of my tasking elders, down on the distant Street, used to be.

Now even the waitstaff had to break their solemn gaze and smile. Indeed, among the whole party, only Mr. Fields was able to preserve his customary gruff aspect, save the glow in his narrowed eyes. It was late now. My father bid each of his guests to quarters throughout the old house and we were dispatched to make sure each of them was comfortable. When all the guests were settled, we retreated into the Warrens exhausted, knowing that our duties would begin again in mere hours, for all the guests would expect their breakfast prepared and waiting when they arose.

The Monday morning following that party, I was helping Thena prepare the wash when I was called away by Roscoe and sent to see my father off in the side parlor. I first went to my room, washed, put on a set of house clothes, then wound my way up the back stairs until I emerged in the central corridor, and then, walking down that corridor, found my father standing, as if he'd been waiting on me. Behind him, I saw Maynard seated at a desk writing and a gentleman standing over him. The gentleman was Mr. Fields, who tutored Maynard three times a week. He wore a look of pained frustration, and Maynard's own face was stricken.

My father smiled at me, but this does not convey the look he gave, because my father had a variety of smiles—smiles of displeasure, or disinterest, or shock and amazement—indeed he smiled so much it made him hard to read, but I knew the smile I saw that morning because it was the same smile I'd seen, mere months ago, down near the Street, down in the fields where he'd flicked me the copper coin.

"Good morning, Hiram," he said. "How are you?"

"Fine, sir," I said.

"Good. Good," he said. "Hiram, I want you to spend some moments with Mr. Fields. Would you do that for me?"

"Yes, sir," I said.

"Thank you, Hiram," he said.

And with that, my father looked at Maynard, still smiling, and said, "Come on, son."

I saw an immediate look of relief extend over Maynard's face as he left his work. He didn't look my way as he and my father left the room. We were, Maynard and I, at a distance at that time in our lives. We spoke only in banalities, with no acknowledgment of what we were to each other.

Mr. Fields spoke with an accent, one I had never heard before, and I immediately imagined it might hail from the Natchez my elders spoke so much of.

"The other day," he said, "that was some trick." I nodded silently, still not sure of his intentions. There were penalties for the Tasked who'd learned to read, and it now occurred to me that my "trick" might bring some sort of wrath. But my trick didn't hinge on reading, because I could not read. I had simply filed away what I had heard of Maynard's own fumblings and matched them with the cards left scattered on the table. But Mr. Fields knew nothing of that technique, and I was not quite sure how, or whether, I should explain.

He regarded me for a moment and then pulled out a set of regular playing cards and handed them to me.

"Examine them."

I pulled cards from the deck one after the other, taking time to examine each one, and furrowing my brow more for effect than out of any sense of labor. When I was done, Mr. Fields said, "Now place each of them face-down on the table."

This I did in four neat rows of thirteen. Then Mr. Fields took one card at a time from the table so that only he could see the face, and asked that I confirm its suit. This I did with each one. Mr. Fields's face did not alight.

Now he reached into his bag and produced a box. When he opened it, I saw that it was a collection of rounds, small ivory discs, with a carved face or animal or symbol on each. He laid these rounds on the table face-up, asked me to look at them for a minute, and then he turned the rounds over so their blank bottoms showed. And when he asked me to find the round with a portrait of the old man with a long nose or the pretty girl with long locks or the one with the bird perched on the branch, it was as though he'd never turned them over, and they were right there facing me.

Finally, Mr. Fields pulled a sheet of paper from his satchel, and then he pulled out a book filled with drawings. He turned to a drawing of a bridge and he told me to look at it, to concentrate on it, and after a minute, he closed the book, handed me a pen, and told me to draw the bridge myself. I had never done anything quite like this, and unsure of Mr. Fields's intentions, and knowing, even then, that the Quality resented the pride of the Tasked, unless that pride could be fitted to their profit, I gave him a puzzled look, and pretended that I did not quite understand. He repeated himself, and then watched as I took the pen, gingerly at first, and began my sketch. For effect, I would glance up, as though straining to recall the picture in my mind. But there really was no need to recall, for it felt to me that the bridge was right there, on the blank paper, and all I need do was trace the lines to reveal it. So I traced the stony arch, the small opening at the right end, the arch over-top, the rocky outcropping in the back, and the tree-filled ravine over which the bridge spanned. And now, seeing this, Mr. Fields's eyes grew wide. He stood and adjusted his jacket. Then he took the sheet, told me to wait, and walked out.

Mr. Fields returned with my father, who'd pulled from his assortment of smiles one which spoke of his own self-satisfaction.

"Hiram," my father said. "Would you like to work with Mr. Fields on some regular basis?" I looked to the ground, and pretended to turn the question over in my head. I had to, because what I then felt was the avenue opening before me, light streaming through. I did not wish to be found too eager. Lockless was still Virginia—the epitome even. I could not yet acknowledge all that this moment portended.

"Should I, sir?" I asked.

"Yes, Hiram," my father said. "I think you should."

"Then yes, sir," I said. "I will."

So the lessons began—reading, arithmetic, some oratory—and my world bloomed with them, my ravenous memory filling with images and, now, words, which were so much more than I had before believed, words with their own shape, rhythm, and color, words that were pictures themselves. We would meet three times a week for an hour, my time always following Maynard's, and though I know that he tried his best not to show it, I could always see the relief in Mr. Fields's eyes when Maynard departed and I entered. This moment became a source not just of pride but of quiet derision—I was better than Maynard, given so much less yet made of so much more.

He was clumsy. He squinted constantly, as if always searching for the next foothold. He was negligent and rude. My father would have guests over for tea and Maynard would think nothing of bursting in and speaking whatever thought then possessed him. He loved to jest, and that was the best part of him—but even that quality betrayed him into telling crass jokes to the young daughters of Quality. At supper he reached across the table for rolls, and spoke with a mouth full of food.

I was certain my father saw things as I did, and I wondered how wrong it must have felt to see the best of you emerge in this way, in the place you didn't expect, indeed in the place your whole world depends on it never appearing.

I tried to remember the Street and Thena's admonition, *They ain't your family*. But seeing the estate as I now did—rolling green hills in summer, woods blooming in red and gold in fall, and then in winter a snow dappling everything, and seeing, though living below, the main house of Lockless, the great columns of the portico, the setting sun casting itself through the fanlight, seeing the winding corridors, and seeing the grand portraits of my grandfather and grandmother, my eyes in theirs, I began, in my quiet moments, to imagine myself in their ranks. And there was my father, who would pull me aside and tell me of our lineage stretching back through his father, John Walker, back through the progenitor, Archibald Walker, who walked here with a mule, two horses, his wife, Judith, two young boys, and ten tasking men. Would tell me these stories as if granting in these asides a teasing share of my inheritance. And I never forgot.

There were evenings, the Task complete, when I would wander to the far eastern edge of the property, past the sprawl of timothy grass and clover, and stand reverent before the stone monument that marked the spot where the first plots that became Lockless were cleared. And when my father told me the stories, passed from his grandfather, of chasing off catamounts, of hunting bear with a Bowie knife, of felling great trees, hauling up stones, and diverting creeks, and by his own hand bringing forth the estate I then beheld, how could I not want to claim this, the courage and wit and all the glory it built with its strong arms, as my inheritance?

But too, with all of that imagining, the facts of Lockless began to make themselves manifest. There were of course the tales of Pete and Ella, their invocations of Natchez and Baton Rouge. There was the tragedy of Big John, of my mother. And to all of this, I now began to add my own stray readings, when left in my father's office, of *De Bow's Review,* which harped constantly on the falling price of tobacco, and then finally the conversation of the Quality themselves. It was tobacco that made for the largess of Lockless, indeed the largess of Elm County. And every year the tobacco yields shrank, the entail of those high families of Virginia shrank with them. The days of tobacco leaves large as elephant ears were no more, not in Elm County at least, where crop after crop had exhausted the land. But out west, past the valley and mountains, on the Mississippi banks, down Natchez-way, there was land in need of improvement, in need of masters to superintend, and men to harvest and hoe, men such as those in the diminishing fields of Lockless.

"Used to be they was shamed to sell a man," I'd heard Pete once say, while I was working in the kitchen.

"Easy to have shame when you got the harvest," Ella answered. "Try shame when you a dirt farmer."

These were the last words I ever heard from Ella. A week later she was gone.

My young way of understanding all of this was singular, a sense that what really had doomed Lockless was not the land but the men who managed it. I began to see Maynard as an outrageous example of his entire class. I envied them. I was horrified by them.

As I learned the house, and began to read, and began to see more of the Quality, I saw that just as the fields and its workers were the engine of everything, the house itself would have been lost without those who tasked within it. My father, like all the masters, built an entire apparatus to disguise this weakness, to hide how prostrate they truly were. The tunnel, where I first entered the house, was the only entrance that the Tasked were allowed to use, and this was not only for the masters' exaltation but to hide us, for the tunnel was but one of the many engineering marvels built into Lockless so as to make it appear powered by some imperceptible energy. There were dumbwaiters that made the sumptuous supper appear from nothing, levers that seemed to magically retrieve the right bottle of wine hidden deep in the manor's bowels, cots in the sleeping quarters, drawn under the canopy bed, because those charged with emptying the chamber-pot must be hidden even more than the chamber-pot itself. The magic wall that slid away from me that first day and opened the gleaming world of the house hid back stairways that led down into the Warrens, the engine-room of Lockless, where no guest would ever visit. And when we did appear in the polite areas of the house, as we did during the soirées, we were made to appear in such appealing dress and grooming so that one could imagine that we were not slaves at all but mystical ornaments, a portion of the manor's charm. But I now knew the truth—that Maynard's folly, though more profane, was unoriginal. The masters could not bring water to boil, harness a horse, nor strap their own drawers without us. We were better than them—we had to be. Sloth was literal death for us, while for them it was the whole ambition of their lives.

It occurred to me then that even my own intelligence was unexceptional, for you could not set eyes anywhere on Lockless and not see the genius in its makers—genius in the hands that carved out the columns of the portico, genius in the songs that evoked, even in the whites, the deepest of joys and sorrows, genius in the men who made the fiddle strings whine and trill at their dances, genius in the bouquet of flavors served up from the kitchen, genius in all our lost, genius in Big John. Genius in my mother.

I imagined that my own quality might someday be recognized and then, perhaps, I, one who understood the workings of the house, the workings of the field, and the span of the larger world, might be deemed the true heir, *the rightful heir,* of Lockless. With this broad knowledge I would make the fields bloom again, and in that way save us all from the auctions and separation, from a descent into the darkness of Natchez, which was the coffin, which was all that awaited, I knew, under the rule of Maynard.

One day I came up the back stairs to the study for my instruction with Mr. Fields, and I was excited because we had just then begun our study of astronomy, and star maps, starting with Ursa Minor, with more to come in our next session. But when I came into the study, I found not Mr. Fields but my father there, seated alone.

"Hiram," he said. "It's time." A deathly fear overcame me at these words. I had been studying for a year now with Mr. Fields. It occurred to me that perhaps this was merely the fattening, perhaps I would go the way of Ella. Maybe they had heard my thoughts somehow or seen the hazy dream of usurpation in my eyes. Maybe they'd done the math themselves and realized my learning could only end in a coup.

"Yes, sir," I answered without even knowing what it was now time for. I clenched my teeth behind my lips, trying to hide the fear now pulsing out from my gut.

"When I saw you down in that field, and I saw your parlor tricks, I knew there was something to you, boy, something that the others down there couldn't see. You had a particular talent, one that I thought could be useful, for these are not prosperous times, and we need all the talent we can get up here in the house."

I looked at him blank-faced, concealing my confusion. I simply nodded, waiting for the thing to clarify before me.

"It's time for you to take on Maynard. My days will not be forever, and he will need a good manservant—one such as you, who knows something of the fields, and something of the house, and even something of the larger world. I have watched you, boy, and what I know is you never forget a thing. Tell my Hiram something once, and it is as good as done. There ain't too many like you, ain't too many of such quality."

And now he looked at me and his eyes gleamed a bit.

"Most of the folks up here would take a boy like you and put him on the block. Fetch a fortune, you know. Nothing more valuable than a colored with some brains in him. But that is not me. I believe in Lockless. I believe in Elm County. I believe in Virginia. We have a duty to save our country: the country your great-grandfather carved out of wilderness will not return to the wild. You understand?"

"Yes, sir," I said.

"It's our duty. All of us, Hiram. And it begins right here. I need you, boy. Maynard needs you at his side and it is your great honor to be there."

"Thank you, sir."

"All right," he said. "We'll start tomorrow."

And in that way my lessons came to an end just as their purpose was revealed. I was tasked with Maynard, his personal servant for the next seven years of my life. It may seem strange now, but the insult of it all did not immediately dawn on me. It accumulated slowly and inexorably over the years as I watched Maynard at work. And so much hung in the balance—the lives of all those whom I'd left down in the Street, and even those of us now in this gleaming, collapsing palace, all of it depended on Maynard maturing into a competent steward of it all, however unjust the entire edifice. But Maynard was not that man.

It all finally came cascading down upon me the evening before that fateful race-day. I was nineteen. I was standing in my father's second-floor study, having filed away his correspondence into the cubbies of the mahogany secretary, and under the silver arms of the Argand lamp I found myself carried away by the latest volume of *De Bow's Review*. I marveled at the volume's presentation of Oregon country, a region I knew from the maps strung aimlessly across the house, but now brought alive for me in these pages as a kind of paradise, a land rich enough to hold all of Virginia many times over, a land of hills, valleys, forests, teeming with game and black soil so fertile it nearly burst out of the earth.

I still remember the words that brought me up: "Here, if anywhere, must be the seat of liberty, prosperity, and wealth." I stood. I closed the volume. I paced back and forth. I looked out the window, far across the river Goose, and saw the Three Hills to the south, looming like black giants in the distance. I turned and spent a few minutes looking at an engraving on the wall. A chained Cupid and a laughing Aphrodite.

And then I thought of Maynard, my brother. His blond hair had grown long and unruly. His beard was an array of mossy patches. Social instinct and grace had not found him in manhood. He gambled and drank to excess, because he could. He fought in the street, because no matter how throttled, he could never be throttled from his throne. He lost fortunes in the arms of fancies, because the labor of the Tasked—and sometimes their sale— would cover all his losses. Visits from family still in Elm often turned to the fate of Lockless, and when Maynard was out of earshot, I would hear them cursing his name and considering all manner of schemes to find another heir to run the family stead. In fact no heirs were present, for when these cousins searched the Walker lineage what they found was everyone of Maynard's generation had gone to where the land was rich and blooming. Virginia was old. Virginia was the past. Virginia was where the earth was dying and the tobacco diminishing. And so with no suitable heir, the Walker masters looked to Lockless with worry.

My father had plans of his own—find Maynard a talented and

suitable partner, and thus engage another family in the struggle to save Lockless. And incredibly, he found one in Corrine Quinn, who was then perhaps the wealthiest woman in all of Elm County, having inherited a fortune from her deceased parents. There were rumors among the Tasked as to the nature of this inheritance, rumors about the way in which Corrine Quinn's parents had met their end. But among the Quality, she was regarded as superior to Maynard in every way. But she needed a husband because Virginia still operated on the code of gentlemen, meaning there were still things beyond her, places she could not go, deals she could not be party to. And so these two needed each other—Maynard an intelligent partner to save his land and estate, Corrine a gentleman to represent her interests.

That night I walked out of the study, disturbed and shaken, and wandered the house until I found myself at the threshold of the parlor, from where I could see the glow of the fireplace and hear Maynard and my father in conversation. They were speaking of Edwin Cox, patriarch of one of the oldest and most storied families of the region. Last winter, he'd wandered out of his home and was caught in a great blizzard, which had just that morning come up over the mountains and blanketed the county. He had somehow lost his way and was found the next day, frozen solid, only a few yards from the mansion of his forefathers. I stood in the shadows outside of the parlor for a moment and listened.

"They say he went out to check on his horse," my father said. "He loved that damn thing, but when he got out into it, he could not tell a stable from the smokehouse. I walked out on the porch that same day, and that wind, by God, I tell you I couldn't see my own hand held out in front of me."

"Why ain't he send his boy?" Maynard asked.

"He'd let nearly all of them loose the summer before. Took them up to Baltimore—he has kin up there—and left them to their own devices. Poor fools. Doubt they made it a week."

At that moment Maynard spotted me outside the doorframe.

"What are you doing out there, Hi?" he said. "Come freshen up the fire."

I walked in and looked to my father, who regarded me as he so often did those days—as though he was between two notions and could not decide which to give voice to. He had settled on a particular smile for me—a half smile held frozen in a macabre rictus. I doubt he meant it to seem as sinister as it did. I don't think he much thought about it. Howell Walker was not a reflective man, as much as he might have thought he should be one, having been born to a generation who fashioned themselves after the Revolutionary scholars of their grandfathers' era—Franklin, Adams, Jefferson, and Madison. All over the house of Lockless were the instruments of science and discovery—great maps of the world, electrostatic generators, and the library that had so often been my home. But the maps were rarely referenced, the devices mostly used for party tricks, and if the volumes were in any way limber it was due to my hand. My father's reading was constrained to useful things—*De Bow's Review, The Christian Intelligencer, The Register*. To him, books were fashion, signatures of pedigree and status, which marked him off from the low whites of the county with their dirt-floor hovels and paltry homesteads of corn and wheat. But what did it mean to find me, a slave, dreaming amid those books?

My father had begun his family at a later age than most. He was now in his seventieth year and losing his vigor. His blue eyes, always intense and regarding, were encroached by the bags beneath them and the crow's-feet extending out from them. There is so much in the eyes—the flash of rage, the warmth of joy, the pooling of sadness—and all of this my father had lost. I suppose he was a handsome man once. Perhaps I just like to think of him that way. But what I remember from that day, along with those lost eyes, are the worry lines carved into his face, the hair unkempt and swept back, his beard everywhere and wiry. He still had the dignified dress of a gentleman of Quality, the silk stockings, the many layers—shirt, vest, bright waistcoat, black frock. But he was the last of a particular species, and the dying was written all over him.

"Races tomorrow, Daddy," said Maynard. "I'm going to show them this time. I'm going to put a passel on that horse Diamond, and bring home the whole acre."

"You needn't show them anything, May," my father said. "They don't matter. All that truly matters is right here."

"Hell I don't," said Maynard, flashing anger. "That man had me tossed from the jockey club, then pulled a pistol on me. I'm going to show them. I'm going to ride out in that new Millennium chaise and remind them . . ."

"Maybe you shouldn't. Maybe you should avoid it all."

"I'm going. And damn them. Somebody gotta stand for the Walker name."

My father turned back toward the fire with a barely perceptible sigh.

"Yes indeed," Maynard said. "I think tomorrow will be something."

Through the shadows I saw my father, exhausted by the need of his first-born son, give me a pained and sideways look and then tug at his beard, and this was a gesture I could read. *Guard your brother,* it said, and I knew it for I had seen it for half my life.

"Best start getting ready for tomorrow," Maynard said. "Hi, go check on the horses."

I walked down the steps into the Warrens and then out to the tunnel. I inspected the horses and then returned to the house the way I came. Maynard was gone, but I saw my father still there, seated before the fire. It was his custom, sometimes, to fall asleep there until Roscoe woke him up and prepared him for bed. Roscoe was not around. I moved to put another log on the fire.

"Let it die, Hiram," my father said. "I'm almost finished here."

"Yes, sir," I said. "Anything I can get you?"

"No," he said.

I asked if Roscoe was still attending.

"No. I let him go early," he said.

Roscoe had two young sons that lived ten miles west of us, and whenever he could, he went over to see them. Sometimes, if my father was in the mood, he'd release Roscoe early from his duties to spend a few extra hours with them.

"Why don't you sit with me a moment," my father said.

It was an unusual request to make to a tasking man, but was not so unusual between us, at moments when it was only us, and each day it seemed there were more moments like this. He'd sold off half the kitchen staff in the past year. The smithy and the carpentry workhouse were empty now. Carl, Emmanuel, Theseus, all the other men who once tasked there had been sent off Natchezway. The ice-house had been fallow for two years. One maid, Ida, worked the entire house, which meant the order that I remembered from childhood was no more, but more than that, meant that the warm smile of Beth and the laugh of Leah and the sad, vacant eyes of Eva were no more. In the kitchen, there was a new girl, Lucille, who seemed totally lost, and so she often suffered Maynard's rages. Lockless had begun to feel desolate and gray, and it was not just Lockless but all the manors along the Goose, now drained of their vigor as the heart of the country shifted west.

I took my seat, the same that Maynard had abandoned, and for a few long minutes, my father said nothing. He just stared into the fire, which was dying, so that all I could now see was a diminishing yellow trace on his face.

"You will mind your brother, won't you," he said.

"Yessir," I said.

"Good," he said. "Good."

And then there was a brief pause before he spoke again.

"Hiram, I know that there is not much I have been permitted to give you," he said. "But I believe that in what I have been permitted to give you, I have made it known how high you sit in my esteem. It is not fair, I know it, none of it is fair. But I have been damned to live in this time when I must watch my people carried off, across the bridge and into God knows where."

Again, he paused and shook his head. Then he stood, and walked over to the mantel to turn up the lamp-light, so that the parlor portraits and ivory busts of our forefathers were now illuminated in the flickering shadows.

"I'm old," he continued. "I can't reconstruct myself for this new world. I will pass with this Virginia, and these troubled times will fall to Maynard, which means they will fall to you. You have to save him, son. You have to protect him. I don't just mean to-morrow at race-day. There is so much coming, so much trouble coming for us all, and Maynard, whom I love more than anything, he is not ready. Mind him, son. Mind my boy."

He paused and looked directly at me. "Mind your brother, do you hear me?"

"Yes, sir," I said.

And we sat there for perhaps another thirty minutes, until my father announced his retirement for the evening. I took my leave and went down into the Warrens, to my room. I sat on the edge of my bed and thought of that day my father called me up from the fields—the day he'd smiled and flipped the copper coin my way. Everything about my life flowed from that decision. It kept me from seeing the worst of our condition. Almost any tasking man at Lockless would have traded his life for mine. But there was a weight of being so close to them, the weight that Thena had tried to warn me about, but something more, the crushing weight of seeing how the Quality truly lived, in all their luxury, and how much they really took from us.

That night I dreamed that I was out in the tobacco fields again, out there with the Tasked, and we were, all of us, chained together and this chain was linked to one long chain and at the end of it stood Maynard, idling lost in his own thoughts, almost unaware that he was holding all of us in the palm of his hand. And then I looked around and I saw that we were all old, that I was an old man, and when I looked back I saw Maynard, not as the young man I knew, but as a baby crawling in a bowling green, and then I saw the Tasked slowly disappearing before me, their familiar faces and bodies fading and fading, one by one, until it was only me, an old man held and chained by a baby. Then everything fell away, the chains, Maynard, the field itself, and I was enveloped in the blackness of night. And then the black branches of a forest sprang up around me, and I was alone, and afraid and lost until looking up I saw a sliver of moon, and then the heavens blinked out from the blackness, and among them I could distinguish Ursa Minor, the mystical bear who secreted away the old gods. I knew this because Mr. Fields had shown me a star map on our last day together. And looking at the tail of the bear, I saw something else: the mark of my future days, wreathed in brilliant but ghostly blue, and the mark was the North Star.

· 4 ·

I AWOKE SHAKEN AND TREMBLING at the dream. I sat up in my bed for a moment, then lay back again, but found no more sleep. I took my stone jar from the corner and walked out of the tunnel, out into the morning darkness, and down to the well, hauled up the water, filled the jar, and walked back through the crisp autumn air to the Warrens.

I thought back on the dream. All those other souls chained with me, who vanished, might one day include my own family, all in Maynard's loose hand, to be pulled this way or that, or dropped on a whim. It pained me. I was of the age when it was natural to seek out a wife, but by then I had seen tasking women promised to tasking men, and then seen how such "promises" were kept. I remember how these young couples would hold one another, each morning before going to their separate tasks, how they would clasp hands at night, sitting on the steps of their quarters, how they would fight and draw knives, kill each other, before being without each other, kill each other, because Natchez-way was worse than death, was living death, an agony of knowing that somewhere in the vastness of America, the one whom you loved most was parted from you, never again to meet in this shackled, fallen world. That was the love the Tasked made, and it was that love that occupied my thoughts when time came to tend to Maynard—how families formed in the shadow and quick, and then turned to dust with the white wave of a hand.

Now, walking out of my quarters, then through the Warrens, I passed the doorway of Sophia, which was open, so that I saw her there knitting by the lantern-light. And stopping at the door, I saw her in profile—her small nose, the soft outcropping of her mouth, the twists of her hair peeking out from beneath the fabric wrapped around her head. She was sitting on a stool, her back straight as a stone wall, the light of the lantern casting her shadow out into the corridor, her long spider arms winding two needles back and forth, fashioning the yarn into something that had not yet taken discernible form.

"You come to say goodbye," she asked. This startled me a bit, for she did not turn, but kept her eyes on that inscrutable whatever suspended between her two needles. I mumbled something garbled and confused. And at that she turned and I saw her sun-drop eyes alight and her soft mouth break into a warm smile. Sophia was conspicuous among the Tasked, because she seemingly did not task at all. She loved to knit, and I often saw her walking among the gardens and orchards, working her needles, so that this knitting might be taken to be her only labor. But all of Lockless knew better. She belonged to my uncle, my father's brother, Nathaniel Walker. None needed to guess at the nature of this arrangement. But if I had had any doubts, they were quickly extinguished when I was given the task of driving her to and then retrieving her from Nathaniel's property each weekend.

This "arrangement" was not unusual, was indeed the custom of the men of Quality. But something in Nathaniel revolted against concubinage, even as he committed himself to it. And like the dumbwaiters and secret passages that the Quality employed to mask their theft, Nathaniel too employed means to take as though not taking, and transfigure robbery into charity. So he had Sophia live down here in the Warrens of his brother's plantation. He insisted she dress like a lady of Quality when visiting, but use the back road of his estate to enter. He kept tabs on who visited her and let it be known among the community of the Warrens that he did so, to ward off tasking men, all, as it happened, save me.

"Did you come to say goodbye, Hiram?" she said again.

"No, uhh, more like good morning," I said, recovering myself.

"Ahh, well, good morning, Hi," she said. Then she turned away from me and back to her knitting.

"Forgive me, I'm guessing I got it backwards," she went on. "Funny thing is, I was thinking of you just now, just before you wandered past. I was thinking of you and the young master, and race-day. I was thinking how glad I was to not be there, and in my thinking, I had had a whole conversation with you, and it was like you was here. So when I seen you there at the door, I was thinking it was the ending of something."

"Uh-huh," I said. I felt myself barely able to muster words. I feared what I might say. I thought of the dream from last night— the dream in which we grew old while Maynard remained young, and held us all chained.

She exhaled hard, as though frustrated with herself, and said, "Don't mind me none."

Now she looked up at me again and a look of realization crossed her. She said, "All right, I am here now. How are you, Hi?"

"I'm good," I said. "About as good as can be expected. Rough night."

"You want to talk?" she asked. "Sit a spell. Lord knows I am always talking to you, filling you with my stories and observations on the world."

"No," I said. "Gotta get to the young master. I'm all right."

"You don't look it," she said.

"I look fine," I said.

"And how would you know?" she asked and then laughed.

"Don't worry bout how I know," I said, returning her laugh. "How bout you worry bout your own looks."

"And how do I look this morning?" she asked.

I just stepped back into the corridor, away from the door, and said, "Not so bad. Not so bad, if I do say."

"Thank you," she said. "Well, since you are not in a conversing mood, what I want to say to you is, you have yourself a pleasant Saturday. And don't let the young master trouble you none."

I nodded, and then I walked up that back staircase of awful secrets into that house of bondage. And as I mounted each step, I felt the terrible logic of the Task, my Task, snap into place. It was not just that I would never be heir to even one inch of Lockless. And it was more than knowing I would never be a subscriber to the fruit of my own labor. It was also that my own natural wants must forever be bottled up, that I must live in fear of those wants, so that more than I must live in fear of the Quality, I must necessarily live in fear of myself.

We left late that morning in the Millennium chaise, turning out the main road of the property, and past the orchards, the workshop, and the wheat fields, out of Lockless, and turning down the West Road and driving past what remained of the old estates—Altbrook, Lowridge, Belleview, names that then still rang out across Virginia but are now, in this electric era of telegraphy and elevators, just dust in the wind. Maynard talked the whole way, and there was nothing new in this—just the usual fare of who he would show up and how. I listened for a bit, and then just let him go on while I retreated into my private thoughts.

And then we were crossing the bridge and turning our way in to Starfall, and it was such a beautiful and crisp November day, so that you could look west and see the last turning of the trees, bits of orange and yellow exploding off the mountains. We hitched our horse and chaise, then walked toward Market Street and were met by a parade of Virginian splendor. They were all out there, the Quality, out there in their masks and garments, the ladies in powdered faces, white gloves, and silk scarves, their bosoms heaving and their parasols held up by colored girls to preserve the ivory sheen of their skin. The men all seemed in uniform—black coats, cinched at the waist, gray trousers, horsehair stocks, stove-pipe hats, walking sticks and calf-skin Wellingtons. As always, they left the captain's share of glamour to their women, trussed in corset and bodice so that they walked slow, measuring all their movements. But there was still a dance in how they moved, with their swanning necks and their swaying hips. I knew they'd been learning to walk like this all their lives, under mistresses and mothers, because it was never the costume that made the Quality, but how the lady wore it. The Northerners from New Hampshire and the pioneers of Paducah and Natchez and the low whites of Elm, all walked with them, but seemed to watch more than walk as this parade of the beautiful and divine made its way down the main avenue of our Starfall, looking as though they would never die, as though Virginia would never die, and this empire of tobacco and bodies would shine like some old city on the hill, so that all the world would wonder why it did not live in the eternal splendor of these first families of Elm County.

I recognized many among them, and remembered even some to whom there was no introduction, remembered them by some stray remark or act. And then there were those whom I knew quite well, men like my old tutor, Mr. Fields, whom I spotted walking alone in the parade. He seemed to be studying the crowd, and when he saw me, he offered a small, thin smile and tipped his cap. I hadn't seen him since our last lesson so many years ago, though I know now that our ending, on the tail of Ursa Minor, was itself a sign. I looked over to see if Maynard had seen Mr. Fields, but he was hypnotized by the glamour, his eyes wide as dreams, a toothy smile spreading across his face. He was not like them, and I can remember feeling ashamed for my part in this. I had done my best for him that morning, fitting him into his clothes, but between his proportions and his habit of pulling at his waistcoat and collar, no ensemble ever properly fit. Still, he was so very happy to be there. All year he'd nursed his indignities, but now he hoped, through his merits as a sporting man, he would be returned to the fold. They were *his people,* his by regal blood, and so there he stood before that parade, with no power to distinguish his own place in it. He pulled at his shirt collar again, laughed loud, and then waded out into the slow parade of Quality, all moving toward the races.

Maynard sighted Adeline Jones, whom he'd once wooed, as much as Maynard had ever wooed anyone. I had heard that she'd quit Elm County, quit all of Virginia, for a lawyer up North. But the races had brought Adeline back, I assumed, if only to take in the changes in her old home. She was a kind woman, and Maynard had always taken this kindness as an invitation to her affections. Now he angled his way through the crowd, waving his hat, and approaching her said, "Hey there, Addie! How are you this day?"

Adeline turned and greeted Maynard with an edgy smile. They talked for a few minutes and then started walking again with the processional, Adeline ill at ease, and Maynard excited to have attached himself to someone. I shadowed them from the edge of the avenue, as all the other tasking men shadowed their charges, watching at a distance as Maynard grew more excited in conversation and Adeline's tolerations were taxed. But she bore it well, as the ladies of Quality were trained to do. Her mistake had been appearing here without a gentleman at her side, one who could shield her from Maynard's conversation, which was now so boisterous that I could hear it above the din of the crowd. He was going on about Lockless, about its prosperity and charms, about her mistake in not succumbing to them, and he did this in tedious jests that were only lightly concealed boasts, and Adeline was forced to bear all this with a smile.

When they reached the racetrack, I watched as she was at last rescued by a passing gentleman, who extended his hand to Maynard and then quickly, sizing up the shape of things, rushed her away. Maynard paused at the gates, and then looked up into the stands to the jockey club, just beginning to fill with subscribers, where he'd once held forth but had been unceremoniously ejected. I walked closer now, with Adeline gone, then stood off to the side and looked to Maynard, who was now lost in a world of painful longing, for race-days past when he was welcomed, or at least allowed, among the gentlemen of the county. And then I saw the insult compound as Maynard's eyes shifted from the gentlemen to the area demarcated for the ladies of Virginia, so that they need not suffer the gambling, coarse talk, and cigars of the men, and in that region I saw Maynard's intended, Corrine Quinn, who seemed to have suffered nothing in her standing for her association with Maynard. And Maynard was no longer smiling, for he felt himself henpecked. There was his future wife, elevated to a standing higher than his own.

I peered into the ladies' club as subtly as I could to get a better look at this woman. Corrine Quinn was out of another time. She spurned the ostentation of the parade, the garments that, in their great extravagance, in their defiance, testified to the dying soil, the tasking families divided, the diminishing tobacco, the fall that was all around. She stood in the stands, in calico and gloves, talking to one of the other ladies, while Maynard watched with scornful eye. Then he shook his head and walked off to take his place, not among the gentlemen, but in the motley of low white men, a class whose position in this society of ours always amazed me. The low whites, men such as our own Harlan, were tolerated publicly by the Quality, but spurned in private; their names were spat out at banquets, their children mocked in the parlors, their wives and daughters seduced and discarded. They were a degraded and downtrodden nation enduring the boot of the Quality, solely for the right to put a boot of their own to the Tasked.

My place was among the coloreds, some Tasked, some free, seated on the waist-high wooden fencing, just off from the stables, where still other colored men tended to the racehorses, feeding them and looking after their health. I knew a few of them—including Corrine's man, Hawkins, whom I saw sitting on the fence with some of the others. I nodded in greeting. He nodded back, but did not smile. That was his way, this Hawkins. There was something cold and distant about him. He perpetually wore the look of a man who suffered no fools, but felt himself surrounded by them. He scared me. There was something hard about him, and I knew just by his manner that he had endured some terrible, unspeakable portion of the Task. I looked over and watched as the other colored men along the fence shouted and laughed with still others working the stables. And watching this silently, as was my way, I marveled at the bonds between us—the way we shortened our words, or spoke, sometimes, with no words at all, the shared memories of corn-shuckings, of hurricanes, of heroes who did not live in books, but in our talk; an entire world of our own, hidden away from them, and to be part of that world, I felt even then, was to be in on a secret, a secret that was in you. There were neither Quality nor Low among us, no jockey clubs to be ejected from, and this was its own America, was its own grandeur—one that defied Maynard, who must forever carp about his place in the order.

It was early afternoon now, cloudless still, and the races were about to begin. But when the first flight of horses galloped off, I was not watching them, I was watching Maynard, who had, it seemed, forgotten all the insults and slights and was now laughing and boasting with the low whites, and it seemed that Maynard had, in spite of himself, found his people. Or they'd found him. The prospect of a high-born Walker frolicking among them allowed these low whites, too, to bask in the glamour of the day. This esteem only increased itself when Maynard's time came and his own horse, Diamond, running among the other horses in a great cloud of brown and black, everything noses and legs, emerged from it all, taking a clear lead from the cloud, and holding this lead all the way to the finish. Maynard exploded. He screamed and hugged everyone around him, threw his arms into the air, and then pointed up in the box, toward the jockey club, and yelled something haughty and rude. And then sighting his Corrine in the ladies' box, he did the same. The men in the jockey club stood there stoic, their lovely sport having been desecrated by this oaf who was born among them, but whose every win lowered the entire game.

After the last race, I met him back off Market Street. I had never seen Maynard more happy in all of his brief life. He looked at me with a huge smile, and said, "Hot damn, Hiram, I told you, didn't I? It was my day, I said it."

I nodded and said, "You did call it."

"I told them," he said, climbing into the buggy. "I told them all!"

"You did," I said.

And then, mindful of my father's admonition, I turned the chaise back out of the town toward home.

"No, no! What are you doing?" he said. "Go back! I want to see them. I told them and they did not heed me. We have to show them! They have to see!"

And so I turned back around and headed toward the center of town, where, by then, the gentry had gathered themselves, along the streets for the last bit of intercourse before parting for the day. But when we rode past in the Millennium chaise, instead of any show of respect, the men and women of Quality glanced our way, nodded without smiling, and went back to their conversation. I don't know what precisely Maynard wanted or why he expected to get it. I don't know what was in him that made him believe that this time they would at last acknowledge the merit of his blood, or forgive his impulses and outbursts. But when it was clear he would find no satisfaction, he growled and ordered me to turn to the far edge of town, where I was to leave him at the pleasure house and recover him in an hour.

I was now alone, and grateful for the privacy of my thoughts. I hitched the horse and began to wander the town. I was recalled again to recent events, to my dream, to the realization of the unending night of slavery, to that morning, when I watched the daylight of Sophia fade like dying sun over the blue Virginia mountains. I do not claim to have loved Sophia then, though I thought I did. I was young and love to me was a fuse that was lit, not a garden that was grown. Love was not concerned with any deep knowledge of its object, of their wants and dreams, but mainly with the joy felt in their presence and the sickness felt in their departure. And in Sophia's own private moments, did she love me? I did not think so, but in another world, a world beyond the Task, I thought she might.

There were two roads leading to such a world—buying one's freedom and running. What I knew of the first consisted of a cluster of free coloreds, living in the southern corner of Starfall, who, in the era of red earth and booming tobacco, were allowed to save some small wage and then buy back their bodies. But that road was closed to me. Virginia had changed. Even as the old lands of Elm County, of Lockless, declined, the luster of those who tasked among them increased. What was lost in their labor upon the land could be recouped in their sale, at a premium, Natchez-way, where the land still bloomed. So where once the Tasked could work their way to freedom, they were now too precious to be granted the right of paying their own ransom.

If the first road was blocked, the second was unthinkable. Every single person I'd ever known who'd run from Lockless was either returned by Ryland's Hounds, the patrols of low whites who enforced the order of the Quality, or they had lost their heart and returned themselves. In any case, so total was my ignorance of the world beyond Virginia that running seemed insane. But there was one who was said to know more.

No man was more esteemed among the coloreds and the whites of Elm County than Georgie Parks. He was the mayor, the ambassador, the dream, though the dream took its meaning from whatever vantage it was glimpsed from. Back when he was tasked, Georgie worked the fields and, much like Big John, seemed to have a preternatural understanding of agriculture and all its cycles. He could spend an hour walking among your wheat fields and tell you about the harvest three years from now or put his hand on your tobacco hillocks, feel for the heartbeat of the earth, and reveal whether your tobacco ears would be elephants or mice. And he had warned the Quality of what they courted with their love of tobacco, in a sideways manner so that his warning was not remembered by them in spite, but with a good-natured regret. But there was a tantalizing shadow about Georgie. He would disappear for long periods or be seen out in Starfall or glimpsed in the woods at the oddest of hours. We had an explanation for these mysteries. Georgie was tied to the Underground.

And what was this Underground? It was said among the Tasked that a secret society of colored men had built their own separate world deep in the Virginia swamps. What powers guarded them there, I did not know. What I knew were the tales of Ryland's Hounds sent off on expeditions to discover the Underground and root them out, tales of how these expeditions returned, reduced in number, scarred and battered, testifying of snakes, strange ailments, poisons, and root-doctors marshaling crocodiles and catamounts into the fray. And this Underground, I was told, would, from time to time, take on new recruits who preferred the wild freedom of the swamps to the civilized slavery of Elm County. It seemed perfect that noble Georgie, praised and esteemed by the whites, and held to have some secret life by the coloreds, would be their man.

I was pulled out of my ruminations on Georgie by the sound of gunfire. I was at the southern end of the town square. I followed the sound and saw a gentleman, in his formal black uniform, laughing uproariously with his shotgun pointed in the air. The tenor of the day was changing. Clouds now crowded the sky. I watched two men stumble fighting out of a pub and into the streets—one older with a long scar across his cheek—and when the older man was bested, in seemingly a single motion, he pulled out a long knife and sliced the face of the younger man. Then two more men raced out of the pub and jumped the older fellow. I hastily walked away as they started to thrash him. On the next block, I watched as a low white woman grabbed a Dutch girl by her hair and slapped her. Her male companion laughed, pulled out a flask, took a drink, and then emptied the rest on the Dutch girl's head. I walked on. This was the riotousness that my father had warned me of, that he begged me to keep Maynard distanced from. But it was always like this with them, a race of cackling Alice Caulleys. Like the parties of Lockless, race-day would start off in high pageantry, and then the drinking would start and the festive spirit would darken, and all the masks of fashion and breeding would fall away, until the oozing, pocked face of Elm County would lie revealed.

There were no other colored people out, because we all knew what came next—the ill feeling descending on the whites would soon be turned upon us. It is odd to say this, but it was the free coloreds who had the most to fear under such circumstance. We who were Tasked belonged to someone. We were property and any damage inflicted on us must be done under the orders of our owner, for you could no more beat another man's slave than you could beat another man's horse. But even from my relative safety, I felt uneasy. And in that state of mind, I endeavored to make my way away from the square to Freetown, and the home of Georgie Parks.

It was a small community, clustered together so tight that I knew everyone who lived there. I knew Edgar Combs, who'd once worked iron at the Carter place, and now did the same for the blacksmith in town, and Edgar was married to Patience, whose first husband had died when the fever hit all those years ago. And across from there was Pap and Grease, brothers, and next to them was Georgie Parks. So I walked out of the madness of the square and to the southern end of the town, and there found myself before Ryland's Jail, which marked the beginnings of the free colored section of Starfall.

It was all planned this way, it had to be, for Ryland's Jail was not a jail for criminals. Sprawling two city blocks, it was a warehouse for the Tasked who'd been caught running away or were being held before being sold. The jail was a daily reminder that no matter their freedoms, these coloreds of Starfall existed in the shadow of an awesome power, which, at a whim, could clap them back into chains. Ryland's Jail was run and staffed by the Low. These men became rich off the flesh trade, but their names were of too recent vintage and their work of such ill repute that they could never rise above their designation. It was the strong association between the jail and the low whites who fed and served it that gave them the name Ryland's Hounds. We feared them and hated them, perhaps more than we feared and hated the Quality who held us, for all of us were low, we were all Tasked, and we should be in union and arrayed against the Quality, if only the low whites would wager their crumbs for a slice of the whole cake.

Georgie's wife, Amber, greeted me at the door, smiling. "I thought you might be making your way past here today," she said. "And timed right, just before supper. You hungry, Hiram?" I smiled and greeted Amber and then stepped into the one-room hut, and that is what it was, barely better than what I enjoyed down in the Warrens. The smell of ash-cake and pork wafted over me and I realized I was indeed hungry. Georgie was there, seated on the bed, next to his just-born son, who lay there pawing at the air.

"Why, look at you," he said. "Rosie's boy gettin' big."

Rosie's boy, that is what they called me down in the Street, though I had not heard a greeting such as this in some time, because there were so few left who still remembered me as such. I embraced Georgie and asked how he was and he smiled and said, "Well, I got me a woman, and now I got me a little boy," and he walked over and rubbed the baby's belly. "So I reckon I'm doing just fine."

"Why don't you take Hiram out back," Amber said.

We stepped outside into a small area where Georgie kept his garden and chicken coop and seated ourselves on two upturned logs. I reached into my pocket and pulled out a small wooden horse that I had carved for Georgie's son and handed it to Georgie.

"For your boy," I said.

Georgie took the horse, nodded a thank-you, and put it in his pocket.

A few minutes later Amber came out with two plates and the cakes and fried pork on each of them and handed one to me and then one to Georgie, and I sat there eating wordlessly. Amber went back in and then returned with her cooing boy cradled in her arms. It was now late in the afternoon.

"Ain't had nothing today, huh?" asked Georgie, smiling large, his reddish-brown hair seeming to flame against the dying light of that late autumn afternoon.

"Naw, guess I haven't," I said. "Somehow it just slipped me."

"Something else on your mind, mayhaps?"

I looked up at Georgie and started to speak. But then, fearing what I knew I wanted to say, I stopped. I set the plate down next to the log. Amber had gone back inside. I waited for a moment and heard muffled laughter and the baby squealing, and I reasoned that Amber was now out front enjoying the company of some other visitors.

"Georgie, how'd you feel when you walked off Master Howell's place for the first time?"

He swallowed half a mouthful and took a moment before answering. "Like a man," he said, and then chewed and swallowed the rest. "Which is not to say I wasn't one before, but I had never truly felt it. My whole life depended on me not feeling it, you know?"

"I do know," I said.

"I don't need to tell you this, or maybe I do, because they have always favored you in a particular way, but I'll say it anyhow and you may make what you feel of it. I now rise when I want and I sleep when it is my will. My name is Parks because I said so. I pulled the name from nothing—conjured it as a gift to my son. It got no meaning except this—I chose it. Its meaning is in the doing. Do you get me, Hiram?"

I nodded and let him continue on.

"I don't know if I ever told you, Hiram, but we was all crazy in love with your Rosie."

I laughed.

"She was a beautiful girl, and there were so many beautiful girls down there in the Street. Wasn't just Rose, you know, was her sister—your aunt Emma too. Such beautiful girls." Emma another name like my mother's, lost in the smoke; I knew she was my aunt, that she'd once worked in the kitchen, that she was a beautiful dancer, but she had otherwise disappeared into the flat words of others and the fog of my mind. But Georgie had it all. The past unfolded itself in front of him like a map, and I saw his eyes glow as he recounted his travels through every mountain pass and gully and gulch.

He said, "Man, I think back to them days, and how we used to stomp the floor. Good golly. Your momma and Emma was as opposite as could be—Rose quiet as Emma was loud, but when they got down to Deep Meeting you knew the same blood was between them. I am telling you I was there, all those Saturday nights. I was there with Jim the Phenomenal and his boy Young P. We had the banjo, jaw-harp, fiddle all going, pots and pans ringing out, and sheep bones clacking, and when it got hot, Emma and Rose would get to it. And it was something, I tell you, with the jars of water on their heads, going back and forth until a splash of water fell from one of their pots. Then they'd smile and curtsy, and whichever one of them had come out on top would look out for any other who should like to step in the ring."

"But no one did." Georgie laughed loudly and asked, "You ever water dance, Hi?"

"Naw," I said. "Wasn't my thing."

"Shame, shame," Georgie said. "Shame to have all that beauty and not pass it on. And it was so much beauty back there. Beautiful girls. Beautiful boys."

Georgie was finished eating by now. He set down his plate and blew out a long stream of air.

"And I think of all that beauty sometimes, how it withered in them chains. . . . Man, I tell you, when I took up with Amber, I vowed I would get her out. Whatever it took, I did not care. I think I might well have killed a man to get her out, Hiram. Anything to not watch her . . ."

And Georgie pulled up there because I think he then realized the import of what he was saying, what it meant for me, and what it meant for my momma.

"And you are out now," I said. "You have done it. You out."

Georgie laughed quietly and then he said, "Ain't nobody out, son, you hear? Ain't no out. All gotta serve. I like serving here more than at some other man's Lockless, I will grant you that, but I am serving, of that I can assure you."

We sat there quiet for a few minutes. The voices out front subsided and I heard the front door close and then the back one open. Amber came out and took Georgie's plate and then my own.

She looked at me, raised an eyebrow, and said, "Georgie filling you with lies again?"

"Tough to tell," I said.

"Mmmm-hmm," she said, walking back into the house. "Watch him, I say. Watch Georgie. He is slippery."

From Georgie's back garden, I could see the far edge of the Goose River. The sun was now dropping low in the sky and clouds were calling up and the day grew cooler. It would soon be time. Maynard would be ready. So I decided to say something to Georgie Parks that would alter my life.

"Georgie, I feel that I must go."

I think he caught the meaning, and then decided he did not, and said, "I guess so. Got to get back across the river, huh?"

"No," I said. "I am telling you that I am getting up in age, and I am watching people disappear, carried off Natchez-way, and I can see the whole place going down. The land is dead, Georgie. The soil done turned to sand and they know it, all of them. I was just walking here and I seen a man knifed and a girl beat in the street. Ain't no law. I like to think there was law once, the older folks speak of such a time, and though I have not known it, I can feel all the changes. A man is blooming inside me, Georgie, and I cannot shackle him. He know too much. He seen too much. He has got to get out, this man, or he cannot live. I swear I fear what is coming. I fear my own hands."

Georgie started to say something, but I cut him off.

"It is said that you are a man of knowledge, that you know more than this little free quarter, that you are connected with people who operate in such things. I want the railway, Georgie. I want the railway out, and I have been told you know of such things."

And now Georgie stood and wiped his mouth, and then wiped his hands on his overalls. Then, never looking at me, he sat down again.

"Hiram, go home now," he said. "Ain't no man blooming in you. It done bloomed already. This is who you are. This is your condition and if you is planning to change it, you must do it as I did."

"Don't work no more," I said. "Ain't no tasking man capable of out-earning Natchez."

"Then your life is your life. And may I say it is a good one. Your

61

only charge is that dumb brother of yours. Go home, Hiram. Get yourself a wife. And make like you happy."

I did not answer. He said it again, "Go home."

And so that was Georgie's command and I followed it. But what I believed, right then, was that Georgie had lied to me, that he was as they had claimed him to be—an officer of freedom, of some other life, of an Oregon for a colored man. He had not even denied it, and so the matter to me then became simple—I had to prove to him who and what I was, that I could not, at that late hour, be talked out of it, and I was certain I could do this, and so as I walked back to Maynard and the chaise, back past the square, I knew that Georgie would help me, I knew that he would get me out, because there was no future here and I saw this even in my short walk back through the refuse of the day. There was trash all out in the streets. A man of Quality, whom I recognized by his garment, lay passed out face-down in manure while his compatriots, stripped down to the shame of their shirtsleeves, laughed at him. I saw torn hats and the flowers that once adorned them. I saw azure scarves in the street. I saw men tossing dice along the side of the pub, and then out front two cocks being fitted for the fight. This was their civilization—a mask so thin that for the first time in my life, I wondered what I myself had ever aspired to in those days back down in the Street, with my trick of memory, designing to catch the eye of the Pharaoh of Lockless, and not for the first time I saw that I had set my sights much too low. Because we in the Warrens lived among them, we knew first-hand that they took the privy as all others, that they were young and stupid, and old and frail, and that their powers were all a fiction. They were no better than us, and in so many ways worse.

Maynard was outside the fancy house with his fancy girl, waiting, and next to them I saw Corrine's man again. Hawkins. Maynard was laughing at some joke, while Hawkins regarded him with a muted loathing Maynard was too drunk to detect. When Maynard spotted me, he laughed even harder, started toward me, and stumbled to the ground, taking the girl along with him. I helped the girl up, while Hawkins quickly moved to help Maynard, whose breeches and waistcoat were now soiled with mud.

"Goddamn it, Hiram!" he cried. "You suppose to catch me!" Indeed. I had always caught him.

"The girl is my own tonight," he yelled. "She's mine, goddamn it! Like I told them, Hiram! Like I told them all! Like I told all the girls!"

Then he looked over to the loathing Hawkins. "Not a word of this to your mistress, boy. Not one word. You understand?"

"A word about what, sir?" Hawkins said.

After a moment of squinting, Maynard laughed again. "Yessir, we gonna get along well, me and you."

"Like family should," said Hawkins.

"Like family should!" Maynard yelled, climbing into the chaise. I helped the girl in and then we were off, headed out the way we'd come in. But then, and who knows why, a moment of clarity struck him, a shame that had defied him all his life, and he ordered me back, away from the town square, out toward Dumb Silk Road. And so we left Starfall in this fashion, left the world as we had known it, for as I rode out of town and the buildings gave way to trees, bursting in gold and orange, as I heard the crows in the distance, the horse clopping in front, and felt the wind in my face, I knew that I had seen every inch of the only world I'd know. I knew how my span of days would end. Someday my father would pass on from this earth and what remained would fall to Maynard, and when that day came, I knew that all paths led to Natchez.

I rode out in thrall to those feelings of the past hours, the dream, the terror, the rage, the unending night, the sun of Sophia fading over the mountains, my lost mother and my aunt Emma. And too there was a want, a desire for an escape from Maynard and the doom of his mastery. And then it came.

I caught sight of the river Goose, and saw a strange mist coming up off the water—a thin fog and now rain that echoed the day's dark turn. And there it was, a blue mist coming up, obscuring the far end of the bridge. And then, and I remember this most directly, because we had been moving at a good clip, the steady and quick clopping of the horse's shoes faded. I could see the horse right there before me pulling us along but without a sound, and I thought perhaps it was me, some temporary deafness, but I did not think much because I wanted to get home, I wanted to be free of Maynard, if only for what remained of that evening, and we were on the bridge, and the thin fog had suddenly parted, and that was the moment when I saw her, saw the woman, saw my mother water dancing on the bridge, water dancing out of the blackness of my mind, and I tried to slow the horse, I remember this, pulling at the reins, but the horse barreled on, though I wonder now if I was even pulling the reins, if I was even there in that space, on that bridge, because even now, having done the thing, I cannot say I truly understand the entirety of Conduction, save this essential thing—you have to remember.

· 5 ·

I WAS IN THE WATER, and then falling into the light, guided by my dancing mother, until the light overwhelmed, and when it dimmed, and faded away, my mother was gone, and I felt the land under my feet. It was night. I saw the fog drawing back like a curtain, until the sky was clear and the stars blinked in and out above. When I turned back, looking for the mist-covered river out of which I had just emerged, all I saw was high grass waving black in the wind. I was leaning on a large stone and in the distance, past the field, I could see the forest, looming. I knew this place. I knew the distance from this stone to the trees, I knew this grass, that it was a field of fallow, my Lockless. And I knew that the stone was no random place-mark, but was the monument to the progenitor, Archibald Walker. My great-grandfather. The wind gusted through, shivering me, so that my waterlogged brogans were like ice against my feet. I took a step forward, wheeled, fell, and down there in that grass I became aware of a powerful desire to sleep. Perhaps I had entered a kind of purgatory, modeled after a world I knew, that must be endured before my reward was revealed to me. And so I lay there shivering, making no effort to move. I reached into my pocket for the coin I carried everywhere, feeling its rough edges, as darkness closed in around me.

But there was no reward. At least none of the sort the old ones spoke of down in the Street. I am here, telling this story, and not from the grave, not yet, but from the here and now, peering back into another time, when we were Tasked, and close to the earth, and close to a power that baffled the scholars and flummoxed the Quality, a power, like our music, like our dance, that they cannot grasp, because they cannot remember.

It was our music that I followed out from the darkness, out from three days, as I was later told, of straddling the line between life and death, of senseless murmuring and frightful fevers. My first note of consciousness was someone humming softly in what seemed to be the distance, and then the hummed melody repeating itself, trailing away for a minute or two, and then returning, and then came the dim realization that I knew the melody, and I began matching the words in my mind:

> *All the heavenly band a-churning*
> *Aubrey spying and good girls turning.*

There was the smell of vinegar and washing soda, so sharp I could taste it, the warmth of a blanket, the softness of a pillow under my head, and then, blinking open my eyes, I saw that I was in a room awash in sun. I could not move. My head was propped against a pillow and cocked to the side. I looked out from an alcove bed, the curtains drawn away. There was a bureau across the room, and on the bureau I saw the bust of the progenitor, and next to that a mahogany footstool, and seated there, her back straight, her neck long, I saw Sophia, working two needles between a spool of yarn, her arms winding back and forth. I tried to move, but my joints were locked. I panicked, for at that moment I feared I had suffered some injury and thus become a prisoner in my own body.

I watched desperately, hoping for Sophia to look over at me; instead she stood, still humming the old melody, still knitting, and walked out the door.

How long did I lie there in that great terror, wondering if I was now entombed in my own body? I can't say, but darkness came again, and this time when I awoke the paralysis had lifted some. I could move my toes. I could open my mouth and roll my tongue. I was able to turn my head and now my arms returned to me, so that pushing, with great effort, I was able to sit straight up in the bed. I looked around and, again seeing the sun, the bust, the light, I knew that I was in Maynard's room. I looked past the footstool and saw his wardrobe, his bureau, the mirror where, only that last morning, I had him stand while dressing him. And then I remembered the water.

I sat there trying to speak, trying to call for someone, but the words were lodged inside me. Sophia walked back into the room, head down, still knitting, and hearing my heaving attempt to speak, looked up, dropped her yarn, ran over and caught me in her long spider arms. Then she pulled back and looked at me.

"Welcome back to us, Hi," she said.

I remember trying to smile but my face must have twisted into some pitiful mask, because all the joy dropped from her. Sophia brought her hand to her face and covered her mouth. She put one hand on my shoulder and the other on my back and guided me back down into the bed.

"Don't dare talk," she said. "You may think yourself out of the Goose, but the Goose ain't yet out of you."

I lay back and the world faded in the same order it came to me— the light of the room disappearing, then the washing-soda smell, and finally Sophia, whose hand I could feel on my brow, whose gentle humming I could still hear. And then I fell asleep and into a dream of my plunge in the Goose. The whole scene now played out at a distance. I saw my head bursting out through the water, scanning the terrain, and deciding that I had found my doom. And

Maynard was there, struggling against the water, struggling to save himself. And I saw the blue light part the sky and reach down for me, and this time I reached for Maynard, my only brother, tried to save him, but he yanked his arm away, cursed me, and then faded into the darkness of the depths.

When I next awoke, my arms still ached, but I felt my hands, limber and loose. The smell of vinegar lingered in the room, but fainter now. I sat up with little effort and saw the white curtains of the alcove drawn closed around me, and through them I could see the rough silhouette of someone seated on the footstool, in lonely vigil. I remembered that Sophia had last been there and felt my blood quicken at the possibility. I heard the song of morning birds and was suddenly filled with a great joy at the fact of having been alive. But then I pulled back the curtains and saw that the silhouette was my father, seated on the footstool with his elbows on his legs and hands cuffing his face, and when he looked up at me I saw that his small eyes were bloodshot and heavy.

"We have lost him," he said, shaking his head. "My Little May is gone and the whole of this great house, the whole of Elm County, is grieving." Then he stood, walked over, and sat on the edge of the bed. He reached out and gripped my shoulder tight. My eyes wandered down to my own body and I saw someone had dressed me in a long nightgown, which I recognized as Maynard's. I looked back up to my father and saw a kind of realization crawling over his face, and we were, in that moment, in a kind of secret communication that can only exist between a parent and child, no matter how monstrous the relation. I saw his small eyes, red with grief, squinting, as though straining to comprehend a message, straining to understand how it came to be that all that remained of him was here before him, was a slave. And when this realization was complete, he pulled back, buried his head in his hands, stood, weeping loudly, and walked out.

I stood and walked to the window. The day was clear and I could see, from the back side of Lockless, clear to the hills, hazy in the distance. I turned away from the window and saw my father coming back to the room. Behind him was Roscoe, who'd brought me up all those years ago from the Street. And across his aged, creased face there was a look of gravity and concern, and I remembered that there had been people who knew me and loved me, elders, who delighted in my song and games. Roscoe laid a set of clothes on Maynard's dresser—my clothes. Then he stripped the bedding, wrapped it into a bundle under his arm, and walked out. My father sat again on the footstool.

"We have sought his body in the river, but the water . . ." he said, his voice trailing off. He was trembling now.

"When I think of my boy at the bottom of that river . . ." he said. "And I cannot but think of anything else, do you hear me, Hiram? When I think of him engaged to that bottom . . . Forgive me. I can but imagine what you saw out there. But I must confess, for none other is fit to hear it: Maynard was all I had of his mother. When his eyes went gleeful, I saw hers. When he was forgetful, I saw her habit. When he was compassionate, as he was always, I saw her."

He was crying now. "And now he is gone, and I am twice departed."

Roscoe returned, this time with a washcloth, a small basin of water, and a larger empty one, and set it all on the dresser.

"Well, so it is, son," my father said. "Some arrangement shall be made. The memory of him does not die, wherever his body might make its rest. What you must know, what you surely know, is that Maynard loved you, and I do not doubt he gave his very life so that you might get out of that river."

When my father left, I took the washcloth and water and cleaned myself, but my hands shook while I juggled the madness of his last words. *Maynard loved you*. This notion—that Maynard loved anyone, that Maynard would give his life for anyone, much less me— was astounding me. But then as I dressed, and turned it over, I came to an understanding—my father believed this insanity. He had to. Maynard was him, was his wife, and this glorified portrait somehow lived right along with the admonition my father had always communicated to me—that Maynard must be watched, that he was not to be trusted with his own life. Walking down the back stairs, I knew that my father's statement could only be reconciled through the peculiar religion of Virginia—Virginia, where it was held that a whole race would submit to chains; Virginia, where this same race held the math that molded iron and carved marble to exact proportion and were still called beasts; Virginia, where a man would profess his love for you one moment and sell you off the next. Oh, the curses my mind constructed for my fool of a father, for this country where men dress sin in pageantry and pomp, in cotillions and crinolines, where they hide its exercise, in the down there, in a basement of the mind, in these slave-stairs, which I now I descended, into the Warrens, into this secret city, which powered an empire so great that none dare speak its true name.

When I got back to the Warrens, I found Thena standing just outside her door, in the dim light, talking to Sophia. Thena looked at me hard. I smiled at her. She walked over to me, shaking her head. Then she put her hand on my cheek and locked eyes. She didn't smile, only regarded me from my head to feet, and I had the feeling that she was making sure every part of me was in its place.

"Well," she said. "Don't look like you fell in no river."

She was not a warm woman, Thena, this other mother of mine. There was a general belief that if she wasn't cursing you or shooing you off, she might, at least, have a good feeling for you. I generally returned this good feeling with my own muted affection. And there was no offense in that. We had our own language to affirm what we were to each other.

But that day, without thought, I spoke a different language. I wrapped my arms around Thena and pulled her close, and held her tight as though venting all my joy at being alive, and held her tight like she were flotsam and I were back in the Goose.

After a few seconds, she pulled back, looked me up and down again. Then she turned and walked off.

Sophia watched her go, then when Thena had turned a corner, she looked at me and laughed.

"That ol' gal know she love you," she said.

I nodded.

"I mean it. She don't much talk to me. But after you went under, she kept asking questions, side-like, trying to get what word on you she could."

"She come see me?"

"Not once—and that's how I know she love you. I'd ask her and she'd get all flustered and I knew what it was—she couldn't see you like that. It's hard, Hiram. It was hard even on me, and I don't like you, much less love you."

At that she slapped my shoulder and we laughed quietly together, but my heart tumbled in my chest.

"So how are you?" Sophia asked.

"Been better," I said. "But glad to be getting back to where I belong."

"Which is to say not looking up from the Goose," said Sophia.

"That is about the fact of it," I said.

There was a silence between us for a few moments that began to feel uncertain and then rude. So I invited Sophia into my quarters. She accepted. I pulled out a chair for her, and when seated, she reached into her apron and produced a ball of yarn and needles and started knitting one of her inscrutable things. I sat on my bed, our knees now almost touching.

"Glad to see you shaping up," she said.

"Yes, I am coming together," I said. "Ain't waste no time getting me out Maynard's room, did they?"

"It's better that way, ain't it?" she said. "Can't say I'd want to be in some dead man's bed."

"It is better that way," I said.

By instinct, I reached into my pocket for my coin, but the coin was not there. Likely it was now lost, and the fact of this saddened me. It had been my charm, my token of the Street, even if my great plans had come to nothing.

"How'd they find me?" I asked.

"Corrine's man," Sophia said, still knitting. "You know him? Hawkins?"

"Hawkins?" I said. "Where?"

"On the shore," Sophia said. "This side of the Goose. Face-down in the muck. No idea how you made it out of there, cold as that water be. Got somebody watching over you."

"Maybe," I said. But I was not thinking of how I got out. I was thinking of Hawkins—how I'd seen him twice on race-day and then how he'd been the one to find me.

"Hawkins, huh?" I repeated.

"Yep," she said. "Corrine and him and her girl, Amy, been here most days since. Sure would be nice to thank him."

"Sure would," I said. "Guessing I will."

She rose to leave and I felt now the soft pain that came to me whenever she did.

After Sophia left, I sat on the edge of my bed contemplating the shape of events. Something did not fit. Sophia had said that Hawkins found me on the riverbank. But I had the most distinct memory of falling down in the fallows. I remembered seeing the monument there, the stone left to mark the first works of the progenitor, Archibald Walker. But the fallows were two miles from the river, and I had no memory of walking the distance between the two. Perhaps I had imagined it all, in the throes of near-death, conjured up this last vision of my ancestry—my dancing mother, the monument of the progenitor—as some farewell to this world.

I stood and walked out of my quarters. I had a notion to head out to the fallows, to the monument, hoping to find something there that might resolve my memory with Hawkins's story. I turned down the narrow passage along which I lived, passed Thena's quarters, and then into the tunnel that led outside. The sunlight beaming in blinded me. I stood there, looking out, my left hand formed over my brow like the brim of a hat. A team of tasking men walked past, with cross-back bags and spades, and among them I saw Pete, the gardener who was, like Thena, one of the old ones who had through his own ingenuity escaped Natchez.

"Hey, Hi, how are you?" Pete said as he passed me.

"Fine, fine," I said.

"Good to hear," he said. "Take it easy, son, you hear? And make sure . . ."

He was still speaking but the distance and my own thoughts overtook his words and I just stood there watching as he and his men disappeared into that blinding light, and at that moment I was, for reasons I do not know, struck by a great panic. It was something about Pete—something about how he disappeared like that into the sunlight, as I had felt myself to be disappearing only days before, but disappearing into a blindness. I rushed back to my quarters with this panicked feeling in me and lay down across my bed.

Again, by instinct, I reached in my pocket for the coin that was not there. I lay there for the rest of the day. I thought back to Hawkins's story, of finding me on the shore. I was certain I had been in the high grass, I remembered it clearly, remembered seeing the great stone monument before falling under, and my memory never failed.

As I lay there I heard the sounds of the house, this place of secret slavery, rising with the hours into the afternoon, and then falling away, indicating evening had come. When all was silent, I walked back out of the tunnel, past the lantern-light, into the night. The moon looked out from behind a spray of thin black clouds, so that it seemed a bright puddle against the sky pinpricked by the stars.

At the edge of the bowling green, I watched as someone crossed the low grass, and as the distance closed, I saw that it was Sophia. She was wrapped from her head down in a long shawl.

"Little late for you to be out," she said. "Especially given your condition."

"Been in that bed all day," I said. "I need air."

Sophia pulled the shawl tighter as a wind pushed gently out from the bank of trees to the west. She was looking down the road as though something else had taken over her.

"I should let you be," I said. "Think I'm gonna take a walk."

"Huh?" she said, now glancing back at me. "Nah, I'm sorry I have this habit about me, I'm sure you seen it. Sometimes a thought carry me away and I forget where I am. Come in handy sometimes, I tell you that."

"What was the thought?" I asked.

She looked back at me and shook her head and laughed to herself.

"You say you walking?" she asked.

"I did."

"How bout I walk with you."

"Suit me just fine."

I said it as though it were nothing, but had she seen me at that moment, she would have known it was much more. We walked silently down the winding path, past the stables, toward the Street, the same path I had run up all those years ago in search of my mother. And then the path opened and I saw the long row of gabled cabins that had once been my home.

"You used to live down here, huh?" she said.

"In that cabin right there," I said, pointing. "And then later when I took up with Thena, farther down."

"You miss it?" she asked.

"Sometimes, I guess," I said. "But if I'm honest, I wanted to come up. I had dreams back then. Big dumb dreams. Dead and gone."

"And what do you dream of now?" she asked.

"After what I just came up from?" I said. "Breathing. I just dream of breathing."

Looking down toward the cabins, we watched as two figures, barely shadows, emerged, stopping just outside. One shadow pulled the other close, and stayed that way for a minute or two, until they released each other, slowly, and one shadow went back inside, while the other turned toward the back side of the cabin, disappeared, then reappeared in the fields, darting now toward the woods at the far edge. I was certain that the shadow now running was a man, and the shadow gone into the cabin was his wife. It was a normal thing to see back then because so many marriages extended across the wide miles of the county. When I was small, I would wonder why any man would impair himself so. But now, watching the shadow bound through the fields, and standing there with Sophia, I felt that I understood.

"You know I'm from somewhere," she said. "I had me a life before all of this. I had people."

"And what was your life?"

"Carolina," she said. "Born there the same year as Helen, Nathaniel's woman. But it ain't about her or him, you know. It's about what I had down there."

"And what was that?" I asked.

"Well, in the first place, I had a man. A good one. Big. Strong. We used to dance, you know. Go down with the folks to this old broke-down smokehouse on Saturdays and stomp the floor."

She paused, perhaps to savor the memory.

"You dance, Hi?" she asked.

"Not even a little," I said. "I am told my momma had the gift. But look like I favor my daddy in that capacity."

"Ain't about 'favor,' Hi, it's about doing. Best thing about the dance is it really didn't matter who had it and who did not. Only crime you could commit was to spend that whole night all lonesome against that old smokehouse wall."

"Is that a fact," I said.

"Yes, it is," she said. "Now, don't misunderstand: I was a caution. Every time I shook, I put some hen out her happy home."

We both laughed.

"I'm sorry I didn't get to see it—didn't get to see you dance," I said. "Everything had changed here by the time I came up, you know. And I was a different kind of child. Even now, a different kind of man."

"Yeah, I see that," she said. "Kinda remind me of my Mercury. He was a quiet one too. Was what I liked about him. No matter what happened, I knew it was between us. I should have known that it could not stand. But he danced, see. Man, in those days we'd dance before we would eat. Used to tear that old smokehouse down, and my Mercury, in brogans thick as biscuits, was light as a dove."

"What happened?" I asked.

"Same as happening up here. Same as happening everywhere. I had people, you know, Kansas, Millard, Summer . . . People, you know? Well, you don't, but you understand."

"Yeah," I said. "I do."

"But wasn't none like my Mercury," she said. "Hoping he resting easy. Hoping he found himself some thick Mississippi wife."

Now she turned without a word and started back.

"I got no idea what for I am telling you all this," she said. I nodded and listened. It was always like this. People talked to me. They told me their stories, gave them to me for keeping, which I did, always listening, always remembering.

The next morning, I washed and walked out, just as the sun made its way over the trees. I passed the bowling green, then the orchards, where Pete and his team—Isaiah, Gabriel, and Wild

Jack—were already picking and gently depositing apples in their burlap satchels. I walked until I was in the fallow field, covered with clover, walked until I saw the stone monument. I stood there for a moment, letting it all come back to me—the river, the mist, the high grass waving, black in the wind, and then the sudden appearance of the progenitor's stone. I circled the monument once, twice, and then saw something glinting in the morning sun, and before even reaching down, before picking it up, before fingering its edges, before putting it in my pocket, I knew that it was the coin, my token into the Realm—but not the Realm I'd long thought.

· 6 ·

I HAD BEEN THERE IN the fallow field. And if I had been in the field, then all of it—the river, the mist, the blue light—must bear out too. I stood stock-still amidst the timothy and clover, the coin now in my pocket, and felt a great pressure in my head, so that the world seemed to wheel and spin around me. I knelt down in the high grass. I could hear my heart pounding. I pulled a handkerchief from my vest and mopped the sudden drizzle of sweat from my brow. I closed my eyes. I took in several long, slow breaths.

"Hiram?"

I opened my eyes, to see Thena standing there. I wobbled to my feet and felt the sweat now running down my face.

"Oh my," she said and then put her hand to my brow. "What are you doing, boy?"

I felt faint. I could not speak. Thena threw my arm over her shoulder and began walking me back to the fields. I was aware that we were moving, but through my fever, everything seemed a rush of autumnal brown and red. The smell of Lockless, the fetid stables, the burning of brush, the orchards we now shuffled past, even the sweet sweat of Thena, were suddenly acute and overpowering. I remember seeing the tunnel into the Warrens flitter before me in a haze, and then I was doubled over, retching into a basin. Thena waited for me to recover.

"All right?"

"Yeah, yeah," I said.

Back in my quarters, Thena helped me take off my outer garments. Then she handed me a fresh pair of drawers and stepped outside. When she returned, I was lying on my rope bed with the blanket pulled up to my shoulders. Thena took the stone jar from over my mantel and walked out to the well. When she came back, she set the jar on the table, took a glass from the mantel, poured water into it, and then handed the glass to me.

"You gotta rest," she said.

"I know," I said.

"If you know, what was you doing out there?"

"I just . . . how'd you find me?"

"Hiram, I will always find you," she said. "Taking these clothes for the washing. I'll have them back to you by the Monday next."

Thena stood and walked to the door.

"I gotta get back to it," she said. "Rest. Don't be no fool."

I fell quickly into sleep, and into a dream world, but one of memory. I was once again out in the stables, my mother just lost to me. I peered into the eyes of the Tennessee Pacer, peered until I disappeared into them and came out in that loft where I had so often played among my young childhood thoughts.

The next morning, Roscoe came to my quarters. "Take it light," he said. "They'll be working you hard in time. Rest yourself now."

But lying there, all I found were questions and paranoias that rattled around in my head—the deceptions of Hawkins, my dancing mother on the bridge. Work was the only escape. I dressed and walked out of the tunnel, rounded the house, only to be greeted by Corrine Quinn's chaise crawling up the main road. This had become a regular occurrence since Maynard's passing. Corrine would arrive with Hawkins and her maid Amy, and then spend an afternoon leading my father through prayer. There had never before been anything observant about the house. My father was Virginian, and like the relics of his Revolutionary fathers, a certain godlessness testified to the old days when everything seemed in question. But now he had lost his only heir, his legacy to the world, and his Christian god seemed all that was left. I backed into the tunnel a bit and watched as Hawkins helped his mistress out of the chaise, and then her maid, and the three walked up to the house. I did not then know why I found them so forbidding. All I knew was in their presence I felt something more terrible than any Holy Spirit.

I thought to return to my childhood habit of trying to fit in where I might be needed. But as I walked from kitchen to smokehouse, then from smokehouse to stable, then from stable to orchard, I was greeted with woeful looks, and it was clear that someone—Thena, Roscoe, or both—had dictated that I not be put to labor. So I resolved to find work myself. I returned to my quarters and changed out of my suit of house clothes into a pair of overalls and brogans. Then I walked out to a brick shed at the start of the woods just west of the main house, where my father kept a collection of lounges, footstools, bureaus, roll-top desks, and other old furnishings awaiting restoration. It was late morning. The air was cold and damp. Fallen leaves clung to the bottom of my brogans. I opened the shed. A block of light cut through a small square window, shining on the collection. I saw an Adams secretary, a camelback sofa, a satinwood corner chair, a mahogany highboy, and other pieces nearly as old as Lockless itself. I decided to work the mahogany highboy, on sentiment. It was here that my father had once kept secret and valuable things, a fact I knew because Maynard routinely rummaged through it and liked to detail his findings. Having decided upon my target, I went back to the Warrens. I took a lantern into the supply cupboard, and rummaged until I found a can of wax, a jar of turpentine, and an earthen pot. Just outside the shed I mixed the turpentine and wax in the pot. I left this solution to sit and then, with no small exertion, moved the highboy outside. I felt slightly faint then. I bent over with my hands on my knees and breathed deep. When I looked back up, I saw Thena looking out from the lawn into the trees.

"Get back in them quarters!" she yelled.

I smiled and waved. She shook her head and stalked off.

I spent the rest of the day sanding down the highboy. It was the most peace I'd had in days, as a kind of mindlessness fell over me.

I slept long and deep that night, dreamless, and awoke filled with the anticipation of renewing yesterday's labor and achieving again that mindless focus. After dressing, I walked back to the shed and found the solution of turpentine and wax ready. By late morning the highboy was gleaming in the sun. I stood back to take in my work. Just as I was about to walk back into the shed, in hopes of discovering another suitable target, I saw Hawkins coming across the grass in my direction. Corrine had obviously returned while I was working.

"Morning, Hi," Hawkins said. "That is what they call you, right?"

"Some do," I said.

At that he smiled, a gesture that had the effect of underscoring the crisp, bony architecture of his face. He was a thin man of mulatto complexion with skin drawn tight, so that you could see in select places the green outline of blood vessels. His eyes were set deep in his skull like gems in a tin box.

"Was sent out here to fetch you," he said. "Miss Corrine would like a word."

I returned with Hawkins to the house, where I retreated to my quarters and changed out of my brogans and overalls into a suit and slippers. Then I walked up the back stairs, pushed open the hidden door, and emerged into the parlor. My father was seated on the leather chesterfield, Corrine at his side. He was holding her hand in both of his, with a pained look on his face, seemingly trying to peer into her eyes, an effort frustrated by the black veil of mourning Corrine wore over her face. Hawkins and Amy stood off to each side of the chesterfield, at a respectful distance, watching the room, awaiting any command. Corrine was speaking to my father in an almost whisper, but loud enough that I caught snatches of the conversation across the long room. They were speaking of Maynard, sharing in their longing for him, or at least some beautified version of him, for this Maynard—held by them as a sinner on the verge of repentance—was not one I recognized. My father nodded as she talked, then he glanced over to me, and released her hands. He stood and waited for Hawkins to draw open the sliding parlor doors. He gave me one last look, still pained, then walked out. Hawkins drew the door closed and I wondered if I'd misjudged the conversation, for I had the foreboding sense that the subject had not been Maynard alone.

I noted then that they were all in black, Hawkins in a black suit, Amy in a black dress and, like Corrine, a veil of mourning, though less ornate. Standing there, Corrine's staff seemed extensions of her deeper mood, ethereal projections of her widow grief.

"You are acquainted with my people," she said. "Are you not?"

"Believe he is, ma'am," said Hawkins, smiling. "But when last I saw this boy he was barely acquainted with his life."

"I should thank you," I said. "I was told that I would have died if you hadn't seen me on the shore."

"Just happened to be out wandering," Hawkins said. "And I see a large steer laid out. And I walk up and sees that it is in fact a man. But you needn't thank me. It was you who got yourself out, which is quite a thing. Get caught in that Goose? Brother, it will carry you off. Man pry himself out? Well, that is quite a thing, quite a man. Goose is powerful, mighty powerful, even this time of year. Carry you off."

"Well, I do thank you," I said.

"Wasn't nothing," said Amy. "He just did whatever any man would for one fixing to be family."

"And we were to be as family," said Corrine. "And I think we should still. Tragedy should not break us. A man starts down a particular road. He remembers his steps, no matter what deluge may call upon the bridge.

"Woman is made for the completion of man," Corrine went on. "Our Father has made it this way. We take hands in matrimony and the rib is returned. You are an intelligent boy, all know this. Your father speaks of you as one would speak of miracles. He speaks of your genius, your tricks, your readings, but not too loudly, for envy rots at the bones of man. For envy, Cain slew his brother. For envy, Jacob deceived his father. And so your genius must be hidden from them. But I know, I know."

The light was low in the parlor, and the drapes half-drawn. I could see only the outline of Corrine's and Amy's faces. Corrine's speech quavered under itself, such that it sounded like three voices trembling at once, a kind of perverse harmony, flowing out from whatever darkness lurked behind the veil of mourning.

And it was not just the tenor of her voice but the very nature of her address that felt unusual. It is hard to convey this now, for it was another time replete with its own rituals, choreography, and manners among the classes and subclasses of Quality, Tasked, and Low. There were things you said and did not, and what you did marked your place in the ranks. The Quality, for instance, did not inquire on the inner workings of their "people." They knew our names and they knew our parents. But they did not *know* us, because not knowing was essential to their power. To sell a child right from under his mother, you must know that mother only in the thinnest way possible. To strip a man down, condemn him to be beaten, flayed alive, then anointed with salt water, you cannot feel him the way you feel your own. You cannot see yourself in him, lest your hand be stayed, and your hand must never be stayed, because the moment it is, the Tasked will see that you see them, and thus see yourself. In that moment of profound understanding, you are all done, because you cannot rule as is needed. You can no longer ensure that the tobacco hillocks are raised to your expectation; that the slips are fed into those hillocks at the precise time; that the plants are weeded and hoed with diligence; that your harvest is topped and the seed is filed and saved; that the leaves are left on the stalk, and the stalk spiked and hung at the proper distance, so that the plant neither molds nor dries out, but cures into that Virginia gold which moves the base and mortal man into the pantheon of Quality. Every step is essential and must be followed with the utmost care, and there is but one way to ensure that a man takes this care with a process that rewards him nothing, and that way is torture, murder, and maiming, is child-theft, is terror.

So to hear Corrine address me in this way, to attempt to draw some human bond, was bizarre and then terrifying because I was certain that the attempt itself concealed some darker aim. And I could not see her face, and thus could not look for any sign that might betray this aim. *I know,* she had said. *I know.* And recalling the story Hawkins told, and the truth of what had happened, I wondered then what, precisely, she knew.

Now I fumbled for words—"Maynard had his charms, ma'am," I said—and was duly checked.

"No, not charms," she said. "He was crude. Do not deny it to me. Put no flattery upon my ears, boy."

"Of course not, ma'am," I said.

"I knew him well," she continued. "He had no enterprise. He had no device. But I loved him, for I am a healer, Hiram."

She paused here for some moments. It was late morning. The sun blinked through the green Venetian blinds and there was an unnatural silence in the house, usually busy with the labor of the Tasked. I badly wanted to go back to the shed, to attend to the secretary or corner chairs perhaps. I felt that it was only a matter of moments before some trapdoor fell out from under me.

"They laughed at us, you know," she said. "All of society cackled—'the duchess and the buffoon,' they called us. Perhaps you know something of 'society.' Perhaps you know something of men who mask their earthly aims in piety and pedigree. Maynard did not. He had no charm, no guile. He could not waltz. He was a boor at the summer social. But he was a true boor, my boor."

When she said this, her voice quavered in still another measure—a deeper grief.

"I am broken, I tell you," she said. "Broken." I heard her weeping quietly under the mourning veil and it occurred to me then that maybe there was no device, that she was as she appeared, a young widow in mourning, that this urge to reach out to me was simply the need to touch those who had been close to him, and I was his slave but still his brother, and thus carried some of him with me.

"You, I think, perhaps, have some sense of how it might feel to be broken," she said. "You were his right arm, and without his guidance and protection, I wonder what you now make of yourself. I mean no unkind word. They say you safeguarded him against impulse and iniquity. I am told you counseled him in trying times. And I am told that you are an intelligent boy. And fools despise wisdom and instruction. And he was your instruction, was he not? And now, the good Howell Walker tells me that you can be seen wandering these grounds, all hands and no direction.

"Are you taken as I am, marking your time in any activity, hopeful of moving your thoughts from him? Woman is not so different, you know? All have their task. And so I wonder if you, like me, see him in all your works. He is all around me, Hiram. I see his face in the clouds, in the land, in my dreams. I see him lost in the mountains. And I see him hemmed in by the river, in those last terrible moments, in noble struggle with the depths. This is how he was, was he not, Hiram?

"It was you who last saw him, who alone can give account. I do not question his passing, for I lean on my Lord, and never my own daily understanding. But I am miserable in my ignorance and imaginings. Tell me that he died as befitting his name, honoring his station. Tell me he died in the true word in which he lived."

"He saved me, Miss Corrine, that is the fact of it." I don't know why I said this. I had spent very little time in the person of Corrine Quinn and everything about her rattled me. I was speaking out of instinct and what it told me was to soothe her, to ease her pain as best I could, for my own sake.

She brought her gloved hands up and under the veil. Her silence forced me to speak again.

"I was going under, ma'am, and I reached out," I said. "I felt the water around me like great knives, and I surely believed I was done. But he pulled me up, until I was strong enough to swim on my own. When I last saw him he was right with me, but the cold and the tide was too much."

She was silent for some moments. When she next spoke, her quavering voice was an iron rod. "You told none of this to Master Howell?" she asked.

"No, ma'am," I said. "I have spared him the details, for the very name of his departed son is hard upon his ears. The story grieves us all. I say it only now because you have so heartily requested and I hope that it shall bring you some portion of peace."

"Thank you for this," she said. "You do yourself more credit than you can know."

Again, she said nothing for a moment. I stood there awaiting her next request. When she spoke, her voice shifted upward. "So your master has left you. You are young, still—but idling as I hear it. What shall you now make of yourself?"

"I go where I am called, ma'am."

She nodded. "Then perhaps you will be called to my side. Maynard loved you so. Your name was the subject of anticipation. My champion was your champion. He gave his life for you. Perhaps, in due course, you too shall give of yourself. Do you see this, Hiram?"

"I do," I said.

And I did see, if not in that moment, then in the hour of reflection after. The grief and weeping might be true, but more certain was her dark intent—to pry me from Lockless and claim my services, my body, as her own. You have to remember what I was: not human but property, and a valuable property—one learned in all the functions of the manor, of crops, read, capable of entertaining with my tricks of memory. I was known for my industry, for my steady disposition, for my rectitude. And it would not be hard. I had, through her union with Maynard, been promised to her anyway. And now she would simply appeal to my father to leave this portion in place, to have me given over as terms of bereavement and mourning. And where would I find my home then? It was known that Corrine had property in Elm County but also farther west, across the mountains in the less developed portion of the state. This was the seed of her fortune, for through the management of multiple interests—timber, salt mines, hemp—it was said she had avoided the fall that now overtook Elm County. Whatever it was, I knew after that meeting I faced a new danger, not Natchez, but a parting from Lockless, the only home I'd ever known.

Maynard's body was never found. But it was decided that all the far-flung Walkers who were able would assemble at Lockless that Christmas to share their memories of the departed heir. The whole month before, we prepared. We cleaned out, swept, and mopped the upstairs salon, which had fallen into disuse in the years after Maynard's mother died. I dusted mirrors stored in the shed, repaired two old rope beds, and had them, along with a small piano, moved into the house. At night I worked down in the Street with

Lorenzo, Bird, Lem, and Frank. It was good to be back there, for they had been my playmates as a young boy. We worked restoring cabins that had gone empty as the number of Tasked declined. We fortified roofs, swept out birds' nests, and brought down covers for pallets, for we knew that we would have to house not just Walkers but all the Tasked who came with them.

I let my mind go numb with the labor, which now assumed a kind of intimate rhythm, so strongly felt that it compelled Lem to call out:

> Going away to the great house farm
> Going on up to where the house is warm
> When you look for me, Gina, I'll be far gone.

And then he called it back again, this time leaving space for his chorus, which was all of us, to repeat each line. And then we took turns adding on from other renditions or from lines all our own, building the ballad out, room by room, like the great house of which we sang. When it came to me, I hollered out:

> Going away to the great house farm
> Going up, but won't be long
> Be back, Gina, with my heart and my song.

And then it was decided by the elders that we too must have a feast, and a table fit for one. A tree was brought down, stripped and finished and then installed with legs, and in that fashion we had a feasting table. It was hard work, but forced all the difficult and thorny questions from my mind.

On Christmas Eve morning, I stood on the house veranda, looking out, and just as the sun peeked over the mountains, which had turned bare and brown, I saw, arriving with sunrise, the long snaking train of Walkers coming up the road. I counted ten wagons. I walked downstairs exchanging greetings and then began, with the tasking folk who'd come up, to help unload the baggage. I remember this time as happy, because there was, in this train of Walkers, colored people who'd known me as a child, who'd known my mother, and spoke of her with a great fondness.

As was the Holiday tradition then, we were all given an extra share of victuals—two pecks of flour, and of meal, thrice the share of lard and salted pork, and two slaughtered beefs for the whole of us to do with as we wished. From our gardens, we brought up cabbages and collards, and all chickens fit for eating were slaughtered and plucked. On Christmas Day we divided ourselves, half preparing their feast up at the house, and the rest working together for our feast, that night, down in the Street. I worked most of the morning chopping and hauling wood, both for the cooking and for the bonfire. Then in the afternoon, I walked up through the woods and brought back ten demijohns of rum and ale. By early evening the sun had set, and the savory smells of our late supper—fried chicken, biscuits, ash-cake, and potlikker—hung over the Street. Men and women from Starfall, with relations still at Lockless, brought up pies and treats for dessert. Georgie and his wife, Amber, smiled as they unveiled two freshly baked apple-cakes. I helped the men haul out the long benches that we had hewn only days earlier, but we had more people than seats. So we retrieved boxes, hogsheads, logs, stones, and whatever else we could find and positioned them around the bonfire. After the kitchen staff had made its way down, prayers were said, and we ate.

Then, by the light of the bonfire, with everyone stuffed and bursting at the seams, the stories began of the ghosts of Lockless, of all our lost and gone. Zev, my father's first cousin who'd gone to Tennessee, returned with his man, Conway, a child-mate of mine, and Conway's sister Kat. They'd seen my uncle Josiah, who now had a new wife and two little girls. They'd seen Clay and Sheila, who, through some incredible magic, had been sold off the land but sold together, and so had that as comfort. And there was Philipa, Thomas, and Brick, who'd been carried off with Zev and were now old, but still alive. Then the talk turned to Maynard.

"That boy May was mourned in death more than he was loved in life," said Conway. He was sitting by the fire with his hands extended to warm them. "The lies come like gospel to these folk. Why, I tell you, they used to talk about that boy like he was the fall of nature. Now they telling us he was Christ risen."

"It's a homecoming," said Kat. "Suppose they should detail each of his sinnings?"

"Would be a start," said Sophia. "When I go, don't want no lies spoken over my body. Tell them—start to end—what I was."

"Way it go for us folk," said Kat, "don't nobody say nothing, 'cept 'Get to digging.'"

"Whatever it takes," said Sophia. "Just no lying. No gossamer. I came here rough, lived as such, and will die the same. Ain't much more needing to be said."

"Ain't about Maynard," said Conway. "It's about them who is putting him to rest, about excusing themselves after a man they kicked around got himself drowned in the Goose. I tell you, it got even me. I used to riddle that boy something silly. I never got to see him as a man. Way I'm hearing it, Maynard ain't much change. And if that is so, I bet they full of guilt and need to share."

"Y'all niggers just as dumb as they say," said Thena. She was standing near the bonfire, looking directly into the flame. "Y'all think this about Maynard?"

No one replied and now Thena looked up and scanned her audience. The truth is everyone was afraid of her. But the silence that now emerged from this fear only agitated her more.

"Land, niggers! Land! This here land right here! They flattering that man Howell," she said. She paused again and looked around. I was close enough to see the shadow of the bonfire dancing off her face and the wintery clouds of her breath. "It's his bequest they after. Land, niggers! Land and us! This whole thing is a game and the winner get to take hold of this place, get to take hold of us."

We already understood. But this was our farewell too, perhaps the last time we would gather in community. And none wished to ruin the moment by loudly trumpeting this fact. But Thena, owing to her particular injuries and disposition, could not smile, could not lose herself in jest and reminiscence. So she shook her head and sucked her teeth, then pulled her long white shawl around her and stomped away.

Everyone sat there, eyes now downcast, stunned back into the reality Thena had put upon them. I waited a few minutes and then walked down to the far end of the Street, until I reached the farthest cabin, the one set off from the others, the one where Thena once stood with her broom, running off children, where I had appeared all those years ago, sensing that this woman, in particular, would understand the betrayal I felt. And now I saw her standing before her old cabin, lost in her own particular thoughts. I walked over and stood close enough so that she knew that I was there. She looked over at me for a few seconds, and I saw that her face had now softened, then she turned back to the cabin.

I stood with her for a moment and then walked back up, leaving her to her thoughts. When I returned, the conversation had turned back to stories, now reaching into a deep past, as much myth as memory.

"Ain't no such thing," said Georgie.

"I say it is," said Kat.

"And I say it ain't," said Georgie. "If any coloreds had ever walked down to the Goose and vanished, I tell you I'd know it."

Now Kat spotted me, and said, "You know it, Hi. It was your grandmother, was your Santi Bess."

I shook my head and said, "Never met her. You know about as much as I do."

Georgie shook his head, and waved his hands at Kat and said,

"Leave that boy out of it. He don't know nothing. I am telling you, if some slave woman walked off this here Lockless and took fifty-odd of us with her, I would know. I'm tired of hearing of this. Every year it's the same."

"Was before your time," said Kat. "My auntie Elma was about these parts back then. Say she lost her first husband when he walked down with Santi Bess into the Goose. Said he went back home."

"Every year," Georgie said shaking his head. "Every damn year it's the same with y'all. But I'm telling you—I'm the one who'd know, not none of y'all."

I felt everything go quiet just then. It was true. At every gathering there was this dispute about my mother's mother, Santi Bess, and her fate. The myth held that she had executed the largest escape of tasking folk—forty-eight souls—ever recorded in the annals of Elm County. And it was not simply that they had escaped but where they'd been said to escape to—Africa. It was said that Santi had simply led them down to the river Goose, walked in, and reemerged on the other side of the sea.

It was preposterous. That was what I had always thought, what I had to think, because Santi's story came to me in a mix of rumor and whisper. And this faulty narration was fractured even more by the fact that so many of her generation, and the one following, had been sold off, so that by my time, not a single person left in Elm County had seen Santi Bess for themselves.

My thoughts were with Georgie—I doubted she even existed. But it was not Georgie's assault on Santi Bess that made everyone quiet, it was his certitude—"I know," he had said.

Kat walked over until she stood directly in front of Georgie. She smiled and said, "And how's that, Georgie? How would you know?"

I looked hard at Georgie Parks. The sun had set long ago, but the light of the bonfire showed his whole face, frozen in discomfort.

Now Amber sidled up beside him. "Yeah, Georgie," she said. "How you know?"

Georgie glanced around. All eyes were fixed on him. "Don't none of y'all worry," he said. "I. Know."

There was a rumble of nervous laughter. And then the conversation switched back to Maynard and more news from all the far-flung places that our people now called home. It was late now, but the spirit was such that none wanted to part. And I am not sure how it happened, or when, because I was not watching for it, my mind was still on Thena, but by the time I caught wind it was all already in motion. I heard the beat but paid it no mind, until a few began to gather on the farther end of the bonfire, and looking over there I saw that one of the tobacco men, Amechi, had pulled a chair out from out of the quarters and a wash-pan and sticks and with this he was tapping out a beat, something up and happy, and then two then three tasking folk began clapping and slapping their knees, and then I saw Pete, the gardener, walk over with a banjo, and then strum the strings, and then it felt like it all happened at once, spoons, sticks, jaw-harps, the dance was upon us, had bloomed seemingly of its own accord, and there was now a circle just off from the fire, and there was a girl with her hand on the end of her skirt swaying her hips to the beat, and what I now saw was an earthen jar on the girl's head, and looking down to her face, I saw that the girl was Sophia.

I looked up into the starry cloudless night, and judging by the half-moon's journey across the sky, I knew that it was somewhere close to midnight. The fire roared high, beating back the December chill, and before I knew it, everyone was in the Street dancing. I slowly backed away until I had a view of everything. There were dozens of us down there. It was an entire nation in movement. Some of us paired off, others in small semicircles, others alone. I looked over toward the quarters and saw Thena seated on the steps of one of the cabins, nodding to the beat.

I watched Sophia, a flurry of limbs, but all under control, and the jar seemingly fused to her head, never moving, and when one of the men got too close, I watched her pull him in and whisper something, which must have been rude, for the man stopped there and simply walked away. And then she looked and saw me watching her, and at that she smiled and walked toward me, and as she did, she angled her head so that the jar slid, and reaching up with her right hand, she caught the jar by the neck. Now standing in front of me, she sipped from the jar and then passed it to me. I drew it to my lips and recoiled at its taste, for I had assumed it to be water. She laughed and said, "Too much for you, huh?"

Still holding the ale, I looked at her and drew it to my lips again, keeping eye contact, and drank, and drank, and drank, and then handed the empty jar back to her. I did not know what made me do such a thing, at least not then I did not, but I knew well what it meant, even if I tried to deny it to myself. She knew too. And cutting her eyes, she put the jar down, jogged over to the far end of the table, disappearing among the shadows, then came back with a full demijohn, and handed it to me.

"Let's walk," she said.

"All right," I said. "Where we going?"

"You tell me," she said.

And so we did walk, and let the sound of the music die behind us as we moved up from the Street, until we were back near the lawn, and the main house of Lockless. There was a small gazebo off to the side, below which was the ice-house. We sat with the demijohn of ale, passing it back and forth silently, until our heads were swimming in it.

"So, yeah," she said, breaking the silence. "Thena."

"Yeah," I said.

"Wasn't no lie, though, was it?"

"Nope."

"You know what happened to her?"

"You mean to make her this way? I do. But I feel like it's her story to tell."

"But she told you, huh?" she said. "She always been soft with you."

"Thena ain't soft with nobody, Sophia. Even before whatever happened happened, I suspect she was never soft on any of her folk."

"Huh," she said. "And what about you?"

"Hmm?"

"You hard on your folks too?"

"Most generally am," I said. "But of course, depend on the folk."

Then I took another drink from the demijohn, and passed it to her, and she was looking at me now, not smiling, just studying me. It was clear to me that I had gone into the Goose one way and come out the other. I wondered how I had endured all those rides to Nathaniel's seated next to her, wondered if I had somehow been blinded. She was such a lovely girl, and I wanted to be with her in a way that I would never want anyone again, in a way that age and experience rob you of, which is to say I wanted all of her, from her coffee skin to her brown eyes, from her soft mouth to her long arms, from her low voice to her wicked laugh. I wanted it all. And I was not thinking of all the terror that came with that, the terror that had swallowed her life. All I was thinking about was the light dancing in me, dancing to some music I hoped only she would hear.

"Huh," she said. Then looked away. She took another drink and set the ale at her feet, and looked up to the starry sky, and when her eyes moved away, I felt jealous of the heavens themselves. And with that feeling, a range of thoughts came to me. I thought of Corrine and Hawkins, and how these well could be my last days at Lockless—gone not to Natchez, but gone all the same. I thought of Georgie and all that he might know. I felt Sophia's hand slipping its way through my arm, until our arms were locked. She sighed, her head on my shoulder, and we sat there watching the stars over Virginia.

· 7 ·

HOLIDAY PASSED AND WE said our final goodbyes, more final than any on this earth, and then the New Year, and with it, our diminished numbers. Corrine was still in the habit of her daily visits and murmured intimations of my fate, and I knew then, given the sway she held with my father, that it would not be long before these intimations became real. My days at Lockless were numbered.

My father had taken note of the restored highboy. And so it came down from Roscoe that my task would now be the resurrection of furniture pieces from ages past. I read documents from my father's study that detailed the precise date each piece was fashioned or purchased, some stretching all the way back to the progenitor, so that these pieces came to represent a story of my ancestry. An ancestry that would end with me, a slave, sold away from this land, unable to save it or the people who'd built it and burnished it and made it thrive, who would be broken apart and scattered to the wind, but still in chains. The old thoughts of Oregon thickened as I read. I could not save Lockless, but another scheme was growing hotter in me. Should I be divided from Lockless, perhaps I might be divided on my own terms. And that led me back to thoughts of Georgie Parks and precisely what he might know.

It was just a notion in my mind, when I walked out that early Friday to complete my ritual drive of Sophia to Nathaniel's place. I walked over to the stables, and hitched two horses to the pleasure-wagon. It was still dark, but I had done this so often before, and was so used to working before dawn, that I was able to perform the necessary exercise blind. I had just finished the hitching when I looked up and saw her.

"Morning," Sophia said.

"Morning," I said.

She was fully dressed in her outfit—bonnet, crinoline skirt, long coat. I wondered at what hour she had risen to make it all work. And watching her delicately move, with the aid of my hand, into the chaise, it occurred to me that Sophia's ability to take on the trappings of a lady wasn't an accident. It had been her life's work to dress Helen Walker, Nathaniel's late wife, to move through the difficult ritual of creams and nail polishings, of corsets and bodices. She knew this ritual better than Helen knew it herself.

Halfway through our ride, I looked over and saw Sophia looking out at the frozen trees, lost in her own thoughts, as was her tendency.

"What you think?" she asked. I had been in her company long enough to be familiar with this habit of beginning conversations in her head and then continuing them out loud.

"I think so," I said. Now she faced me and a look of incredulity came over her face.

"You got no idea what I'm talking about, do you?" she said.

"I do not," I said.

She laughed to herself and said, "So you was just gonna let me talk as though you knew?"

"Why not?" I said. "Figure I'd catch on soon enough."

"And what if it was something you ain't wanna hear?"

"Well, seeing as how I won't know till I hear it, guess that's a risk I'm taking. Besides, you already in it. Can't back out now."

"Mmm-hmm," she said, nodding. "I guess so. But it's personal, Hi, you see? Goes back to the times before I come to Lockless."

"Back to them Carolinas," I said.

"Yep. Good ol' Carolina." Sophia said this softly, blowing out each word.

"You was a maid to Nathaniel's wife back then, right?" I asked.

"Wasn't just any old maid," she said. "Me and Helen, we were friends. At least we was friends, once. I loved her, you know. I think I can say that—I loved her, and when I think of Helen, I think only of the best times."

She was wistful as she said this, and I felt I understood how it happened for girls like her, how it began for them as children, when they played together with their one-day mistresses, caring nothing for color, and were told to love them, as they would love any other playmate. They grow together, and as the play hours decline, the ritual changes. They are both weaned on the religion of society, of slavery, which holds that for no particularly good reason one of them will live in the palace, while the other will be condemned to the dungeon. It is a cruel thing to do to children, to raise them as though they are siblings, and then set them against each other so that one shall be a queen and the other shall be a footstool.

"Our games used to carry us off," Sophia said. "We used to make ourselves up as the grand ladies would in their big dresses. We would play together in the fields back in Carolina. Once I fell and rolled right into some briars. I must have yelled to the devil and back. But she was right there for me. She gathered me up and got me back to the home-place. I am powerfully remembered to her, Hi, and when I see the briars now, I don't think of the pain, for I am thinking only of her."

She said this looking straight at the road.

"I am telling you that we were us before we were him," she said. "We were something to each other, and that is now smoke. The man she loved wanted me. It was not for any love of me, Hiram. I was jewelry to him. I knew it. And then my Helen died, died bearing his child, and I cannot tell you the pain and guiltiness that came over me."

She stopped there and we rode along and all that was heard was horse and wheels crunching against the frozen road. I had the feeling that this was coming to some terrible revelation.

"Do you know, I still see her in dreams," she said.

"I ain't surprised," I said. "I still see Maynard, though I confess my recollections don't have half the magic of your own."

"Ain't no magic, though," she said. "Sometimes, Hi, sometimes . . . it is my feeling that she got away and left me with . . ."

Now she turned to me, breaking her gaze into the woods.

"He'll never let me loose till I'm used up, you see? Then he'll send me out of Elm somewhere, and take up another colored girl for his fancy. We really ain't nothing but jewelry to them. I always known this, I think. But I am getting older, Hi, and knowing something is a far measure from truly seeing it."

"Takes some time," I said.

She was quiet again and for a few moments there was nothing but the gentle clopping of the horse along the road.

"You ever wonder about the rest of your life?" she said. "You ever wonder about young'uns? About any life that might be out there waiting for you?"

"Lately," I said, "I wonder about everything."

"I think of young'uns all the time," she said. "I think of what it must mean to bring someone, a little girl perhaps, into all of this. And I know it's coming, someday. That it ain't even up to me. It's coming, Hiram, and I will watch as my daughter is taken in, as I was taken in, and . . . I am trying to tell you that this all has me wondering about something else, about another life, past the Goose, maybe past them mountains, past . . ."

And her voice trailed off and she was looking off to the side of the road again, and I think now that this is how the running so often begins, that it is settled upon in that moment you understand the great depth of your peril. For it is not simply by slavery that you are captured, but by a kind of fraud, which paints its executors as guardians at the gate, staving off African savagery, when it is they themselves who are savages, who are Mordred, who are the Dragon, in Camelot's clothes. And at that moment of revelation, of understanding, running is not a thought, not even as a dream, but a need, no different than the need to flee a burning house.

"Hiram," she said, "I don't know why I come to you with this. All I know is you have always been one who saw more, who knew more. And then you met the Goose. We thought you was dead. You were there at the gates, and I watched you turn away and I wondered how a man could come back looking upon the world the same."

"I know what you are speaking of," I said.

"I am speaking of facts," she said.

"You are speaking of goodbye," I said. "And to where? How could we live, in any way, out there?"

She placed a hand on my arm. "How can you come up out the Goose alive and, in any way, still live here? I am speaking of facts."

"You can't even name it," I said.

"But I can name this and every kind of life that will come after," she said. "We could go together, Hi. You are read and know of things far past Lockless and the Goose. You must have some need of it. You must have found yourself dreaming of it, waking up now and again gripped in it. You must have some wanting to know all that you, all that we, might become out from under here."

I did not answer. We could now see the great opening in the road that marked Nathaniel Walker's place. I drove past this opening, and turned down a side path, which was our customary approach. I stopped the horse at the end of the path. Through the trees I could see Nathaniel Walker's brick main house. I watched as a well-dressed tasking man came down the way. He nodded when he saw us, then motioned wordlessly for Sophia. She stepped out of the chaise and looked back at me. I noted, right then, that she had never done this before, instead she usually walked right on with her escort. But now she paused and looked back and what she said in that silence was something resolute, certain. And I knew then, looking at her, that we must run.

As I pulled away from Nathaniel Walker's place, my mind now focused again on Georgie Parks. I must find him. I had known Georgie all my life and I understood that he might fear for me as a father fears for the son about to go off to war. I understood. Georgie had seen so many hauled down to the block and sent Natchez-way. I even sympathized. But still I had to run. Everything seemed to point me to it—the library volume, scheming Corrine and bizarre Hawkins, the fate of Lockless itself, always chancy, but now heirless, dire. And Sophia, who seemed to share in my desperation, in my need to see whatever lay beyond those three hills, past Starfall, past the Goose and its many bridges, past Virginia itself. *You must have some need of it*. I did. But the only route I then knew must be walked by the light of Georgie Parks.

The following Saturday afternoon, I worked on the drawers of a cherry secretary, and satisfied that they were again running easy, I washed, put on a change of clothes, and made my way to the home of Georgie Parks. I was not far into Starfall when I spotted Hawkins and Amy just outside the inn, both still in mourning black. They were distracted by their own conversation and did not see me, and so I kept my distance and watched Hawkins and Amy for a moment, before continuing on my way. I wanted no conversation, for their habit of picking at all the details of my life and my intentions had become intolerable to me. All of their questions gave way to other questions.

I found Georgie standing in front of his home, a short walk

from Ryland's Jail. I smiled. Georgie did not. He motioned for me to walk with him. We kept to the road for a bit, then turned off onto a smaller path where the town began to give way to the wilderness, and then took a dirt path, which brought us through some tangled green that opened to a small pond. Georgie said nothing during our short walk and now gazed at the pond for a moment before speaking.

"I like you, Hiram," Georgie said. "I really do. If I was so lucky as to have a daughter about your season, you would be my only choice. You are smart. You keep your mouth where it should be, and you were more better to Maynard than such a man ever deserved."

He rubbed his red-brown beard, turned and looked up into the trees. His back was now to me. I heard him say, "Which is why I can't for the fact of things understand how a man such as you would come to my door looking for trouble."

When he turned back to me, his deep brown eyes were simmering. "What would a respectable man like you want with this?" he asked. "And by what reasoning have you got it figured that I am the one who shall award it?"

"Georgie, I know," I said. "We all know. Perhaps you have hid it away from the Quality, but we have always been smarter than them."

"You don't see the half of it, son. And I am telling as I have told you before—Go home. Get a wife. And get happy. Ain't nothing over here."

"Georgie, I am going," I told him. "And I ain't going alone."

"What?"

"Sophia going with me."

"Nathaniel Walker's girl? Have you lost it? You take that girl and you might as well spit on that man. It is a high offense against any white man's honor."

"We are going. And, Georgie," I said with only a hint of the anger I now felt in me, "she ain't his."

It was not only anger in me. I was nineteen, and a guarded nineteen who'd worked to feel nothing in this direction, so that when I did feel it, right there in that moment, when I did feel that I loved her, it was not with reason or ritual, nor the way that makes families and homes, but the way that wrecks them, I was undone.

"Now, let's get one thing straight here," Georgie said. "She is his girl. They all his girl, you get it? Amber his girl. Thena his girl. Your mother was his girl—"

"Careful, Georgie," I said. "Real careful."

"Oh, it's careful now, huh? That's what it is? You telling me about careful, son. They *own* you, Hiram. You a slave, boy. I don't care who your daddy is. You a slave, and don't think that just because I'm out this way, out here in this Freetown, that I ain't some kind of slave too. And as long as they own you, they own her. You got to see. We are captured. Been captured. And that's the whole of it. What you are talking here done got men a whole week in Ryland's and beat within a prayer of they life. You have got a feeling in your heart and I respect it. I done felt it myself, what young man ain't? But you almost died, Hi. You do this, and you will wish you had."

"Georgie, I am telling you that this is not a choice. I cannot stay. And you have got to help."

"Even if I was what you have me figured to be, I would not."

"You ain't understanding," I said. "I am going. That is a fact. I am asking you to aid me, because I believe you an honorable man devoted to the honorable path. I am asking you, Georgie. But I am going."

Georgie paced for a moment, executing his own internal calculations, for he knew now that with his help or without, I was going and I was going with Sophia. What I could not know as he regarded me there, his eyes widening with realization, was that he must have been figuring on the consequence of such an action, and his conclusion made clear, and whatever his hatreds, whatever his loves, especially his loves, he now saw but one path forward.

"One week," he said. "You got one week. You meet me here, on this spot where we now stand, with your girl. You should know that I would not do any such thing if not for what you have told me here and determined yourself to do."

My power was always memory, not judgment. I walked away from Georgie's home fixed only on my own suspicions, never suspecting how much beyond those the fact of things truly ranged. And even when I, again, came upon Amy and Hawkins, this time seen straight by them right outside the general store, I could not see how the pieces fit.

There had been no way to avoid them this time, for I had been so lost in thoughts of Georgie, of Sophia, that they had seen me before I saw them.

"How you carrying it, small stepper?" Hawkins said.

"Well and fine enough," I said. It was now early evening and dusk had begun to fall over the town. The locals of Elm County who'd come into town for business now drifted out on their pleasure-wagons and chaises. I regarded Hawkins warily, trying to find the quickest road out of conversation.

"What you got bringing you into town?" he asked, and to this he married his characteristic thin-lipped smile. I didn't answer and I saw by the shift in his face that he now knew that he'd assumed a familiarity that was not there. But this did nothing to stop him.

"Aw, I'm sorry," he said. "Don't mean to cause no injury or offense. Lady say we should be as family, though, right?"

"Calling on a friend," I said.

"Friend like Georgie Parks?"

There were all kinds of ways to task in Virginia, ways beyond the fields, the kitchens, or the shed. Some tasking was not so material. Offering entertainment, sharing wisdom. And then there were even darker tasks. To be their eyes and ears, their intelligence among the other tasking men, so that they, the masters, knew who smiled in their faces and scoffed behind their backs, who stole from them, who burned down the barn, who poisoned and who plotted. The effect of all this was a kind of watchfulness among the tasking folks, in particular toward those you did not know. This worked the other way too, so that if you were new to Lockless or any of these other houses of bondage, you took things slow, you did not question or inquire on people's affairs, for if you did you might then be thought to be among those who were eyes and ears, who tasked beyond the Task, and this was a dangerous place because then you yourself might be poisoned or plotted against. But Hawkins took no care, which gave his question a sinister import.

"Ain't nothing," he went on. "My sister, Amy, got people tasking this way. Say she see you over at Georgie's from time to time."

Amy stood eyeing us both. And I saw now that she seemed nervous about something that was soon to happen or an event she would like to not miss.

"Yeah," I said, still uneasy. "Georgie is known to me."

"Uh-huh," he said. "Georgie's quite a fella."

I looked back to Amy, who was no longer shifting her eyes nervously, but casting them a block away. Following her gaze, I saw my old tutor, Mr. Fields, coming toward her. This was now twice in three months, twice after having not seen him in seven years. What was more, Mr. Fields was clearly walking toward Amy, as though he had some appointed rendezvous with her and Hawkins. He saw me before he reached her, and froze for a moment. I had the sense that some plan of his had gone awry and he would very much like to change direction. But instead he once again doffed his hat as he had those months ago at race-day. Hawkins followed my eyes to Mr. Fields, who by now was standing at Amy's side. They were watching us and in some state of confusion. And Hawkins was no longer smiling, indeed he looked quite nervous himself, watching them watch us. But then he turned back to me and the smile was recalled.

"Well," he said. "I guess that's my folks calling on me."

"Guessing it is," I said. And then it was my turn to smile, and I am not sure why, except to say that it was my feeling that Hawkins had been lying to me, lying about where he'd found me, lying about the motive of his questions. And I felt I had at last caught him unawares, and managed to drag some portion of his secret machinations into the light. And his discomfort at this made me smile. I stood there and watched him walk over to Amy and Mr. Fields, and then tipped my hat, once again, to the whole party as they walked off.

I should have thought more on those events. I should have wondered at the familiarity between two tasking folks and a learned man of the North. I should have seen the connections with Georgie Parks. But my mind was swimming in the ocean of possibilities opened up by Georgie's assent. And more my great concern was not with uncovering the plotting of others, but with how I might best conceal my own.

The next day I rode back to Nathaniel's estate to retrieve Sophia. Fifteen minutes into my ride, not far from home, I was stopped by the patrol of low whites—Ryland's Hounds—who haunted the woods in search of runaways. I produced my papers for them, and seeing Howell's name upon them, they quickly allowed me on my way. But the event shook me, for I had by then completed a shift inside of myself. I'd already gone from Tasked to fugitive. I so greatly feared that they would see it in me, in some misbegotten smile or unlikely ease. But Ryland's Hounds were white—low whites, but white all the same—so that their power blinded them.

Sophia and I rode back in silence, saying nothing. But just before reaching Lockless, I stopped the chaise. It was late morning and cold. No one was on the road and the only sound was the wind whipping through the bare branches, that and my pounding heart. I wondered if Sophia had been taken in on some design. Phantoms flittered before me like moths and for a moment I saw

them all in concert together——Howell, Nathaniel, Corrine, Sophia, even Maynard, who did not die, who presided over my
dreams where he rose up out of the icy teeth of the Goose detailing the roster of my sins. But when I looked over and saw her,
brown eyes looking out into the forest, as she often did, not even
noting our pause, when I saw her there, seeming so cool and far
above the cares of the world, the feelings in me welled up and
overwhelmed.

And then she spoke.

"I got to get out, Hi," she said. "I will not be an old woman
down in the coffin. I will bring no child to this. Ain't no society
here. No rules. No prohibitions. They took it all with them to
Kentucky, Mississippi, Tennessee. Ain't nothing left. It's all gone
Natchez-way."

She paused for a moment and then said again, slower this time,
"I got to get out."

"Right," I said. "Then let's get out."

· 8 ·

I AM SO MUCH OLDER now, old enough to understand how a tangle of events can be unraveled to reveal a singular thread. So as to my freedom, the events stood thus: I knew that I would never advance beyond my blood-bound place at Lockless. And I knew that even if I did, Lockless, whatever its past glories, was falling, as all the great houses of slavery were falling, and when they fell I would not be freed, but would instead be sold or passed off. And I knew by then that my genius would not save me, indeed my genius would only make me a more valuable commodity. I was convinced that this was what had attracted Corrine, that she, aided by the mendacity of her people, was making an early if still mysterious claim. And my own view of this claim, of everything really, was altered from the moment I walked out of the Goose. And all of that—my knowledge, my destiny, my escape from death—taken together was like a bomb in my chest, and Sophia, and her intentions, were the fuse. That was how I saw her back then, as the necessary end-point of my calculations. It all made sense to me, but would have made more had

I considered that Sophia was a woman of her own mind, with intentions, calculations, and considerations all her own.

She came upon me later that week, while I was outside working a set of corner chairs, and when I saw her, the fuse burning in me, I felt a kind of daring.

She stopped and smiled, looked at the corner chair, and then began walking into the shed.

"Don't think you wanna do that," I said. "Ain't really no place for a lady."

"Ain't no lady," she said, walking inside.

I followed her in and watched as she wiped away the cobwebs and ran her fingers against the furniture to judge how much she could accumulate in one swipe. She walked among the pieces, passing the maple drunkard's chair, then the Hepplewhite table and the Queen Anne clock, the light from the small window cutting against the dark.

"Huh," she said, turning to face me. "This all yours to work?"

"I guess."

"Howell's word?"

"Yep. By way of Roscoe. But really I just got sick of laying up there waiting for them to tell me something. 'Sides, this is how it was when I was a boy. Used to get in where I could. Work where I was needed."

"Could still go out to the fields," she said. "They always looking for hands."

"Did my share of that, thank you kindly," I said. "How bout you? Ever been in them fields?"

"Can't say that I have," Sophia said.

She was now closer and I noted this because I noted everything about her now, in particular the precise distance she maintained from me. There was a part of me that knew this to be all wrong, but it was the discredited part, the part that had believed a coin could reverse Virginia against itself.

"Not the worst," I said. "Don't have these folks watching every little thing you do."

She was closer still.

"What kind of things you might like to hide?" she said, moving closer so that I now felt my balance slipping away. I put my hand down on a piece of furniture, I can't remember which.

She just looked at me and laughed, then walked back out of the shed.

"Can we talk some more?" she said, almost whispering. "About all that."

"Yeah, we can," I said.

"In an hour," she said. "Down by the gulch?"

"Sound good to me," I said.

I don't know what work happened in the time before that meeting. I spent the whole of it thinking only of Sophia. Slavery is everyday longing, is being born into a world of forbidden victuals and tantalizing untouchables—the land around you, the clothes you hem, the biscuits you bake. You bury the longing, because you know where it must lead. But now this new longing held out a different future, one where my children, whatever their travails, would never know the auction block. And once I glimpsed that other future, my God, the world was born anew to me. I was freedom-bound, and freedom was as much in my heart as it was in the swamps, so that the hour I spent waiting on our meeting was the most careless I had ever spent. I was gone from Lockless before I had even run.

"So how's this suppose to go?" she asked. We were down by the gulch, looking past the wild grass to the other side of the woods.

"I don't quite know," I said.

Sophia turned to me with a doubtful look.

"Don't know?" she asked.

"I put my faith in Georgie," I said. "That's all I got."

"Georgie, huh?"

"Yeah, Georgie. I ain't ask a whole lot of questions—you must understand why. This thing Georgie got himself into, well, I imagine part of the deal is you don't talk too much. So my notion is simple. We bring ourselves, and nothing more, at the appointed time and place and then we go."

"Go into what?" she asked.

I looked at her hard for a moment, then looked back over the gulch.

"The swamps," I said. "They got a world down there, a whole Underground, where a man can live as a man should."

"And what about a woman?"

"I know. I thought on it some. Perhaps not the ideal place for a lady—"

She cut me off and said, "Told you once today, Hi, I ain't no lady."

I nodded.

"I get along just fine," she said. "Just get me out of here and I'll get the rest figured myself."

That last word—*myself*—hung in the air.

"All by yourself, huh?" I asked.

She looked back at me unsmiling.

"Look, Hiram, I need you to understand something. I like you, I really do." Her eyes were hard on me, drilling their way in, and I felt that what she was saying now was from the deepest of possible places. "I like you and I do not like many men, and when I look at you I see something old and familiar, something like what I had with my Mercury. But I will like you a heap less if your plan is for us to get to this Underground and for you to make yourself up as another Nathaniel. That ain't freedom to me, do you understand? Ain't no freedom for a woman in trading a white man for a colored."

I noticed then that her hand was on my arm. And that she was squeezing it firmly.

"If that is what you want, if that is what you are thinking, then you must tell me now. If it is your plan to shackle me there, to have me bring yearlings to you, then tell me now and allow me the decency of making my own choice here. You are not like them. You must do me the service of giving me that choice. So tell me. Tell me now your intending."

I remember her ferocity in that moment. It was such a peaceful day. Late in the afternoon now and the sun was setting in this season of long nights, the perfect season, I would soon learn, to run. I heard no birds, no insects, no branches in the wind, so that all my senses were focused on Sophia's words, words that for the first time in my life I experienced without pictures, for reasons I could not fully then understand. What I did understand was that she was terribly afraid of something—something in me, and the thought that I would, in any way, exist to her in the way of Nathaniel, that she would fear me as she feared him, scared and shamed me all at once.

"No," I said. "Never, Sophia. I want you to be free and I want any relating between us, should there ever be relating, to always be one of your choosing."

She loosened her hand now, so that her grip became just a touch.

"I cannot lie," I said. "I hope that you will some day, at some time, choose me out there. I confess it. I have dreams. Wild dreams."

"And what do you dream of?" she asked. Her grip was again tight on my arm.

"I dream of men and women who are fit to wash, feed, and dress themselves. I dream of rose gardens that reward the hands that tend to them," I said. "And I dream of being able to turn to a woman for whom I got a feeling, and speak that feeling, holler that feeling, with no thought beyond me and her as to what that might mean."

We stood there a little longer and then walked up from the gulch together and then out of the woods. By then the sun was setting over Lockless. We paused at the edge of the woods. Sophia said, "I had best go ahead alone." I nodded and watched her walk out and disappear. And then I came out, up from the forest toward the house, until I could see the tunnel beneath into the Warrens. And standing there in that tunnel, with her arms crossed, was Thena.

Thena was also transformed by my new vantage. I was running off, a young man with a young girl, toward a new life, the first true life we'd ever have, one that these old coloreds were afraid to pursue. I had tried to save them, save the whole of Lockless, but that was over now. They were lambs waiting for the slaughter. The elders all knew what was coming. They knew what the land whispered, because none lived closer to the land than those who worked it. They lay awake at night, listening to the groaning ghosts of tasking folk past, those who'd been carried off. They knew what was coming and still they waited for it. And all of this sudden shame and anger, rage and resenting for they who let this happen, who stoically watched their children carried off, all of this I now heaped upon Thena, so that when she saw me there coming up from the woods, and I saw her, with her arms crossed, waiting for me as I approached, and I saw the disapproving look on her face, I felt an incredible anger.

"Evening," I said. She rolled her eyes in response. I walked into the tunnel and toward my quarters. She followed me. When we were inside, she turned up the lamp on the mantel and then shut the door. She sat in a chair in the corner and I saw the flame of the lamp casting shadows on her face.

"What is with you, son?" she asked.

"Don't know what you mean."

"You still fevered or something?"

"Thena . . ."

"Been mighty strange these past few weeks, mighty strange. So what is it? What's got you?"

"Don't know what you mean."

"Alrighty, lemme ask it like this. What in all of creation done possessed you to run round Lockless with Nathaniel Walker's girl?"

"I ain't running round with nobody. Girl choose her company, sure as I chose mine."

"That's what you think, huh?"

"Yep, that's what I think."

"Then you as dumb as you seem."

What I now did was cut my eyes at Thena, in a gesture I had learned from children rebellious against their parents. And I was a child, I know that now, a boy overrun with emotion, undone by a great and momentous loss. And I felt it, just then, though I could not name it, I felt all that I had lost when my mother fell into that black hole of memory, because standing before me was someone whom I stood to lose again. And I could not bear to lose her, to look her in the eye and confess my plan, to leave the only mother I had ever known. So when I spoke, it was not with sadness or honesty but with anger and righteousness.

"What I done to you?" I asked.

"Huh?"

"Whatever, in all of creation, have I done to you to speak to me so?"

"Speak to you so?" she said, and the look became almost bemused. "Hell you care bout how I speak to you? You fell to me out of nothing, I never asked for any of it, but what I do every evening, after breaking my back for these folks? Who fry up your bacon and corncakes? That girl ever done that for you? Who guard you against what these folks try to make of you with all their schemings? And what have I asked from you, Hiram? Whatever have I asked?"

"And why start now?" I said. Then I fixed Thena with a long hard stare. It was not a look fit for anyone, nor any woman who had loved me, and certainly not the woman who had so cared for me.

Thena looked back at me as though I had shot her. But the pain quickly passed. It was as if her last hope that this wicked world would admit some justice, some light, had vanished before her and what was left was the crooked end she had expected all along.

"You gonna regret all this one day," she said. "You gonna regret it more than any evil that come along with that girl, and evil will come to you, I assure you. But this moment here when you speak as such to those who loved you when you was most frail, you gonna regret." Then she opened the door, looking back only to say, "Boy like you should be more careful with his words. Never know when they the last ones he might put upon a person."

I didn't have to wait long for the promised regret to bloom inside me, but in that moment it was overwhelmed by another portion of me, the one that thought only of my impending flight from this old world, with its dying land, its fearful slaves, and its low and vulgar whites. I would leave it all behind for the freedom of the Underground, and made no exception for Thena.

The remaining days passed until finally it came, the morning of Georgie's fateful promise, came like life itself, long and quick. I woke to that day filled with unease. I lay awake in my bed, hoping that the day might remain there with me, but then I heard the shuffling of the Warrens and the hum of the house above, and this awful music announced that the day was a fact, and my promise was a fact, and it could not be backed away from. So I rose to the darkness and walked with my earthen jar toward the well and saw Pete on my way there, already dressed and on his way to the garden, and I remember this because it was the last time I ever saw him. Outside in the distance, I saw Thena at the well, all alone, drawing water for laundry. It was such hard work—hauling up the water, firing up the wood, beating the garments, preparing the soap—and she did all of it. I remember standing there, knowing how I had wronged her, scorned her, heaped on disrespect, feeling the sharp shame of it, and beating it back with my anger, with my "Who does she think she is?" I waited for her to finish and watched from the tunnel as this old colored woman hauled the water all alone, knowing even then that I would regret this, that for the rest of my life, those last words to Thena, when I stood apart from her, would haunt me.

When all was clear, I walked to the well and filled my own gourd, then walked back and cleaned myself and dressed. I came to the mouth of the tunnel and watched the sun come up over Lockless, and for one final, weighty moment pondered the step now standing before me. I thought of oceans and all the explorers of whom I had read during those long summer Sundays in the library, and I wondered what they had felt stepping up off the land and onto the deck, looking out over the sea, the waves, which they must cross into some unknown realm. I wondered if fear took them, if they ever were compelled to run back into the arms of their women, to kiss their young daughters, and remain there among them in the world they knew. Or were they like me, aware that the world they loved was uncertain, that it too must fade before time, that change was the rule of everything, that if they did not cross the water, the water must soon cross over them? So I must go, for my world was disappearing, had always been disappearing—Maynard called out from the Goose, Corrine from the mountains, and above all, Natchez.

I jogged myself out of the reverie. I walked up the stairs and spoke with my father, who had now found a task for me—work in the kitchen with the remains of the wait staff, beginning tomorrow. "One last day of freedom," he said. But I was, by then, past any care for such things. I simply nodded and then assessed him for any sign that he had caught on. But he was cheerful, more cheerful than I'd seen him in weeks. He spoke of Corrine Quinn, and her promise to visit later that week, and I felt an incredible relief at the fact that I would by then be gone.

I walked to the library. I thumbed through the old volumes of Ramsay and Morton. Then I walked back down toward my quarters. For the rest of the day I kept out of sight. I could not bear to eat. I could not bear to see anyone else. I was by then done with all the reminiscences and fantasy. What I most wanted was for the appointed moment to come. And it did, I tell you, it did. The sun set, bringing on the long winter night, and then the house quieted and the hum of the day faded until all that was left was the occasional creaking. I brought nothing with me save ambition, not clothes, not victuals, not books, not even my coin, which I now pulled from the pocket of my overalls, rubbed one last time, and deposited on the mantel. I met Sophia at the edge of the peach grove. We used the road to mark our path, but stayed in the woods, out of sight, in case we were spotted by any of the patrols. We talked and laughed in our normal easy way but with lowered voices, until the road bent and then in the distance we saw the bridge across the Goose. And feeling that this was the moment, the place from which none would dare turn back, we were quiet, struck dumb by fear and awe. We stood there looking out at the bridge, which was but a long dark span against the greater dark of the night. I heard the creeping things of the earth calling out to each other. The night was starless and overcast.

"So it's freedom then," I said.

"Freedom," she said. "Mend it or rip it. No more treating. No more in-between. Die young, or not all."

And so we walked out from the woods and onto the path, and in open view of the night, I took her hand and I was aware that her hand was steady and mine trembled. We had put our lives on the honor of Georgie Parks. We believed in the rumor, in the Underground. We crossed and did not look back, and made for the woods, steering clear of Starfall. I had, in the days prior, taken time to wander among the back-paths, and had found a way to bring us to Georgie's meeting place with both speed and discretion. When we reached the small pond where Georgie and I had stood one week earlier, we relaxed a bit.

"What will you do when you get there?" I asked.

"Don't know," she said. "Don't know what a gal do in a swamp. Would like to work—work for my own. That is my highest ambition. How bout you?"

"Get as far as I might from you, I figure."

We both laughed.

"You know you crazy," I said. "Got me out here, running. I say if we make it through—when we make it through—I will have had all I need of Sophia's schemings."

"Uh-huh. Might be nice to lighten my own load," Sophia said. "Men ain't brought me and mine nothing but a heap of trouble."

We laughed a little more. I looked up at the starless sky, then looked over to Sophia, who was backing away, backing toward the pond. And then I heard footsteps, and conversation, and I could tell that whoever was approaching was not alone. I thought to hide then, but I distinctly heard Georgie's voice among the men, and this stayed me. Then the voices went quiet and all we heard were the footsteps crunching against the ground. I took Sophia's hand and looked through the opening in the wood. I saw the darkness framing the figure of Georgie Parks.

I smiled, I remember that. And I tell you, as I have always, that I remember everything, but here perhaps, I am playing tricks upon myself because it was a starless night, and I could not see Sophia as little more than a silhouette before me, but I swear that I remember seeing the face of Georgie Parks, and his face was pained and was sad and I did not know why. And then I heard the footsteps again and I saw five white men emerge, one by one from the darkness, and I saw that one of them carried a rope between his hands. And when they were out, they stood before us for what seemed like forever and I heard Sophia moan, "No, no, no . . ."

And then I watched one of the men touch Georgie's shoulder

and say, "All right, Georgie, you done good." And at that Georgie turned his back on us and walked back into the forest, and these men, with their rope, turned to us.

"No, no, no," moaned Sophia.

I swear they were like phantoms, glowing against the night like specters, and I knew by their outline and bearing exactly what they were.

· 9 ·

Ryland's Hounds brought us up by pistol-point, brought us through that moonless and starless night, through a darkness thick enough to touch, thick as the ropes knotted around our hands. And I was suddenly aware of the cold, of the wind swinging like a sword, so that I then began to shiver and this became a fact of great amusement for our captors, and though I could not see them, I could hear them laughing at me, mocking me—"Time for shivering past, boy"—for they took me to be in fear of what they might do. It was true that Ryland's Hounds were fearsome and the fact that I was not in total terror can only be attributed to the flight of emotions—shame, anger, shock—that now raced ahead of fear. They could have done anything to us out there, done anything to her, for this was the normal path of things. It was the necessary right of the Low, who held no property in man, to hold momentary property in those who ran, and to vent all their awful passions upon them. And from the moment I saw Georgie disappear, and Ryland float out of the woods like wraiths, I felt that this venting must come. But it did not. They just led us out of the woods, into Starfall, until we were at the jail, and there they replaced rope with chains, and left us in the yard, like the animals they took us to be, dressed in cold irons, for what must be our last moments together, our last moments upon this earth as we knew it.

I remember the heaving weight of the chains, a center-line extending from the collar around my neck, down to a smaller chain and cuffs around my wrists, through another chain and cuffs clapped around my ankles. And this lattice of cold iron was looped around the bottom rail of the fence that bracketed the jail, so that I could neither straighten my back nor take a seat for relief, and was thus permanently stooped. All my life I had been a captive. But whereas the particulars of my birth had allowed me to feel this bondage as a mark or symbol, there was nothing symbolic in this hulking web. I could angle my neck in one direction, and there I found pain of a different sort, for I caught sight of Sophia, fastened just as I was, perhaps a few yards away. I wanted so bad to say something as radical as I felt the moment then demanded. I wanted to tell her of my great sorrow at having led her into this deeper, truer slavery. I wanted to hold myself to her account for this great betrayal. But when I spoke, I had nothing but the most impoverished of words.

"I . . . I am sorry," I said. I had turned my head back down to the ground. "I am so very sorry."

Sophia did not answer.

What I badly wanted, right then, was a blade, and with it, I would slit my own throat. I could not live knowing what I had done, what I had brought to Sophia. And it was so very cold out there. I could feel my hands turning to rock, and my ears disappearing into the night, and I knew I was crying, because I felt those quiet tears freezing on my cheeks.

At that moment, lost in my own shame, I heard a low rhythmic grunting, and I saw that with each grunt the bottom rail of the fence shook a little. And now looking over I saw that it was Sophia who was grunting. She was pulling the weight of the chains and, one foot at a time, sliding closer and closer, for what I could not be sure. Perhaps she wanted to be closer so that she might whisper some ancient curse, or rend one of my ears between her teeth. She moved with great force, and with her every upward heave, the rail heaved with her. I had no idea she was this strong. She began slowly, breaking between each slide, but as she approached, the heaves became faster and greater, so that I thought her plan might be to the snap the railing itself and free us. But when she reached me, she stopped, exhausted, panting from her great effort, and she was close enough that I could see all of her features and she looked upon me, tender at first, so tender that, at least for that moment, my shame slid away. Then, straining against the chains, she angled her head forward a bit, past the fence, past the jail, and though I could not see it, I knew that her indication was aimed toward Freetown. And she looked back at me and what I saw was a look so hard that I knew that she too wished for a knife, though the throat she wanted it for would not be her own. Now I saw her face tighten and her teeth bear down. Sophia gave one last heave until she was right next to me, so close that I could feel her breath on my cheek and her arm close against mine, so close that she could lean in against me, as she did now, so close that I could feel her warmth, so close that icy darkness retreated, and I shivered no more.

II.

Were I to tell you the evils of slavery . . .

I should wish to take you one at a time and

whisper them to you.

WILLIAM WELLS BROWN

· 10 ·

Ryland's Jail was my home now. Sophia was parted from me that next day, for where I did not know—sold to the fancy trade? Sent back to Nathaniel? Natchez?—and what I was left with was that portrait of her, which I see even now, fighting against the chains for that moment of contact, focusing her hateful gaze, not inward, not on me, not on herself, but on the base treachery of Georgie Parks. Even then I did not know how deep the treachery went. But I knew enough to husband a hate thick as winter stew. Later, years and years later, I would understand the impossibility of Georgie's standing, the way the Quality had narrowed his choices until he lived on a thin chancy reed called Freetown. But just then I hated him and succored myself on the miraculous notion that Georgie would someday be subject to my wrath.

I was thrown into a dank cell, with a filthy cover and straw pallet for bedding, and a bucket for relief. Each day I was brought out early, made to exercise, and then washed. Blacking was applied to my hair, oil to my body. And then I was made to stand, with all the others, stripped down to my skin, in the front parlor of the jail. The flesh-traders, vultures of Natchez, entered and had their way with me. They were a ghastly sight, the lowest of low whites, because unlike their brethren, these men, while originating in that bottom file, had grown wealthy from the flesh trade, but seemed to revel in their debased roots, their slovenly dress, their missing teeth, their foul odors, their habit of spitting tobacco wherever they wished, as a kind of absurd show. The Quality shunned them, for slave-trading was still held as disreputable business. They did not host the traders in their homes nor invite them into their Sunday pews. Time would come when gold would outweigh blood. But this was still Virginia of old, where a dubious God held that those who would offer a man for sale were somehow more honorable than those who effected that sale.

This shunning caused a great resentment in the traders, a resentment they vented on us. They took glee in their work, so that in that parlor, they seemed to dance as they approached, and when they gripped at my buttocks to check their firmness, they did it with vim and vigor; and when they twisted my jaw in the light, checking my skull against their theories of phrenology, they never failed to smile a little; and when they stuck their fingers in my mouth, probing for rotten teeth, or struck my limbs searching for old injuries, they hummed a melody to themselves.

I would fall into myself during these "examinations," because I quickly learned that the only way to survive such invasion was to dream, to let my soul fly from my body, fly back to Lockless and another time, when I called out the work songs—"Be back, Gina, with my heart and my song"—or stood before Alice Caulley, watching her gleam as I recited her history, or sat under the gazebo, passing a jug of ale and nursing all my wants and desires. But it was only a dream. And the fact was I was there in the awful now, being handled by men who gloried in their power to reduce a man to meat.

So I was now under it, down in the coffin of slavery, because whatever I had endured back at Lockless, it must be said, was not this and was nothing like what surely was to come. And I was not alone. There were two others in my cell. The first was a boy with light brown hair, barely twelve I guessed, a boy who did not smile and never spoke and maintained the hardened aspect of a man long tasked. But he was a boy, a fact revealed at night by the fearful whimper in his sleep, by his small yawn in the morning. Each night, after our supper of scraps, his mother called on him. And I guessed from her garments, which were above the heavy osnaburg of the Tasked, that she was free but had somehow lost possession of her child. She would sit on the floor outside the cell holding his hand through the iron bars and they would pass the moments silently, hand-in-hand, until Ryland dismissed her. There was something achingly familiar in this ritual, something that an old forgotten part of me recognized, like a scene from some other unrecalled life.

My other cellmate was an old man. His face was lined by the ages, and upon the ocean of his back I saw the many voyages of Ryland's whip. Whatever my miseries during that time in Ryland's Jail, nothing I endured approached what was put on this old man. The math of profit shielded me and the boy. But this old man, his days of use over, with only pennies to be wrung for him, was meat for the dogs. At any moment in the day, whenever the mood struck, these men would pull the old man out and compel him to sing, dance, crawl, bark, cluck, or perform some other indignity. And should his performance dissatisfy any of them, they would wail on him with fists and boots, beat him with horse reins or carriage whip, hurl paperweights and chairs at him, or reach for whatever else was at hand. And I felt the rawest shame beholding this, though I did not recognize it as such, shame in myself in having no ability whatsoever to help.

These were dark times of the soul. My sympathy for these two was quickly swallowed by the sense that it was these same dumb sympathies that had brought me to this moment. My mind was frantic with suspicion. Perhaps it was all conspiracy. Maybe Sophia was in on it. Perhaps Thena had warned them. Maybe they were all sitting up somewhere, laughing with Corrine Quinn, laughing with my father even, at my foolish dreams of freedom. And so shame and sympathy quickly gave way to a hardness that has never left me.

It was night. I was lying on the damp stone floor. The little boy's mother was gone. I could hear Ryland up front in a drunken game of poker.

Tonight the old man, for some reason, felt the need to speak. His voice came to me in the darkness. He first told me in a croaked whisper that I reminded him of his son. I ignored him and tried to snuggle between my pallet of straw and a moth-eaten blanket, looking for any warmth I could find. And so he said it again, in a tone that communicated the privileges of his age.

"Doubtful," I responded.

"Doubtful that you are him, certainly," he said. "But I have marked you and know that you are about his age and bear that taint that he must surely wear. We are parted from each other, but at night when I dream of him, I dream of a man betrayed. And that man wears a look much like you."

I said nothing.

"How do you come here?" he asked.

"By way of flight," I said. "I ran from the Task and took with me another man's fancy."

"But they ain't kill you," he said, wholly unmoved. "Must be some task still to be gotten from you. Though likely in another country where none know your name and your boastful sins shall strike them as the lies of a man shackled and diminished."

"Why they lay it on you so?" I asked.

"Amusement, I suppose," he said.

He chuckled in the dark at this.

"I'm bout ready for the ox," he said. "Can't you tell?"

"No different than the rest of us," I said.

"Not you. Not yet. And not that one over there," he said, waving at the boy. "Yes, indeed, a homecoming is calling me back to my peoples. I know I am fated to die here, in torment, for I am wholly dressed in the worst of sin."

He was now into it and though it was night I could see the old man sitting up and staring out toward the parlor, where we could see lantern-light licking back shadows from the other room, and could still hear Ryland exploding into occasional laughter. Now and then the little boy's soft breath curled into a light snore.

"I lived as I should," he said. "I did not live alone. And when I found myself out there, the last man, with no society to enforce true law, I knew that my time had come.

"The world is moving, moving on without this here country. Time was that Elm County was like the only son, best loved by the Lord. Time was this country was the height of society, and the white people was all regale and splendor, grand balls and gossip. I was there. I was out, very often, on the riverboat with my master. I saw how they made revelry. You are born into these fallen years, but I remember when they lived feast to feast, their tables heaving under fine breads, quail and currant cakes, claret, cider, and all other manner of delights.

"None of it for us, I grant you, but we had our gifts. Our gift was the steady land under our feet. That was a time when a good man could make himself a family, and could witness his children, and children's children, the same. My grand-daddy saw it all, yes he did. Brought here from Africa. He found the Lord. He found a wife and generations came under his survey. It was not our season, but the season was so certain, such that even a tasking man could count out the steps of his life. I could tell you stories, boy. I could tell you about the races, and the day Planet flew out his shoes. But never mind it. You have asked why they put it upon me so, and I will tell you."

I had heard the stories before. It had become common to package the feeling of those days, the relative solace taken in knowing one's mother, in having cousins on the nearby estate, of Holidays that still stand tall in memory. But that solace is not freedom, and one can be certain but never be secure. It was the certain system that gave Sophia to Nathaniel, that made me. There was no peace in slavery, for every day under the rule of another is a day of war.

"What is your name?" I asked the old man.

"What do it matter?" he said. "What matters is that I loved a woman, and in that love I forgot my name. That was my sin, the cause by which I am found here, with you, and with this boy, and left to the mercies of these low-down whites."

He was trying to stand now—using the iron bars to pull himself up. I stood to help but he waved me off. He managed to lean against the bars, with his left arm looped through for support.

"I was wedded as a young man and lived for a great many years in all the happiness that a man and a woman might ever hope to know. We lived among the Task, you see, but the Task never lived in us. We had a son. He grew upright and Christian. He was taken in high regard by all around—Quality, Tasking, and Low. He worked the land like it was his own, and thought our masters might be so struck to grant him freedom, perhaps upon their dying.

"He was a boy of big thinking. All knew it. Girls fought over that boy's legacy. He would not marry. He held for one of high honor and would accept none who measured less than his mother. But she died, my wife, my whole heart, yes she did. Fever took her from me. Her last injunction upon me was simple—'Keep that boy safe. Let him not sell his legacy for wood.'

"I kept to that. I kept him right under true law. And when he took a wife, a girl from up in the cook-house, it was like the spirit of his mother returned, for the girl was honorable, and worked her task in the same spirit as my son.

"Years passed us by. We was re-formed into something new, another family. I was blessed with three grandchildren, but only one, a boy, made it past yearling. When they died, we grieved hard together, for the love flowed between us all was strong, something like that river James, and all of that love was given to that one who survived.

"But the land was not what it had been, and the Quality took up a new trade, and the trade was us, and each week when we counted we saw hands fading away.

"Then one evening, after the count, the headman come and address me alone. He say, 'All of us round these parts done long felt you a good man. You and your folk are as children to us, near to our heart. But you have heard the soil that is now bearing a song of death. It breaks me all to pieces to say this, but we must part with your boy. I am sorry. It is for the good of us all. I come to you to tell you first, so that I am honorable. We have done all we can to assure him some comfort. Best I can do is send his wife and boy along with him. It's all I got.'"

I was now standing myself. I was watching the old man, for fear that he might tumble. The light from the parlor was still glimmering. The laughter had grown a little lower and there were fewer voices to be heard now.

"When they told me that, I went to nothing," he said. "I walked back to my quarters. I was trembling. My sight was going black. I walked out into the woods to address the Lord. But I tell you, I could not speak. I slept out there and did not come to the fields in the morning. They must have known I was grieving, for the headman never came for me.

"That day I wandered the near-country with only my thoughts. I walked, but never ran. A notion gnawed in me. These people were so low that they would divide a father from his only son. I knew what I was. My whole life was purchased on time. I was born in the varmint trap. There was no way out. It was my life. But no matter how much I said it, a powerful part of me had never believed. Then they took my boy.

"I come in that night and face him. I told him what they said. His face was a rock, yes it was. He ain't show no fear, he was too strong, and his strength broke me down and I wept. 'Don't cry, Pap,' he said. 'Some way or the other, we shall have our Grand Meeting.'

"Two days later, the headman send me on an errand to town. But before I go, I see a familiar buggy and horse up at the house. And out from that buggy come Ryland—and I knew the time of our parting was upon us. I walked off trying to comfort myself in the knowing that my boy would have a good wife and they should blossom as natural.

"But when I get back, his wife was still there and my boy was gone. At night I come to her, a rage growing in me, and she say they took my son and her baby, that Ryland would not carry them all. And that girl broke down right there in front of me—crazed, wailing. When she regained herself, when she stood, I did not see her face, I saw a haunt of my wife. And I then recalled her injunction upon me—'Keep that boy safe.' That's how I knew my time was all about done. For a man that can't honor his wife's dying wish ain't even a man, ain't even a life.

"The girl said she could not live. She had other family, and seen many of them go that way, down Natchez. None could know who would be next. By what cause should we live out of connection? The tree of our family was parted—branches here, roots there—parted for their lumber.

"We were crazed in our grieving. I tell you, the girl took my hand and when she turned I again saw the face of my wife. She led me out into the night. She walked to the cook-house and I knew just what she planned. They would have skinned us alive. I dragged her back and put her to bed. When morning came she was back to herself, and she put on that very same costume that all us tasking folk must wear to live."

I knew the ideas of the old man's son, and saw myself in his ambitions, in his notion that he might prove himself noble and thus achieve his feeling. It was not so hard to understand. But the Task does not bargain, does not compromise, it devours.

"Time came she was grateful for my wisdom, if you might name it such. We were joined by our grief. Our families gone from us. And living each alone, in Virginia, was a life we could not do."

And here the old man paused and I had that awful feeling of knowing precisely what he would say before he said it.

"It was natural that I love her. It is natural for man and woman to make family," he said. "Upon that great stead, with all our people shipped out from us, it is natural that we would be together. And we were together for some years. I will not disavow it. I will not denounce her. I will say I have sinned in a world of terrible sinners, that this world is constructed to divide father from son, son from wife, and we must bite back with whatever a blade we have at hand.

"One day a white man who'd long moved his property to Mississippi returned. Said he'd sold his plot for he could not reconcile himself to such a savage people. He returned with men. And among these men, I learned, was my beloved son.

"Right then, right there, I knew I could not live. A man returns from the grave to find his father has taken his wife. It could no way be me. That night, I went to the cook-house, as my daughter, as my new wife, had once thought, and set it to flame. I knew what they would do to me. It must be done. But before they did, I would atone for my portion. And I would bite back."

"And so they beat you on instruction of your master?" I asked.

"They beat me because they can," he said. "Because I am old, and will fetch no price. Someday the ghost shall give me up. I know it. But who will greet me in that After?"

And now he began to slide down against the bars of the cell. I heard weeping and I went to him, he fell into my arms and looked up at me and asked, "What will the mother of my only son say to me? Will she know that I have done it as best it came to me? Or will she who charged me so, who charged me with a task no colored can bring, turn from me forever?"

I did not answer. I had no answer. I helped him stand and felt his skin like cracked leather that only barely held in his bones. I walked him over to his pallet and laid him back down. And I listened as he wept softly, repeating over and over, "Oh, who will greet me in that After?" And I listened until he fell asleep, and when I fell asleep after him, I dreamed again of that same field I'd seen months ago, a field of my people with Maynard, who was my brother, holding the chain.

The boy went first. I saw him taken in a coffle of coloreds headed west. I saw him from the back courtyard where they had brought us, as they did from time to time, to endure, yet again, our own appraisal and inspection. His mother walked slowly next to the coffle, in step with her son. She was not chained. She was silent and in all white, and when she could, she touched the boy's shoulder, clasped an arm or held his hand. The train disappeared down the road. It was morning. The day was clear. I was still out in the yard—being handled, being molested, violated, robbed. I was trying so hard to fall back into my mind, to not be there. But the sight of that boy, disappearing in the train down the road, and the sight of his mother—so familiar from some other life—pulled me back.

A half hour after the train had disappeared, I was still in the yard when I heard wailing, shrieking, and looking over I saw that the boy's mother had returned. "Damn you child-killers!" she cried.

"Damn you who have murdered my boys! Hell upon you, say I! May a just God scatter all of your animal bones!"

Her wailing cut the air and the courtyard turned to her. She was walking toward us, shrieking, cursing Ryland and all who should enter the savage trade. So many of us who went, went with dignity and respect. And it occurred to me how absurd it was to cling to morality when surrounded by people who had none. And so seeing this woman, crying out, inconsolable, summoning the wrath of God, gave me heart. She seemed to grow as she came toward us, her every step shaking the ground, I thought, so that even these jackals of the South halted their business to look. A young mother had gone down the road. But something else had come back. Her hands were talons. Her hair was alive and enflamed. Ryland met her at the fence. She clawed at his eyes. She caught his ear in her teeth. He yelled with pain. Soon others came, overtook her, threw her to the ground, kicked her, spat upon her. I did nothing. Understand that I saw all of this and I did nothing. I watched these men sell children and beat a mother to the ground, and I did nothing.

They dragged her away, one hound pulling each arm. Her white garments now ripped and dirty. And as they dragged her off, I heard her holler, almost in rhythm and melody, like the old work songs, "Murderer, say I! Auctioneer of all my lost boys! Ryland's Hounds, Ryland's Hounds! May a righteous God rend you to worms' meat! May black fire scorch you down to your vile and crooked bones."

The old man went next. They took him out for their amusements one night, and never returned him. He had made confession before me, and having done as such, he might now go to his reward.

Nothing so simple for me. My task had only just begun. I was there for three weeks. I was starved and thirsted. They kept us just hearty enough to make us work, and just hungry enough to make us miserable. I was rented out across the county for various tasks.

I cleared frozen ground. I emptied outhouses and drove night-soil. I hauled corpses and dug graves. In those weeks I watched a great number of coloreds—man, woman, and child—brought through and sold off. I was surprised to have remained so long. I began to suspect that I had been singled out for some especial point of torment. I was young and strong and should have fetched a price within days. But the days went on, and people went on, and I remained.

Finally, just as the first hints of spring made themselves known, a buyer appeared. Ryland brought me out in chains. I was blindfolded and gagged. I heard one of my jailers say, "Well now, fella, you have paid quite the price, I know, but I reckon that you have got the upside of this entire bargain. This boy is young, healthy. Should be worth ten hands out in the field."

There was a silence for a moment, then another of my jailers spoke: "We held him far longer than any man should. We had most of Louisiana looking after this boy. Hell, Carolina too." I felt rough hands on me. Someone was inspecting me, I had adjusted to it by then, and that alone is the worst of it—that a man could feel his violation as natural. But it was different now because I was blindfolded and could neither see the prospective buyer nor anticipate where he might place his hands.

"And you have been well paid for your time, and any troubles," the buyer said. "But not for your manners nor conversation. Leave me with what is justly mine and I shall leave you to your work."

"Just making talk," he said. "Just making it all cordial."

"But no one asked you," said the man.

All conversation ended there. I was hoisted, like the thing I was, into the back of the carriage. I saw nothing through my blinds. But I felt the carriage moving at a rapid clip, and for hours there were no words or whispers from the driver, just the random sounds of the woods and the road rumbling beneath us, until we reached a portion of the path where the carriage slowed. And I could feel us going up and over several hills. And then we came to a stop. I was hoisted out. Hands worked at my bindings. My arms were freed. My eyes unmasked.

I was on the ground. I looked up and saw it was night. And then I saw my capturer. I had imagined him a giant. But now I saw him to be average-sized and unremarkable—an ordinary man. The dark was too thick to make out any features, and at all events, there was no time to make a survey. I tried to stand but my legs went wobbly and I fell. Then I stood again, but this time my capturer gave a gentle shove and I fell back, but instead of hitting the ground where I might have expected my feet to have been, I fell farther. And looking up again, I saw that I was in a pit. Then I heard the door to the pit into which I had fallen close over me.

Again I rose, my feet unsure, the ground wobbling under me, barely upright before my head touched against a hard earthen roof. I reached out and found walls of roots and wood, which kept the earth around me at bay. I took the measure of my dungeon. It was about my height, perhaps double in length and width. The darkness was total, beyond blindfolds, night, and perhaps blindness itself. A kind of death. I thought of *Marvell's Book of Wonders,* the entry for oceans, how their mass could swallow whole continents, which themselves could swallow some innumerable quantity of me. I saw myself as a child, on the library floor, marshaling all my powers to count the breadth of the ocean, until my head throbbed at the limits of perception. And I felt, at that moment, down in that darkness, in that seeming death, that I was lost in an ocean, a body sinking in the great surf.

I had heard stories of white men who bought coloreds simply to enact their wildest pleasures—white men who kept them locked away for the sheer thrill of being able to; white men who bought coloreds for the ecstasy of murder; white men who bought coloreds to cut on them for experiments and demon science. And I felt then that I had now fallen to such a white man, that I was now subject to the perfect vengeance of Virginia, Elm County, my father, and Little May.

· II ·

TIME LOST ALL MEANING. Minutes could not be discerned from hours, and with neither sun nor moon, day and night became fictions. At first I took note of the odor of the earth, the occasional sounds above, but soon enough—it is impossible to say when—they became useless noise to me. The wall between sleep and the waking world dissipated, so that dreams were indistinguishable from the figments and illusions that now began to bedevil my mind. I saw so many things down there, so many people. And among those visions, one in particular assumed a special importance, because among all the visions that came over me, this one would soon reveal itself to be no device, but true memory.

We were young, and I was in my first year of service to my brother. It was a long summer Saturday and the masters of Lockless had become bored, which brought to their normal oppressions an element of novelty and whimsy. And so Maynard, who was then a child, had the perverse notion to gather all the Tasked up from out of the Warrens and have them assemble on the bowling green. He ordered me to spread the word. So I did this and within half an hour or so I had them all out on the green, where it was announced by Maynard that the gathered Tasked—old and young, some freshly exhausted from the field, others in the overcoats and polished shoes of the house—would race each other for his amusement. On the possible scales of humiliation and measured against all the troubles put upon us back then, this would not be the worst. But it *was* humiliation and what doubled it for me was that I had not yet understood my place among things, for as I watched Maynard organize them into packs to run against each other, he called to me, "What are you doing, Hi? Get down here."

I looked for a moment, not comprehending.

"Get down here," he said again. And it occurred to me what he meant. I was to run too. I had just that year been brought out of my lessons with Mr. Fields. I remember the eyes of everyone assembled directed toward me, and what I saw in them was both sympathy for me, perhaps unearned, and disgust for Maynard. So I was lined with three of the others and off we went in the August heat to the edge of the field. By the time we'd turned to run back, I was past them all, for while I cannot speak for them, I really was running, running so hard that when my foot caught itself in something hard protruding up from the ground, a rock, an old tree root, I flew off the ground and straight into the field. I hobbled my way back to the starting line, where I found Maynard laughing in a great mood, organizing the next group. For the next three weeks, I moved through the house discharging my duties limping, and every step I took, the sharp pain in my ankle was a constant reminder of my state.

This vision replayed itself for me as though on some sort of carousel, interspersed with others of Thena, Old Pete, Lem, and the woman dancing on the bridge, my mother. But mostly there was darkness, total darkness, until at some point, hours, days, weeks after I had been deposited there, I saw a slice of light cut its way through the ceiling of my dungeon. I scurried back almost ratlike into the farthest corner of my box. And then there was a sound: something dropping to the ground and a voice bellowing out to me.

"Come out," said the voice above me. "Come out."

I walked over and touched the rungs of the ladder. Looking up, I saw the light of dusk and against it the outline of that ordinary man who'd brought me there, my warden.

"Come out," he said.

I climbed up. When I reached the top, I did not so much stand before this ordinary man as I hunched. We were in a small clearing in the woods. In the distance I saw the last orange breath of the dying sun pushing out over the dark fingers of the woods. In this clearing, my captor had arranged an absurd reception—two wooden chairs, a table between them. He motioned to one of the chairs, but I would not sit. The ordinary man turned, walked toward the other chair, turned back to me and tossed a package my way. I reached to catch it, felt it slip from my fingers, then scoured the ground to retrieve it. A piece of bread wrapped in paper. I gobbled it down and in that instant knew I had never truly experienced hunger until my time down in that pit. However long I had gone without food, it had been long enough that the pangs of famish had faded from me, like a visitor who ceases to knock upon realizing no one is home. But the morsel of bread revived my hunger. I seized up and convulsed and then, looking at the table, I saw more packages and something more essential—a jar of water.

I did not even ask. I scampered over and drank and let the water wash down my throat and around the side of my mouth, down my neck and onto my long shirt and overcoat, which I now caught the pungent odor of. The world of feeling began to come back to me. I was hungry and terribly cold. I unwrapped another piece of bread, quickly devoured it, and then another and was going for another when this ordinary man quietly said, "That will be enough."

I turned and saw that he was seated not too far from me, and though it was dusk, it was already too dark for me to get the full features of his face. The ordinary man sat there in his chair, saying nothing. I waited there, shivering against the cold. Then I saw a light in the distance growing larger and approaching us. I heard wagon wheels crunching against the road until a large covered car and horse stood before us. A man next to the driver held a lantern. The driver stepped off and nodded to the ordinary man, who then beckoned me to board the wagon. I climbed up and saw now that there were several other colored men in the car. And then we were off, rumbling down the road, the wagon shifting and creaking under us. I examined the other men gathered there, and wondered what depredations might now greet us. And there were no chains, who would need them? For had you seen the bowed heads around me, you would have known that these men were more than bound, they were broken. And I was one of them, so tumbled into the pit of despair that all my disparate motives had been reduced to survival. I had been reduced to an animal. Now came the hunt.

We rode for an hour or so, and then were ushered back out of the wagon, placed into file. And we stood there in ungainly ranks, the ordinary man surveying us as a general might review a fresh round of recruits. And though it was darker now, I found that the darkness suited my eyes, as though the time below had somehow changed me so that the moonlight proved enough for me to now take the measure of this ordinary man—his hair hanging long and ungainly beneath his wide-brimmed hat, and a long gray beard, raw and untamed, sprouting out from his face. There were more of us than him at that moment, however beaten down and demoralized we were, but we knew he wasn't alone. Because white men in Virginia are never really alone.

And then the others arrived, announcing themselves by lantern-light in the distance and the approaching clomp and clack of horse hooves and wheels creaking up the road. And now I saw three carriages pulling to a stop before us and from them white men disembarked, holding the lanterns in their hands. The light cast a yellow pall upon them and they seemed otherworldly creatures of another age—demons, gorgons, specters—summoned back to wreak the vengeance of Quality upon our persons. But then I heard them talk, and I heard a particular cadence that told me that I was still in Virginia, and these "creatures" were no conjuration, but a pack of low whites. Their talk was rough. Their coats were worn. Now my heart dropped, and a new wave of fear overtook me. The monsters of myth would have been preferable to these men I knew too well. The low whites enjoyed only a toehold in the craggy face of society, an insecure position, which only augmented the brutal spirit they so often visited upon the coloreds of Virginia. This brutality was the offering Quality made to the low whites, the payment that united them. And it struck me now that this was the point of our evening—a ritual of brutality, in which we, the captured, were to be the sacrifice.

The ordinary man extended brief pleasantries to the low whites and once again walked down the line and made an appraisal of us. There was something theatrical about him now, and whereas before he had seemed solemn and reserved, now he was boastful and preening. He reached into his coat and pulled on his suspenders. He would stop, assess a man, shake his head mockingly, and suck his teeth.

And then, having assessed us again, he spoke.

"Villains of Virginia," he bellowed. "Judgment has now set its blind gaze upon you. Thieves! Robbers! Murderers! Villains who have compounded your crimes by connivance to escape our laws and pass into another land under false and assumed names."

Again he walked the line, but this time he stopped before one of the men farther down the line to my left. "You, Jackson, talked of murder of your master—but talked too much, boy! You were given up and now must stand before Virginia justice."

The ordinary man moved down. "And you, Andrew, thought you could make off with some portion of your master's cotton crop, did you? And when found out, decided you might run."

Andrew stood solemn and silent. The ordinary man moved on.

"Davis and Billy," he said, now walking to the other end of the line. "Why, boys, I am told you were well liked. What would send you to murder a good man in the alley and pilfer his property?"

"Property was ours," yelled out one of these two. "Was the last gift of my uncle, 'fore he was put on the square!"

One of the men in the yellow light cut him off. "Ain't no yours, boy!"

"Goddamn you," said the man on the line. "Was my uncle's! You best not color his name!"

At that the man standing next to him said, "Shut up, Billy. We got enough of it already."

Another man yelled from the yellow light, "Don't you worry yourself, boy, we will feed him his manners well enough."

The ordinary man now walked toward the center of the line.

"You all wished to run," he said. "Well, by God, I was not constructed to stand against the will of any man, or any niggers."

The ordinary man walked back toward the wagon, climbed atop its seat, and stood. "Here is what we're gonna do. You are now in the care of these Virginia gentlemen. They have agreed to give you an allotment of time to go. Outdistance them for the whole of this evening, and freedom is yours. But if they catch you, your whole life is at their mercy. Maybe you'll make it out and your sins will be wiped. More likely, you won't make it an hour before justice finds you. Makes no difference to me. I did my service. Time come for you to do yours."

Then he sat down, took the reins, and the wagon rumbled off.

We stood there, looking around and into the night, looking at each other, for some clue, perhaps waiting, hoping, even amidst our gripping fear, that some jest would be revealed. We were too stunned to move. I looked over at the white men, the apparitions in their wide-brimmed hats, who now stood waiting for us to apprehend the fact of our situation. And then, his patience exhausted, one of these whites broke from the group and walked over to the rough line of us. He was holding a cudgel. He took this cudgel and smashed it over the head of one of the tasking men, now branded renegade. The tasking man seemed in disbelief as it happened, for he made no effort to block the blow. But he screamed out as it took effect, and then crumpled on the ground. The man with the cudgel now turned to the rest of the line and said, "Best to get to getting, boys."

Everyone scattered at once. I ran too, with one look back toward the fallen man, a dark heap against the greater enveloping darkness that now gathered behind me. I ran alone. I suspect we all did. There was no effort among the Tasked assembled there to cooperate—perhaps among those two brothers, Davis and Billy— but if the terror that struck me when that man was cudgeled struck them, if they had been held under as I had, then likely there was no time for thinking, no time for loyalty.

And so I ran—but neither fast nor, as it turned out, far. Hunger stole my will. The cramps turned my limbs to wood. The night wind cut against me, and now more loping than running, I noticed that the ground beneath me was uncertain and wet and even the soft tug of the mud added to my weight.

And where was I now running to? What is North but a word? The Underground, the swamps, but a myth spread by the villain Georgie Parks? And what hope had I to elude this pack of predators? But even in this terror and despair, I didn't think to fall down in the road or to surrender myself. The light of freedom had been reduced to embers, but it was still shining in me, and borne up by the winds of fear, I kept running, bent, loping, locked, but running all the same, with my whole chest aflame.

The night was lit up by the power of my adapting eyes, so that wet and wintery forest was all laid out before me. And I heard my brogans sinking into the ground with every step, the twigs snapping under me. And I heard a shot in the distance and I wondered if they'd caught one of us, killed one of us. The drum in my chest boomed louder. In my path I saw the skinny trunk of a fallen tree, which I told myself to leap over as I ran. But my body gave me up. I fell and there was now mud in my nose, mud in my mouth. And

I remember the feeling of relief coming over me, relief from all my muscles finally at rest. But even then, even down there, I could still see the light of freedom, dim and blue. I heard voices now— a muddle of cries and yells—and I knew that soon they would be upon me. *Rise,* I told myself. *Rise.* Slowly now, my fingers grasped at the mud, my palms pushed in deep, and I was then on my hands and knees. *Rise.* And one knee was up and then another, and then I was standing again.

But no sooner was I up than I felt the cudgel crack across my back. I fell. And they were all over me again, kicking, punching, spitting, cursing, violating. I did not fight them off. I left my body, flew, soared even, back to Lockless, back down on the Street with Thena, back to the garden with Old Pete, back beneath the gazebo with Sophia, so that when they roped my arms and dragged me off, when I felt the wagon wheels rumbling beneath me, I was barely aware of it. I remember everything, I tell you. I remember it all—all except those moments when I gave up memory, when I left my body and flew away.

They brought me back before the ordinary man, all roped and trussed. I did not even look at him. They blindfolded me and tossed me into the back of another wagon, and, after a short ride, tossed me into the same pit from which my ordeal began.

This hunt became my routine. I would be pulled up from the pit, given a pittance of bread and water, put into file with a group of renegades, who were addressed with all their crimes, and then sent to run. I remember the names, how the ordinary man would read them in his low gravelly voice—Ross, Healy, Dan, Edgar. And each night we were made to run. And each night I was defeated. And each night returned to my pit. Had I died? Was this the hell of which my father spoke? Some nights I would be out running for hours and I could swear I saw the soft glimmer of dawn, its borders at my finger-tips. Then I would be taken, beaten, and tossed right back into the box, where the carousel of dreams and visions awaited—I am watching Sophia water dance by the fire, I am watching Jack and Arabella flick marbles in the ring, I am gathering the Tasked for Maynard to run.

But I grew stronger. I grew faster. And this began not with the body but the mind, for I found that when in the right mind, I ran faster and farther, and if I were ever to win this twisted game, I would need all the assets I could manage. And so, in my mind I began to call out the very anthems that Lem and I exchanged that last Holiday:

> *Going away to the great house farm*
> *Going on up to where the house is warm*
> *When you look for me, Gina, I'll be far gone.*

The song powered me, for it reminded me of Lem and the Holiday, Thena and Sophia, and all of us gathered together. Even in the darkness some part of me smiled.

And I felt freedom, brief as it was, in those nights of flight. Even as I was hunted, I felt it in the cold wind cutting against my face, the branch scratching my cheek, the mud under my brogans, the heaving heat of my breath. No Maynard yanking at me. No trying to discern the motives of my father. No creeping fear of Corrine. Out here, it was all so clear. In running, I felt myself to be in a kind of defiance.

And I was growing crafty. I remember being out one night for what must have been hours. And I knew it had been hours because by the time they'd finished with me and hauled me back, pummeled and beaten, to the ordinary man, I saw something incredible—the sun rising over what I could now see as green hills. And remembering the promise made to me of freedom, I knew that I was close. I learned to cover my tracks, to double back over them, so as to confuse them, and learned, too, that I could track them as sure as they tracked me. And I realized that I had a gift that I could bring to bear—my memory. It was always the same crew, and they were unoriginal in their workings. Memorizing the terrain and their habits gave me a sudden advantage. I would find my way to their flank. One night they split up. I felled one, and then pummeled another. They gave me an extra hard licking for that one, and I was forced to confess the limits of my operation. I was running, when what I needed was to fly. Not just in my mind, but in this world. I needed to lift up away from these low whites, as I lifted away from Maynard and the river.

But how? What was that power that could pull a man out of the depths? That could pull a boy out of the stables and into the loft? I began to reconstruct events. Both of those uncanny moments featured blue light and both brought me, in different ways, close to my mother, or to the dark hole in my memory where I'd lost her. The power must have some relation to my mother. And I needed the power because I needed to fly, or I would die trying to outrun these wolves.

Maybe the power was in some way related to the block in my memory, and to unlock one was, perhaps, to unlock the other. And so in those dark and timeless hours in the pit, it became my ritual to reconstruct everything I had heard of her and all that I had seen of her in those moments down in the Goose. Rose of the kindest heart. Rose, sister of Emma. Rose the beautiful. Rose the silent. Rose the Water Dancer.

It was a cloudless night and I was running. I could feel that it was now spring, for the nights were no longer so fierce upon me. My heart no longer pounded against my chest as I ran. My legs were fluid. And the men must have known this, for I had noticed that they had increased their numbers. And whereas before they would split up to pursue the whole line of fugitives, I now began to feel that the entire team was focused on me above all the others. So it was that night that I heard them, closing in. And then the forest opened up and I saw a pond glistening, wide and dark. I had to make an effort around the water. I could hear the cries and whoops of the men behind me. I pushed around the pond as hard as I could, the voices of the men steadily closing, and I dared not look back. And then my foot caught on something, a branch, or a root, I cannot be sure, and a sharp pain, an old pain, shot up through my ankle. I felt myself falling and then I was down in the fens, and I felt the cold muddy water on my face. I crawled for a moment. But delirious with pain, and knowing the hunt was over, I called out, but this time not in my mind but out loud for all to hear:

> Going away to the great house farm
> Going up, but won't be long
> Be back, Gina, with my heart and my song.

What did the men pursuing me see in that moment? Did they even hear me calling out? They were right on me, ready to lay on hands, perhaps reaching at that moment. Did they see the air open in front of them, the blue light of all our stories knifing through the world, illuminating the night? What I saw was the woods folding back against themselves, a rolling mist, and beneath it a bowling green that I immediately recognized as belonging to Lockless. That was my first thought. But then as the scene came upon me—and that was how it felt, like the world was drawing to me more than I was drawing to it—I saw that this was not the Lockless of my time, for there were tasking folk who I knew to no longer be with us. And directing them I saw, as I remembered him all those years, laughing and thoughtless, Little May. He was pointing back at the house, yelling something, and drawn to that direction, I saw that he was yelling at me, not me floating above but me on the ground, in time, in that first year of service, stripped from the instruction of Mr. Fields, still apprehending my place in things.

The moment struck me not as another turn on the carousel, but wholly new. It was like being asleep and never recognizing, no matter the absurdity of things, that you are in a dream. The very nature of logic and expectation was bent, and the absurd struck me as normal, so I simply observed myself, observed Maynard, as we had been, in that other time. Even as I watched this younger me cornered off with another group of tasking folks and lined up to run, even as I saw myself racing off, even as I felt myself to be racing with them, though my legs were not moving, I did not understand. I watched as I separated myself from the line, faster than all of them, and touching the tip of the field, I saw myself turn back, and then trip, scream, and fall, grabbing at my ankle. I remember wanting to comfort this child, this me from another life. But when I moved to him, the world again peeled away and I was back in my own time.

But not in my own place. Pain again shot through my ankle. I was on the ground howling. I tried to crawl. And then I stood. I took one step. It was agony. I fell. And again I felt myself slipping under. I looked up one last time and saw one of the men standing over me.

No. A different one now.

"Quiet down, boy," Hawkins said. "The way you hollering liable to wake the dead."

<h1 style="text-align: center;">· 12 ·</h1>

I WAS BROUGHT BACK BY the pain in my ankle. It was no longer the sharp stab from before, but a dull throbbing. I opened my eyes and saw the daylight, the beautiful daylight that I hadn't seen in weeks, blaring through a window like a horn, so loud that the rest of the world blurred before me. Slowly my eyes shifted so that the blur began to take shape—a table by the bedside with a pipe hooked onto a vase shaped like a ship, a large clock on a ledge across from me, and above my head a canopy, and scarlet-red curtains pulled back. I looked down and saw that I had been fully washed, and fitted in cotton drawers and a silk night shirt. It occurred to me that I might still be down under, and this just another turn on the carousel. Or perhaps I had ascended out of the hell of my dungeon and gone, at last, to my reward. But the dull throbbing of my ankle signaled that the world around me was real. And I saw that I was not alone, for there were figures, too, forming out of the blur. One was Hawkins, the man who had, now twice, found me on the other end of miraculous flight. He was seated in a chair, and next to him, no longer in her mourning clothes, I saw the forsaken bride of Maynard Walker, Corrine Quinn.

"Welcome," she said.

She was smiling, smiling joyously even, and I was aware that I had never seen her smile in such a way before. It was as if she had discovered something lost ages ago, a key perhaps, or the final piece of a puzzle that had so long vexed and discomfited her. But there was something more, something in her manner, for she was smiling *at me,* not smiling *upon me.* Her manner had always been bizarre and unlike anything I had ever seen among the Quality. But this was different still, for there was nothing masterful nor certain, no dominance in her manner, only a deep pleasure, a satisfaction at some unseen goal having been attained.

"Do you know what has happened to you?" she asked. "Do you know where you are?"

There was the smell of spring potpourri—a sharp sweet mix of mint, thyme, and something else—a scent that could never be of Lockless, where a boyish spirit prevailed and didn't allow for such things.

"Do you know how long you've been gone?" she asked.

I said nothing.

"Hiram," she said. "Do you know who I am?"

"Miss Corrine," I answered.

"No 'Miss,'" she said, her joyous smile now relaxing into a look of confirmation. "Corrine. Only ever Corrine."

The unnaturalness of the moment now expanded. I saw, looking over, that Hawkins was not standing in wait, as a tasking man should, but was seated right next to her with his posture upright and erect.

Again she asked, "Do you know where you are?"

"No," I replied. "I don't know how long I have been gone. I don't know where I been gone to. I don't even know why."

"Hiram," she said, "we are going to have an agreement, an understanding. I will be truthful with you. And in turn, you will do the same for me."

Now she stared hard at me.

"You well know why you were sent away," she said. "You ran, taking another with you. Surely by now you have guessed that we have intelligence greater than your own. I will tell you anything, but you must do me the same."

I moved to sit up in the bed and felt a sharp pain in my back and legs. My feet were cracked and sore. I felt my face and found a knot above my left eye. And I remembered the nightly ordeal I had suffered, the hours spent in the pit.

"Yeah, we're sorry about that. Had to be sure." Hawkins now gave a look of acknowledgment and said, "Had some notions, but to be sure, had to carry you off."

We're sorry, he'd said, implying that Hawkins, a tasking man, had some power here, not just in this room but in all the hell that I had journeyed through for what had been, what, a month? Months?

"Hiram," said Corrine. "You went into the Goose River with Maynard. No, you took Maynard into the Goose River. He had no choice in the thing. Perhaps you wanted this, but want or not, you killed a man, and in so doing, sent long-drawn plans to dust. For your impulse and desire, for your crime, great men must now reapportion their lives and whole armies of American justice are now in flight. You do not understand. But I think you shall, for it is my belief that in your wild thrashings there was a design, greater still than even our own."

As she spoke, Corrine unhooked the pipe from the vase with her left hand, and with her right took the top off. The smell of tobacco now wafted out. She lit the pipe, pulled, and puffed out a plume of smoke. Then she handed the pipe to Hawkins, who relit, puffed, and handed the pipe back to her. White smoke fluttered up from them and hung like dust on the sunlight cutting through the window. I thought back to the last conference, in that low-lit parlor of Lockless, where her voice quavered and trembled, and I remembered how odd she was even then, how odd she'd always been, how she seemed to eschew the fashion of the moment for a Virginia of old, and how conspicuous and wrong it all really was. But now I saw the truth so suddenly I wondered how I had never seen it before. It was a lie, the whole thing was a lie, the tradition, the mourning, perhaps even the marriage itself.

I must have lost all my covert powers while away, for Corrine looked at me and laughed and said, "You are wondering how I did it, aren't you?"

"I am," I said.

"Yes, yes, I understand, I truly do," she said. "It is a rare thing for any lord or lady of the estate to truly fool the servant. It is a luxury to be so grandly deceived, to live among perjury and invention. Whatever your aspirations, Hiram, I know that you have never enjoyed such splendor. You are a scientist. You have to be.

"But these fools, these Jeffersons, these Madisons, these Walkers, all dazzled by theory, well, I am convinced that the most degraded field-hand, on the most miserable plot in Mississippi, knew more of the world than any overstuffed, forth-holding American philosophe.

"And the lords and ladies of our country know this. This is why they are so in thrall of the dance and song of your people. It is an unwritten library stuffed with a knowledge of this tragic world, such that it defies language itself. Power makes slaves of masters, for it cuts them away from the world they claim to comprehend. But I have given up my power, you see, given it up, so that now I might begin to see."

She held the pipe in her hand, and shook her head. "Yes, you do see, you do understand, but you are not yet wise. Your pursuit of this design, your embrace of a man who is, in fact, a villain . . . well, this thing with you, this Conduction that pulled you out of the river, you are not the first, you know? You know the story— Santi Bess and the forty-eight coloreds—"

"That never happened?" I interrupted.

"Indeed it did," Corrine said. "And its implications are the very reason you find yourself here before us. Did you know that before her departure, there was no Freetown in Starfall? Did you know that Georgie's entire treachery—a slavery in liberator's clothes—is really the treachery of the lords of this country?"

At the mention of Georgie's name, memories flowed back, old memories of a man who had been as family. Thoughts of Amber and their baby. Had Amber known? I thought of our last conversation, how she tried to dissuade me. And I wondered at what precise moment Georgie decided to hand me off. And I wondered how many he had handed off before me.

"It's a good trick," Hawkins said. "Gotta give him that—they give shelter to Georgie and his pals, and he gives them intelligence and eyes. So the next time a Santi Bess come, he laying in wait."

"But that can't happen, can it, Hiram," said Corrine. "Because Santi worked by a different power—the same power that pulled you out of the river Goose, the same power that freed you from our patrol."

Now I looked around the room. Things began to assemble together, and a set of questions slowly formed but all I managed to ask was one.

"What is this?"

Corrine reached for a handbag. She produced a paper and held it up.

"You were given to me, body and soul, by your father," she explained. "He signed you over because your flight disgraced him. It was another blow to his heart, already weakened by the loss of Maynard, and he answered the blow with rage. He wanted nothing to do with you. But I convinced him that you were too valuable to lose, and so he signed you over to me. For a healthy price, of course."

Now she rose and walked over to the door.

"But you are not mine," she said, and at that she opened the door. I could see stairs and the upper portion of a banister. "You are not a slave. Not to your father. Not to me. Not to anyone. You asked what this was. It is freedom."

These words did not fill me with delight. The questions now overran me. Where had I been? Why was I left in a hole? How long had I been under? What happened to the ordinary man? And more than anything, what had become of Sophia?

Corrine returned to her seat. "But freedom, true freedom, is a master too, you see—one more dogged, more constant, than any ragged slave-driver," she said. "What you must now accept is that all of us are bound to something. Some will bind themselves to property in man and all that comes forthwith. And others shall bind themselves to justice. All must name a master to serve. All must choose.

"We have chosen this, Hawkins and I. We have accepted the gospel that says our freedom is a call to war against unfreedom. Because that is who we are, Hiram. The Underground. We are who you were searching for. But you found Georgie Parks first. I am sorry about that. At great expense, and risking exposure, we retrieved you. This was not done for your benefit, but because we have long seen in you something of incredible value, some artifact of a lost world, a weapon that might turn the tide in this longest war. You know of what I speak, do you not?"

I did not reply. Instead I asked, "Where is Sophia? What happened to her?"

"There are limits to our powers, Hiram," Corrine said.

"But you say you are the Underground," I said. "If you are who you say you are, why didn't you free her? Why did you leave me in that jail? Why did you leave me in that hole? Do you know what has happened to me?"

"Know?" asked Hawkins. "We caused it to happen to you. We authored it. And as for your freedom, there is a reason we are the Underground. And a reason we've lived to fight so long. There are rules. There is a reason you found Georgie before you found us."

"Every night, those men hunted me," I said, the anger growing in me. "And you let them do it. No, worse. You sent them to do this?"

"Hiram," said Corrine, "I am sorry but that hunt was but a preview of your life now. And that dungeon was but a glimpse of the price of your failure. Your life was over the minute you engaged with Georgie Parks. Would you prefer we left you to that? Hawkins speaks the truth. We had to be sure."

"What did you have to be sure of?" I asked.

"That you really did carry the power of Santi Bess, of Conduction," Corrine said. "And you do. Twice now we have seen it made manifest. Surely it was the work of our Lord for Hawkins to find you the first time. And inquiring, we discovered from others that you'd once talked wildly about something much the same happening to you as a child. We needed to wait for it to happen again. We calculated where the power might send you, and we waited for you to arrive."

"Arrive where?" I asked.

"At Lockless," she said. "We thought you might be trying to get back to the only home you've ever known. We had agents watching for you every night."

"And here you are," said Hawkins.

"And where am I?" I asked.

"Somewhere safe," said Corrine. "Where we bring all those newly married to our cause."

She paused for a second here. I saw a hint of sympathy in her face and I knew she was not relishing any of this, that she had some sense of my pain and confusion.

"There is so much that you must understand, I know. We will explain, I promise you this. But you must trust us. And you must trust us because there is no going back. Right now, there is nothing else true in this world. And soon you shall see that there is nothing else truer than our cause."

At that Corrine and Hawkins rose. "Soon," she said as they left.

"Soon you will understand it all. Soon you shall singularly comprehend, and then your comprehension will be a new binding, and in this binding—in this high duty—you will find your true nature."

Now she paused at the door and uttered words that felt like prophecy.

"You are not a slave, Hiram Walker," said Corrine. "But by Gabriel's Ghost, you shall serve."

· 13 ·

THAT EVENING, STILL LYING in bed, I heard voices downstairs and the smell of what I hoped to be supper—I had not enjoyed a proper meal since my flight from Lockless. This all combined to rouse me from my stupor. I saw now that upon the bureau there were two washing pans filled with water, a toothbrush, dentifrice, and a set of clothes. I cleaned and changed and then limped downstairs, across a foyer, and into an open dining room, where I saw Corrine, Hawkins, Amy, three other coloreds, and none other than Mr. Fields.

I stood in the doorway for a moment until he saw me. He was laughing at some story Hawkins was relating, but when he saw me his smile turned grave and he looked to Corrine, who now looked to me, and then the whole table turned to me in the most solemn way imaginable. They were seated before a veritable feast, but all of them, black and white, man and woman, were dressed in work clothes.

"Please, Hiram," Corrine said. "Join us."

I walked in gingerly and took an empty seat near the end, next to Amy and across from Mr. Fields. We had stewed okra and sweet potatoes. We had greens and baked shad. There was salt pork and apples. Some type of bird stuffed with rice and mushrooms. Bread. Pudding. Dumplings. Black cake. Ale. It was the most indulgent meal I'd ever had, but more incredible than the meal was what happened after.

Corrine rose first and then the others, and all together they began to clean the dishes and reset the dining room. It was an incredible sight. There was no division. Everyone moved together, everyone except me. I tried to help but was refused. When the clean-up was done, they all retired to the parlor and I watched as they played blind man's bluff late into the night. It occurred to me both by their jolly nature and their stray comments that this was not the usual evening, that something had changed warranting this celebration, and that the something was me.

I stayed that night in the house, in what was the guest chambers, sleeping long and late into the afternoon. I had never engaged in such luxury, not even during Holiday. I washed and dressed and then walked downstairs. The house was quiet. On the kitchen table there was a pan of rye muffins with a note next to it directing me to indulge. After devouring two muffins, I cleaned my dish, walked out the front door, and took a seat on the porch. From the outside, the house was modest and quaint, covered in white clapboard. There was a garden out front, filled with blooming snowdrops and bluebells. Past the garden there was a bank of woods, and then in the distance I saw the majestic peaks of what I knew to be the western mountains. I surmised that I was likely at the border of Virginia, most probably in Bryceton, Corrine's family stead, the same manse where she'd told me, months ago, she would have me delivered.

In the distance, I saw two figures emerging from the woods. They walked toward the house and I could soon discern that they were two white men—one older, one younger, a father and son perhaps. When they saw me they stopped. The younger one nodded in greeting, but the older man grabbed him by the arm and pulled him back to the woods. I sat there for an hour looking out and at some point fell into a daydream and then, obviously more fatigued than I thought, into an actual dream. And I was back in my cell again, but this time with Pete and Thena, and when the men pulled me out to the front parlor Pete and Thena laughed, and I could hear their laughter through the entire ordeal as men inspected me, violated me. I could not at that time yet see this as such—as violation. It took time to learn how to speak of what was done to me directly, to tell the story of my time in Ryland's Jail as it was, and not feel my manhood fleeting from me. It took time for me to see that the story really was my greatest power. But back then, when I awoke from the dream all I felt was a burning anger. I had never been a violent boy. I did not have much of a temper. But for years after this, I found myself randomly filled up with the most destructive thoughts and feelings, and unable to truly admit to why.

I was awakened by a door closing behind me. I looked back and saw that it was Amy. She walked out and stood on the porch for a moment, looking out as the now setting sun fell over the mountains. She wore neither a mourning gown nor black veil, but a gray hoop dress with a white apron across the front. Her hair was pulled back behind a bonnet.

"I am supposing you have questions," she said.

Yes. I had many. But I offered none of them. It was my feeling that I had asked enough already, by which I mean I had told them enough already, because I'd learned in my first life that interrogation is never one way. Until Amy said, "All right. I understand. I must suppose that were I you, right now, I would not be much for talking myself. Nevertheless, I'm talking. Because there are things about this place, about this new life, that you should know."

Out of the side of my eye, I now saw her looking at me. But I held my eyes on the mountains and the sun drawing to a close over them.

"You have probably guessed where you are—Bryceton. Corrine's place. But you have not guessed, and cannot know, what her place really is. I might as well tell you. You will see it soon enough.

"Bryceton used to belong to Corrine's folks. Seeing as how she was the onliest, when they died, the estate fell to her. I guess you know by now Corrine ain't what she seem. Oh, she is Virginia, through and through. But by cause of what she seen right here, and some knowledge acquired up North, she takes, shall we say, a different view of the slavery question. And her view, which is my view, and my brother's view, is quarrelsome and wrathy."

Here Amy laughed lightly and paused for a moment and said, "I should not laugh. It is not funny, except when it is. Which I must say is all the time to me. It is a blessing to be here, to be at war with them. We are an outpost in that army that you now know as the Underground. Everyone living here is part of that army, though we can give no tell of such things. If you walked with me now, you would see what anyone would expect—orchards blooming, fields all lush. And if we were entertaining, you'd see us all at work, singing and happy. But understand that every single one of those you would see singing and working here are with us, and have dedicated themselves to extending the light of freedom into Maryland, Virginia, Kentucky, and even into Tennessee.

"They're all agents, though they work in different ways. Some of them work from the house. They are read, as you are, and have put that skill to use. Paper is important in this—freedom papers, wills and testaments. It's the house, I know, but believe me they are a wild bunch. The house agents always got an ear to the ground. They study. They know the gossip. They know the journals. They know everyone of influence in their region, but no one in the region really knows them. And then there are others."

Amy paused here, and when I looked over, I saw a half smile had crawled up the corner of her mouth. She was now looking out to the mountains herself, watching as they consumed the last morsel of sun.

"You see that there?" she asked. I did not answer. "That there is what it is. Sitting here watching the sun set on your own time, with nothing over you and no one to command you or threaten a seven and nine. It was not always this way, for me. I was, with my brother, tied to the meanest man in the world and that man married Corrine and, well, that man is not with us anymore and I am here with you able to enjoy small natural things such as this.

"But there are others who cannot be remanded to a house, for they feel the walls pushing in. They are the ones who remember the first time they ran, and it was so glorious to them, to be in defiance against everything they had ever been told. It is the most free they ever felt, and they are left in chase of that freedom. That is the field agent. The field agents are different. They go into plantations and lead the Tasked up off of them. The field agents are daring. The hounds make them feel alive. The swamp, the river, the bramble, the abandoned stead, the loft, the old barn, the moss, the North Star—that's the field agent.

"And we need each other. We work together. Same army, Hiram. Same army."

She went quiet again at that. And we sat there looking at the evening sky and the stars peeking out.

"And what are you?" I asked.

"Hmmm?"

"House or field?" I said. "What are you?"

She looked at me, snorted, laughed, and said, "I'm a field agent, of course."

Then she looked back toward the mountains, which were now just dark blue hulks in the distance. "Hiram, I could run right now, even free as I am, run from nothing, run right past them mountains, past all the rivers, through every prairie, sleeping in swamps, feeding off roots, and then after all that, I could run some more."

⋅ ⋅ ⋅

So I was trained to be an agent, trained in the mountains at Bryce-ton, Corrine's family stead, along with other new agents recruited for the Underground. You will forgive me for not saying much about my fellow agents. Those who are mentioned in this volume are either alive and have tendered their permission, or have gone off to that final journey to meet with the Grand Discerner of Souls. We are not yet past a time when scores are settled and ven-geances sought, so many of us must, even in this time, remain un-derground.

My life now doubled. I resumed my regular interest in wood-working and the crafting of furniture. And I acted as I had, help-ing among the folk who worked at Bryceton, though they worked in a manner then most strange to me. There was no division in labor along any front. The kitchen, the dairy, the mechanic's workshop, were worked by all, regardless of sex and color, so that should Corrine Quinn be without business abroad it was nothing to see her out among the crops, or serving supper with Hawkins in the shotgun dining hall where we together assembled nightly.

After supper, we would return to our barracks and change from our dinner garb to the uniform of the night—flannel shirt, elastic-bound trousers, and light canvas shoes. Then we would report for that first phase of training. We ran for an hour every night, cover-ing, by my estimation, six to seven miles. Mixed in with these miles were breaks for all manner of calisthenics—arm raises, lean-ing rest, hops, etc. And then after our run there was more—sideways lunges, leg lifts, knee bends, etc. The regimen was derived from the German '48ers, men who'd fought for liberty in their old country, and found common cause here in the Underground. Whatever their origins, they made me stronger. The burning in my chest diminished to the slightest discomfort and I found that I could cover wide spans of country without rest.

There were no tasking men among these instructors, only the Quality and the Low. Some of them, I suspected, were among the men who had once regularly hunted me. I don't know if I ever got over this. I felt myself disposable to them, at least to this portion in Virginia who were, to my mind, zealots. And though I know they had to be, that there was no other way for them to be, it meant a certain distance between us, for their war was against the Task, and mine would be a war for those who were Tasked.

As it happened, there was one exception, though I wonder now if this was because he was not Virginian, but a native of the North. That was Mr. Fields, whom I met with for an hour, thrice weekly, after my calisthenics, beneath the house in a sprawling sub-basement, accessible only by a trapdoor, which one accessed by stepping through a large mahogany marriage chest whose bottom had been cut out. Down two sets of stairs, there was another door, behind which lay a musky, lantern-lit study, with two rows of bookshelves on each side, stuffed end to end. In the middle of the room there was a long table with equidistant seats, and at each seat there was pen and paper.

In the farthest corner there were two large secretaries, the pi-geonholes of which were filled with various papers pertaining to the Underground, tools of the house agents who, some nights, I saw down there, at the long table, quietly executing their stealthy craft. I would sit at the table with Mr. Fields, who took up our studies as though nothing had ever occurred between us, as though the span of years had not even happened.

My curriculum now expanded, and I was happy for this: geom-etry, arithmetic, some Greek and Latin. And then for one remain-ing hour, I was given the free run of the offices and left to choose among the volumes. I think now that my own volume, the one that you now hold here, began there in those moments—in that library. For eventually I began not simply to read but to write. At first it was merely a record of my studies. But soon this record expanded to my thoughts, and then from my thoughts to my im-pressions, so that I now possessed, not merely a record of my head, but of my heart. From where did such an idea originate? I guess I must thank Maynard. Among the effects he pilfered from my father's own pigeonholed secretary was an old journal kept by our grandfather, John Walker, who, in keeping with his generation, believed himself to be in the midst of a grand struggle that would alter the face of the world. I didn't have such pretensions, but I did sense, however dimly, that I had, however incidentally, caught on to something significant beyond my small life.

I continued this routine for a month, with little alteration, until one evening, when I went down underneath the house and there was Corrine in place of Mr. Fields.

"And how are you finding things here?" she said.

"Most strange," I said. "It is another life."

Corrine yawned quietly and sat down. She put her elbow on the desk, and her chin in her palm, regarding me with tired eyes. Her hair was pulled back in black curls. The lantern-light tumbled shadows onto her face. Her aspect was of an ancestress though she barely outranked me in years. I recalled her time with Maynard and felt myself becoming enthralled by the breadth of her deception. How little I had known of her then, her intelligence, her savvy, her cunning. Then I felt a shock of fear roil through me. Corrine Quinn, who wore the mask of Quality, was mysterious and powerful. And I had no real notion of her capacities.

"Even you," I said. "It is a lot to consider. I just . . . I would never have imagined. Not in a thousand years."

"Thank you," she said. And she laughed, clearly delighted in the grand sweep of her deception. "Do you enjoy the writing?"

"I have seen so much lately," I replied. "I have felt a need to record it, especially my experiences here."

"Careful with that," she said.

"I know," I said. "It dies with me. It does not leave here."

"Hmm," she said, her eyes now alight. "I have heard that you have made the library your quarters," she said. "And that some nights, you have to be practically dragged from its depths."

"It reminds me of home," I said.

"And would you go back, if you could? Home?" she asked.

"No. Never," I said.

She studied me for a moment now, for what I could not be sure. They were always studying me down there. I could feel it, even my fellow agents in training, it seemed, always probing me with questions, watching me when they thought I was not looking. I answered them with as much silence as possible. But there was something about Corrine that compelled me to speak. There was something to her own silence that communicated a deep and particular loneliness, and though we never spoke directly upon the origins of this feeling, I felt it to be cousin to my own.

"When I was down, back there, back at Lockless," I said, "I had my freedoms—more than most, I should say. But I was still property of another man. Even speaking it as such, here right now to you, lowers me."

"Indeed," she said. "And some of us have been down since the days of Rome. Some of us are born into society and told that knowledge is rightfully beyond us, and ornamental ignorance should be our whole aspiration."

She chuckled and paused a moment, waiting for me to catch her meaning. And when it was apparent that I did, she said, "The mind of woman is weak—this was the word, you see. But now they say that any and all who would aspire to the rank of lady must have some touch of the book. But not too much. No hard study. Nothing that might injure the delicate and girlish mind. Novels. Tales. Proverbs, that sort of thing. No papers. No politics."

Now Corrine stood and walked over to the desk. And from the desk drawer she retrieved a large envelope.

"But I have not let them dictate to me, Hiram," she said, holding the envelope. "And I have not simply read, my boy. I have learned their language and custom—even those that should be beyond my station, especially those that should be beyond my station, and that has been the seed of my liberty."

She walked back over and placed the package before me.

"Open it," she said.

This I did and found inside of it the life of a man. There were letters to family. There were authorizations. There were certificates of sale.

"This is yours for one week," she said. "We can't hold on to this man's effects forever. What we have here is a selection, random enough so that its absence should not yet alarm him."

"And what am I to do?" I asked

"Learn him, of course," she said. "This is a lesson in their customs. A way of comprehending all of those things beyond your station. He is a gentleman, of some education and schooling, as are many of the great slave-holders in this country."

I must have looked confused because Corrine now said, "What do you think you've been studying down here?"

I said nothing. She continued on, "What we do is not idle exercise, nor Christian improvement. First you learn what they know, in the general. And then you learn them in the specific—their words and their hand. Own the man's especial knowledge and you shall own the measure of the man. Then you might fashion the costume, Hiram, and make it yours to fit."

I began my study the very next day. Quickly I ascertained that all the documents were drawn up by the same hand. Studying them, a portrait began to emerge. From the artifacts of the author's life—the balance of his ledgers, his communications with his wife, his journal entries upon certain deaths, the accounting of consecutive harvests—the man, in all his traits and foibles, was summoned before me. I saw his daily habits, his routines, his particular philosophy, and by the final hour, having never known him, I could render nearly all of his features.

Corrine met me again, a week later, in the library. I provided her with all I had ascertained, and under her rigorous interrogation, I provided even more. What was his wife's favorite flower? How regular were their departures? Did this man love his father? Had he yet turned gray? Where did he stand in society? And how ancient was his fortune? Was he given to the infliction of random cruelties? I responded to every query—I had, with my gift of memory, inhaled all the facts of the man's life. But Corrine pushed on to questions that went beyond the facts that might be committed to memory to matters of interpretation. Was he a good man? What did he covet in life? Was he the sort to revel in perceived wrongs? The next night she picked up this line of inquiry and pushed me to construct the man down to the last loose thread of his waistcoat. On the following night of interrogation, I found that the more speculative questions came easier, and then by the last night they were so easy that I felt them to be matters of my own life. And that was the point of it all.

"Now," she said. "You have read well enough to know this man to be in possession of a particular property of which he is most fond."

"The jockey, yes," I replied. "Levity Williams."

"The same," she said. "This man will need a day-pass for the road, a letter of introduction for the further portion, and finally free papers signed by his master. You will provide these."

She pulled from her case a tin and handed it to me. Opening it, I saw a fine pen, and by handling it, I knew it was the same weight as the one so often employed by the object of my study.

"Hiram, the costume must fit," she said. "The day-pass must be done with the same hurried disregard, the letters must have all that official flourish, and the freedom papers the same arrogance that is surely the right of these vile people."

There was still the practical fact of copying his signature and penmanship. But here my memory and gift for mimicry triumphed. It was no different than what I'd done all those years ago, when Mr. Fields showed me the image of the bridge. Harder were the man's beliefs and passions, and my ability to convey them with confidence and ease, as though they were my own. I never forgot that lesson. It was essential to what I became, to what I unlocked and saw.

I don't know if those documents ever loosed Levity Williams.

Everything we did was done under so much secrecy. But still, in forging these documents I felt something new arising in me and the new thing was power. The power extended out from my right arm, projected itself through the pen, and shot out through the wilderness, right at the heart of those who condemned us.

Soon this became regular labor. Every few weeks, Corrine presented me with a new package. And each week I fitted myself to the costume, so that when I finished, I was sometimes unsure of where I ended and where the Taskmaster began. I knew them. I knew their children, their wives, their enemies. Their humanity wounded me, for here too were the bonds of family, and here too were young lovers overrun by the rituals of courting, and here too lay a sorrow, a grim understanding of the sin of the Task. And here too were fears that in the last calculation they too were slaves to some Power, some God, some Demon of the old world, which they had unknowingly unleashed upon the new. I nearly loved them. My work demanded no less: I must reach beyond all my particular hatred and pain, see them in their fullness, and then, with my pen, strike out and destroy them.

Every soul sent to freedom was a blow against them. And we did much more than that. We returned the documents edited and augmented. Our forgeries encouraged feuds. We altered inquests. We lent proof of fornication. My anger was now free and ranged beyond Maynard and my father, aimed now at all of Virginia, an anger I sated each night, under the lanterns, at the long library table.

When done, I would retire to my bed, all worn. In sleep I escaped the men I studied every day and instead dreamed of some far place, a small plot, a stream running to carry away all troubles. I dreamt of Sophia. Those were the good days. On the bad days my dreams were hot, and I saw the jail, the boy, his mother raining down the wrath of God upon Ryland's Hounds—"Ryland's Hounds! May black fire scorch you down to your vile and crooked bones." I saw a man who'd loved a woman and lost his name. And

I saw all of my own betrayal, the cackling, the moaning, the rope. On those days I woke up nursing a different feeling, particular and direct, for I awoke thinking of all the things I would do should I ever again cross the path of Georgie Parks.

But I had not been brought to the Underground for vengeance, nor even mere forgery, but for the power I was believed to bear. If we could only learn to trigger it, to control it and harness it. There was one who knew, one like me, but unlike me she had mastery of this power. In her section of the country, she had become so beloved and famed for fantastic exploits that the coloreds of Boston, Philadelphia, and New York had given her the name Moses. The power she wielded had been dubbed "Conduction"—the same word Corrine used to describe my own power—for how it "conducted," seemingly at will, the Tasked from the shackled fields of the South to the free lands of the North. But this Moses kept her own counsel and declined to give the Virginia Underground any notion of how she worked. And so I was left to my own devices, or more properly stated, I was left to their devices.

We decided to experiment. First, we all agreed that to trigger the power, I needed some kind of stimulation, some kind of threat or pain, even. And too it was thought, from my own testimony, that the power was tied to the indelible moments of my life—and in my own mind I remembered that it might be connected specifically to my mother. But how to summon those memories up and make them serve? Corrine and her lieutenants employed all manner of tricks to draw me out. Hawkins shackled me and asked me to recount, in every detail, the betrayal of Georgie Parks. Mr. Fields blindfolded me, then took me out into the forest and asked for every detail of the day I plunged into the Goose. Amy and I met at the stable and I recounted everything I knew of the crime my father had put upon my mother. I drove Corrine in a carriage, one Saturday, and recalled all that I felt while taking Sophia to meet my uncle. But no blue light of Conduction came to me, and when I finished my story, though my hosts might well be riveted and my own heart in tatters from the memories, I was always exactly where I had begun.

The afternoon after the drive, after another aborted attempt at Conduction, Corrine and I walked together up to the main house and into the dining area. Mr. Fields and Hawkins were there drinking coffee. They greeted us both and then departed. Summer was well upon us with its long days, which meant less cover for our rehearsals. I remember the earth waking up that year and the transcendent feeling that I was waking up with it. But still no Conduction.

We sat at the table and continued our conversation until we had exhausted all the small things. And then Corrine said, "Hiram, the truth is that by the lights of any other standard, you have made yourself into a fine agent. This will be a particular boon to us, because you shall be deployed according to our needs, and not your limits. Perhaps this means nothing to you—but it should. Not everyone makes it here, you know."

In fact the compliment did mean something to me. I had lived the whole of my life in service of my father and brother. Every step I took, any accomplishment fulfilled by me, even those made possible by my father, was received as a threat to the rightful order of things. For the first time in my life, I was aligned with the world around me.

But I wondered what became of those who did not make it, those who'd been entrusted with all the secrets of the Virginia Underground but revealed themselves to be liabilities. I knew so much now—too much, I thought, to ever be released back into the world.

"The truth is we expected none of this," she continued. "We knew you were read. We knew of your gift of memory. We knew you had been raised proximate to society. But we had not counted on how easily you would assume the mask. We knew you had been hunted. But we had not known how much guile you'd truly taken up in your time down under."

She paused here, and I knew that we were entering into the darker portion of her conversation. She was looking down, struggling for her words. I thought then of the mastery she once displayed over me, back at Lockless, back in my father's library, and how it had, in this moment especially, fled from her, and it occurred to me then that it really was all an illusion, that this entire order was engineering, was sorcery, all of it held up by elaborate display, by rituals and race-day, by fancies and parades, by powders and face-paint, it was all device, and now stripped of it I saw that we really were just two people, a man and woman, sitting here. I suddenly wanted to alleviate her obvious discomfort, and so I did that which I so often declined. I spoke.

"And that is not enough," I said. "The running, the reading, the writing, it is not why I was brought here. So it is not enough."

"No," said Corrine. "It is not. Hiram, there are enemies in this world that cannot simply be outrun. And there are a whole assortment of our own held deep in the coffin of slavery, too deep for us to reach—Jackson, Montgomery, Columbia, Natchez. But this power—this 'Conduction'—this is the railroad that might turn a week's journey into an instant. Without it, we can menace our enemy. With it, distance is nothing to us and we might strike at him wherever. In short, we need you, Hiram—not just as Hiram the forger of letters and Hiram the running man, but as one who can return these people, our people, to the freedom given to all."

I understood her well. But I was still thinking of those who failed to meet the expectations.

"And what will you do with me should I never again achieve it?" I asked. "Hold me here forever amongst your forgeries? Haul me back down into the hole?"

"Of course not," Corrine said. "You are free."

Free. There was something in how she said this that caught me. It rankled, though I could not then quite say why.

"'Free,' you say. But I will serve. You said it yourself—and serve as you decide and determine. I do what you want. I go where you say."

"You assume too much of me," she said.

"Who else is there?" I asked. "What is this Underground beyond what I have seen here? Who is being moved? I have not seen them. What about my people? What about Sophia? What about Pete? What about Thena? What about my mother?"

"We have rules," she said.

"Rules for what?" I said.

"Rules for who can be gotten out and how," she said.

"Right," I replied. "Then let me see them."

"The rules?" she replied, puzzled.

"No," I said. "Let me see the action. Let me see these people we are bringing out. No. Much better. You say I have exceeded all expectation. Then let me do the thing myself."

"Hiram," she said. And her voice was now low and filled with worry. I think she knew that she could lose me right there. That if she did not prove to me that this was not all some trick, I would be gone, and any hope of Conduction would go with it.

"Very well," she said. "You want me to show you. I will show you."

"No games?" I asked. "This is for real?"

"More real than you think," she said.

· 14 ·

BUT FOR CORRINE to admit me into the deepest sanctums of the Underground, she had to ensure that I would never leave. For this reason, she demanded something of me to bind me for good to the cause. And what she demanded was the destruction of Georgie Parks.

I had dreamt of such a deed, in jail, in the pit, and then here, had long contemplated all that I might vent upon Georgie. But now I saw that faced with the thing, the sword in my hand, all my wrath faded in the face of the full shape of what must necessarily follow.

"You were not the first he betrayed," said Corrine. "And you were not the last. He is back there at Starfall, right now, plying his devious trade." It was late night. I was down in the library with Hawkins and Corrine. I had just finished my studies for the evening. And I knew, hearing them, that I had not yet come to terms with all that Georgie had done. Some part of me still saw him as he had been mythologized—Georgie the tasking man who'd seized his own liberty. To fully accept his betrayal was to accept the fullness of what had been done to us, how thoroughly they had taken us in, so that even our own heroes, our own myths, were but tools to further maintain the Task.

The plan, they explained to me, was to use our gifts of mimicry and fraud to implicate Georgie in a betrayal. Not a betrayal of the Tasked, but of Georgie's own Taskmasters.

"You know what they'll do to him," I said.

"If he lucky, they'll hang him," said Hawkins.

"And if he ain't," I said, "they'll clap him in chains. Break his family. Send him Natchez-way. And work him worse than anything he know. And God forbid the tasking folk find out why he down there."

"Likely they'll tell 'em," said Hawkins.

"We crossing into something here," I said. "Or y'all done already crossed, and asking me to follow."

"I say we just kill him outright," said Hawkins, marching past my concern.

"You know we can't do that," said Corrine.

She was right—but not out of any moral principle. It was too obvious, and if reprisals did not find us, they would certainly find every tasking soul in the region. No, Georgie Parks must be dealt with and it must be his masters who did the deed. We would simply offer mild encouragement.

"These people, I know them well," Corrine said, shaking her head. "Whatever agreement they have with Georgie, I promise you that they trust a freeman less than the slave. And Georgie is a known liar, even in their service, a man who bends under power. Is it so hard to imagine him bending under another power, still?"

"The Underground," I said.

"Or what they believe the Underground to be," Corrine replied. "And what if some notice might be found in a distinguished home marking the breadth of his sins, his efforts to work both sides, his feckless enslavement to this Underground? And what if then a package of effects—forged passes, free papers, the literature of abolition, and missives indicating a northward journey—were to be located in Georgie's home or on his person?"

"We killing him," I said.

"We are," said Hawkins.

"By the rope or by the chain," I said. "We are setting to kill that man."

"That man meant to kill you," Corrine said, her gray eyes filling with a low anger. "He meant to kill you, Hiram. He's killed many before you and if we do nothing he will keep killing. This is a man who takes the last hope of freedom and burns it for fuel. Little girls, old men, whole families, he burns them all. Have you ever been deep into the South? I have. It is hell, worse than the stories say. Endless toil. Endless degradation. No man deserves this, but if any did, it would be the masters themselves first, and men like Georgie Parks second."

The logic of it all was clear. But I felt myself now slipping into something darker, something far beyond the romance I imagined for myself when I set off that night with Sophia. The Task was a trap. Even Georgie was trapped. And so who was Corrine Quinn to judge such a man? Who was I, who'd run with no higher purpose save my own passions and my own skin? Now I understood the Underground war. It was not the ancient and honorable kind. No armies amassed at the edges of the field. For every one agent, there were a hundred Quality, and for every Quality, there were a thousand low whites sworn to them. The gazelle does not match claws with the lion—he runs. But we did more than run. We plotted. We instigated. We sabotaged. We poisoned. We destroyed.

"It's on us," said Hawkins. "Do you get that it's on us? He is out there breaking families, sending folk to the jails, to the auction, and he is doing it in our name."

"We did not ask for this, Hiram," said Corrine. "You are right, it is not our normal work. But what would you have us do? What is the option we have not yet conceived?"

There was none.

Now Corrine produced another file, and put it before me on the table, and I knew what was within—the usual assortment of stolen documents that might help put me in the mind of the Quality. Then Corrine looked at me and the look was not of pity or sorrow, it was fire.

A month later I walked out of my quarters in my flannels to begin the evening routine. It was full summer now. The nights had shortened and the days had begun their July sprawl. On the path from my quarters, I saw Hawkins approaching with Mr. Fields, both in their day clothes. Hawkins made small talk while Mr. Fields's eyes darted to and fro. I felt that something was coming. Hawkins looked me up and down and said, "No work tonight. Tomorrow neither. Get some rest."

I looked at him a little longer to see if I correctly caught his meaning.

"We got one," he said.

But I did not rest—neither that evening, that night, nor the next morning. I had only the vaguest notions of the Underground's methods in the field, and my mind ran circuits trying to imagine. They met me outside the following evening. I wore a pair of comfortable trousers, a shirt, hat, and the same pair of brogans I had thought to run in. I tried my best to conceal my excitement, but then I met eyes with Hawkins and he laughed.

"What?" I asked.

"Nothing," said Hawkins. "It's just you can't go back. You can't get out. You know that, right?"

"Long past the getting-out point," I said.

"Indeed," said Hawkins. "But it is a load we putting on you. And I'm feeling all that you about to feel, right now, looking at you. And I'm remembering myself when they first brought me into all this. You about to see."

"He can't know," Mr. Fields said. "And besides, what else is there now?"

We walked up from the quarters toward the main house of Bryceton and convened in one of the side-buildings.

There was a table with three cups and a jar, and from the jar Hawkins poured three servings of hard cider. He took a sip, sucked in a stream of air, then said, "In a sense it's an easy one. About a day's journey south of here. And then a day's journey back. Just one man."

"And in another sense?" I asked.

"It's one man, a real man," he said. "This ain't hopping or running or some spell down in the library. This is real patrol, real hounds out there who'd like nothing better than to carry you off."

Hawkins ran his hands through his hair and shook his head. I had the sense that he was more scared for me than I was for myself.

"All right, listen," he said. "Man's name is Parnel Johns. He done did something to get him in bad with the local tasking folks. Had a grift he was running. Stealing from his master and selling it to some of the low whites. His master knew something was off but could not figure on what."

"So he took it out on all of 'em," I said.

"Surely did," said Mr. Fields. "And he did so with interest, working the whole plantation double-time to get it back, beatings if they come up short."

"Johns kept stealing?" I asked.

"No, he stopped," said Mr. Fields. "But it didn't matter. His master just went ahead and now this is the new theory of the home-place."

"Master take it out on the tasking folks . . . ," said Hawkins.

". . . And the tasking folks take it out on Johns," I said.

"With time and a half. He got no people now. His country ain't his country," said Hawkins. "And he want out."

"Sound like a piece of work to me," I said, shaking my head. "Surely there are tasking folks more deserving of justice."

"Course they are," said Hawkins. "But we ain't bringing justice to Johns. We bringing it to his master."

"What?" I said.

"You see, Johns, whatever his cowardly ways, is a hell of a field-hand," said Hawkins. "And he's more than that. He's something of a genius—plays the violin. Even works the wood like you."

"What's that got to do with freedom?" I asked.

"Nothing," said Hawkins. "It ain't about freedom. It's about war."

I paused and looked them both over.

"No, don't start that," said Hawkins. "Don't start thinking again. Remember where that got you last time. There's a bigger thing here. A higher plan."

"And what's that?" I asked.

"Hiram," Mr. Fields said, "it's for your own good. For all of our good. You don't want to know it all. Just trust us on that."

He paused for a moment to see if I could catch on and then he said, "It is hard to trust, I understand. Believe me, I do. All you have been met with since our first meeting are deceptions. I am sorry for that. It is not always an honorable life. And so perhaps it would help if you were given some bit of truth, even if it does not pertain to our journey this night. I want you to know my real name, Hiram. It is not Isaiah Fields. It is Micajah Bland. 'Mr. Fields' is a name I've assumed for my work here in Virginia. I would appreciate you using it for as long as we are down here, but it is not the name to which I was born.

"So I have trusted you now, with something most precious, something that could get me killed. Will you now trust us?"

And so our journey began—Hawkins, myself, and Micajah Bland. We did not run. For all the training, we merely walked. But we took a brisk pace, avoiding main roads, and going through the pathless backwoods and over hills, until the woodlands flattened and I knew from this, and our respective orientation to the stars, that we must be headed east. The land was dry, the night warm. I knew by then that this was the worst season to conduct, simply because of the brevity of the sunless hours when we could travel. Winter was the field agent's high season. In summer, with fewer hours, precision of arrival and departure was everything. We walked for six hours or so roughly to the south-east.

Johns was just where he was supposed to be—at the crossing of two paths in the forest, distinguished by a wood-pile on the right end. Standing in the woods, we saw him pacing in his nervousness. It was my first mission and I was entrusted with making the contact. We worked in teams. But only one man made contact at first. By this method, should we be betrayed, only one of us would fall.

I stepped out from beyond the trees and approached. Johns stopped pacing. He had come just as he'd been told to. No bundles. No extra effects. Only the forged papers in his hand, in case of Ryland. Surveying him, I confess myself mixed. There had always been men like him, those who, for their own amusement, menaced an entire tasking team. In the days of my grandmother, Santi Bess, they had ways of dealing with such men. An accidental fall in the woods. A spooked horse. A pinch of pokeweed. And now I must work to free such a scoundrel, while good men, women, and children lay buried under.

I looked at him hard and said, "Ain't no moon over the lake to-night."

He said, "That's 'cause the lake had its fill with the sun."

"Come on," I said. He paused for a second, looked to the woods and motioned. And then out came a girl, perhaps about seventeen, in field overalls with her hair tied under a cloth. And this is why such men as Parnel Johns were fed to the pokeweed. Every act of normal sympathy was, to them, an invitation to leverage. Give them a calf and they demand the herd. I thought for a moment of leaving them right there. But this was a matter for those more senior than I. So I said nothing and led them back into the forest to the small area where Hawkins and Bland were waiting.

"Who the hell is she?" said Hawkins.

"She with me," said Johns.

"Hell are you saying?" said Hawkins. "We had arrangements for one cargo, now you trying to dump more?"

"It's my daughter, Lucy," he said.

"Don't care if it's your momma," said Hawkins. "You know the plan. What the hell are you doing?"

"I ain't leaving without her," said Johns.

"It's all right," said Bland. "It's all right." Hawkins and Bland were friends. I knew this because Hawkins could make Bland laugh, not just giggle but uproariously laugh, and Micajah Bland did not much laugh.

Hawkins shook his head, frustrated. Then he looked at Johns and said, "If we get even a sniff of Ryland, I am dropping you both. You got it? We know the way North. You don't. If I get a hint of anything strange, we will drop you here and leave you for the hounds."

But there wasn't anything strange—or at least not in the way Hawkins suspected. We kept a good pace for the rest of the night and had made some good distance by daybreak. Hawkins and Bland had scouted the land well. They found a cave for a midpoint rest and we arrived there just as the sun came up over the hills. We took turns sleeping and keeping guard over our cargo. Contrary to what Hawkins said, we could not leave them. We could not risk any word getting out about our methods. If they became too much of a load, I feared what might be done.

We took three-hour shifts. I took the last one—late in the afternoon until nightfall. Everybody was asleep except for me and Lucy, who was having trouble adjusting to the time of things. I watched Lucy step out of the cave and into the open air. I did not stop her but followed just behind. She was not Johns's daughter, that I could tell. They shared not a single feature. He was high yellow and she was dark as Africa itself. But more than that, it was in the way they walked, held hands, and whispered to each other.

"I don't know why he lied," she said.

"Nervous," I said. We were just outside the cave. I was seated on a stump behind her. She was watching the sun as it began to bed down in the west.

"He didn't want to do it," Lucy said. "Don't blame him. It was all me. You know he got a family, right? A real family—woman at the other place, two daughters."

I don't know what it is about me that made people want to unburden themselves. But I knew from her mention of Parnel Johns's family where we were going. And so we went.

"Master Heath, who own us, used to have this young wife," she said. "She was cruel as all hell. I know, I was her serving girl. She was the type to take the whip to you 'cause it rained too hard or the milk was too warm. She was as pretty as she was mean, and all the men in town knew. Master Heath held her tight for fear of losing her. He was the jealous kind. Well, one day that young wife took to religion. Wasn't sincere for what I could tell, but it was a way to see some of the world.

"She got friendly with this old pastor, who'd come around every day and minister the good word. And it got real clear to me—though not to Master Heath—that he was ministering more than that."

Here Lucy laughed at her own insinuation and then turned to me to see if I had caught on, and though I had, there was no real register in me and this somehow made her laugh even more. And then she said, "You know they left one day? Just up and ran out. Picked up and, I'm guessing, started all anew. I hated that girl, and in some just other life, I do declare, I will be holding the whip and she'll be underneath. But I could still see the beauty in it, you know?

"We talked about it," she said. "Dreamt about it—dreamt about it all the time. It was powerful, I tell you. But we knew it could never be us. We was tasking folk."

Now she turned back away, and I heard her crying a bit.

"And then it happened," she said. "Listen, I look young, but I ain't so young. I been left by a man before. I know what it look like. I know that face. And he came to me with that face, and before he said a word he broke down and cried, because he knew that I knew he was gone. Don't blame him. He wouldn't say where. He wouldn't even say how. Just that come the next morning he'd be gone and he'd being going without me.

"They say Parnel's a scoundrel, well, so am I. And he is my scoundrel. His crime is he don't want to live just—and how can a man, when the whole house is wrong? They blame him for what Master Heath do to them. But I blame Master Heath.

"I followed him last night. Caught him out in the trail, some time fore he got to you. And I told him, he either take me or I was gonna go back and tell em he was running. I never would have done it. Ain't built that way but . . . I tell you this to say, it was me. He was too weak to leave me."

"Don't make it right," I said.

"The hell I care about right?" she said. "Hell I care about you or your men? You know what they did to us back there. You done forgot? You don't remember what they do to the girls down here? And once they do it, they got you. They catch you with the babies, tie you to the place by your own blood and all, until you got too much to let go of to go. Well, I got as much right to run as Parnel. Much right as you or anyone."

Lucy was no longer crying now. Unburdened, she walked back to the cave, where the rest were beginning to rise. Hawkins gave me a wary look. I saw him but paid no heed. I focused on Lucy, who had by then walked over to a smiling Parnel Johns and laughingly embraced him.

We made good time that night. By midnight the moon was high, and I could see the mountains in the distance. And I knew then that we were near Bryceton. We kept going right past it. An hour or two later we found ourselves at a small cabin. Smoke rose from the chimney and fire-light flickered in the window.

Hawkins whistled. He waited, then he whistled again. Waited. Then whistled one last time. The fire went out inside. We waited a few minutes longer. Then we followed Hawkins around to the back. A door opened and out came an old white woman. She walked over to us and said, "The two-fifty been late all week."

Hawkins said, "No. I believe the schedule changed."

At that the woman said, "You said it was only one of them."

"Sure did," said Hawkins. "Not my notion. You do with 'em what you will."

She studied the group for a second and said, "All right, y'all get in here quick."

We walked inside and we helped this old woman start up the fire again. Hawkins stepped outside with her. They talked for a few minutes and then returned. Hawkins said, "I reckon it's time for us to make our way home."

Micajah Bland turned to Parnel Johns. I could see the tenderness of his face against the fire-light. "Don't worry," he said. "You'll be fine."

Johns nodded. And then as we walked out he said, "When we safe, can I send word to my daddy?"

Hawkins laughed to himself and turned back. "You most certainly can," he said. "But if the Underground find out, it'll be the last word you ever speak."

With this now done, and with my actions against Georgie Parks, it was felt by Corrine and by others that it was time for me to see more of the Underground's work, to journey out of the country of slavery and into the North. Philadelphia would be my new home.

I was given a few days' notice, and was lucky to have even that. The Underground would give me no chance to reconsider, for though we all dreamed of going north, all sorts of fears might overrun a man when the dream descended into the real. There is always a part of us that does not want to win, wants to stay down in the low and familiar. And so there was no time to think and submit to the cowardly parts of me. I spent my last days in counsel and reflection. I talked with Micajah Bland about what to expect. I walked the woods and thought of all that I once took for normal, but would soon be without.

Those of us working in some new terrain had to take up a new identity and be furnished with papers. The house agent never made his own. They were furnished by other house agents from other stations, for it was thought that no man could author his own life. They began with the root of my occupation—woodworking at a local company that was a cover for the Underground's operations. I was to be a man who'd purchased his freedom, and fled in the wake of certain recent laws that choked the rights of the free coloreds in the South. I was given two sets of working clothes and another set for church. My name stayed the same with one addition—the surname Walker.

There was still the matter of how, precisely, to get there. Ryland's Hounds trawled the roads, harbors, and railways. We were aided by the fact that there would be no runaway report for me, and thus no Ryland searching for a man of my description. We decided on the train. I would be joined by Hawkins and Micajah Bland. Our plan was simple. I was a freeman. Hawkins, a slave belonging to this Bland, a white man, his proprietor. Should I, at any point, find my papers under challenge, Bland would offer testimony as to the identity.

"Act like a freeman," Hawkins advised. "Lift your head. Look them in the eye—though not for too long. You are still colored. Bow before the ladies. Be sure to bring some of them books of which you are so fond. Remember, own the acre, or they will see right through you."

On our day out, I held these notions, and when my nerves came upon me, as when procuring my ticket, as when handing my trunk to the boy for stowing, as when the train pulled off and the South, and everything I had known, fell away, I simply told myself this thing that must become my truth. *I am free.*

I DEPARTED WITH FEW EFFECTS to my name and no real farewells. I saw neither Corrine nor Amy that last evening, and assumed them both involved in some mischief of their own. I left on a hot summer Monday morning, four months after my arrival at Bryceton. We walked most of that day, Hawkins, Bland, and I, and spent that night in a small farmhouse of an old widower sympathetic to our cause. Then, that Tuesday, we set out separately for the town of Clarksburg, where the first leg of our journey would commence. The plan was to cross through the state, by the Northwestern Virginia Railroad, and then in western Maryland we'd link up with the Baltimore and Ohio, proceed east and then north up into the free-lands of Pennsylvania, and find our destination in Philadelphia. There was a shorter route due north, but there had been some recent troubles along the rail there with Ryland's Hounds, and it was felt that the audacity of this direct approach right through the slave-port of Baltimore would not be expected.

When I reached the Clarksburg station, I spotted Hawkins and Bland sitting beneath a red awning. Hawkins was fanning himself with his hat. Bland was looking down the track, in the opposite direction from where the train would approach. A flock of black-birds sat on the awning. On the platform I saw a white woman in bonnet and blue hoop dress holding the hands of two well-dressed toddlers. Some distance away, outside the shade of the awning, a low white with what I guessed to be all his possessions in a carpet-bag smoked a tobacco. I stood off to the side, not wanting to in-spire suspicion with any presumption of cooling shade. The low white finished his tobacco and then greeted the woman. They were still talking when the blackbirds flew from the awning, and the great iron cat roared around the bend, all black smoke and ear-splitting clanking. I watched as the wheels turned slower and slower and came to a screeching stop. I had never seen anything like it outside of a book. I presented my ticket and papers to the conductor gingerly. He barely looked at them. It may be hard to believe now, in these dark days, but there was no "nigger car." Why would there be one? The Quality kept their Tasked ones close the way a lady keeps her clutch, closer even, for this was a time in our history when the most valuable thing a man could own, in all of America, was another man. I headed to the back, walking in the aisle between the two rows of seating. The train idled for a few minutes. I tried not to look nervous. But when I heard the conductor yell, and the great cat roared again, I felt every inch of me loosen and relax.

The entire journey took two days, so that I arrived at Gray's Ferry Station, overlooking the Schuylkill River, on Thursday morning. I stepped off into a crowd of people searching for friends and family. I saw Hawkins and Bland as soon as I was off the train, but they gave me a wide berth, for it was known that even here in the city, Ryland prowled searching for runaways. I had been given no description of my escort. I was told to merely wait. There was an omnibus across the street, hitched to a team of horses. Several of the train passengers stepped on board.

"Mr. Walker?"

I turned and saw a colored man in gentleman's clothes before me.

"Yes," I said.

"Raymond White," he said, extending his hand. He did not smile.

"This way," he said and we walked over to the omnibus and boarded. The driver cracked a carriage whip and we pulled away, in the direction opposite of the river. We did not talk much during the ride, and this was to be expected given the business that had brought us together. Nevertheless, I was able to take the measure of this Raymond White. His dress was impeccable. He wore a perfectly cut gray suit that angled down from his shoulders to his cinched waist. His hair was neat and parted. His face seemed a stone with features cut into it, and for the whole of that ride no expression of pain, annoyance, joy, humor, nor concern moved those features. Yet I thought that I saw a sadness in his eyes that— despite all Raymond's forbearing elegance—told a story, and I knew, if not how, that his life was somehow tied to the Task. And from that sadness I drew that his high manner, his nobility, was no simple matter of birth but of labor and struggle.

The omnibus cut away from the river and into the heart of the city. There were people everywhere on the streets. I could see them out the windows, so many people, so that it seemed to me as though race-day had gathered a hundred-fold, as though the whole of the world had gathered there, gathered to heave between the workshops and fur dealerships and druggists, to walk the stone-chipped streets, to inhale the acrid air. Every rank of person in every configuration—parent and child, rich and poor, black and white. And I saw that the rich were mostly white and the poor mostly black, but there were also members of both tribes in both classes. It was a shock to see it directly, for if whites held the power here, and they did, they did not seem to hold it exclusively. And I tell you, I had never seen more miserable specimens of the white race, and never more luxurious specimens of the colored race, than I saw that day. The coloreds here were not merely surviving, as they did in Starfall, they were sometimes dressed in garments more elegant than anything I'd seen on my father. And they were out there in the churning city, in their hats and gloves, and their ladies under their parasols, moving like royalty.

This astonishing portrait was set against the most offensive odors known to man. I did not smell the air here in this city so much as feel it. It seemed to be born in the gutters, then rose up to mingle with the dead horses in the street, and finally joined the fumes of manufacture and production, until the odor—an orchard left to rot—was an invisible fog that hung over the whole city. I was used to all the malicious odors of livestock, but alongside the gardens, the strawberry bushes, the woods. But the smell of Philadelphia offered no such balance; it hung everywhere, over every street, in the workshops and taverns, and, I would discover, if care was not taken it drifted into homes and bedchambers.

We got off the omnibus after twenty minutes or so and entered into a brick row house on the corner, where we found Bland and Hawkins already installed. They were just past the foyer, in a small parlor drinking coffee with another well-dressed black man. Seeing us, the whole party smiled and looked up. The man whom I did not know stood, strode over, and gave a big handshake and bigger smile. I could tell from his features that he was kin to Raymond White. He had the same stone-face, but not the stoicism.

"Otha White," he said, introducing himself. "No trouble on the rail, right?"

"Not that I can tell," I said.

"Here, have a seat," said Otha. "I'll bring y'all some coffee."

I sat while Raymond and Bland made small talk. Otha returned with coffee and then the conference began.

"Take care of this man, you hear?" Hawkins said, drinking his coffee. "He is the genuine article. This is not idle talk. Seen him buried under a river and dig himself out. He done suffered everything we could throw at him, and he still standing. Should tell you something."

This was the kindest thing Hawkins had ever said to me.

"You know my commitments," Raymond said. "My whole life is given to this. And we gladly welcome his aid in our business."

"We could really use you," said Otha. "I don't know you, Hiram Walker, but I wasn't raised here either. But I learned and I think you will too."

Hawkins nodded, took a drink from his coffee. Hawkins seemed more at ease with Otha, born in slavery, than Raymond, a creature of the North. I think now, through the lens of years, that it was a matter of how we worked. In Virginia, we were outlaws, a matter that soon became our honor, so that we reveled in being beyond the morals of a world we believed to be premised in Demon law. We were not Christians. Christians plied their trade in the North, where the Underground was so strong as to not be an underground at all. I can recall now many nights, sitting in some Philadelphia tavern, listening to men, conducted only days earlier, boasting of the details of their flight. Whole city blocks teemed with fugitives, and these fugitives populated congregations, where they were organized into vigilance committees who guarded each other and watched for Ryland. In the North, the agents of the Underground were not outlaws, indeed they were very nearly a law unto themselves. They stormed jails, attacked federal Marshals, and shot it out with Ryland's Hounds. Men like Hawkins plied their trade in the shadows. Men like Raymond shouted in the town square.

But for Otha, it was different. There was something about him, something about his implied roots and rough manner, that compelled deference from Hawkins, however deeply buried and unacknowledged, for Hawkins was a man given to saving souls, not peering into them, least of all his own. I know enough of what

Bryceton was before Corrine's transformation, of its atrocities, to know that "soul-peering" was a luxury.

"All right," Hawkins said, now rising. "The boy don't know nothing. I am relying on you to fill him in. We have done our part. May he serve the cause here as well as he done served it down there."

I rose and Hawkins turned to me, shook my hand, and said, "Doubtful we'll be seeing each other again anytime soon, if at all. All I can say is be good."

I nodded. Hawkins shook hands with the others, Bland included, who it was decided should remain in Philadelphia a few weeks for business of his own. After Hawkins left, Otha took me upstairs to my quarters while Raymond and Bland remained below to talk. It was a small room, but after months of living in common, and before that living in the hole, and before that the jail, it was heaven. After Otha left, I lay across the bed. I could hear the muffled intercourse of Bland and Raymond floating up from below, and the sounds of what seemed to me boisterous laughter. Later, I took my supper with Otha at a local tavern. He explained that I would have a long weekend to orient myself in the city. Planning the next day to explore, I came straight home and slept. Otha slept here too, in a bedroom next to mine. Raymond stayed outside the city with his wife and children.

I rose early the next morning to see Philadelphia. I walked out onto Bainbridge Street, one of the city's great thoroughfares, just adjacent to our office on Ninth Street, and watched the variety of human life, a menagerie of wants, needs, and intentions, teeming in the streets, and it was only 7 A.M. On the other side of the street, I saw a bakery, and through the window I could see a colored man at work. I walked in and was greeted with a sweet smell, the perfect antidote to the fog of the city. On the counter there was a pleasing array of treats—cakes, fritters, and dumplings of all kinds—laid out on parchment. Behind the counter, more still, stacked on trays suspended in slotted shelves.

"New around here, are you?"

I looked up and saw the colored man smiling at me. He was perhaps ten years my senior and regarded me with a look of pure kindness. I must have recoiled at his question, because he said, "Don't mean to snoop. In fact not snooping at all. I can see it in all the new ones. Just dazzled by the smallest things. It's okay, son. Nothing wrong with being new. Nothing wrong with being dazzled."

I said nothing.

"Name's Mars," the man said. "This is my place. Me and my Hannah. You from over near Ninth Street, right? Staying with Otha over there? Raymond and Otha—they both my cousin— blood to my dear Hannah—and you with them, so that make you family to me."

Still I said nothing. How rude I was back then. How wide my suspicions sprawled.

"How about this," he said. And then, reaching behind him, Mars ripped off a piece of parchment from a roll and went into the back. He returned with something wrapped in the paper. And when he handed the package over to me, it was warm to the touch.

"Go on," he said. "Try it."

I opened the paper and the scent of ginger wafted out. The smell evoked a feeling, all at once, sad and sweet, because the feeling was attached to a lost memory that I felt lurking somewhere down a winding foggy path in my mind.

"What I owe you?" I asked.

"Owe me?" Mars said. "We family. What I tell you? We all family up here."

I nodded, managed a thanks, and then backed out of the bakery. I stood on Bainbridge for a moment watching the city, the gingerbread wrapped in paper still warm in my hand. I wished I had smiled before I left. I wished I had said something to reward his kindness. But I was fresh out of Virginia, fresh out of the pit, Georgie Parks still on my mind, Sophia still lost to me. I walked across Bainbridge, west, across streets that counted up, pondering the absurd size of a town with so many streets they'd apparently run out of names. I walked on until I was at the docks, where I saw a mix of colored men and whites unloading and working on ships.

I followed the river as it bent inward then curved back out. Its banks were crowded with workshops, small factories, and dry docks. The oppressive scent of the city eased some against the cool river breeze. Now I came upon a promenade. There was a large green field dissected by walkways, themselves lined with benches. I took a seat. It was about nine in the morning now. Friday, the end of the working week. The day was clear and blue. The promenade was filled with Philadelphians of all color and kind. Gentlemen in their boaters escorted ladies. A circle of schoolchildren sat in the grass hanging on the words of their tutor. A man rode past on a unicycle, laughing. It occurred to me just then that this was the freest I had ever been in my life. And I knew that I could leave right then, right there, that I could abandon the Underground and disappear into this city, into this massive race-day, float away on the poisonous air.

I opened the paper. I brought the gingerbread to my mouth, and as I ate, something inside me cracked open, unbidden. The path I'd seen back at Mars's bakery, the one called up by that scent of ginger, now appeared before me again and this time there was no fog, and really there was no path, just a place. A kitchen, which I instantly recognized as belonging to Lockless. And I was no longer on the bench, or even near the promenade. I was standing in that kitchen, and I saw on the counter cookies, pastries, and all manner of sweet things, on trays lined with parchment paper, just as they had been back at Mars's bakery. And there was another counter adjacent to that one, and I saw behind it a colored woman, singing softly to herself, kneading dough, and when she saw me she smiled and said, "Why you always so quiet, Hi?"

Then she went back to kneading and singing to herself. Some time passed before she looked up at me again and laughed. "I see you there eying Master Howell's ginger snaps," she said. "You might be quiet but you fixing to get me in a whole mess of trouble."

She shook her head and laughed to herself. But a few moments later, I saw a look of caution on her face as she brought an extended index finger to her closed lips. She walked over to the door and peeked out, then walked back over to the other counter, filled with treats, and pried two ginger snaps loose from the paper.

"Family got to watch for each other," she said, offering these to me. "And furthermost, as I see it, all of this belong to you anyway."

I took the two cookies from her hands. I must have known what was happening. I must have realized, amidst it all, that wherever I then was, it was not the Lockless of now, was perhaps not even the Lockless of then. It was as though I were in a dream. And this woman before me, I could not name her, though I felt a pang of recognition, and a pang of something more—of loss. And so strong was this feeling that I ran to her, the ginger snaps still in my left hand, and hugged her, long and hard. And when I stepped away, she was smiling big as day, big as the baker Mars had smiled at me only that morning.

"Don't forget," she said. "Family."

And then I saw the fog return, float into the kitchen from all around, until the counter disappeared before me, and the trays disappeared before me, and the woman disappeared before me, and she said to me as she faded from my sight, "Now get on."

And then I was back, seated on a bench. I felt tired. I looked at my hands, which were now empty. I looked up and out past the promenade to the river. The man on the unicycle rode past again.

He waved. I looked to the benches to my left and then my right. The line of benches continued on both sides with little difference, save this—three seats down I saw a piece of half-eaten gingerbread on the bench, and in the grass the parchment in which it had been wrapped, blowing gently in the summer breeze.

· 16 ·

Now I knew. That was Conduction. The power was still with me, even if I did not quite understand how to call it forth. I dragged myself, exhausted, back to our building and fell asleep as soon as I returned to my room, with the sun still out, and did not wake again until early the next morning. I thought to try to access the power again, but the fatigue and malady that I now saw accompanied every Conduction dissuaded me. Instead, I decided to visit Mars's bakery again and apologize for my rude manner. Then, perhaps, walk through the city more, to test the freedom, perhaps east this time toward the Delaware River, maybe even across it and into the small hamlet of Camden, where Raymond and his family lived. But just as I pulled on my brogans, I heard a knock at my bedroom door and then Otha's voice.

"Hiram, you there?"

I opened my door and saw Otha already descending the staircase. He looked back up at me, still bounding down, and said, "Gotta go."

I followed him down the steps and into the parlor, where we

found Raymond pacing with a letter in hand. When he saw us, he walked to the door, grabbed his hat, and, without a word, dashed out. We followed him out onto Ninth Street and then to Bainbridge, which was already by then flush with the flow and miasma of Philadelphia.

"The law of our state is quite clear," he said when we caught up to him. "No man or woman can be held under bondage—even if brought here under bondage. Haven, once requested, must be granted. But it must be requested. We cannot induce them to freedom. They cannot be wooed."

"But the masters," said Otha, looking at me. "They keep the law hidden. They tell their people lies, frighten 'em. Threaten their families and friends."

"But when we have someone who clearly states their intentions," said Raymond, "then we are empowered to make sure those intentions are respected. And this Bronson woman has made such a request—one that her captor dishonors. Forgive my rush, but time is short. If we are to make this man honor the law, it must be done right now."

We were headed east now, along the same path I had thought to take earlier that morning. Before long we were at the docks, and I could see the Delaware lapping gently against the ships. It was now Saturday. Hot yet again, hotter in this city than anything I had ever known in Virginia. Shade had no meaning here. The heat followed you as sure as the odor, and the only relief I was coming to find was here at the shores of the city. We walked a few piers to the south until we stood before the gang-plank of a riverboat. We boarded quickly. Raymond surveyed the passengers but did not see anyone matching this Bronson woman he spoke of. Then a colored man said, "They down below, Mr. White."

We walked to the back of the boat and found a set of stairs leading down, and there in the belly we saw another group of passengers. I recognized the "Bronson woman" before Raymond did. I needed no description. I had, in just my two days, seen my share of tasking folks. They were dressed as well as the free coloreds here, perhaps even better dressed, as though their captors sought to conceal the chain that extended between them. But if you watched long enough, you could see in their manner, in the particular way they attended, that some other power held them. And this Bronson woman was well-dressed, costumed even, the way Sophia would be costumed for Nathaniel, and I saw her arm was held tight by a tall thin white man, and that with her other hand she held tighter still to a boy no older than six. I watched her eyes spot Raymond, who was still searching, and then her eyes found mine, and then she looked away, turning her gaze to her son.

By then Raymond had caught on. He walked over and said, "Mary Bronson, I understand you have made a request. We are here to see this request done, in accordance with the law of our state, which shows neither respect"—and now Raymond fixed his eyes on the tall thin man—"nor regard for the customs of bondage."

I was out of Virginia, cut from a world where our work was furtive, where I was a criminal who must respect the very customs I was working to destroy. But here I was in Philadelphia, watching an agent of the Underground operate in the wide open, with no choreography, no costume. Raymond's words went off like a bomb. And the white man who held Mary Bronson felt it.

"Damn you," said the white man, yanking at Mary Bronson's hand, so that she stumbled off-balance a bit. "I mean to return with my property to my home country."

Raymond ignored him.

"You are under no order to obey," he said to Mary. "He will not detain you while I stand, and should you come with me, I assure you the law of this state will reinforce my efforts."

"Damn you, I have her!" said the man. This he said with great force. But I saw he no longer held Mary's arm. I did not know if she had slipped it free or if he, with his wrath focused on Raymond, had simply forgotten. By now a small crowd had gathered near us, some to reinforce, some to see the source of the commotion. They informed each other of the details of the story. They grumbled and motioned toward the man, who did not seem to perceive what little power he had withering around him. But Mary perceived it all. The crowd buoyed her. She took the hand of her child, and walked toward Raymond. The man fumed, called for Mary to return, but she ignored him, positioning herself behind Raymond, and the child behind her.

"Boy," the man said, his eyes raging at Raymond. "If I were home I'd have you in your proper place, and break you good." At this the grumbles grew into taunts, shouts, and threats.

There is a moment in the stormy lives of a few blessed colored people, a moment of revelation, when the sky opens up, the clouds part, and a streak of sun cuts through, conveying some infinite wisdom from above, and this moment comes not from Christian religion, but from the sight of a colored man addressing a white one as Raymond White now did as he turned to the white man.

"But you are not home."

Then he looked back at the crowd, and the man following with his eyes began to understand his predicament. Rage and determination fled from him. Fear and panic closed in. The thin white man seemed to grow paler and thinner by the second. The crowd, agitated by the man's threats, now murmured to each other as to what they ought to do next.

After we watched the boat shove off, Otha and I sat with Mary Bronson and her son back at the Ninth Street house. Raymond had gone off to begin the business of having Mary housed and, hopefully soon, employed. It was the custom in Philadelphia to take an account of the ordeal of all who passed through the Philadelphia station. It was yet another notion that was utterly unimaginable in Virginia, where such accounts might implicate a fugitive.

But Raymond believed himself in the midst of history and felt strongly that all pertaining events should be well recorded.

Otha made coffee and gave Mary's son a collection of toys—cows, horses, and other farm animals rendered from wood. I took the moment to walk over to Mars's bakery, where he introduced me to his wife, Hannah. I managed a smile upon meeting her and did my best to apologize for my demeanor the day before. He handed me two loaves of warm bread and said, "Nothing to apologize for. Like I said, family."

Back in the house, Mary was on the floor of the parlor playing with her son. I went to the kitchen with the bread, searched for a knife, a platter, and plates. There was a jar of preserves on the counter along with a wedge of cheese. With all of this I fashioned a spread and placed it upon the dining room table. Otha served up the coffee for everyone and brought Mary and her son to the table. There was a gentle air of relief and even celebration in the meal.

After the meal, Mary helped us clean up. Then we repaired to the living room for the interview. I watched as Mary's son took a wooden soldier in each hand, made a threatening face, and then crashed the two horses into each other with a loud "Pssshhh!"

"What is his name?" I asked.

"Octavius," she said. "Don't ask me why, I ain't name him. Ol massa decided that like he decided everything else."

Otha offered Mary a seat on the sofa. I went up to my room and retrieved paper and two pencils. Then I sat down at the table. Otha was to ask the questions. I would record.

"My name is Mary Bronson," she told Otha. "And I was born a slave."

"No more, though," Otha said.

"No more," Mary repeated. "And I want to thank y'all for that. You got no idea what I been through down there, what we all been through. I'd have done anything to get out from under that man, I just wasn't sure how. You know this ain't even the first time I been to the city, and it ain't even the first time I had the notion to run. I don't know why I ain't done it before."

"Where you from, Mary?" Otha asked.

"Hell," she said. "I am straight out of hell, Mr. Otha."

"And why you say that?" Otha asked.

"I had two other boys, beside Octavius here, two other boys and a husband. He was a cook just like me. Everybody around the house loved the work I did."

"Did you love your own work?"

"Was never my work to love. But I was different, you see. Fact of it is, I had an understanding with my old master. I did the cooking, but I wasn't the only one in the kitchen. So time to time, my old master would hire me out and split whatever I made with me. Plan was to gather up enough to buy me and mine out. I would go first, so as not to have to split nothing no longer, and then I'd get my man, Fred, that was my husband's name, I'd get him so as to have another hand to work. And then we'd, all together, get the young'uns."

"And what happened?"

"Old master died. Place was carved up and one of them low whites—man you just seen—took over. Then I ain't like my work so much. He took all the money for himself, said he had no notion for any agreement with my old master, nor any banking. So I got crafty. Started working slow and sloppy. But he caught on."

Mary Bronson paused here. She drew herself in, composed herself to continue.

"That's when the beating start. He set a figure for every week. Said if I ain't make that figure he'd take it out on my hide. He threatened to sell my husband, my sons—all my boys. I worked hard as I could, Mr. Otha. He sold them anyway. He spared me my youngest"—she nodded to the little boy, still on the floor playing with the wooden animals—"but that wasn't no sympathy or concern. It was weight. He held that boy over me, so I always had something else to lose."

"Why'd he bring you to the city?" Otha asked.

"He got family up here," she said. "He was bragging to them about my work. Had me working for his sister. In his sister kitchen."

"Up here?"

"Yes, he did. But I done showed him, have I not?"

"Surely, you have."

"Chain is a powerful thing, Mr. Otha, a powerful, powerful thing. I was thinking bout all the times I come north and ain't run. And I was thinking about the grip they got on me. And I knew that boy would be off to the fields in a year or so, and I knew that then they'd have him too."

She sobbed softly into her hands. Otha went over and sat next to Mary Bronson. Then he drew her close, held her, gently patting her back. As he held her, Mary Bronson wailed and I heard in the wailing a song for her husband, her boys, and all her lost.

I had never seen an agent do what Otha was now doing—comforting her, treating her with the dignity of a free woman, not an escaped slave. He rocked her in his arms until she was settled and then he stood and said, "We shall have a place for you and your boy in the next few days. Raymond gone to get all that started. You and your son welcome to stay here until it's all arranged."

Mary Bronson nodded.

"It's a good city, ma'am," said Otha. "And we are strong here. But I understand if you don't want to stay. Either way, we gon help how we can. As you will soon see, finding freedom is only the first part. Living free is a whole other."

There was a moment of silence. I had stopped writing, thinking the interview terminated. Mary Bronson had stopped crying now. She wiped her face with Otha's handkerchief. And then she looked up and said, "Ain't no living free, less I'm living with my boys."

She had composed herself now. I could see that her pain and fear were shifting into something else. "I don't wanna hear about your church. Don't wanna hear bout your city. My boys—they

203

the only city I need. Now you done found a way to get me and Octavius out, and by God, I am thankful for it. I was raised correct—I am thankful. But my other boys, *all my lost boys,* that is my highest concern."

"Mrs. Bronson," said Otha. "We just ain't set up like that. That just ain't in our power."

"Then you ain't got the power of freedom," she said. "If you can't keep them from parting a mother from her son, a husband from his natural wife, then you got nothing. That boy over there is my everything. I run for him, so he might know some other world. Left on my own, I would have died as I was born—a slave. That boy freed me, you see. And I owe him so much. Mostly I owe him his pappy and his brothers. If you can't stop them from breaking us up, as they do, if you can't put us back together, then your freedom is thin and your church and your city hold nothing for me."

That following Monday I began my employment in a woodworking shop, just off the Schuylkill docks, at the corner of Twenty-third and Locust. The owner was an associate of Raymond White's, and a large number of those who labored there were fugitives. I worked there three days a week and three for the Underground.

After work I would usually walk alone through the city, taking in the incredible alchemy of sounds, odors, and sensations, all of which proceeded late into the night. But still and all, among that incredible amalgam of people, I somehow felt alone. It was Mary Bronson who'd done it, her longing, her hunger for a freedom that extended to all of her blood. For what did it mean to be free, in a city such as this, when those you hold to most are still Tasked? What was I without Sophia, without my mother, without Thena? Thena. *Boy like you should be more careful with his words,* she said. *Never know when they the last ones he might put upon a person.* And I should have been, I knew that even then. But I was now aging faster than my years, so that Thena's words redounded with the lamenting of a man much older than my twenty years. My treatment of her was the worst thing I'd done in my short life. I saw now that I had been little more than a boy lusting after a dream. And now the dream was gone, like Mary Bronson's boys were gone, carried off into the deep, far from any means the Underground might muster to recover it.

One Friday morning, as I was leaving for work, Otha approached me and said, "A man can't be too long without family."

I stared back and said nothing.

He smiled. "Still, it might be nice to be with some folks who care, Hiram. Supper? Tonight? At my momma's. What do you say? Whole family'll be there. We good folks, I tell you, and would very much welcome you as our own."

"All right, Otha," I said.

"Lovely. Just lovely," he said. Then he tendered directions and said, "See you tonight."

The White family home was across the Delaware River. I caught the ferry that evening, then walked along a cobbled road until it turned to clay and then to dust. The heat of the city, the air damp and thick, faded behind me, and a refreshing breeze swirled up the road. It was good to be out. It was my first time in anything like the country since my arrival, and I now realized everything that I missed about my old Southern home—the wind in the fields, the sun pushing through the trees, the drawn-out afternoons. Everything happened at once in Philadelphia, all of life one ridiculous crush of feeling.

The parents of Raymond and Otha lived in a large house with a porch wrapping around and a pond out front. I stood for some time on that porch, staring at the front door. Inside, I could hear children and mothers, fathers and brothers, their words and laughter mixing into a happiness that took me back to Holiday down at the Street. Even before I stepped inside the house, all their accumulated affection radiated out. I had felt something like it before.

Under the Goose. Where I was in reunion with a mother whom I could not remember. Where I saw my cousins, and Honas and Young P. And no sooner did I recall this feeling than it all came upon me again. The summer breeze grew chill. I shivered. And everything before me went blue. The door to the Still home expanded into many doors all in a row, and these doors pulled away from each other like bellows. I felt myself falling away. A door opened. I looked in. I saw my mother's hand reaching out from the smoke. She walked toward me, her hand reaching for mine, and when she grabbed it, the blue faded, and the yellow heat of that summer afternoon returned. And in the doorway I saw a woman, who was not my mother, but about the age she would have been. And just behind her I saw Otha, who, seeing me, stopped, waved, and smiled.

"Hiram?" the woman asked. And before I could respond, she said, "That must be you. You look like you seen the devil himself."

She gripped my hand tight and then looked into my eyes. "Uh-huh. Hunger'll do that to a man. What Raymond and Otha got you eating down there? Why, don't just stand there—come on in!"

I followed for a couple of steps until the woman stopped and said, "Viola White. I'm Raymond and Otha's mother. But you just call me Aunt Viola, because that is who I am to you. Any man working with Otha and Raymond is family to me."

I followed Viola White—"Aunt Viola" would take some time with me—into the front parlor and found a crush of cousins and aunts. Raymond stood at the mantel talking with an older man. Mars, the proprietor of the bakery, rushed over and pulled me into a big scrum of family, rendering introductions and discoursing on the effects of that gingerbread.

"That boy try make like he cool, like he wasn't caught," Mars told his wife, Hannah. "But soon as he stick his face in the paper, I knew I had him."

Hannah laughed and I, surprising myself, laughed too. Something was happening here. Walls were falling down, walls I had erected down on the Street. My silence, my watching, was a wall. There was love even on the Street, I tell you, some of the deepest and hardest I'd ever seen. But the Street was brutal and erratic. Passions transfigured into outrages and violence, even among us. But the demeanor that served me at Lockless seemed cruel and unnecessary among the Whites, so I found myself, awkwardly and haltingly, smiling, laughing, and, above all, talking.

After supper, we took coffee and tea in the back salon. There was a piano there, and one of the younger girls seated herself and began to play. What I remember more than any virtuosity was the gleaming pride in all the eyes of the White family at the talents of this child. And I remembered how I had talents, too, as a child, but that my own father wished them to be in Little May. I was an amusement, a source of laughter. Watching that little girl encouraged in her pursuits, rewarded in whatever genius she had—and we all had some—I saw all that had been taken from me, and all that was so regularly taken from the millions of colored children bred to the Task. But more than this I saw, for the first time, colored people in that true freedom that Mary Bronson longed for, that I hungered for walking through the city, that I had glimpsed under the Goose.

I had noticed, throughout conversation, the names "Lydia" and "Lambert," and I knew from how they were spoken that these two were family still held down by the Task. After the young girl's recital, I found Otha seated on the large porch, looking out past the road and into the lush green woods in the light of a summer's twilight. I took a seat and said, "I want to thank you for having me here, Otha. It means a lot."

Otha looked to me and smiled. "It's nothing, Hiram. I'm glad you came. The work can be such a weight."

"Your mother," I said, looking back inside. "I gather she knows."

"They all do. The babies only a little, of course. But how could they not know? They the reason we in the work to begin with."

"Well, you've got a beautiful family," I said.

At that he went quiet for a moment, and his gaze returned to those woods.

"Otha," I asked, "Lambert and Lydia?"

"Lambert was my brother," said Otha. "And Lydia is my wife. Lambert died while I was still down. And Lydia is still there, though I have not seen her in some years."

"Children?"

"Yup. Two girls. One boy. You?"

I paused for a moment.

"Naw, just me."

"Huh. Don't know what I'd do without my young ones. Don't know who I'd be. This whole thing, this Underground, starts with my babies."

Otha stood and looked through the door inside. We could hear the gentle clanging of dishes, rumbling and somber talk broken by the occasional giggling of children. Then he walked to the side of the porch and seated himself there against the wooden railing.

"I'm not like them. Wasn't raised up here," he said. "My daddy is old and stooped now but he was something in his day. Born to the Task. But in his twenty-first year he walked up to his old master and told him straight—'I'm grown now. And I shall sooner die as have the yoke.' And the old master thought on it for a day, and when he next saw my pappy he had a rifle in one hand and Pappy's papers in the other. And he told my pappy, just as straight as my pappy had told him, 'Freedom *is* a yoke, boy. You'll soon see.' Then he handed Pappy the papers and said, 'Now get off my land, for the next time you and I meet, only one of us shall walk away.'"

Otha laughed at that. "But there was this girl Viola—Momma—who was tasking there too. There was two of us by then—myself and my brother Lambert. Daddy had it figured that he would get up North, get some work, and then buy us our freedom. He

208

started out at the docks, saving for the day he could get us all out. But Momma had her own notions. She ran with me and Lambert, took the Underground as it was back then. Shocked the life out of Daddy when she showed herself down at the city docks.

"They married proper and two more was born—Raymond and Patsy. That's Patsy's daughter who was at the piano. Girl can sing like a bird. The old master let my daddy walk—don't ask me why—who can figure white folks? But for my mother—a girl—to take mastery of her life, as she did, well, it was too much. Maybe it was how she did it—just up and leaving. Or maybe it was us. Momma was the goose. But we was the golden eggs.

"That man sent the hounds up to the city. They bagged me, my brother Lambert, my momma, Raymond, and Patsy—the whole family save my daddy. We was carried back. When we got there Momma made it out as though the escape was all Daddy's idea. Told the old master she never wanted no part in running anyway. Flattered him into believing he was good white folks. And I guess the old master believed her. Maybe he needed to believe her, needed to think that he was doing some kind of good, dividing a family and holding 'em down.

"Anyway, wasn't long after that Momma ran again. Went different this time, though. She woke me up in the dead of night. I must have been about six, Lambert about eight, but I can still see it, like it's all right in front of me—the memory is sharp as an axe. She was at our bedside when she told us. 'Baby, I got to go. I gotta go for Raymond and I gotta go for Patsy. They gon die down here. I am so sorry, baby, but I gotta go.'

"I know why she done it, now. I knew why she done it, even back then. But it burned in me, a low heavy hatred. Can you imagine hating your own mother, Hiram? After that, the old master sold us south—two lost boys sent down into the deep. They did it to punish my momma, to show her that whatever plans she had of coming back for me and Lambert was done. I had a whole other life down there. I met a girl—my Lydia—and we made a family. I tasked hard. I was a man well regarded in slavery, which is to say I was never regarded as a man at all.

"Lambert knew. Maybe 'cause he was older, he knew all that was taken from us. And the hate in him was so strong, it just ate him. So Lambert . . . Lambert died down there, far from home, far from the mother that birthed him and the father that reared him."

And here Otha caught up. I could not see his face, but I heard the halting in his voice, and I felt a halo of agony burning all around him.

"There are so many holes in me, so many pieces cut away. All those lost years, my mother, my father, Raymond and Patsy, my wife and my kids. All my losses.

"Well, I got out. My master needed the money more than he needed to hold me, and through the kindness of others, I got out. I came up to this city searching for my family, for I was left with rumors of where we had been. And soon I heard from the coloreds that this man Raymond White was a good one to know, should you be searching for family. I sought him out."

"Y'all recognize each other?" I asked.

"Not even a little bit. And I had no surname. He sat with me, just like we sat with Mary Bronson a few weeks back, and I gave him my whole story. Later, Raymond told me that he trembled with every detail. But you know Raymond, he is a rock. So I'm sitting there telling him all that I know. And I'm wondering how he's taking it, because the whole time, he just real quiet. Then he tell me come see him again tomorrow. Same time.

"Next day I come back and there she was, Hiram. I knew her right away. I didn't even need to search myself or think no time on it. It was my momma. And then Momma tell me that this man, this rock, was my brother. It's the only time I seen tears in Raymond's eyes.

"When we was young Lambert and me had all kinds of schemes for seeing our way out. We knew our people were somewhere free. But when all of our plans fell to pieces, despair fell over us like a shadow. You see, we was different than men such as you, Hiram. We had known, since the day our mother vanished, that we were born to the title of freedom. And if freedom was my momma's right, and freedom was my daddy's right too, then somehow it must be ours."

"I think we all got it fixed that way," I said. "For some it's just buried far deep."

"But it was never buried for us. Lambert remembered everything from that last night. He remembered Momma's caress upon his forehead, the last stroke of her hand. When Lambert died, Hiram, I knew that I could not. I knew that I must, somehow, live and then get back out. And I knew that any anger in that venture was a waste. I think back to my momma's words the night she left. I think about them all the time in this work, in my time on the Underground. 'I gotta go for Raymond and I gotta go for Patsy,' she said. 'I am so sorry, baby, but I gotta go.' And I, being young and loving my momma, I said, 'Momma, why can't we go with you?' And my momma she said . . . she said, ''Cause I can only carry so many, and them only so far.'"

· 17 ·

THE CONDUCTIONS WERE MORE frequent now. The world would suddenly and randomly fall away and moments later I would return, dumped into back-alleys, basements, open fields, stock rooms. Every Conduction seemed activated by a memory, some whole, some mere shards, like the vision of a woman who snuck me ginger snaps. But with the glue of tales swapped down in the Street, I assembled a rough picture: The woman who'd slipped me ginger snaps was my aunt Emma. I remembered the stories of her prowess in the Lockless kitchen. And I also thought it was no mistake that this Aunt Emma was the same aunt who would water dance out in the woods with her sister, my mother.

I began to feel that something was trying to reveal itself to me, that some part of my mind, long ago locked away, was now seeking its liberation. Perhaps I should have greeted the unraveling of a mystery and new knowledge with relief. But Conduction felt like the breaking and resetting of a bone. Each bout left me fatigued and with a somehow deeper sense of loss than the one I'd carried into it, so that I was in a constant low thrum of agony, a melancholy so deep it would take every ounce of my strength to rise out of bed the next morning. For days after each Conduction, I would still be working my way through the most sullen of moods. This no longer felt like freedom, not anymore.

And so one day I walked out of the Ninth Street office set upon the intention to leave Philadelphia and the Underground, leave the triggers for these memories that threw me into depression. I did not meditate on this decision. I did not gather any effects. I simply walked out the door with no view of ever coming back. I reasoned that my initial exit would alarm no one, since it was known that I enjoyed walking through the city. But then I would just keep walking.

I turned away from the office and made my way over toward the Schuylkill docks. Of all the people I saw in the city, the sailors seemed the most free, tied to nothing save each other, bound by boyish jabs and indecent mockery that always elicited a host of laughter. Sometimes they fought. But whatever their quarrels, these men seemed a brotherhood to me. Even in their freedom they still somehow reminded me of home. Maybe it was their hard black faces, their rough hands, bent fingers, bruised and worn-down nails. Maybe it was how they sang, because they sang as the Tasked did.

I stood at the dock watching them work, hoping one might call out to me, perhaps asking for a hand, and when no one did, I left, and that whole day I just wandered. I crossed the river, passed a cemetery and some railroad tracks, and stopped before an alms-house to watch the indigent of the city gather. I walked more until I stood before Cobbs Creek and a forest at the south-westerly recesses of the city. By now it was late. I had no plan and it was getting dark. I really had no way out, no way to escape the Underground nor the binds of memory. So I turned around, and these were the thoughts that clouded me on my way back to Ninth Street, back to my fate, the notions that kept me from watching as I had been trained to do. Suddenly I was face to face with a white man who seemed to materialize out of the night itself. He asked me something, but I could not hear. I leaned closer, asking him to repeat himself. And then I felt a sharp blow fall across the back of my head. There was a bright flash. Another blow. And then nothing.

When I awoke I was, once again, chained, blinded, and gagged. I was in the back of a drawn cart and could feel ground moving beneath me. I cleared my head and knew exactly what had befallen me, for I had heard all the stories. It was the man-catchers—Ryland's Hounds of the North—who'd gotten me. They were known to simply grab colored people off the street and ship them south for a price, with no regard to their status as free or in flight from the Task.

I could hear them laughing with each other, doubtlessly counting up their haul. I was not alone in the cart. Someone near me was weeping, quietly—a girl. But I was silent. I had wanted out of the Underground and now I had it. There was some small part of me that felt relief, for I was, at least, returning to the Task I knew.

We rode for several hours, across the back-country roads. Ryland, I reasoned, would like to avoid towns, toll-roads, and ferries, for as sure as we feared Ryland, Ryland feared the vigilance committees, allies of the Underground, which stood watch for man-catchers who sought to drag freedmen down. We stopped to make camp and I felt rough hands around my arms—I was pulled along for a moment and then tossed to the ground. "Take care, Deakins," I heard one of them say. "Damage that boy and I'll damage you." This man, Deakins, propped me up against a tree. I could move my fingers but nothing else. I was listening to their voices, attempting to calculate their number, when I saw a brightness through my blindfold. A campfire. The men gathered around and traded their small talk. I now counted four voices, and from their words and general commotion, it became clear that they were eating. Their last meal.

I never heard him approach and doubtless neither did Ryland. There was the crack of a pistol shot—twice—a scream, a struggle and then two more cracks, then a bit of whining, like a child's but not the child I'd heard in the wagon, another crack and then nothing for a moment. And then I heard someone rummaging for something, and again I felt hands upon me. The click of a lock and the chains loosened. With a furor that shocked me, I pushed the hands away as well as their possessor and pulled off my blindfold and gag, and by the fire-light I saw him—Mr. Fields, Micajah Bland, regarding me with the most stolid and unmoved face.

I stood and leaned against the tree to settle myself. There were two others, bound and manacled as I was. Bland worked quickly, moving among them. I looked away and saw four bodies on the ground. How do I explain what happened in that moment, the blinding, unconscious rage I felt? It was as if I had been lifted out of myself to behold the scene. And what I saw was me kicking one of the corpses with all the power I could muster. Bland came over to stop me, and I pushed him away again and kicked the dead man—Deakins perhaps—even more. Bland did not try to stop me this time. In that moment all the rage of everything from my mother to Maynard to Sophia to Thena to Corrine, all the lies, all the losses, all that they had done to me in the jail parlor, all the violation, all my impotence for the little boy in my cell, for the old man who loved the wife of his son, for the days they'd chased me into the woods—all of it came up there and vented itself on a dead man.

Finally tired, I doubled over on my knees. The fire was now burning low. But I could see Bland standing there with a girl and a man, and the man stood in front of the girl to shield her from my anger, and it occurred to me then that the man was the girl's father.

"Are you finished?" Micajah Bland asked.

"No," I said. "Not ever."

We are all divided against ourselves. Sometimes part of us begins to speak for reasons we don't even understand until years later. The voice that took me away from the Underground was familiar and old in me. This was the voice that conspired to come up off the Street. This was the voice that consigned my mother to the "down there." It was the voice that had spoken to Thena, and so callously left her behind. It was the voice of freedom, a cold Virginia freedom—freedom for me and those I chose. But now a new voice was rising, one enriched by the warmth of the house of Viola White, and the ghost of my aunt Emma who from somewhere deep within admonished me, *Don't forget, family.*

We walked through the woods until we reached a town where Bland had left his horses, carriage, and a cart. I was aware now of the blow I'd taken earlier, as my head was pounding steadily, seemingly in rhythm with every step we took. I sat in the cart with the girl and her father. Morning was just beginning to break over the horizon in a fan of orange and blue. We had gone a few miles when we stopped. I turned and saw Bland talking to a small woman standing in the road, her whole body wrapped and covered in a shawl. Then she turned and began walking to the back of the cart. When she was close enough, she put a hand on my cheek, and then my forehead and then the back of my head, which was sore to the touch. I could now see that she was, judging by her countenance, only slightly older than me, and yet in her approach, in her confidence and command, I sensed someone much senior.

"Got 'em, did you?" she said, calling back to Bland, even as her hand was still on my face.

"Yes," Bland said. "They had not even made it that far out and the fools decided to stop and have a banquet."

She turned to Bland and said, "Glad they did." The she turned back to me and said in a soft voice, "But you, boy, what were you doing? And what kind of agent let them hounds get under him like that? Mmmm-hmmm. Almost carried you off."

I said nothing but felt my face burn. She laughed and pulled back her hand.

"All right," she said to Bland. "Y'all get gone."

The cart began to creak as the horses moved. The woman waved to us and then walked off into the woods to our rear. I could feel some excitement in the cart now. The man and the girl started chattering with each other. When I didn't join in, the man leaned over to say, "Don't you know who that was?"

"Not particularly," I said.

"Moses," he said. He waited for a moment as if to recover from the effect that speaking the fact of things had on him.

"My God . . ." And he paused again. "That was Moses."

There seemed to be as many names for her as legends. The General. The Night. The Vanisher. Moses of the Shore, who summoned the fog, and parted the river. This was the one of whom Corrine and Hawkins had spoken, the living master of Conduction. I did not register all of this at that moment. Too much had happened, and I was mostly in shock at all that had befallen me.

An hour later, the girl was asleep in her father's lap. Bland pulled over the cart and called for me to join him in the front. We rode for another few minutes in silence. I broke it with a question.

"How did you find me?"

He snorted and laughed. "We are all watched, Hiram."

"If you were watching," I said, "why you ain't stop them before they socked me and dragged me out the city?"

Bland shook his head. "The men, the ones who grabbed you, they've operated in Philadelphia for some time now. They prey off the free coloreds. Children are especially prized. We can't really stop them. But sometimes we get a chance to send a message as to just how dangerous the man-catching business can truly be."

"So you planned it all?" I asked.

"No. But you asked why we didn't stop them. And this is

why—to send a message, a warning. To make their cohort understand the perils of their trade. We could not send such a message in
the confines of the city. But out here in the open country, with no
one to tell . . ."

"Murder," I said.

"Murder? Do you know what they were going to do to you?"

"Yeah, I do know," I said. And at that moment I was back at
that terrible night, chained to the fence, with Sophia at my side.
And I was recalling how badly I wanted to give in to it all, to die
right there, and how she held me up, and spoke to me without
speaking, how strong she was when I needed her most, and how
foolish I had been when she needed me. And now she was gone,
and they, Ryland, the hounds, had done God knows what with
her.

I said, "You only got half the story about me. You know about
the girl—Sophia—the one I ran with. But you don't really know
the feeling I had for her, and how much it aches me that they have
her now while I am up here, breathing the free air. All I can tell
you is she was better than me. Fact is, sometimes I think you got
the wrong one for an agent. Shoulda been her."

I began to weep. Softly and quietly, but enough that I had to
stop and collect myself.

"She saw so much in me," I said. "But I fell. And Sophia fell
with me. And here I am, up here, in the North, and she is . . . I
don't even know where she is. What I know is she deserved better
than me. She deserved more than a man who would lead her right
into the jaws of Ryland."

And at this there was no control. I was weeping openly. It was
all out there now. I had led a woman I loved right into the maw.
And the weight that this put upon me was now open and known.
Bland made no effort to conciliate. He kept his eyes on the road.
And when I had stopped weeping, he spoke.

"You know that feeling you had for this woman Sophia?" he
asked. "You know how it rips you to pieces wondering what be-

came of her? You know all the moments you've lost wondering how you might have done things different? And you know all the nights you've sat up wondering if she were even alive? Hiram, that is the feeling that marks an entire nation held down. A whole country looking up wondering for their fathers and sons, for their mothers and daughters, cousins, nephews, friends, lovers.

"You say I murdered those men back there. But I say to you that I saved the lives of so many unknowable others. Those who would murder you—strip you away from all your family and friends—and remember nothing of it. They cannot live, not without some fear, some specter, and if murder is what you must name it, then I gladly accept the claim."

We rode in silence for a moment.

"Thank you," I said. "That should have been the first thing I said. Thank you."

"No need to thank me, Hiram. This work, this war, it gives my own life meaning. I don't know what I'd be without it. And I must say that I think if you gave it a chance, you might well find meaning . . ."

Bland was still talking, but the headache overpowered everything, and soon, to my great relief, the world faded away and I slipped out of consciousness.

Late that next day, I awoke with a dull ache all over my body. I dressed, walked downstairs, and found Raymond, Otha, and Bland all in conference. They summoned me over and I sat down before them. Scanning their faces, I had the sense that they were ashamed of something almost—my foolishness at being captured, perhaps. And I thought then that they had been called to do something awful yet necessary.

"Hiram," Raymond said. "Bland is an old friend to me. I trust him as much as my own family, and to be truthful with you, more than certain members of that family. He is not, as you well know, an exclusive agent of this station. He has his acquaintances across the Underground and, in his dealings with those acquaintances, has, on occasion, taken up projects that would not have met my approval. I understand that you were among those projects."

I began to feel a shift in the temperature of things.

"I know well the methods and reputation of Corrine Quinn. They are not my methods, Hiram, no matter their aim."

Raymond shook his head now and looked to the ground. "This ritual burial, the hunting, the chasing, it is all abhorrent to me. In that spirit, I am compelled to say that you are owed an apology. I feel that what was done to you, no matter the aims, was wrong."

"It was not you who did it," I said.

"Yes, but it is my cause. It is my army. And while I cannot balance Corrine's accounts, I can tend to my own. And it was wrong, not just on her behalf, but to our cause"—and here Raymond paused a moment before looking back at me—"no matter what power may beat in your breast."

"I understand," I said. "It is nothing. I understand."

Now Raymond took in a deep breath. "No, Hiram," he said. "I do not think you truly do."

"I know more than you give me credit for, Hiram," Bland said.

"What do you mean?" I asked.

"I mean, I knew it all. I knew about Sophia, all about your feelings. It is my business to know. And that is why I know not just how you felt then, nor just how you feel now. I also know exactly where Sophia is being held."

"What?" I said. My head throbbed with almost the same force it had throbbed last night.

"We had to know," Bland said. "What kind of agents would we be if we didn't know exactly who you ran with and what became of them?"

"I asked Corrine," I said. "She said it was out of her power."

"I know, Hiram, I know. It was wrong. I can't defend it. I can only tell you what you must already know—that when you are operating as Corrine Quinn does, on the other side of the line, the math is different. It has to be. You were part of that math."

I screened out the headache and said, "Where?"

"Your father's place. Lockless. Corrine prevailed on him to take Sophia back."

"But you didn't get her out? All the power held by your Underground and you . . ."

"Virginia has its rules. We took what we could from them. We could not take it all."

"And so that's it," I said. "You're going to leave her to it?"

"No," Otha said. "We don't never leave nobody to it. Ever. They have their rules. And by God, we got ours."

"Hiram," Raymond said. "We don't mean to just offer you an apology. It is not just words we bring, but action to match them."

"You see, we don't just know where Sophia is," Bland said. "We know precisely how to bring her out."

· 18 ·

For those next few days, walking the streets of Philadelphia, or at work with chisel and lathe, at work forging the letters and passes, I thought of little else but Sophia. I thought of her water dancing by the fire. I saw us under the gazebo, trading the jar of ale. I remembered her long fingers, brushing against the dusty furniture in the workshop. I thought of us down by the gulch and I, very badly, wished I had embraced her there. And I thought of all the possibilities of a life up here—of a family of our own, of gingerbread memories, and daughters who sang after dinner, and long walks by the Schuylkill. And I wanted badly to show this world to her, wondered what she would make of it all—the trains, the crush of people, the omnibus—all of which were, day by day, more and more familiar.

Two weeks after I was taken by the man-catchers, I was summoned out to Raymond's home across the river. He met me on the porch and told me he was alone. His wife and children were in the city, and I gathered from the look on his face that this was by design. There were always so many secrets.

We went into the home and climbed up to the second level, where he reached up and grasped a metal ring, attached by a hinge in its wooden housing in the ceiling, and pulled gently, until the ceiling opened up and a ladder slid down. We then climbed up the ladder, into the rafters of the home. Raymond walked to a corner where I saw several small wooden crates. He selected two. We carried them back down out of the rafters, closed up the ceiling again, and took them down to the drawing room.

Raymond opened the crates and said, "Have a look, Hiram."

Reaching in, I found an assortment of paper, correspondences with fugitives—filled with kind words, familial reports, and grave intelligence on the movements of Ryland's Hounds, the plots and intrigues of the Slave Power, and most often, requests for the liberation of relatives. I saw that he marked those that he had acknowledged and those he hoped to. There was great value in these papers, and he had crates of them, much to be learned about the actions of our enemies, but should our enemies ever acquire them, much to be learned of our own. In the wrong hands, countless agents would be exposed.

"The stories here are beyond anything anyone could ever believe—even those of us who are actually party to them," Raymond said. I was still filing through them, amazed at the array. It seemed that there was a testimony from nearly everyone who'd ever run from the Task and been rescued by the Philadelphia station. It occurred to me that my own interview with Mary Bronson likely was contained there. "It is good to remember why we do what we do. I have worked with agents of all persuasion and I cannot say that they are moved by the purest of motives."

"Possible that none of us is pure," I said. "Possible we all got our reasons for doing what we do."

"Indeed," Raymond said. "Can I say that without the connection of my family, I would be here right now? Involved as I am? Of course not. And family is what we promised you, is it not? Your beloved Sophia—who ran with you, in a manner not so different from all those stories contained in my files, indeed, not so different from my very own parents."

"Somewhat different," I said. "We never got to a point of seeing things clear. We were very young. It's odd to say it as such, I know. Ain't even been a year since I was captured. But there was something there, something we were nursing that I do believe would have bloomed into family. But maybe not. Maybe I imagined it all."

"Well," he said. "At the very least, you are owed a chance to find out."

"I believe so."

"It is not the simplest of matters, this business with Sophia. But you have been toyed with too much, Hiram, and so I will make the statement concerning you directly and then give you the rest of it after."

I took a deep breath, preparing myself.

"We have yet to make contact with her—it is a delicate matter, as you can imagine, one that will require some time. But Bland has devised a plan for her conduction. Indeed, he has volunteered to handle the thing personally. But there is a complication here—not with Sophia, but with us. You have caught us at a particular time, as we are occupied with another operation," he said. "Otha has spoken to you of his wife?"

"Lydia?" I asked.

"Yes, Lydia. And not just Lydia but their children . . . my nieces and nephews. It has long been our plan to see them out. Otha appeared to us as though out of a dream. We had thought him lost. But through fortune and the grace of God, he returned to us. And as happy as he has been to be back among us, and as happy as we have been to have him, we are not whole.

"Lydia is in Alabama. Her owner has defied all our entreaties to pay for her freedom. And worse, we believe those entreaties have only raised his suspicions and made him watchful. Lydia and the children are truly in the coffin, Hiram, and with each day there, the coffin closes a little more."

"I understand," I said. "Everyone—but everyone in their time."

"Yes," Raymond said. "Everyone in their time. But there is more still. This operation is not just personal, but costly. We need someone to assist Bland, someone to ensure he can leave for Alabama at the appropriate time."

"Of course. It's why I'm here."

"No, this is personal. This is not the Underground as you understand it, and this is certainly not Corrine. There are those who would object to this and so I need you to understand—this is of your own free will. Indeed if you cannot help us in this, we will still proceed with the rescue of your family. As I've said, it is my feeling that you have endured more than what was just. We do this for you as a way of bringing matters into balance, no matter Corrine's feelings on things."

"Yeah, I figured," I said. "This ain't really Corrine's sort of deal. She is a good woman, I think. And they are, no doubt, in a good fight. But what I have seen up here, what I have seen of your momma, your cousins, your uncles, ain't just the fight. I have seen the future. I have seen what we are fighting for. I am thankful for Corrine. I am thankful for the fight. But I am most thankful to have seen all that is coming."

And now here, I did something very curious—I smiled. And it was an open and generous smile, one that rose up out of a feeling with which I was so rarely acquainted—joy. I was joyous at the thought of what was coming. I was joyous at the thought of my role in this.

"So I am in, Raymond," I said. "Whatever that means, I am in."

"Excellent." Raymond smiled and said, "And you're welcome to remain here as long as you like with these correspondences. As you saw, there are more upstairs. My wife will return soon and the children in the afternoon, but don't let that stop you. Explore as you need. May we never forget why we do this, Hiram."

I spent the rest of that day lost in Raymond's files, as thrilling as any *Ivanhoe* or *Rob Roy*. In the evening I joined the family for dinner and accepted an invitation to stay the night and thus continued my reading by lantern-light. I left the next morning after a small breakfast. I felt myself unbalanced by all that I had so quickly consumed, for it was only now, through those files, that I came to understand the great span of the Underground's operations, and the lengths to which its clients had gone to escape the Task. There in my hands, in those files, legends came alive—the resurrection of "Box" Brown, the saga of Ellen Craft, the flight of Jarm Logue. These stories were incredible, and taken together they gave me some sense of why Raymond and Otha would dare such a thing as a liberation up out of the Alabama coffin. They had dared so much already. In Virginia what mattered was immediate and invisible. And while Raymond would not wish these files to be exposed to the world, not just then, the safety of a free state made him bold. Freedom was what mattered to him. Freedom was his gospel and his bread.

Leafing through the pages, I felt the stories come alive before me. I saw them as though I was right there, so that on the walk to the ferry, on the ferry itself, and then all the way to the Philadelphia station, legions of colored people, panoramas of their great escapes, overlay the geography, so that I saw them all before me, saw them coming up from Richmond and Williamsburg, from Petersburg and Hagerstown, from Long-green and Darby, from Norfolk and Elm. And I saw them fly from Quindaro, to take haven in Granville, then bed down in Sandusky, and rejoice just west of Bird in Hand, not so far from Millersville, a small pass to Cedars.

And I saw them fleeing with Irish girls, absconding with mementos of lost children, running with salt pork and crackers, running with biscuits, flying with cuts of beef, inhaling the last of the master's terrapin soup, taking drags of his Jamaican rum, and then out into winter, thoughtless and shoeless, but freedom-bound. Black maids running with dreams of holy union, running with double-barreled pistol and dirk, so that when confronted by hounds, they pulled out, yelling, "Shoot! Shoot!" They fled with young children dosed into slumber, with old men who shuffled out into the frost, who died exposed in the wood with these words on their lips: "Man made us slave, but God willed us free."

And in all of these words, and each of these stories, I saw as much magic as anything I'd seen in the Goose, souls conducted as surely as I was out from its depths. And I saw them coming up on railroads, barges, river-runner, skiff, and bribery coach. Coming up on horseback over hard snow and March melting ice. They were fitted in ladies' dress and came up, in gentry clothes and came up, in dental bandage and came up, in sling and came up, in rags not worth the laundry lady's washing, but came up. They bribed low whites and stole horses. Crossed the Potomac in wind, storm, and darkness. Came up, as I had, driven by the remembrance of mothers or wives sold south for the high crime of standing contrary before lust. They came up devoured by frost. They came up with tales of hard drinkers and overseers who took glee in applying the lash. They came up stowed like coffee in boats, braving turpentine, scarred and singed by salt-water anointing, guilt-racked for finding themselves so broken that they should bow before their own flogging, for having held their brothers down under the master's lash.

In the stories that day, I saw them running out into the forest, clutching a Brussels carpet bag, yelling, "I shall never be taken!" I saw them boarding ferries, singing low and only to themselves:

> *God made them birds and the greenwood tree*
> *And all has got their mate, but soul-sick me.*

I saw them that day at the Philadelphia docks, praying, "Hide the outcast, betray not him that wandereth." I saw them wandering on Bainbridge and crying for all their dead, those who had taken ship for the final harbor from whence none shall return. All of them came to me, from the papers, from the memories, all of them drawn up from Pandemonium, up from Slavery, up out of the jaw of the Abomination, up out from under the juggernaut's wheels, singing before the sorcery of this Underground.

The following evening, I went to Micajah Bland. I was still shaken from being stolen off the streets of the city. I analyzed everyone from afar. When people walked close behind, I stopped to let them pass. Low whites of a particular style and dress became particularly suspicious to me, as hounds so often drew allies from their ranks. And there were low whites all over Philadelphia, indeed they were the largest class—and they were found especially near Bland's home, by the Schuylkill docks. There were coloreds here too. I stood catercorner from Bland's house, watching for a full ten minutes. I saw a shabbily dressed colored man dart out of the row house next door. He moved down the hot street with speed, and right behind him I saw a colored woman chasing and yelling all manner of vulgarity. And then behind her an older black woman yelling after and giving chase, and finally two little colored girls standing in the doorway wailing. I thought that I might should do something, and then the older woman—a grandmother perhaps—returned and shooed the little girls inside, the door still open.

I had heard stories of coloreds like this, different than Raymond and his family, living penny to penny, beaten and run off jobs for daring to apply themselves to that which was held to be "white man's work." I had not noticed them at first because it was the relative opulence of all the other coloreds that struck me. But watching there, across the street, I remembered that Otha had warned clients of the Underground of this fate, for these coloreds were usually runaways themselves, men and women who made no connection with society, with certain churches, and thus found freedom hard upon them. And it occurred to me then that this fear that I felt, this study I put on every face, was their lifetime and worse, for if they were caught by the hounds, no Bland would rally to them.

As for the man himself, I found him at home expecting me. A young woman answered the door, smiled, and then called out his name. She introduced herself as Laura, and mentioned that she was Bland's sister. It was a modest house—one of the better ones in the quarter but not as nice as Raymond's or the White family home on the other side of the river. But it was clean and well-appointed.

We shook hands and there were the usual pleasantries. I felt a deep relief at having completed the small task of walking to Bland's home unmolested. And having done that, I was now aware of a gnawing impatience to set upon the work of freedom for Lydia, and thus, in turn, freedom for Sophia, *my Sophia*. She existed in my mind not as one with her own notions and ideas but as an idea herself, a notion herself, so that to think of *my Sophia* was to think of a woman for whom I possessed a true and a sincere feeling, but, too, was to think of *my dreams* and *my redemption*. It is important that I tell you this. It is important that you see how little I knew of *her dreams,* of *her redemption.* I know now that she had tried to tell me, and I, who so prided himself on listening, simply could not hear.

At all events, this was the spirit, anxious and rash, that I brought to Micajah Bland, so that no more than five minutes after taking my seat I said, directly and abruptly, "So how we gonna do it?"

"Get to Sophia?" Bland asked.

"Well, I was thinking about Lydia and the kids. But we can start with Sophia if you like."

"Sophia is the easy one. I have to prevail upon Corrine and marshal some resources, but it will be done."

"Corrine . . ." As I said her name, my voice trailed off. "She's the one who left Sophia there."

"It is her station, Hiram. She deserves notice, and more, deserves consultation."

"Corrine . . ." I shook my head.

"You know the full story on that woman?"

"No," I said. "Except that she has left Sophia down in the coffin."

And now something happened, something that I was not aware of at the time. I do not know if it was a kind of possession, but I know that I felt an anger rising in me, an anger related to me, related to my violation, related to the jail and what had been done to me. But it was not my anger. And the voice that now spoke was not mine so much as one recently imprinted upon me. And the voice now said, *You know what they did to us back there. You done forgot? You don't remember what they do to the girls down here? And once they do it, they got you. They catch you with the babies, tie you to the place by your own blood. . . .*

At that moment, the usual calm repose of Bland's face broke and gave way to something in him I had never seen before and never saw again—fear. And then the walls fell away and in their place there was a great and borderless nothing. The table and chairs were still there and they, along with Bland himself, were wreathed in a now-familiar blue. I was aware of myself, and aware of a deep anger—but more I felt a low guttural pain—one that had been with me since the day I'd left Maynard to the deep. Most important, I was, for the first time, aware of exactly what was happening as it was happening, so that I now thought to try to steer it, direct it, the way you might direct a dream. But the moment I did this, the moment I attempted to directly affect my surroundings, the world reverted back. The great nothing shimmered, until the outlines of walls returned. The blue faded and I saw now that we were seated again, except that we had changed places and I had taken Bland's seat while he had taken mine. I stood and touched the walls. I walked out of the room, stumbled into the foyer, then leaned against the wall. There was that same disorientation, though the fatigue was less. I returned to the dining room and took my seat.

"That's it, isn't it?" I said. "That's what Corrine wants."

"Yes, it is," he said.

"Have you seen it before?"

"Yes," he said. "But not like that."

For long minutes, I said nothing. Bland himself now stood and left the room, and I took this as charity for it seemed to me that he knew that I needed a moment to collect myself. When he returned, his sister Laura was with him. She mentioned that it would be time for supper soon and asked me to stay.

"Join us, Hiram," said Micajah Bland. "Please."

I agreed.

After the meal, we took a walk together, silently strolling through the evening Philadelphia streets. And then I finally asked, "Who'd you see do it? Moses?"

He nodded.

"And that was her, the other night?"

"Yes."

"And that was how you saved us?"

"No. We didn't need anything so otherworldly for that bunch."

"Bland, if Moses can do this, why not send her after Otha's family?"

"Because she is Moses, not Jesus. She has her own promises to keep. There are limits to everything. I respect Corrine. I respect what she wanted to do with you. But she does not really understand the power, nor how it works."

We walked some more, wordlessly. The sun was setting behind us. I had not been out for an evening walk since Ryland's Hounds had tackled me near the docks. But I felt a kind of safety with Micajah Bland. The fact was he was my oldest friend on the Underground, to the extent that I had any. And it was he who had, in his own particular ways, believed that there was indeed something in me.

"How in God's name did you get tangled up with Corrine?" I asked.

"You have it backward," Bland said. "When I met Corrine she was a student, a girl at an institute in New York, where these Virginians of a certain class would often send their daughters for a lady's education—French, housekeeping, art, a little reading. But Corrine was precocious and the city entranced her. She would often sneak out and attend the lectures of abolitionists. That is how she and I met.

"You see, there were those of us then who'd long felt that we'd like to expand our war into the South. She was easily recruited, and then cultivated as our chief weapon to stab at the heart of Demon Slavery itself. And she was a weapon—their prim Southern belle, an ornament to their civilization, turned back against them. She has proved herself repeatedly, Hiram. You cannot imagine the sacrifice."

"Her own parents," I said.

"Sacrifices, Hiram," he said. "Tremendous sacrifices, the kind that Raymond and Otha, and even our Moses, would never approve of, nor would I ever ask them to. This was about the time I met you. I was then in the business of reconnaissance, under the guise of Mr. Fields. It was there at Lockless that I first heard the stories of Santi Bess, but even then I did not make the connection between you, the boy with the invincible memory, and Conduction. Lockless was one among the ancient houses that Corrine targeted, but the only one featuring an heir who we believed could be deceived with relative ease. But as she closed in she realized that the Virginia station stood to gain control not just of an ancient Elm County estate but of one who could bring a great power into our control."

"But you had Moses," I said.

"No, Hiram," he said. "No one has Moses. Certainly not Corrine. Moses has her loyalties and they are tied most strongly to the station here in Philadelphia. Corrine sought similar power, but tied to Virginia."

"So everyone clean, huh? No one to blame?" I said.

"No, Hiram. She is not clean. She is right. Have you ever thought about what they would do to her if she were found out? Do you realize what, particularly, they would do to a woman like that, who'd mocked their most sacred principles, and sought to destroy their whole way of life?"

We had by now wound our way back to the front of the Ninth Street office, my home. It occurred to me, then only emerging from my feelings, that Bland was seeing me home. I looked at him, laughed quietly, and shook my head.

"What?" he said. "We cannot have you getting blackjacked and bound yet again."

I laughed again, a little louder this time. At this Bland threw his arm around my shoulder and laughed with me.

· 19 ·

THAT NIGHT, I SAT up replaying the small Conduction I had brought about in Bland's home. The power was within me, but it was not in my hands so much as I was in the hands of the power, for when it made itself known, when the blue glow came over and the curtains of fog fell upon me, I was but a passenger in my own body. I needed to understand, and for that I needed someone who already understood, and the only such someone was Moses.

But first, the fate of Lydia White and her children. I found myself, the next day, with Micajah, Otha, and Raymond in the parlor, discussing the various means by which we might bring them out.

"We need a set of passes," Bland explained. "And they need to be in the name of this man Daniel McKiernan. Hiram, it was McKiernan who once held Otha, and now holds his family. We need these as precise as we can make them. They have a long way to travel, and our agents, they fall on the smallest things—being

234

out on the roads at an hour forbidden by obscure law, confusing the arrival time for the local ferry, or just bad luck."

"I can fabricate the passes," I said. "But I need an original sample of his style. As many as possible. Perhaps Otha's free papers?"

"Nah," Otha said. "That don't work. I intrigued with another man to have myself bought from McKiernan, and it was that other man who gave me my papers."

"There is another way," said Raymond. "There was a time, not too distant, when just across the river, it was legal to own a man—in some ways, it still is. Nevertheless, among the men who most advantaged themselves through slavery, there was one of particular importance to my family—Jedikiah Simpson. Mr. Simpson owned me, my mother, my father, and Otha."

"This was the man your mother ran from?" I asked. "The one who sold Otha south?"

"The same," Raymond said. "Now Jedikiah Simpson is long dead. But his son has taken possession of the old place. He also owns a home here in the city, just north of Washington Square. Elon Simpson, on account of his wealth, is held to be a gentleman in the city's most respectable circles. But we know that he is not respectable at all. We know, for instance, that he kept his investment in slavery by selling his slaves farther south."

"Have you ever crossed paths with him?" I asked.

"No, not yet," Raymond said.

"But we got eyes on him," Otha said. "Both here in the city and on his place down South. And from that we know Elon Simpson still has business with Daniel McKiernan."

Everyone was quiet for a minute, waiting to see if I had yet seen the plot. But they need not have waited, it was forming as they spoke. So I looked to Otha and nodded to confirm my comprehension.

"A letter, a receipt of sale, anything," I said. "I just need some correspondence between Simpson and McKiernan. A break-in, perhaps?"

"No," Raymond said. "Bland has a more delicate option."

They were all three smiling now, like children holding on to a secret.

"Tell me," I said.

"How bout I show you," Bland said.

And so that night I found myself standing in an alley with Bland, watching the street through the glow of gas-light, positioning ourselves in such a way that the street could not watch us. Our eyes were set on the home of Elon Simpson. We were right off of Washington Square, a part of the city marked by well-appointed brownstones with shuttered windows and a park hailing back to this country's birth. Here was the seat of this city's Quality—and the seat of our dead.

I had, by then, done my share of reading on Philadelphia, so I knew that, in another time, when the Task was here in Pennsylvania, the city had fallen victim to a wave of fever. And among the men who combatted this fever was Benjamin Rush, a famous doctor, which is hard to countenance given the theory he put forth in defense of the city. Colored people were immune to the fever, he told Philadelphia, and more than immune, their very presence could alter the air itself, sucking up the scourge and holding it captive in our fetid black bodies. And so tasking men were brought in by the hundreds on the alleged black magic of our bodies. They all died. And when the city began to fill with their corpses, its masters searched for a space far from the whites who were felled by the disease. And they chose a patch of land where no one lived, and tossed us into pits. Years later, after the fever had been forgotten, after the war had birthed this new country, they built rows and rows of well-appointed houses right on top of those people, and named a square for their liberating general. It struck me that even here, in the free North, the luxuries of this world were built right on top of us.

"How did you come to this?" I asked. We had been standing there for hours, Bland and I, watching the house.

"You mean to ask how a white man comes to the Underground?"

"No. You particularly. How did you come to this?"

"My father died when I was a child, and my mother could not carry us. I did what I could. I worked whatever job was presented, even at that age. But Laura and I were split from each other, and as soon I was old enough, I got as far away from home as I could. I was a young man in search of adventure. I went south and fought in the Seminole War, and was forever changed. I watched men burn Indian camps, shoot down innocents, and steal children. My own struggles, I realized, could be dwarfed by even greater struggles.

"I became aware of my lack of sophistication as to why men fight. I had always been curious about the world, but had not had the chance to achieve an education. But then my mother died, and I returned home to care for Laura. I took work over at the docks. But whenever I had a spare moment, I could be found in the reading rooms of the city. And it was there that I found the cause of abolition, and eventually the Underground. I worked across the country—Ohio, Indiana, Massachusetts, and then New York, which brought me to Corrine Quinn and then to Lockless."

Bland was about to say more, when, at last, the whole reason for our vigil appeared before us. A white man stepped out from the home of Elon Simpson, stood out on the sidewalk, and waited. At this Bland pulled a cigar from his coat and lit it. He took a puff and then turned to me, and against the small light from the cigar, I saw him smile. Bland then walked out of the alley and stood in the street. The man moved swiftly toward Bland. Bland turned back to the alley. The man followed him.

"They told me you'd be alone," the man said. "They told me this would be quick and easy."

I wondered for a minute if this were Elon Simpson himself, but even there in the dark I could see that he was not outfitted as a gentleman would be.

"Nothing in life is quick and easy, Chalmers," Bland said. "Nothing important, at least."

"Yeah, well, I did my part," he said, and at that he handed Bland a package.

"We need to have a look at these," Bland said. "Let's go inside."

"Like hell," Chalmers said. "Quick and easy, that was what your people said. You already wronged me by bringing *him* with you, now you want me—"

"I want you to take us inside," Bland said. "It really is simple. You promised papers addressed to a certain person. I need to verify that those papers are what you claim. To do that, I need to be able to read them. To read them, I need light, and the nearest light is inside your master's home."

"Mr. Simpson ain't my master," Chalmers said angrily.

"You're right, he isn't. I am. And you're going to take us inside to verify these papers. And if you don't, we are going to send our own papers to this man, this Elon Simpson, who is not your master. And these papers will alert him to the exact nature of all of those unchaperoned walks you seem to be in the habit of regularly taking with his sister whenever she visits the city. I'm sure he'd very much enjoy hearing how you have decided to make the scandalizing of his family a part of your regular work."

It was too dark to see his expression, but I saw Chalmers take a step back. I imagined what he might be feeling right then—the impulse to run. Perhaps all of his effects were packed. Perhaps this sister had already been alerted. Or perhaps she had not and he would simply leave her to bear the consequences of the report. Perhaps there was a coach waiting for him that would take him into the merciful arms of family farther north. Or maybe he would adventure out into the Oregon of my imaginings, or take up in the free company of the sailors I loved.

"Think carefully, Chalmers," said Micajah Bland. "You can take your chances with a gentleman of vast resources. Or you can take us inside. No one else has to know. It can all be as a dream. No one has to know, I say. It is just us. We can finish this right now. Quick and easy."

Chalmers hesitated a moment and then began walking back toward the house. We followed him up the stairs, then into the foyer and past the salon and then into a back-room that served as Elon Simpson's study. Chalmers drew up the lamp-light, and Bland sat down behind the desk to read. There were several papers in the bunch and Bland shuffled through them quickly.

"No," he said. "None of these will do. Not one."

"They said you needed some of Mr. Simpson's papers," said Chalmers. "They told me, I do this one thing, and I am free."

"No, I think they told you a good deal more," Bland responded. "Did you even bother looking to whom these papers were addressed?"

"They said bring you papers. I brought you papers."

"Well," Bland said, fixing his eyes on me. "We're going to need more."

Bland nodded in my direction, stood, and began inspecting the room with the aid of the lamp. Knowing my part, I sat at the desk and began sifting through the drawers. I flipped through a personal journal, scanned a few letters to acquaintances, looked over some invitations, yet found nothing bearing an address to or receipt from McKiernan. But when I looked up again, I saw that Bland was now focused on a small oak chest in the corner. He knelt down and rubbed his hand over the iron lock. Then, standing again, Bland reached into his pocket and produced a small satchel, and from the satchel he drew a wire. I watched Bland work at the lock, and then looked over to Chalmers, who was now seated in a high-back armchair, fiddling nervously. Bland worked the lock for a minute or two, then he looked over to Chalmers and smiled as the top of the chest groaned open.

Reaching in, Bland retrieved a large stack of neatly opened envelopes and put them on the desk. As soon as I began to sort through them, it was clear that these letters were a different sort of communication. They were records of transactions—records of people managed, bought, and sold. The volume of business was brisk and the numbers appended to the people made it clear that these dealings were the root of Elon Simpson's wealth. I had never seen either Simpson. But I could not help but imagine the son here among the Northern Quality presenting himself as a man of society, a man of good breeding, reputable connections, and respectable business. But shut away in that foot-locker was his unwashed life—the proof of a great crime, evidence of his membership in the dark society that underwrote this opulent home, which was, itself, built upon a sprawling grave, in the heart of this alleged slaveless city.

There were several letters from McKiernan. I took all of them. The more samples I had, the better.

"But he'll know they're gone," Chalmers protested.

"Only if you tell him," said Bland.

Chalmers followed us to the door.

"Someone will be in touch with you next week. We have good intelligence that Mr. Simpson, your not-master, will not be back before then. The letters will be returned to you. Put them back into the chest and close it up," Bland said. "And then you'll be done with us. Quick and easy."

It only took a couple days for me to write the passes, along with a few letters testifying to Bland's references in some of the more treacherous regions where he'd be traveling. We had the documents back to Chalmers a day later, and we never heard from him again. Even after things went as they did, nothing was ever traced back to Raymond, Otha, or anyone else at our station. Bland headed to Alabama shortly after. I didn't get to say farewell. I have so rarely been afforded the right of farewell. But this one seemed more significant as the full plan was made good to me by Raymond.

It was the most daring rescue anyone in Philadelphia had ever undertaken. The plan would send Bland west, where he'd take up haven with one of the more capable agents in Cincinnati. He would scout the Ohio River, and find some sort of appropriate landing either in Indiana or Illinois. Once Bland had found a safe landing, he would venture deep into slave country, into the heart of the coffin—Florence, Alabama—and make contact with a Hank Pearson, an old and trusted friend of Otha's still on the McKiernan place. Hank would then bring Lydia, who would know Bland by the possession of a shawl she'd given to Otha as a remembrance of her. Then, posing as their owner, Bland would lead the family back out. Should they become separated, the passes would certify the right of Lydia and her children to be on the road. The plan was not simply daring in its steps, but in its timing. It was early August—a long way from those seemingly endless winter nights that offered an agent of the Underground so much cover. But it had to be done just then, for it was said that McKiernan was on hard times, and might, at any point, start selling off hands, and then our knowledge and planning would be lost.

· 20 ·

IT WAS NOW THE end of summer, the slow season for rescues, so
that we would have had little to do but await news of Bland's
mission. But fortunate for us, the time coincided with an annual
gathering of all those who made legitimate and open war against
slavery—concerned citizens who through the journals, oratory,
and ballot fought for abolition. We in the Underground fought a
secret war, covert, mystical, violent, but were quietly allied with
the open one, and the August meeting was the only time when our
two factions, hailing from across the country, could meet. The
prospect of a reunion with Virginia, with Corrine, filled me with
apprehension. After Bland's departure we began to make our preparations and two weeks later we were off, Raymond, Otha, and I,
aboard a private stage, so that as Bland now made his way south,
we endeavored to make our way farther north, into the mountain-
ous region of New York.

I was coming to understand that Raymond and Otha fought on
both fronts of the war, were leading lights among the abolitionists
while keeping their hands in the darker business into which I had

been drawn. No station east of the Mississippi conducted more coloreds into freedom than those brought through Philadelphia. Adding to that fame was the odyssey of Otha from the depths of Alabama, from the depths of orphanage, into the waiting arms of his family. But on the second night of our carriage ride, we were joined by one whose regard outstripped us all. Moses.

I now knew her not simply as a creature of legend, but through the many exploits detailed in Raymond's files. Still, when she stepped into the coach carrying with her the air of all her adventures, I was so dazzled I barely managed a greeting. She exchanged warm pleasantries with Raymond, nodded at Otha, and then held her gaze on me.

"How you holding up, friend?" she asked. It took a moment before I remembered that when she'd last seen me, I was recovering from Ryland's assault.

"Well," I said.

She had with her a walking stick, as she did that same night I'd seen her out in the woods, and now, in the daylight, I could see that it had across its body a series of carvings and glyphs. She saw me studying the thing and said, "My trusty walking stick, stripped from a branch of the sweet gum tree. Goes wherever I do."

The coach rolled on. I found it incredibly difficult to not stare. Even without her power of Conduction, she was the most daring agent on the Underground. I had seen enough of the world, had read enough of Raymond's files, to know that hers was a soul scarred, but not broken, by the worst of slavery. And I thought then back to my burial in the hole, the time in the jail and those nights when I was hunted as prey. Perhaps I needed it. Perhaps I had to see more of it, to know for myself how low and evil it all really could be. Raymond called this woman Harriet, a name she claimed to prefer over all her other titles. But still he gave her all the respect a soldier might give a great general, answering all her questions while posing few of his own in return, waiting upon her constantly though she rarely requested anything.

A day later, we rolled into the Convention, a campsite nestled in a cleared field, not far from the border with Canada. The land belonged to one of the great benefactors of the Underground, who it was said had plans to resettle a community of coloreds here to task only for themselves. Rain had come a day before our arrival, and as we unloaded from the coach, we sloshed in our brogans. The three of us claimed a space on the outskirts of this camp, toward higher ground, and then dispersed, each to his own way.

I looked out and saw mud-streaked tents extending to the edges of the woods, and then, walking amongst them, saw convention-eers in humor and debate, and then in the larger tents, I saw orators of reform preaching their cause from makeshift platforms. The orators loved spectacle, and seemed to be vying with each other to bring followers to their cause. I waded through the throngs of listeners and paused before a white man in calico breeches and top-hat, who just at that moment was weeping uncontrollably into the sleeve of his coat. Through his tears, he told a tale, which held the audience rapt, of how rum and lager had stripped him of his home and family, until all he had were the clothes in which he was now dressed. And he was resolved, he said, now recovering himself, to remain garbed in this same costume until the curse of spirits was purged from the land.

I walked farther. I stopped before a crush of people and watched as two women, both in overalls, with shaven heads, declaimed on the rights of women to appear with all the freedoms of men, in all the same spheres. And as the women went on, their pitch and volume grew, until not even the gathered audience was spared, for the women now asserted that until we too resolved to take up the cause of suffrage, in this very assembly, we were partners in that vast conspiracy to pillage half the world.

And this pillage continued, I realized, moving farther to still another tent, where a white man stood beside a silent Indian in traditional dress. And the white man spoke of the great depredations he had seen, the iniquitous lengths these Georgians, Carolinians, and Virginians would commit themselves to, in the name of land. And by then, I well knew what would be done upon that land, how the sin of theft would be multiplied by the sin of bondage.

Farther along I went, until I caught sight of a line of children who stood behind a man raging against the factories of this country. The children had been sold into drudgery by parents who could no longer afford them, until they were saved by the beneficence of the society the man represented. Solely through these efforts of charity, the children would be bound to school and rescued from the evils of capital. And farther still, I found that this argument was cousin to another made from a trade unionist, who insisted that the titles of all factories should be stripped from their luxuriating owners and given to those who toiled in them.

And still farther was another related argument made that day, that the factory be rejected in total, that society be condemned a dead letter, and that men and women organize themselves in new communities where all worked together and owned everything in common. And even this was not the pinnacle of the Convention's radicalism, for at the farthest edges of camp, I found a spinster who insisted that I and everyone rebuff even the bonds of marriage, which was itself as a kind of property, a kind of slavery, and ally myself with the doctrine of "free love."

It was late morning now. The sun beat down out of the cloudless August sky. I wiped my brow with my jacket sleeve, and sat for a moment on a tree stump away from the fray of conventioneers and tents. It was all so much—an entire university out on that green. New ways of being, new ideas of liberation, now intruded upon me. Only a year ago, I would have rejected them all. But I had seen so much now, so much beyond even all that I had beheld in my father's books. Where did it end? I could not tell, and this fact both pained me and filled me with joy.

When I looked up, I saw a woman just older than me, standing at the edge of the camp area from where I had just emerged, regarding me closely. When our eyes met, she smiled and approached directly. She had a delicate light brown face, framed by thick black hair that flowed down her cheeks and then to her shoulders.

I stood out of respect and her smile now disappeared. She surveyed me from head to foot, as though trying to be sure of something, and then she said the last thing I expected to hear.

"How are you, Hi?"

Had I heard this elsewhere, under other circumstances, it would have been a relief, for I would have been filled with thoughts of home. Immediately I began shuffling through a deck of questions, uppermost being how this woman had gotten hold of my name.

"It's all right," she said. "It's all gonna be all right now." Then she extended a hand and said, "I'm Kessiah."

I declined her greeting, but she continued on, registering no insult.

"I'm from your place—Elm County, Virginia. Lockless. You don't remember me. You remember everything, but you don't remember me. It's all right. I used to look after you when you were a baby. Your mother would leave you with me when she had to—"

"Who?"

"Your mother—Momma Rose, we called her—she would leave you with me. And the way I have heard it, you know mine—Thena is her name. She lost her children some years ago. All five of them sold on the racetrack of Starfall, sent off to God knows where. But I am here now with the Underground, and I have heard that there was one who was here too, who came up just as I did, and I have heard that that one is you."

"Can we walk?" I asked.

"We surely can," she said.

I led her farther away from the Convention toward that outer portion of the green, on higher ground, where we had tied up our coach and pitched our tent. I helped her into the seat and then climbed up and seated myself next to her.

"It's true," she said, looking straight ahead. "It's all true. I can tell you how it happened if you like."

"I most certainly would like," I said.

"Well, it's as I told you, you know? I'm Thena's baby—her oldest one. We lived down on the Street and I have some fond memories of that time. My daddy was a big man in those days, a headman on the tobacco team, and that is to say he was about as big as you can be when you was Tasked.

"We had our own house at the end of the Street, set off from the others and bigger too. I thought this was all on account of my daddy and the high esteem in which he was held by those up top. He was a hard man. I do not remember him speaking much, but I recall that when the Quality came down to address him they spoke with him in a kind of respect that they accorded no other tasking man."

And Kessiah paused here, and a look of realization came over her. Then she said, "Or perhaps that is all in my mind. Perhaps it is the memory of a child, trying to recall things as I would have liked it to have been. I do not know. But I do have it that way, I tell you. I remember the games we used to play. I remember the marbles. I remember the ball and string. I remember playing the Knight and the Whistle. But mostly, I remember my momma, who was as warm and lovely a woman as I ever did know. I remember Sundays, just laying up in her bosom—all five of us—like kittens. My daddy was a hard man, but I think I knew even then that something about him had protected us, that he was doing something, or had done something, for all of us to have that cabin, set off at the end. We had our own garden out back, our own camellias. And that was my life."

Kessiah was looking out over toward the tents we had just left, lost in a reverie. I was lost in my own, remembering Thena all those years ago, puffing on her pipe and recalling that man she loved, Big John. It seemed incredible to me that this Kessiah could be their daughter, could be here of all places.

"But I got bigger and was soon put to work—at first carrying water out to the folks in the field, and then after that in the fields myself. But I did not mind, all my friends were there too and I was close to my daddy. It was hard labor, that I knew, but I was always inclined to hard labor, it's what put me here on the Underground. But back then my world was the fields and the Street, and the Street is how I knew you, Hi, and knew your mother and knew your aunt Emma. On weekends the older folks would go down to the woods for their little dances and would leave me to watch over the babies, and you was one of those. I am not so surprised to find you here. You were always different. You just watched, watched everything, and I was thinking when I spotted you up here how you have not changed, how you were just watching. It is my blessing to find you, to meet you again out here, so far from the Task.

"It was such a different time, and it amazes me, shames me almost, to say that I was happy back there, but I do believe I was, for a time, and I recall when the feeling changed. It was when my daddy fell. Fever, you know. That hit my momma hard. She was still warm as ever, but she was so grieved. Would cry every night and call us to her, 'Come in and rest with your momma,' she would say, and we—all of us kittens—would lay there with her and she would just cry, and all of us would cry with her. But I tell you, Hi, this was nothing measured against what was coming. Least when my daddy passed, we had each other. But, well, soon we ain't even had that—was like all of us passed from each other, like all of us died and was damned to a different hell."

Kessiah now turned to me and said, "They say you knew my momma, a little."

I nodded and intended to say no more, for I could not yet bring myself to fully accept the story. But I could see Kessiah regarding me with expectant eyes. An expectation I knew well.

"She was not exactly as you say it here," I said. "But I believe it was the same woman. And more I believe she had reason to be as she was, as I knew her. But I don't think that much matters. What matters is that she was good to me. That, for me, Thena was the best part of Lockless."

Kessiah cupped her hands and brought them to her face so that they covered her nose and mouth and she cried gently and quietly.

And then she said, "So you know about the racetrack?"

"I do," I said.

"Imagine that. All of us, my brothers and sisters, taken out there and sold. Do you know I never saw them again? Do you know how hard I have tried to find them? But there are so many gone, Hi. Like water between my fingers. Gone."

"I . . . I know," I said. "I did not always know. But I know now. Your mother, she tried to tell me. But I did not always know what it meant to be handled as such. But I am seeing it now."

"They used to say your daddy was a white man."

"He was," I said.

"Didn't save you, did it?"

"No. Don't save none of us."

"No, it don't, and I am here before you only on a chance. Most of mine was taken Natchez-way, but I was carried off up to Maryland and put to work out in the timbers, and not so long after, I met this man, Elias, and we took a shine to each other. Elias was a freeman who worked for his own wage and he planned to buy me off so that I might live free too.

"Timbers was hard labor, but I found me another family. I refashioned myself for that new life, formed myself around that man, and I got to something close to happy. I knew that I could never again be a girl. And I knew that I was marked, very harshly, by what had come before. But I found something, and just when I did, Hi, I tell you they endeavored to put me right back on the block. But I had something for them this time, you see. I had married into a family of a particular sort, and among that family there was the one who you know as Moses."

And Kessiah was now laughing to herself at the thought of it.

249

"You should have seen it. Me and Elias had said our farewells. It had been so hard. And then the day of, he shows up in the auction and starts bidding. And my heart is leaping because it's him and some other man all the way from Texas. And they go back and forth until my Elias look at me with the saddest eyes. And I know he done lost, and Texas done won. And Texas pays his money and shuts me up in a cell. You should have heard him and all his intentions. He was so high and mighty. Sunrise we'll be off, he tells me. Hah! Sunrise. He don't know. Sun came sure enough. But Moses got there first."

Moses, I thought. Conduction.

Now Kessiah looked at me. "It was a plan, you see. They bid me up as high as they could. Made the man pay and then got me out. My Lord, after I seen that, after I seen what Moses had done to them, I could not go back to that life. I thought of all the hell they had given to me. And I thought of how good it felt to give some back in good measure. And I thought of all my pains and how many more there were like me, and all I wanted thereafter was to be on this Underground.

"I been with Moses ever since. Was how I heard about you, Hi. Some boy, they tell me, come up from Virginia—Elm County, *my county*. And I start to checking and I hear your name, and I could not believe it, but my God, it was you. Soon as I seen you here wandering and watching, I knew it was you."

At that she threw herself on me and embraced me, and when she did, much to my surprise, I was warmed. I had been away from home so long. And now, there I was with some memory of it, with someone else who had made the same journey. It was getting late and we each had to find our people. We stood and embraced again and she said, "We'll have more time, you and I. We will have more days here."

Then she looked at me and said, "Oh my, I don't know how I forgot to ask, been talking so much myself. How is Momma Rose? How is your mother?"

Soon I was walking again among the tents and saw that exhortation had given way to amusements. There were teams of jugglers who tossed fruit and bottles amongst each other. There were daredevils who extended a thin cable between the heights of two trees and walked across once, and then danced their way back again while singing a tune. There were acrobats who tumbled and twisted and leaped in mid-air.

And how was my mother? How fared Momma Rose? I still had no recollection of her, only the stories assembled from those like Kessiah who'd known her, so that when I thought of her, it was like a scene sketched of some ancient myth, not like I remembered Sophia, not like I remembered Thena—Thena who had never been more alive to me than she was in that moment with Kessiah, with the recollections of the daughter mixing with my own. And I felt that I now understood so much, that I knew why she had been so hard with me. Her injunction: *I am more your mother standing right here now than that white man on that horse is your father.*

We all joined for supper—Otha, Raymond, Kessiah, Moses, and I—and afterward, with the sun now low in the sky, a group of colored folk assembled around a bonfire. They began, in the slowest, most haunting voices, to sing the songs that could only be made down in the coffin. I had not heard these songs since I had left, and hearing them now, I felt them tugging at me, I felt myself swaying in the August heat. It was all too much. I left and went to roam, with my thoughts, among the muddy byways between the rows of tents.

I sat down on a patch of dry grass just beyond the tents, where I could still hear my people singing in the distance. I was reeling from the day—Kessiah, the memories of Thena and Big John, the arguments and ideas about women, children, labor, land, family, and wealth. It occurred to me that an examination of the Task revealed not just those evils particular to Virginia, to my old world, but the great need for a new one entirely. Slavery was the root of all struggle. For it was said that the factories enslaved the hands of children, and that child-bearing enslaved the bodies of women, and that rum enslaved the souls of men. In that moment I understood, from that whirlwind of ideas, that this secret war was waged against something more than the Taskmasters of Virginia, that we sought not merely to improve the world, but to remake it.

I was pulled out of my thoughts by a man milling around nearby. I was greeted by a messenger who handed me a parcel, with a seal, which I immediately recognized as the mark of Micajah Bland. My heart leapt. My greatest urging then was to open this letter. But it was Otha's family, and it should be he who first understood their fate. I found him with Raymond, still near the bonfire, still enraptured by the slave songs that were ringing out. I handed the letter to Raymond, who was the better reader. On Otha's face, alight with the bonfire's glow, was all the trepidation we could expect. But then Raymond smiled and said, "Micajah Bland has Lydia and the children. They have passed out of Alabama. At the time of this letter, they were traversing Indiana."

"My God," said Otha. "My God."

He turned to me and said, "It's gonna happen. After all of these years, my Lydia, my boys—all of them—my God, I wish Lambert had made it to see this."

Otha then turned back to Raymond and burst into tears. Raymond broke his usual solemn mask, and held Otha close as they wept. I turned away, thinking they needed their time, overrun by a day filled with more wonders than I could fathom.

ONCE I'D DREAMED OF ruling, as my father had done, back at Lockless, and it is tough to say it as such, that it was my dream, even if I had not thought it all through. But I had found the Underground, or the Underground had found me, and for this fact I was at last happy. On the Underground, I found meaning. In Raymond White, in Otha, in Micajah, I found family. And now in Kessiah, I felt that I had even found some lost part of myself.

The next evening, after another day of exhortations and amusements, I decided to walk through the woods, high into the hills above the field, and that's where I saw her, Moses, seated on a large rock, her legs folded. She was still and at peace and I thought perhaps to leave her to her thoughts, but when I began to walk away I heard her voice cut through the quiet night air.

"Evening."

I turned and saw her already walking toward me, her eyes fixed on my head. When close enough, she reached out to feel the spot where I had taken Ryland's blow. Then she stepped back, smiled, and said, "I knew we would have our time to speak, and it is good to do so out here, far removed from them. Heard a lot about you," she said. "And then Kessiah said you spoke more just yesterday."

"Yes," I said. "We're from the same home-place, as it happens."

"Uh-huh, she told me as much. Good to see someone from home, ain't it? Give you some sense of roots. It must be hard on you to be so far from your roots."

"Aren't we all?" I asked.

"No," she said. "Me, I'm home fairly often, even if the masters would like it different. I work in one place, and it is the place I know best—the far shore of Maryland, my home. Someday I shall return there for good, but not like this, not as no agent, but in the bright and open sun. But in the by-time, I am there fairly often and it is good to get back, good to remember."

"I remember plenty," I said.

"I know you do. Way I hear it, your talent is such that you are as good working in the house of Philadelphia as you were in the fields of Virginia. And I have heard it whispered that you, particularly, might be able to work even more."

"I've heard that too," I said. "But it's all horse and no saddle."

"Huh," she said. "Give it time."

"I think it ain't really up to me. I want my people out. But I see it. There are so many people. And I can see them all now."

"Oh, I am so glad to hear you say that," she said. She was smiling at me mischievously. And I felt, in fact knew, that I had just then enrolled myself into something. "Here is the thing, friend, I work small and I work alone. I move by my own time and my particular vigilance. But for this one job I need a man who runs least well as he writes, and I am told that you are one of the few, this side of the Underground, who qualifies."

"Can't see why you need any help from me. I know they call you Moses. And that name comes out of a majestic power, don't it?"

"Majestic," she said. "That's a big word for something so simple."

"But the stories," I said. "I know what they say. Moses tamed oxen as a girl and harrowed the fields like a man. Moses talk to the wolves. Moses brought the clouds to earth. Knives melt upon the garments of Moses. Bullwhips turn to ash in the slave-master's hand."

She laughed. "That what they say, huh?"

"That and a lot more."

"Well, here is what I will tell you," she said. "My methods are not for the offering. It's the Underground, not the Overground. This ain't no show. I don't advertise like Box Brown. Put before something they can't understand, people got a tendency to talk— and also to make something bigger than what they actually saw. However it play, understand that talk don't come from me. I speak no more than required, and leave the passenger to their colors and wide tales. And as for names, I answer to one—Harriet."

"So no Conduction, then?" I asked.

"Big words. Big words," she said. "All I want to know is you ready to work. I'm headed back home. And you have been recommended to me as one who could well do a turn. So do you wish to work, or do you want to while away the hours quizzing me?"

"Of course I want to work. When do we leave and who are we after?"

It was only then that I heard the eagerness in my own voice, the powerful desire to work with this woman of whom I had heard so many stories.

"I am sorry," I said. "I stand ready whenever you would have it."

"Go on back to the camp," she said. "Enjoy the show."

She then walked back to her boulder and, turning away from me, said, "We be moving soon enough. Might even get you that saddle."

The next morning, I woke up to a grand commotion outside the tent. I heard Otha's voice, lost in a kind of hysteria. And then I heard Raymond and some others, whom I did not recognize. They were trying to calm him and I think right then I must have known, because no matter our troubles, Otha almost never was one for such commotion. Something truly terrible must have come. I stepped outside the tent. It was barely first light, but I could clearly see Otha's head buried in the shoulder of his brother, and he was swaying almost, barely able to stand.

Raymond saw me first. His eyes widened and he shook his head. Otha, perhaps sensing me there, broke away from his brother and turned to me. I saw an entire funeral on his face.

"Have you heard?" Otha asked me. "Have you heard what they done did?"

I did not answer.

"Hiram," Raymond said. "We can explain it all later. We have to . . ." And at that Raymond just shook his head in disbelief, and tried to guide Otha away. "Come on, Otha," he said. "Come on . . ."

"Come on where?" Otha said. "Where can we go, Raymond? For the doing of what? It's over. Can't you see that it's over? They got Lydia in the coffin. Where we gon go? Micajah Bland is dead. Where can any of us go?"

And then Otha turned to me. "Did you hear that, Hiram?" he asked. And I saw that his face had gone from pain to rage. "Did you hear what they did? They killed him. Chained his body, bashed in his head, and threw him in the river."

And Otha burst into tears as he said this, and Raymond and several of the men pulled him away from the tent. He nearly came to blows with them at first. He yelled and screamed and kicked, until Raymond took hold of him. Now they led him, almost carried him, away and I could hear Otha yelling the whole time, "Did you hear what they done did? Micajah Bland is in the water! And what we gon do now?"

I stood there rooted, until I could no longer see them. And then I stood there longer, struck wholly dumb. When I came out of it,

I saw that there was a commotion all around me. The news was spreading across the camp. I could see people talking amongst each other in groups and those groups shifting among others to share whatever rumor or intelligence they'd garnered of Micajah Bland's fate. And then I looked down and saw a satchel not far from where Otha and Raymond had stood. On instinct I reached for the satchel and carried it back into my tent, and when I opened it, I found a collection of newspapers, detailing the saga of Micajah Bland and Lydia White. The first item told the tale—"Runaway Negroes Taken." The second confirmed that it was, indeed, the family of Otha White. My hands trembled as I thumbed through the third—"Thief of Negroes Returned to Alabama." And then finally a dispatch from an Indiana agent, who wrote with great sorrow, communicating the news—the body of Micajah Bland had that morning washed up on the shore. Head stove in. Hands bound behind him in chains.

By then, I had been trained to package away misery. And so what I thought of in that moment was not Micajah Bland, but the simple task of getting those papers back to Raymond and Otha. I moved among the crowd. A few people, knowing my affiliation with the Philadelphia station, tried to stop me and ask what I might know. I ignored them, and scanned among the tents for a clue as to where they might have taken Otha. I saw some of the agents of the western Underground before a tent. One of them waved to me—"Here," he said. Then another parted the entrance for me, and walking in I saw Otha seated there with Raymond. Otha was calmer now, though still smoldering. There were a few others whom I recognized as clearly senior within the loose leadership of the Underground. Harriet was there, and most shockingly, seated calmly—Corrine Quinn.

There was not much time to weigh her presence. The conversation halted when I entered.

"I am sorry," I said, walking over to Raymond, "but I thought you might need these."

Raymond thanked me, and I took my leave, allowing the meeting to continue. I walked away from the camp, back toward the woods where I'd met Harriet a day before. I sat there, on that same boulder where Harriet had sat. Would that I could open a door right here in the woods, I thought, and pull the cotton fields of Alabama to the forests of New York. But I had nothing. A power was within me, but with no thought of how to access it or control it, I was lost.

I returned and found the camp still in mourning. It was afternoon by then. I went to my tent and lay down. When I awoke, Otha was there seated in a chair next to me. Otha was a man of true feeling, but never wild in his passions, or flagrant in his rages. I had never seen him as he was two days before in joy, nor as he was that morning in agony.

"Otha," I said. "I'm sorry. I . . . I don't even know what to say. I have never met Lydia or your children, but I have heard so much of them now that I feel them as family."

"He was my brother, Hiram," Otha said. "Micajah Bland was not my blood, but he was so much my brother that he would die for me and mine. I am not young to any of this. I lived divided from my blood, and made brothers wherever I lived, and grieved every time we were divided—and we were *always* divided. But I have never, for an instant, shied away from connection, from love.

"I am sorry about my anger this morning. Raymond did not deserve it, and I am sorry you saw me as such."

"There's no need, Otha."

He was silent for a few minutes. I said nothing, thinking that this was Otha's time.

"I want to tell you a story about dreaming. I want to tell you, specifically, because I know you have struggled to see your place, struggled to touch that power they all say is in you. And if in this pain I can give something to you, that would well soothe me too."

I sat up in my pallet and listened.

"I met my wife, Lydia, shortly after Lambert died. Lambert was

258

older, stronger, and braver. He was my heart, and my faith, and whenever I fell to despair, it was his unflagging belief that set me straight. And then to see him go under as he did, feeling that we would never get home, that God had truly indeed blighted us. A torrent of ugly came over me. I spent many nights in the very state that you saw me this morning. Perhaps you know about this, a pain that reaches out and falls over your heart like night.

"I found my only balm was in the work, Tasked though I was. My mind disappeared into my hands and I was soothed by the fields. The whites thought it was my great morality. They thought me gracious under the lash. But I hated them all, Hiram, for as sure as they had ripped me from the cradle, they had right well murdered my brother.

"In this state I met Lydia. Perhaps, having been born into Alabama, she knew more about the weight, and was better fitted to carry the great burden of a bonded life. I would rage and she would laugh, and soon enough I found myself laughing along. And then I would be angry that she had diminished me to laughter. And I would laugh at the whole heap of the thing again. We were to be married, and I felt myself come back to the world. I was tied to something, you see.

"A few days before we were married, I came to see Lydia and found her back-sore. She was well-liked and highly valued by all the Quality, and had never been condemned to a seven and nine. She told me it was the boss's headman. He had been hot after her. She would not submit. And so he whipped her, claiming it done on account of her sassing him.

"When I heard that, my blood got up. I stood to leave without saying a word. She asked what I planned to do. I said, 'Kill him.'

" 'Don't you dare,' Lydia said.

" 'Why not?' I asked.

" 'Because they will shoot you and you knows it,' she said.

" 'I'll see that as it comes,' I said. 'But on my manhood, I gotta make this right.'

"'Damn your manhood and every inch of you to hell if you touch one hair on that white man's head.'

"'But you are mine, Lydia,' I said. 'And it's my duty to make you protected.'

"'And you gonna protect me from under the ox, too?' she asked. 'I picked you for a reason. You done told me your story, and I know that you have some notion of a place beyond this. Otha, it's got to be about more than this. It's got to be about more than anger, more than manhood. We got plans, me and you. And this is not our end. This is not how you and me die.'

"Those words have never left me, you understand that, Hiram. I dream about 'em—*This is not our end,* she say. *This is not how you and me die.* She had taken the whip. But I was the one who was claiming to be wounded. I was supposed to love her. But all I was truly loving was my own regard.

"I know you can picture what horror we saw through our union, what horror, at this very moment, my Lydia, my children, must still see. But what I want you to see is what I am trying to now save, what sent Bland down under, and that is all that my Lydia and me built together—the jests that belong to only us, our children who are an honor upon us, a feeling so deep that it calls across this whole continent. Lydia saved my life, Hiram, and I will give anything to save hers.

"Micajah Bland knew all of this. And they killed him for it. I grieve more than you know."

Now he rose and held open the slit of the tent.

"My Lydia will be free," he said. "This is not how we die. My Lydia will be free."

· 22 ·

That next morning, it came the hour to decamp, and having gathered my affairs in my carpet-bag, I wandered through the field and watched as this wondrous city of new ideas, of visions and liberated futures, of men and women, which sprung up in the fields, fell back into nothing. I took a walk in the woods, so as to enjoy the country air one last time before my descent into the smoke and filth of the city. When I returned, Raymond, Otha, and Harriet were all finishing their preparations. I saw Kessiah nearby tightening the strap on a traveling piece. When she saw me, she put her hand to her mouth, walked over, pulled me close into a hug, and said, "I am so sorry, Hi. I am so deeply sorry."

"I appreciate it," I said. "But no concern should be put upon me. Not with Otha's family still lost."

"I know. But I also know Micajah Bland was something to you," she said. And she gripped my arm tight, almost as a mother would a child.

"Before you," I said, "he was my closest connection back to the old place. Not that I would ever wish it, but it is truly something for him to leave me just as you came."

"It is," she said. "Maybe someone is watching for you."

She smiled and I felt a warmth between us. I had met Kessiah only three days before, but already I had been drawn into her. She was the elder sister I had never thought to need, the plug in the hole that I had not even known was there.

"Thank you, Kessiah," I said. "I hope I shall see you soon. In fact, should you have some time, please put down a few lines for me."

"I'd surely like to," she said. "I am of the field, though, so I cannot say I can match eloquence with one such as you. Anyway, I shall be traveling to Philadelphia with you—me and Harriet. Micajah Bland's going as he did has changed some things. Likely we will have to change too."

We embraced again. I reached down for her bag and carried it over to the coach and stowed it away. When I looked back, I saw that Raymond and Otha and Harriet had been joined by Corrine and, to my surprise, Hawkins and Amy. They were all in deep conversation and exchanging embraces and affectionate words for Otha. I had never seen them so soft with each other, but too I had never seen the Underground in mourning for one of its own. Corrine looked different. She had traded in the mask of Virginia—her hair flowed down to her shoulders. Her ivory dress was plain. She wore neither powder nor rouge. When Hawkins spotted me, he nodded and gave, as much as was possible for him, a look of concern.

We rode in a caravan of three coaches. Otha, Raymond, and I in the first coach, Corrine, Hawkins, and Amy in the second, and finally Harriet, Kessiah, and their driver, a young man conducted recently by Harriet, who swore himself to her. We bedded down that night at a small inn about an hour's ride north of Manhattan island. But sleep brought me not one measure of peace, for no sooner had I closed my eyes than I found myself lost in baneful nightmares, so that I was out in the water, out in the river Goose, bursting through the waves, and when I came up I saw, all again, May drowning before me. And I thought myself back there, and seeing, already, the blue light gathering around, and knowing that the power was in me, I decided that this one would be different. But when I reached out, Little May turned and I saw it was not him but Micajah Bland.

I awoke with a dreadful thought. I had created the passes, I had forged the letters of introduction. The fault for all this must lie with me. I thought of Simpson. I thought of McKiernan. I thought of Chalmers. I ran through all the events of that night. I thought of the days following and all the practiced forgeries. And I remembered that it was sometimes perfection that gave up the house agent, that sometimes the passes were too good, too practiced, and aroused suspicion. It had been me, I was certain of it.

I had killed Micajah Bland. I had nearly killed Sophia. Perhaps I had doomed my mother, somehow, and maybe that is why I could not remember. I felt my chest tighten. I could not breathe. I rose from my bed, dressed, and then stumbled outside. I sat on the back porch and bent over and breathed and breathed and breathed. Sitting up, I saw a garden in the back. It was still late evening. I walked through the garden, and as I approached I heard familiar voices. Hawkins, Corrine, and Amy were there all seated on a circle of benches, each of them smoking a cigar. We exchanged brief greetings and I took my seat. By the moonlight, I saw Corrine inhale and then breathe out a long stream of smoke. And for a few long minutes there was only the night music of insects. Then Corrine took it upon herself to speak what was in all of our minds.

"He was an uncommon man," she said. "I knew him well—and liked him very much more. He was so uncommon. He found me all those years ago. He saved me. He showed me a world that I had not even glimpsed. I am not here without him."

There was now more silence and I watched as the faces around me alighted in the glow of the cigars. Guilt took hold of me, and I said, "He saved me too. Saved me from Ryland. Saved me from all those dumb notions of the swamps. Was he that first introduced me to books. I owe him more than could ever be known."

Amy nodded and then reached into her pouch. She offered a cigar. I took it and nodded a thank-you, then played with it between my fingers. Then I leaned into Hawkins, who struck up a light. I inhaled deep and said, "But I have learned. I tell you I have learned some things."

"We all know, Hiram," said Hawkins. "Somebody say you headed down Maryland-way, goin down with Moses, as they say."

"If she still would have me."

"Oh, she will," Hawkins said. "Moses would not stop for Bland, no more than Bland would have stopped for her. Might wait a few, but she is going. It is truly a terrible thing. But it also just as he would want—an uncommon man, as you say—but he went just as every one of us would want."

I felt sick at that moment. I remembered my dream. I said, "And how was that?"

"Sure you want to know?" Amy asked. She said this softly and somehow this caused the whole blow to land with even greater effect. But I did want to know. As much as possible, I did, and my guilt stripped me of all my guile, so that as I inhaled this time, I began to cough and choke, and this gave Hawkins a great laugh, and then the whole party of them laughed together. And I watched them laughing until they all settled back into their silence. And when they had, I calmly said, "The papers. I did the papers. I believe it was me who got that man killed."

This was the cause for more laughter, but this time only from Hawkins and Amy.

"I did the papers," I said again. "No other way a man like Bland would have gotten caught, except by my hand."

"What you mean ain't no other way?" asked Hawkins. "All kinds of ways."

"Especially in Alabama," said Amy.

"The papers," I said. "That got him caught."

"No. That is not what happened at all," Corrine said. "It had nothing to do with his papers."

"What then?" I asked.

"He was so close," Corrine said. "So close. He spent all those weeks scouting the shore along the Ohio River, until he found the perfect landing. We don't precisely know how he did it, but he found Lydia with her boys and rowed down the Tennessee posing as their owner until he was in the free country of Indiana. But then, as I understand it, one of the children got sick, and it became hard on them to continue their travels by night."

"That's how they got picked up," said Hawkins. "White man stopped 'em for questioning. Thought Bland's story was funny and took 'em to a local jail, waiting to see if it was any word on runaways."

"There was," said Amy.

"Bland could have left right there," Hawkins said. "They had nothing on him. But as we've got it from the papers and dispatches of agents in the area, he kept trying to get to Lydia and the kids, until they jailed him too."

"We do not know how he was ultimately killed," Corrine said. "But knowing Bland, he would have continued looking for an escape. And I suspect that his captors realized that the delivery of their Negroes, and the claiming of a likely reward, would be easier without an agent fixed on getting those Negroes away."

"My Lord, my Lord," I moaned.

"And damn y'all for sending him," Hawkins said. "Alabama? All kinds of ways to get caught. Into the coffin for some babies?"

I could have told Hawkins all that I had learned. I could have told him about Otha White. I could have told him about gingerbread. I could have told him about Thena and Kessiah. I could have told him how much more there was to the Underground, more than math and any angle, more than movement.

But Hawkins was grieving in his own way, I knew. I was feeling it more even now, for the levels of grief and loss now began to unspool. Sophia, Micajah Bland, Georgie, my mother. I was not even angry about it. By then I knew that this was part of the work, to accept the losses. But I would not accept them all.

· 23 ·

Back in Philadelphia, I returned to my routine, alternating between my woodworking and the Underground. There was not much time for mourning. It was now September and the high season of conduction would soon be upon us. There was some concern that Bland had somehow been betrayed. We reviewed our entire system. Codes were changed. Methods of movement revised. Certain agents came under scrutiny. Relations with the western Underground were never the same again, for it was thought that they might have, witting or not, played some role in Bland's destruction.

I saw Kessiah quite a bit that month. This was the only good thing to come out of the moment, for it truly was like the discovery of some relative long lost. At the start of October, Harriet called on me. She suggested a walk through the city. So we headed toward the Schuylkill docks, then across the South Street bridge toward the western boundaries of the city.

It was a cool, crisp afternoon. The leaves had begun to change and the people to bind themselves up in their long black coats and woolen scarves. Harriet wore a long brown dress, a cotton wrapper around her waist, and a bag across her body. For the first twenty minutes or so, we spoke only of bland things. Then as we moved farther out and the people began to fall away, our conversation veered toward its true destination.

"How you holding up, friend?" Harriet asked.

"Not so good," I said. "I don't know how anyone holds up against this. Bland was not the first, was he? Not the first agent you lost, I mean. Not for you."

"No, friend, he was not," said Harriet. "And he won't be the last. You had better get that."

"I do," I said.

"No, you don't," she said. "This is war. Soldiers fight in war for all kinds of reasons, but they die because they cannot bear to live in the world as it is. And that right there was the Micajah Bland I knew. He could not live. Not here, not like this. He put it all on the line—his life, his connections, his sister's heart—because he knew that that is exactly the line on which all the rest of us must live."

We stopped walking here for a moment.

"I know that you don't understand," Harriet said. "But you will adjust yourself to these facts. You will have to. There will be more. Could be you. Could be me."

"No, never you," I said, now smiling.

"Someday it will be me," she said. "Just hoping that the only hounds I answer to are held by my Lord."

The talk quickly turned to the business at hand.

"So you're with me, friend," said Harriet. "It ain't the coffin, this is true, but Maryland is still Pharaoh's land. I know what they say about me, but understand that this is never what I say about myself. We all the same when the hound got the scent. That axe swing and any man might be lumber. And with that, all that I have learned shall be nothing, shall be dust upon the long road. You will not find me believing in my own miracles, but in the strictest principles of the Underground."

And then she smiled softly and said, "But there are so many miracles. As when I was told of a man who did not merely conduct but self-resurrected, who hoisted himself out of the ice, a man who, pursued by the hounds, felt a longing for home so fierce that he blinked and he was there."

"That what they say, huh?" I asked.

"That's what they say," she said. "I never told you what happened with me, did I?"

"You don't tell much of nothing about yourself at all. Ain't much for giving out stories, as you said."

"Yeah. I did say that. So we'll wait on that one. Don't matter much, either way. What I am asking is that you put more trust in me than your own failings."

We turned around and headed back toward Bainbridge Street, again walking mostly in silence. When we got back home, we sat in the front parlor.

"So, Maryland," I said.

"Maryland," she said. Then she reached into her bag and produced a file of letters.

"I need two things: First a pass, drawn from the shadow of this hand. I need the pass to be for two."

I started scribbling notes.

"Then I need a letter in slave-hand. Remit it to Jake Jackson of Poplar Neck—Dorchester, Maryland. From his brother Henry Jackson. Beacon Hill, Boston. Give him all the loving tidings a brother would, and do it whatever way should come to you. But note this portion particularly: *Tell my brothers to be watchful unto prayer and when the good old ship of Zion come along, be ready to step onboard.*

I nodded, still scribbling.

"Have that letter off by tomorrow's post. We got to give the thing time to land and make its effect. Then we are on our way. We leave in two weeks. One night's journey."

I stopped and gave a puzzled look.

"Wait," I said. "One night? Ain't enough time to get to Maryland."

She just looked back and smiled.

"Nowhere near enough time," I said.

But two weeks later, in the dead of night, I walked out of the Ninth Street station, down Market Street, where all was asleep, and met Harriet at the docks of the Delaware River. We headed south past the coal depot, past the South Street pier where the Red Bank ferry bobbed in its moorings, until we stood before an array of older, battered piers that were little more than rotted wood groaning and creaking as they swayed in the night-black river. I looked farther down the docks and saw that these shadowy ruins diminished into mere stakes jutting out of the water.

The October wind blew up off the river. I looked up and saw that clouds obscured the stars and moon, which so often guided us. Fog rolled up. Harriet stood at the pier, looking out into the night, out through the fog, toward the invisible banks of Camden, but in fact far past them. She was leaning on her trusty walking stick, the one I'd seen her with on our way to New York. She said, "For Micajah Bland." And then she began to walk on the shattered pier before us directly out into the river.

That I followed, and did not question, tells you exactly how much faith I had placed in Harriet by then. She was our Moses and I believed even in my fear that she would somehow split the sea that now stood before us. And so I walked.

I heard Harriet say, "For all those who have sailed off to the port from which there can be no return."

I heard the wet wood of the pier groan under my weight, but the planks felt sturdy beneath my feet. I looked back, but a fog had encircled us on all sides, and thickened so that I could no longer see the city behind me. I looked forward and saw Harriet still walking out.

"We forgot nothing, you and I," Harriet said. "To forget is to truly slave. To forget is to die."

And at that Harriet stopped in her tracks. There was a light growing now, out of the darkness. At first I thought Harriet had lit a lantern, for the light was low and faint. And then I saw that the light was not yellow but a pale spectral green, and I saw that this light was not in Harriet's hand, but was in Harriet herself.

She turned to me, with eyes of the same green fire that had grown up out of the night.

"To remember, friend," she said. "For memory is the chariot, and memory is the way, and memory is bridge from the curse of slavery to the boon of freedom."

That was when I saw that we were in the water. No, not in it, over it. We should have been under it, for I knew that the pier was gone and there was no longer anything of this world beneath our feet. The Delaware River is deep enough for a steamer to come into harbor. But the water barely lapped against my boots.

"Stay with me, friend," Harriet said. "No exertions needed. It's just like dancing. Stay with the sound, stay with the story and you will be fine. And the story is as I have said, offered up for all those given over to the maw of the Demon. We seen it all our lives, yes we have. Starts when you young, with but the barest sense of the world, but mayhaps even then, you got some sense that it is wrong. I know I did."

What happened then was a kind of communion, a chain of memory extending between the two of us that carried more than any words I can now offer you here, because the chain was ground into some deep and locked-away place, where my aunt Emma lived, where my mother lived, where a great power lived, and the chain extended into that selfsame place in Harriet, where all those lost ones had taken up their vigil. And then I looked out and saw them, phantoms flittering, flittering like that baleful day out on the river Goose, and I knew exactly what the phantoms were and what they meant to Harriet.

So when I saw the boy off to the side of us, out in the mist, wrapped in spectral green, no older than twelve, I knew that his name was Abe, and I knew that he was among those gone Natchez-way, sent across "the river with no name." And now I could hear Harriet's voice again, in that deep place where the chain was anchored and rooted.

"You were not acquainted with this Abe," she said. "But by the light of this Conduction, you shall know him right well. I regret that he will not be joining us on the way back. It is regrets of Abe that sent me to the Underground."

Now the light of Harriet opened with some brightness, and I saw a path before us, across the water that was not water. There was no dock in the distance, but in and out of the darkness I saw the phantoms of Harriet's memory—dancing about, as they would have been in that time when they were known to her. And as we approached and passed each one, the phantoms fell away.

"You know me well, friend," she said. "I was made under the lash. I was only seven when Master Broadus sent me trapping varmints in the swamps. I might like to lose a limb out there. But I come back whole—out the cage, not the jungle. When I was nine, they call me up to the Big House and I was given the entirety of the parlor's care. My errors were many. My mistress beat me, every day, with a rope. I began to think that this was God's plan. That I really was the wretch they made me out to be, and deserved no more than the abuses I received.

"Now, for all my humiliations, the fact of it is that there was some corners of hell to which I, thankfully, received no invitation. I speak now of the crossing of the nameless, of the long walk to Natchez, the mournful march to Baton Rouge. I saw it all, friend. Why, my uncle Hark lost half an arm just thinking of the nameless, just watching them white men watch him a little too closely.

272

So one morning he got up, and thinking how hard it'd be to sell a cripple, raised his axe with one hand, and gave the other hand over to the Lord. 'I might be lame,' Hark say. 'But I shall not be parted.'

"Hark was uncommon. Most just took the walk, leaving in their wake wailing wives, broken husbands, and orphans. And then there was our boy Abe—whose wide wondrous face I see before me right now, easy as I did in that other life—a well-mannered boy who done only as he was told. His momma died in the birthing, and his daddy was long sold away. Whatever pains he felt over these partings, he never shared. He spoke only as a child should—when induced by elder folk—and these elders, knowing his pain, however hidden, were soft upon him.

"But for those who were hard, for those who worshipped the seven and nine, Abe was a caution. I tell you, friend, that boy could not be held. Would have made a hell of an agent, for he ran like he had the lungs of a lion. The moment Master Broadus even thought of correction, the boy would fly.

"Sometimes the headman would call us up to help hold him. We might make some motion as such, but in our hearts we were with Abe. You know what it is—the Tasked must take they victories as they come. And if you saw Abe, as we did, blazing through the wheat field, hurtling through the high corn, you would have seen our deepest unspeaking—freedom, friend, freedom. In those moments running, he was free, unweighted by the partings, unbroken by the seven and nine. And watching him is how I got my first taste of Conduction, of the great power in even the smallest of escapes."

Harriet paused here for some moments and we moved again in silence. I was gripped by her telling and could see the events of her narrative open up before me. And so full was the brilliance beaming out from her that all features of our path stood in green relief.

"I stood outside the town emporium, minding my own. And like lightning, I seen young Abe streak by. He bounded a bench, shot under a wagon, got himself proper, and flew on. And then right behind him, I seen old Galloway, stumbling over himself, panting with every trot.

"Galloway called out to a tasking man, 'You there, boy! Come bind this fellow.' They cornered Abe, but might as well have cornered the air. He dashed out and slid right under Galloway's legs, easy as the boat under the bridge, and Galloway cried out, cursing his very hands. I should have been going on then, but I was fixed on the story now playing out before me. And the longer it went, the more men came, until I seen the Tasked, the Low, and Galloway all bent over, panting, heads bent over in their humiliation.

"Now, Galloway would like to give the thing up, but there was a crowd now and so his pride kept him going. Can't no slaver have his niggers in defiance. So Galloway gathered himself and bounded on. I watched them dance a little more, and then Abe turned toward me. My particular feelings upon slavery were not yet whole. Surely I would like to be a gal working on her own time. But I was young. I had no religion but felt Abe in flight to be my own jubilee.

"So Abe darted my way. And then I heard Galloway call to me, as he called to all the others, 'Bind that boy!' I could not. I would not. I was nobody's headman. And if I was, I should know better than to make my marbles upon the taking of a boy like Abe. He cut away, ran, and then cut back toward me again. And out of his own unthinking frustration, Galloway grabbed a weight and hurled it at Abe. Don't know what he was thinking, for Abe had eyes in the back of his head.

"No such luck upon young Harriet."

By now Harriet burned with the brilliance of twenty lanterns, and the pale green extended out into a full white. There was no water. I could not feel my legs. I could not truly feel any part of me. I was now merely a presence, an essence following a voice.

"The weight sailed right past Abe and caught me in the head. Crashed through my skull. And then the Lord's long night came all over me.

"I did not wake in Dorchester but in some other time. I saw Abe racing across the land and his foot-tracks set the trees to fire. The forests burned to cinder. The ash fell to the ground. And then the ash rose with the wind, until it formed itself into a whole company of black men in blue, black men with rifles upon their shoulders. And I was there with them, Hiram. And we were a multitude. In the eyes of this army assembled before me, I beheld the humiliations of slavery burning like fire. And each of these men had the face of young Abe.

"I stood upon a high bluff, soldiers arrayed around me. Below we saw the great range of our shackled country, its crops, rooted in flesh and watered with blood. And a song rose up among these men—this legion of Abes—as they stood in ranks, and the song was that old feeling put to hymn, and on my sign we fell down upon this sinful country, and our battle-cry was as mighty as a great river conducted through a high and narrow valley.

"I awoke. I saw my momma crying. I had been down under for months. All thought me lost. None knew that I had been found. All that year my body recovered. Whole weeks would pass, and I would not speak. But there were words aplenty in my head. And I knew, at that young age, that someday the season of running would pass, we would take our victories as we wanted, not as they were given, and we would fall upon this country in the spirit of all those taken over the nameless. And we would scourge this Natchez. And we would burn this Baton Rouge."

The light of Harriet began to dim now, gradually as it had arisen. And I felt my body slowly coming back to me—my thumping heart, my heaving lungs, my hands, my legs, my feet, all now landing, not on water, but solid ground.

"Young Abe. I have not forgotten you. Before Undergrounds and Conductions, before agents and orphans, before Micajah Bland, when I was but a girl you gave me the first feeling of what it might mean to be free. I heard they captured you by Hampton's Mark, not so far from Elias Creek. They say you were at last worn down, but still and all, it took a town to tackle you. I do not believe them. All who have seen you know the truth. You might be lamed, but you shall never be parted."

Now the light had fallen back to palest green. My eyes were restored. I looked out. The docks, the river, the piers, were all gone, and looking up I saw, where there had once been clouds, a clear sky and the North Star blinking out. I was on an outcropping with a small bank of woods behind us and a large empty field in front and below. I looked back along the path to see from where we had come, but there was nothing but the woods. I heard Harriet moan and I saw she was leaning on her walking stick. With a trembling voice she said, "Horse . . . Saddle."

She took a step back and tumbled backward to the ground. I ran to her and held up her head. Her eyes rolled back and she moaned softly. That was when I heard the horn. I laid Harriet softly upon the ground and turned and looked out across the field and I saw them there, if only as shadows—tasking folk making their way out. And I knew we were not in Philadelphia anymore. A door had opened. The land had folded like fabric. Conduction. Conduction. Conduction.

· 24 ·

I WAS IN NEW COUNTRY—THE trees, the smells, the birds—and just then I saw the sun breaking, and all of it coming alive. I could not take to the roads. Ryland would be watching. And too there were tasking folks of uncertain loyalties who might want to claim the grand bounty that forever hung over the head of Moses. I stood there for a moment, looking down from the outcropping. The sun was just beginning to blow yellow over the horizon. I gathered up Harriet and slung her, gently as I could, over one shoulder. Then I squatted down and took her walking stick in hand. I pushed back into the woods, slowly but deliberately, clearing the branches and brambles with the stick, then walking into the space I'd opened. After an hour of this, with some intermittent rest, I spotted a dry gully beneath some shrubbery. I saw that there was just enough space here to lay Harriet, but not enough for me. Her safety was uppermost. I could be left to chance. I pushed deeper into the woods, thinking that should I be taken, I would like to be taken alone. At nightfall, I would return for Harriet, who I hoped would have roused herself by then.

In the early afternoon, I heard woodsmen from a nearby timber camp come out for scouting. I was perfectly still, which was nothing when measured next to the time I'd spent confined in that Virginia burial pit. Later, I saw two low whites and their hounds out for hunting. But I had sprinkled graveyard dust all around, which I knew would conceal my trail. I saw a group of children—some Quality, some Tasked—out at play and wondered if they might take my hiding place for their own. But they scooted on. And then, after the longest day I had ever lived, I rejoiced as the shade of night drew over the earth. The moon flew up high, and its rise was carried as much in the firmament as in my nervous heart.

I walked back to the gully, and pulling away the brush, I saw Harriet still lying there, as I left her, walking stick across her chest, like a pharaoh entombed. I reached to touch her face, as she had so often touched mine. It was cold to the touch. I looked down and saw her lungs heaving strong, and when I found her face again, I saw that her eyes were open. She smiled and said, "Evening, friend."

She was up in minutes. It was as if the whole thing was but a nap. We walked for some time, following a dirt road, but keeping ourselves to the woods, so we would see any patrol long before it was upon us.

"My apologies, friend. I thought I had enough spirit to make it without one of those bouts," she said. "The jump is done by the power of the story. It pulls from our particular histories, from all of our loves and all of our losses. All of that feeling is called up, and on the strength of our remembrances, we are moved. Sometimes it take more than other times, and on those former times, well, you seen what happened. I have made this jump so many times before, though. No idea why this one socked me so."

We walked and the woods opened into a clearing where men from the timber camps had been at work. Across the field I saw a cabin and, through a window, the flickering of a hearthfire.

"That there's our place," she said. "But I suppose you must have some questions. There will not be much time after this, so I suggest you ask now." We sat on a pair of stumps. The night was cool. A slight wind blew out from the forest and across the fields.

On the Street we lived in a world of stories and tales, of hoodoo and professed conjuration, of prohibitions—no hogs slaughtered under moonlight, the floor never walked with one shoe. I did not believe in that world. Even as I knew what had happened to me, how I had come to Thena, how I had come out of the Goose, I thought the whole explicable, comprehendible through books. And maybe it is all explicable, and maybe this is that book. But nevertheless, when I was conducted, I underwent a drastic revision of the world around me, and what wonders and powers it held.

"My grandmother was a pure-blood African. Went by the name of Santi Bess," I said. "It was said that this Bess could unwind an African tale with such effect that sometimes a first frost would feel like a prairie heat."

Harriet, seated upon the stump, said nothing.

"And Bess's gift for stories was so prized that the Quality would bring her up during their socials and she would put her stories to songs and rhythms that they had never heard. They were amused by her and would toss coins. Bess would smile and scrape the coins into her apron. She never kept them. She gave them to the children in the quarters. She claimed to have no need and I think I now know why.

"As the story goes, Bess came to my momma one night, and told her that she must walk to a place where Momma could not follow. They were born to two different worlds, she told her—Momma's was here, but my grandmother's was far gone. And now Bess must tell a story, the oldest story she knew, one that would turn back time itself, and journey her back to that place where her fathers were buried in honor, and her mothers gathered their own corn. That night Bess walked down to the river, in the middle of winter, and disappeared.

"And Bess ain't disappear alone. That same night forty-eight of the Tasked walked off from their plantations to never be seen again. And every one of 'em was pure-bloods, just like Santi Bess.

"I have never known how to feel about this story, Harriet. My momma was left out of connection. Her father was sold off. Then she was sold off too. I thought I was done with all of that. I can barely see her face, for I have no memory of her now. But that story, and this Santi Bess . . ." I trailed off—shrinking back from the words forming in my throat. I turned to Harriet, stunned. "How have you done this?"

"Sounds as if you already know, friend," said Harriet. "Imagine the islands in a great river. And imagine that normal folks must swim from island to island—imagine that is their only method. But you, friend, you are different. Because you, unlike the others, can see a bridge across that river, many bridges even, connecting all the islands, many bridges, each one made of a different story. And you cannot just see the bridges, you can walk across, drive across, conduct across, with passengers in tow, sure as an engineer conduct a train. That is Conduction. The many bridges. The many stories. The way over the river.

"It was a known practice among the older ones. And I have heard tell that even on the slave ship, folk leaped to the waves and were conducted, conducted back to their old African home." Harriet sighed, shook her head, and said, "But we are here now. And we have forgotten the old songs and lost so many of our stories."

"There's so much," I said. "So much I can't remember."

"Seems to me you remember quite a bit," Harriet said.

"I do. Everything. Every little small bit, but there is a gash in the thing, a gash in me, a gash where my mother should be. When I look back, I can see my childhood playing out like a stage show right here in front of me, but the main player is fog."

"Huh," she said. Then she leaned on her stick and stood. "Ever consider you don't really want to see?"

"No," I said. "Not really. I feel that it is the opposite, in fact. Like I am really straining to see."

Harriet nodded and then handed me the walking stick. I turned it in my hand, looking at the glyphs on each side.

"Those markings won't mean nothing to you. It is written in the language that only I hear. And what is important is not the markings, but the stick itself. Stripped from the sweet gum tree. Reminds me of them days when they put me out to the timbers. Worst days of my life. But they was the days that made me. I think about 'em sometimes, think about all that happened out there, and I like to break down and cry. It is a painful thing, what they have done to us. And there is a part of me that would like to forget. But when I grip that branch of sweet gum, I cannot help but remember.

"I can't say what done happened to you, Hiram. But if I were to venture a guess, I would say that there is some part of you that wants to forget, that is trying with all its might to forget. And what you need is something outside of yourself, something beyond you, a lever to unlock that thing you done shut away. Only you know what the thing might be. But I think if you can find that lever, then you can find your mother, and when you find your mother you will find that bridge."

"That how it worked for you? You put your hands on that sweet gum branch and everything was there?"

"No. That's not how it worked. But I am not like you. Kessiah told me some of it. We both mighta tasked, but we ain't tasked the same. See, when I came up from that deep sleep, I ain't just remember, I heard colors, I saw songs, I felt all the various odors of the world. Voices assaulted me from all over, and remembrances old as ancestors did not dim but burned bright as torches. I would watch them play out before me, and everywhere I walked, was just like you said, a whole stage of memories was with me.

"They used to say I was touched. So I learned to regulate the power, to summon some voices and then make others diminish. Sometimes they were too strong and they would tumble me down, just as they did last night. But when I rose after, I rose upon different earth. It was the bridge, Hiram," she said.

"Conjured up?" I asked.

"No," she said. "The story is always real. It is not made by me. It is made by the people. And the story is fit to certain points, like the base of a bridge, which cannot be altered by me, nor Santi, nor you."

"I don't know," I said. "Feels chancy to me. Like this thing can take me at any point—in the stables, on an actual bridge, in a field. Anywhere."

"Was it a trough in that stable?" she asked.

"Sure was," I said. "Filled with water. Felt like it sucked me right in."

"Bet it did," she said. "Nothing chancy about any of that."

"I ain't understanding."

"Don't you see it, friend? You was standing at the ramp of the bridge. In every one of these stories—Santi into the river, you out of the Goose, us over the pier . . ."

I sat there dumb.

I still wasn't getting it. And at that Harriet laughed.

"Water, Hiram. Water. Conduction got to have water."

My mouth must have dropped, because Harriet started laughing even harder. And she had a right to laugh. It seemed so obvious now. Every time I'd felt the pull of the thing, felt the river of Conduction rushing along—from the water trough in the stables, to the Goose that pulled Maynard and me off the bridge, to the Schuylkill near Bland's home—there had always been water within reach. And now I thought of all of Corrine's absurd efforts to access the power, and never once had we noted that element that now seemed most obvious.

"Why didn't you use it for Lydia?" I asked. We were now walking toward the cabin.

"Because, to tell a man a story, you gotta know how it end," said Harriet. "I never been to Alabama. Can't jump to an end I ain't never seen. And even knowing beginning and end, I have to know something of who I'm conducting in order to bring 'em along. Don't usually have that luxury. Which is why my normal means are as any other agent. This time, though, it's folks I know."

We walked over to the cottage and found those people. The door opened as we approached, and warmth breathed out. It was now deep into the night, but inside the cabin, everything teemed. We were greeted by a motley group of four men, all of them in task-ing clothes. Two of these men had an aspect similar enough to Harriet that I knew they were kin. A third tended the fire that I'd seen burning through the window. My eyes lingered on the fourth, sensing something amiss, and then I realized that this one was a woman with her head nearly totally shorn. I thought of the two white women at the Convention who preached equality in every sphere, but I knew that this was a scheme of a different sort.

"Hiram, this is Chase Piers," Harriet said, gesturing toward the man tending the fire. "He is our host and we are thankful for his part in this."

Then, smiling at the other two men, whom I took to be kin, she said, "No such kind words for these two rascals." Then she hugged them both and they all laughed.

Harriet said, "These are my brothers Ben and Henry. Finally got some steel in these boys, took 'em long enough. But I guess if Henry had not stayed down this way he never woulda met his wife."

And now Harriet went over to the woman whose hair was shorn, rubbed the round egg of her head, and laughed.

"Every whit of this is your making," the woman said, smiling but annoyed. "Why, I knows the Lord must be carrying us up out the coffin, for he would not have a girl give away a blossom of hair such as mine for still another chain."

"Worked, didn't it?" said Harriet.

The girl nodded and smiled, less annoyed.

"This is Jane," Harriet said. "She's Henry's wife."

Jane now smiled at me. The absence of hair put the focus on her striking face, the sharp angles of her cheeks, her small eyes and large ears. And there was a boisterous faith in her, a feeling shared among all who gathered before the hearth. By then I had been party to enough rescues to know that this was not normal. Fear was normal. Whispers were normal. But this group laughed like they was already North. It was nothing like I'd seen in Virginia or even among those who'd come through the Philadelphia station. The difference was Harriet, who by way of Conduction, by weaving of legend, was now her own one-woman war against the Task, and in particular against the county that had her so. And seeing this, even after having seen Conduction, I decided that the stories really must be true. Harriet really had pulled the pistol on the coward. She really had conducted across a river in winter. The whip really had melted in the overseer's hand. She was the only agent never to fail at a single rescue, never to lose a passenger on the rail. And though that is the story, it was known, even then, among those huddling in the warmth of that cabin. For when they spoke of their departure, they spoke of it as divine right. Here they were on the cusp of a realized prophecy, and before them was their prophet, Moses, filling them up with certainty.

Harriet now unspooled the plan. "It is the tradition that a rescue be kept simple and small, and not just the tradition, but wisdom," she said. "But you are all known to me, every one, and I have agreed to your terms and you have agreed to mine, which are simple—*none shall turn back*."

I felt, in this moment, perhaps more than in the Conduction itself, that all the sobriquets that attended Harriet were earned. Her manner, calm and steely, would have been enough. But it was the effect she had on the others. None spoke. It seemed as though the night itself froze and there was only Harriet holding our attention. And when she offered her edict—*none shall turn back*—it didn't fill us with fear, for it did not seem a threat but prophecy.

"Jane and Henry, you shall remain here at Chase's place. Keep indoors until tomorrow night. On account of it being Sunday, should be some time before they figure you two done picked up and left. Ben, I know you won't be tasking, but do me a favor and make yourself seen—just in case. We don't want old Broadus and his people seeing the threads until the web is all around them. About this time tomorrow night, we shall meet at Daddy's place, rest a taste, and then we are gone."

She paused, drew herself back, and then stood with the aid of her walking stick.

"Now, here we arrive upon the complication. Hiram, there is one who ain't among us. My brother Robert has a baby coming, and would not like to go at all but for the fact that Broadus is ready to put him on the auction block. Robert got to run, but he insisted that he remain with his wife until the last second he could. It was not my wish to leave the thing as so, but family gets ahold of your heart and starts to twisting, and, well, what comes of that often is not wise.

"But I have agreed, only on the notion that he be kept in the dark as to the whole of our plans. I'll tell him like I'm telling the rest of you, when I get him under my eyes. So Robert must be gotten and you, Hiram, must do the getting, friend."

The charge was new, though not wholly without expectation. Harriet had pointedly been round-ways in her description of what we faced. Perhaps it was to prevent me from thinking too much and carrying any apprehension. This was not Virginia and I would be going it alone.

"I'd like to go myself," she said. "But Robert is upon the home plantation and my workings there are very much suspected.

They'll be looking for me. You will be less likely to be suspected, and if you are, you have your passes that shall give you and Robert the right to the road."

I nodded. "So when shall I leave?"

"Right now, friend. Right now," she said. "You must make it to Robert's place before the daylight. Then wait, keep yourself out of range, and then soon as night fall, you and Robert head to my daddy's—Robert will know the way."

"I got him," I said.

"One more thing, Hiram," said Harriet. She turned to Chase Piers and said, "Chase, get him that thing."

Chase went into a small cupboard and pulled out something wrapped in fabric. He handed it to Harriet, who then unwrapped the fabric, and I now saw that she held a pistol that glinted in the fire-light. "Take this," she said, handing the thing to me. "It's for them. But more it's for you. If you have to use it, then it will likely be too late and you will want it for both."

So I walked back out into the woods, moving as instructed. There were secret signs guiding my path. And though it was night, the signs were visible by moonlight, more so because I knew what to search for—a star carved into the bark of black oak; five felled branches all fastened to the ground, two of them pointing east; a large stone with a crescent moon drawn on top and a spade underneath. I missed a few of these, found myself turned around, but nonetheless, I was at Robert's place before sunrise and thus with time to spare. The Broadus plantation was not as lush as my Lockless, and the quarters were little more than hovels arranged haphazard in the forest. Broadus had not even bothered to have the trees cleared from around. And I thought that if this chaotic arrangement gave any tell as to what it was like to task down here, I well understood why Harriet would like to forget.

It was now Sunday morning, which meant no Task, and no

Task meant no count, so the headman would not notice Robert's parting until the next day. We'd be in Philadelphia by then, with Raymond and Otha, plotting on the next step to Canada or New York. The plan, as much as I knew of it, called for Robert to step out of his quarters just before sunrise, whistle once, and then walk to the woods where we would meet. Once Robert approached, I was to speak a phrase to let him know my intentions, and he would respond with his own. Failing any of that, I would know that something had gone wrong and would immediately then head off myself back to Chase Piers's cabin. And so I waited, at some distance, until I saw a dark figure step outside and look around. I heard a whistle and then watched the figure begin making its way out from the cabin into the woods. I walked toward the figure and said, "The Zion train is upon you."

"And I should like to be aboard," Robert said. He was a normal-sized man, with a sad countenance holding none of the joy or confidence that Harriet's other family had offered. There was weight to him, and rarely had I seen a man woeful at the prospect of rescue from the Task.

"We leave at nightfall," I said. "Make all your arrangements, and then meet me here."

Robert nodded again and headed back to his cabin.

I retreated deeper into the woods. Though there would be no tasking this day, I did not wish to attract any attention. So I walked until the woods rose upwards and, climbing up a hill, found a cave where I kept peace until dark. Then as the appointed hour approached I made my way back. But Robert did not appear. I waited longer, and when he did not show, I wondered if Robert had staked out the wrong time, because I knew I had not. I thought to leave without him, for Harriet would make no exceptions, and I think, were I back in Virginia, I might well have done it. But the months had changed me, and I thought often during those days since the New York Convention of how Micajah Bland had died, of how he could have left Lydia and made his way back. And I thought of how he would have rather faced Otha in the next life than in this one having done such a thing. And I still had my passes should I need them. So there alone I made a decision to return with Harriet's brother Robert or not return at all. I left the wood to check on his cabin.

As I approached I heard a woman yelling, and through the open door I saw the woman pacing about and Robert on the bed with his head hung between his hands. I watched from outside for a moment as the woman inveighed against Robert with a mixture of rage and pain.

"I know you are leaving me here for some social with that Jennings girl," she said. "I know you, Robert Ross. I know you are leaving me, and you had better be an honorable man and say it as such."

"Mary, it's just like I done said—I am going to see my brother and my ma and pa," said Robert. "Ain't nothing but a Sunday. You know this. Look, there's Jacob"—and at this Robert motioned out the door toward me—"I told you bout him. From the Harrison place. He got people that way too, ain't that right, Jacob?"

Mary turned to me, standing outside, looked me over, and rolled her eyes.

"I ain't never seen no Jacob," she said.

"He right there," Robert said.

"You ain't never need any kind of partner for the walk before," she said. "What done changed? I never seen this man before. I know he ain't from around here. How bout I walk with you stead of him. I know what you doing, Robert Ross. I know all about that Jennings girl."

I was in the doorframe of the quarters. I now stepped inside. And saw Mary fully—a small woman with a righteous rage all over her. She really did know Robert, even if she did not directly know which way he was now heading. She looked me over again and said, "Jacob, huh? How bout I march over to the Jennings place and ask about you."

"We ain't doing that," I said.

"Ain't no 'we.' I do it by my lonesome, right now."

"No. I can't let you."

"Really. So you saying you gonna stop me?"

"My ambition, ma'am," I said, "is that you will stop yourself."

Mary shot me an incredulous look. I had to move fast.

"You right," I said. "Ain't no Jacob around here. But should you act as you now claiming to would bring pain upon you and everyone you love in a kind of way that go far beyond finding Robert sneaking around with a girl."

Behind me I heard Robert moan and say, "Baby . . ."

"Mrs. Mary," I said. "It is apparent to me that you have not been given the full shape of things. You are right. Robert is stealing away. Robert got to steal away, and there ain't a thing you should want to do about it."

"Damn if I shouldn't," she said.

"No, ma'am," I said. "I really don't think you should. I know he ain't been straight with you, but I will tell you directly. Broadus bout to put this man on the block. And when he do, you will have a better chance of walking on water than seeing your husband in this life again."

"He been running that business for a year now," she said, "and Broadus ain't done nothing. Robert work too hard for them to move."

"Robert working hard is the first reason to move him. Strapping man like that fetch a good price. And what nigger ever been saved on account of working hard? You got that much faith in these people? I been giving this place a good survey. It is teetering. I done seen many a farm like it before. They selling folks off 'cause they got to. I seen it before. And I am telling you now, telling you straight, that your Robert got two choices—the auction block with Broadus, or to run with me."

If there was an official rulebook for the Underground, I was in violation of its most primary articles. Agents worked hard to be seen only by those they were conducting. And they never identified their true business, preferring any number of other stories. But I had given it all up, in hopes, with time against us, of swaying Mary to let us go.

"The Underground offers the chance at reunion," I said. "I hate to divide you. I know what it is, I tell you, I do. I am divided myself—got a gal down in Virginia who I think of every minute of every hour of every day. I was forced from her. But better to be forced north by the Underground than be forced deeper into the coffin. This is the only way, I am telling you.

"I have heard the two of you are new with child, and I know what must weigh on you. I was an orphan, Mrs. Mary. My momma was sold away and my daddy wasn't worth spit. I know you must be fearing that child coming up without a daddy, and I have a feeling for that stronger than you can know.

"But you have got to get this, ma'am. Your Robert will be taken—either by us or by them, but he will be taken. You know who we are. You know what we do. And you know our sign. We are people of honor, ma'am. And I tell you, upon my word, we will not rest until you and your Robert are brought into reunion."

She stood there dazed and fell back a step. She moaned, "No, no," and shook her head. And I remembered, in that moment, Sophia moaning when the hounds closed in. But just as swiftly I remembered something else—back in Virginia, at Bryceton, before we were to leave to rescue Parnel Johns. I remembered how much I distrusted it all, and how Isaiah Fields became Micajah Bland, and how his trust in me gave me trust in all the everything that followed. That was the spirit I summoned up just then.

"My name," I said. "My name is Hiram, ma'am. Your Robert Ross is my passenger and I am his conductor. On my life, ma'am, he shall not be lost. And nor shall you."

A soft tear rolled down Mary's cheek. She gathered herself a moment and then brushed past me. "I swear, Robert, if this is a girl, I will find you, and I am telling you that this man, this Hiram and his high words, they will not save you."

I felt I should look away. They deserved the moment, for there would not be another in some time. But thinking back on all that I said, thinking back on Virginia, thinking back on Sophia, I could not move.

Robert pulled her close. He kissed her warm and soft. "Not running to no girl, Mary," he said. "I'm running for a girl, and that girl is you."

That fight with Robert and Mary set us back some. Without it we could have done the trip across the backwoods, and been to Harriet's parents' place well in time for our departure. But now we must take the roads, which was not ideal. Harriet, prophet that she was, had foreseen this—I had the passes. So it was to the roads then. I was trusting to Robert, who now directed us to the home of their mother and father, Ma Rit and Pop Ross. Harriet had kept every portion of the plan in its own box so that should any of us be taken, none—no matter how beaten and whipped—would be able to sketch the full picture.

Robert was quiet for the first portion of the trip, reserving his words solely for directions. I let him be. Whatever my curiosities, the parting had been hard enough and I had no intentions whatever of asking him to relive it. But then it happened as it always does with me. At a certain point, Robert just started talking.

"You know the plan was to leave her, don't you?" he said.

"Yep. And that's precisely how it played," I responded.

"Ain't what I mean," Robert said. "Plan was to leave her for good. For me to get on by my lonesome, and find a new life up in the North."

"And your child?"

"Ain't no child—not of mine at least. I know that. And she know that."

We were quiet for a minute.

"Broadus," I said.

"Broadus son," Robert said. "Him and Mary bout the same age. Played together as kids. Then was parted, as we all are. I guess he had a thing for her even back then. And now a man, he thought he would make good on those feelings, no matter how fixed and honest Mary was. Maybe she felt the same. She surely ain't stop him."

"And how was she to do that?" I asked.

"Man, I don't know," Robert said in frustration. "How anybody do anything down here? But I am telling you, I'd be damned if I was gon be raising some white man's child."

"So you run then."

"So I run then."

"Broadus wasn't bout to sell you, was he?"

"No, he was. I ain't know when but he was. For a while I thought that might well be a relief from my position. I did not have any desire to see Natchez, but if it helped me forget Mary, and my humiliation, perhaps it was for the best."

"A man being sold ain't never for the best."

"Yeah, I know," Robert said. "Harriet and the family got to me, pulled me out of my despair. Told me that some other life might yet await me in the North. They ask about Mary and the baby of course, and I tell Harriet no way I'm going with some other man child. She ain't like that, ain't like that much at all, but I tell her either it's gonna be new life in everything, or I'll just take my chance with Broadus.

"But when time come to leave, when I really had to face up to what it mean to leave my Mary, I . . . I don't know. Best I can say it is I got weak and started thinking maybe some of the old ain't so bad. And then you come in and make your promise—"

"I'm sorry about that, I thought—"

"Nothing to be sorry about whatever. Fact is, you was saying what I was feeling. I can't live without Mary. I don't want no freedom that ain't about some place with her. . . . It's just that child,

raising some other man's baby, it grind on a man in a kinda
way. . . ."

"Yeah, it do," I said. And I felt it. I understood. But I also had
begun to understand more, for I was thinking not just of myself
and my Sophia and not just of Robert and Mary, but that day,
upstate, the day I met Kessiah. And I was thinking back to that
great university of slaveries and tasks, and of the women in overalls, and the vast conspiracy to pillage half the world. And I was
thinking of my part in that pillage, of my dreams, of the Lockless
I had built in my mind, built mostly out of *my Sophia*.

"We can't ever have nothing pure," Robert said. "It's always out
of sorts. Them stories with their knights and maidens, none of
that for us. We don't get it pure. We don't get nothing clean."

"Yeah," I said. "But neither do they. It is quite a thing, a messy
dirty thing, to put your own son, your own daughter, to the Task.
Way I see it, ain't no pure and it is we who are blessed, for we
know this."

"Blessed, huh?"

"Blessed, for we do not bear the weight of pretending pure. I
will say that it has taken some time for me to get that. Had to lose
some folk and truly understand what that loss mean. But having
been down, and having seen my share of those who are up, I tell
you, Robert Ross, I would live down here among my losses,
among the muck and mess of it, before I would ever live among
those who are in their own kind of muck, but are so blinded by it
they fancy it pure. Ain't no pure, Robert. Ain't no clean."

· 25 ·

B Y NIGHT WE'D ARRIVED at a small path, which led into a clearing and then to the Ross place. I saw a house and then a stable
behind it. I remembered then that Harriet's parents were free, and
their children were not.

"Can't see my momma," Robert said.

"Why not?" I asked.

"She wear her feelings out front, and if she was to see me, if she
was to know, she'd holler like a baby, and when the white folks
come to ask what happened, no way my momma could lie. Harriet
left here ten years ago. I seen her since then, but she ain't spoke to
momma. Ain't 'cause she don't want to. But how could she?"

At that Robert gave a whistle. After a few minutes, an older
man, who I took as his father—Pop Ross, he called him—walked
out and, looking in no particular direction, waved toward the
back of the home. We circled around, picking our way through
the surrounding woods. Partway around we caught a vision,
through the window, of Ma Rit sweeping the floor. Robert

paused, suddenly aware that he might never see her again, then he kept weaving his way back. Around the back we found the stable, and opening it there, I found the entire party seated and silent inside. We did not speak. Harriet emerged from the corner. Her eyes were glued on Robert. She took his lapels, shook them, and then pulled him close into the strength of her embrace. And there we sat in the stables, waiting upon the safety of the deepest part of night. Some took to the loft and slept. Pop Ross brought us food. But opening the door, he turned his head away without looking in and extended his right arm, waiting for whoever to take the tray.

Twice I saw the old woman venture out to the entrance of the road, look off into the distance, only to return. I wondered if she had some notion of Robert coming.

Now the rains started up. Ben and Robert peered through a crack in the stables, which framed the back window of the main house, and through that window they could see Ma Rit lit up by the fire, puffing on a pipe, with the forlorn weight of her missing children all over her face. Harriet, who had not seen her mother in years, did not want to see her now. She did not look through the crack. She would risk no farewell, even a distant one.

Finally, Ma Rit extinguished the fire and went to bed. I looked out and saw that a heavy fog had rolled in. Now Harriet inspected each of us. It was time. We walked out. I saw Pop Ross at the door, blindfolded.

"When they ask have I seen any of you," he said, "I shall answer, with my word upon God, that I have not."

We walked out into the fog. Jane took one of the old man's arms. Henry took the other and we fell into the muddy woods. And as we walked, Harriet's father hummed quietly to himself, then took up the familiar tune of departure and one by one they too picked up the song and it was delivered in a low quiet murmur through our party.

Going up to the great house farm
Going on up, for they done me wrong
Day so short, Gina. Night so long.

Then the woods broke and we came upon a wide pond, the length of which we could not see past through the fog and the dark. The voices lowered until the only sound was the rain against the leaves above, and the falling water rippling against the still water.

"Well, old man," Harriet said, turning to her father, "time for me to take over."

I think they must have all gotten some understanding of what was to happen, because as soon as Harriet said that, Jane and Henry broke their embrace and everyone stepped into the water. Henry, Robert, and Ben formed a line at the front facing out onto the pond. Jane took my hand and pulled me right behind them. I looked back and saw Pop Ross standing there, blindfolded. Harriet walked over to him, circled once as if to take up every inch of him for her memory, then kissed him gently on the forehead. Then she touched his cheek and I saw the green light of Conduction pushing out from her hand, and by that light I saw the tears streaking down Pop Ross's cheek.

They stood like this for a few seconds. Then Harriet turned and took her place in front of her brothers and started walking out into the depths. Her brothers followed silently, and Jane and I followed them. Only I looked back and when I did I saw Pop Ross there, still blindfolded. And as we moved deeper into the pond, I watched him slowly slip away from us, slip away as memories sometimes do, into the darkness, into the fog.

When we walked into the water, just as before, it was not water at all. By then Harriet was shimmering. She looked back past her brothers to me and said, "Don't you fear a spell. I got a chorus this time. And the chorus got me."

She walked forward, burning brighter with every step, breaking the fog before us like the bow of a ship breaking the sea. Then she stopped, and the small procession behind her stopped too. Harriet said, "This here journey is done all on account of John Tubman."

"John Tubman," hollered Ben.

"Who, to my eternal heartbreak, could not join us. This is for Pop Ross and Ma Rit, who I well know shall be with us in the by-and-by."

"By and by!" Ben hollered. "By and by!"

"We have found ourselves upon a railroad."

"By and by!"

"Our lives be the track, our stories the rail, and I be the engineer, who shall guide this Conduction."

"Conduction," he shouted.

"But this ain't no bitter tale."

"Go head, Harriet, go head."

"For I done my grieving in a time far past."

Now Harriet's other brothers took up the response.

"Go head. Go head," they yelled.

"John Tubman, my first love, onliest man I found fit to follow."

"That's the word."

"I have put my name on it for fact—Tubman."

"That's the word! That's the word!"

"It began when I was a small pepper, for slavery make my child hands into grinding stones."

"Hard, Harriet! Hard!"

"A touch of measles nearly put me down."

"Hard! Hard!"

"The weight stove me in. And vigilance came."

"Conduction!"

"I walked out into the woods. Testified. Beheld the path."

"Conduction!"

"But could not walk it till I was fully grown."

"By and by! By and by!"

"I worked the labors of men."

"Well, go head, Harriet, go head!"

"Got me an ox team."

"Harriet got a ox!"

"Hired myself out. Broke the fields."

"Harriet got a ox! Harriet break the land!"

"The Lord put travails before me. Made me hard as Moses before Pharaoh."

"Go head, Moses, go head!"

"But I sing of John Tubman."

"Tubman!"

"Man don't like to be outshone by woman."

"Moses break the land!"

"John Tubman was not that kind."

"There it is!"

"My strength honored him. My labors made him soft before me."

"Go head, Moses! Go ahead!"

"And I love him because I know, a girl got to love who love you."

"Moses got a big bad ox!"

"John Tubman love my strength. Loved my labor."

"Strong, Moses! Strong!"

"So I know he love me."

"John Tubman!"

"We planned for freedom on the slow steady grind of work."

"Hard, Moses! Hard!"

"We had plans. Our land. Our kids. By my ox."

"Moses got a ox!"

"But there was one who loved me more than John Tubman."

"That's the word! That's the word!"

"The Lord give me vigilance. The Lord light the path."

"Conduction!"

"The Lord called me to Philadelphia."

"Conduction!"

"But my John would not come."

"Hard! Hard!"

"I made my moves from the North. I saw new things."

"Moses got a ox!"

"And when I come back I was not the same girl."

"Moses break the land!"

"But I was fast to my word."

"Strong Moses."

"And I came back for my John."

"Yes, you did!"

"And found him taken up with some other gal."

"Hard, Moses! Hard!"

"I stewed on that. I thought to find them both and make a mess of the thing."

"Moses got a ox!"

"Didn't care how loud I was. Didn't care if Broadus heard me in full fury."

"John Tubman!"

"Didn't care if I was put back under slavery's chain."

"Hard! Hard!"

"But one man stop me."

"Strong, Moses!"

"My daddy, Big Ben Ross. He grab me up and say Harriet got to love who love Harriet."

"Go head, Pop Ross! Go head!"

"And brothers, I shall tell you, like Pop Ross told me—got to love who love you."

"Go head!"

"And it was my Lord who always loved me most."

"Go head!"

"My John left me, brothers. But I knows it was I who left that man first."

"John Tubman!"

"My soul was captive of the Lord, for it was Him who, over all again, loved me most."

"Moses got a ox."

"John Tubman."

"Strong, Moses."

"Wherever you are."

"Strong, Moses, strong."

"I know your heart and you now know mine."

"Strong Moses."

"May no vice come upon you. May your nights be easy."

"Strong."

"May you find your peace, even down in the coffin."

"By and by."

"May you find a love that love you, even in these shackled times."

"That's the word."

· 26 ·

AND THERE WE WERE early that next morning, before sunrise, down at the Delaware Avenue docks, on the other end of Conduction. Fog rolled off the water, obscuring the city. I looked back at the party and found a weakened Harriet with an arm slung around the shoulders of Henry and Robert. I took command and guided the group to our appointed meeting, a storehouse but a two-minute walk from where we had appeared. There we found Otha and Kessiah waiting for us. Henry and Robert laid Harriet down on a row of crates. She said, "Now, don't you start fussing over me, you hear? I told you I was fine long as I had my folk. Served me well, don't you think?"

"That was beautiful, Harriet," I said. "I ain't never seen nothing like it."

"You'll see it again, friend," she said, fixing her eyes to mine. "You'll see it again."

Kessiah rubbed Harriet's brow softly for a moment and then she turned to me. She smiled silently and nodded her head, and in that moment, I felt the import of all that I had just seen wash over me in a great wave of grieving and joy. Something I had long been searching for, a need that I felt but could not name, now clarified before me. It was Harriet, her brothers, her father, an entire family warring to exist as such. And I felt then that there could be no holier, no more righteous war than this. And now looking upon Kessiah, who was my bridge back to Virginia, my bridge to my mother, my bridge to Thena, I felt her to be family, so that it was natural to do as I did in that moment, to take her by the shoulders and pull her close and hold her tight, and inhale the floral smell of her hair and feel the softness of her cheek against mine. It was all so new. And I was so very new. A weight was falling away, and the weight wasn't merely the fact of the Task, its labors and conditions, but the myths beneath—my father as my savior, my plot to leave behind the Street, my notion that Lockless could be redeemed by my special hand. My forgetting. I forgot my mother. And then went off into the house of Lockless like I had no mother. And then I was conducted, brought up out of the coffin, brought up out of slavery. And now I felt myself shedding the lie, like old skin, so that a truer, more lustrous Hiram emerged.

Kessiah said, "It's all right, Hi. It's all gonna be all right." And I felt her patting and rubbing my back, in the way that one soothes a child. I tasted salt on my lips, and became aware that I was crying, and now I was sobbing in her arms, and realizing this, I was ashamed. But then I looked up and saw that everyone else around me, the entire party Harriet had brought, Otha and Kessiah, everyone, was hugging and sobbing too.

We went in shifts, by horse and buggy, to the Ninth Street office, so as not to arouse undue attention. We were all there assembled by sunrise. Everything was timed perfectly. Raymond poured coffee and served rye muffins, brown bread, and apple tarts from Mars's bakery. We were, all of us, famished, and while doing our best to maintain manners, we fed ourselves to our hearts' content.

"So this is what it is, huh?" Robert said. He was standing off in the corner of the parlor, by the window, watching the others as they ate.

"This and more," I said. "Some good. Some bad."

"But on the whole, better than being held, huh?"

"On the whole, yeah," I said. "Still. There are parts of life that can't be gotten out of, and I have had to learn, here, that we are all, at the end, held somehow. Just that up here you get to choose by who and by what."

"Thinking I could work that," Robert said. "And I must say that I am even thinking that I must be held again by my Mary."

"Gotta love who love you," I said.

"So it seems."

"You talk to Harriet?"

"I have not. Don't know how to ask . . ."

"I'll ask. Was I who made the promise."

Raymond took in each of the passengers for interview. I took notes. It lasted the whole day. At night everyone was dispatched to a different home in the city or out in Camden. They were advised to stick to indoors, for by now their escape would be known, and Harriet would be the prime suspect. By the end of the week, Philadelphia would be prowling with Ryland, but too, by then, they would themselves be headed farther north. That evening I sat down in the parlor. Harriet was upstairs in my room, fast asleep, as she had been since our arrival at the Ninth Street office.

Raymond was about to walk out with Jane and Henry to secure them in their lodging. But just before he left, he said, "I thought this might wait until your return." Then he handed me a letter and said, "Hiram, I want you to understand that you don't owe anyone anything anymore. Not me. Not Corrine."

I sat in the parlor holding the letter. I saw that it bore the mark of the Virginia station and thus knew what it said before even opening it. I was being recalled to the muck. I appreciated Raymond's words, but there was no way I was not going back. By then, I felt myself to truly be on the Underground. It was who I was and I had no idea what I would make of my life without it. And there was a promise I had made only a year ago, though it felt like ten years, a promise to bring Sophia out. And even with Bland gone, I was starting to see a way to do it.

An hour or so after Raymond left, Harriet ambled down the stairs holding her walking stick. She sat on the sofa and inhaled deeply.

"So that's about the whole of it?" I asked.

"Yep," she said. "That's about it."

"Well, not all of it."

"What you mean?"

"I ain't tell you, but to get your brother Robert out, I had to make a promise. It's Mary. She wasn't letting him go. I told her everything."

"Everything?"

"I know. It was not smart."

"Nope. Not really," Harriet said. Then she cut her eyes away from me and let out a deep breath. We sat there in silence for a moment.

"But, I will say that I was not there. I told you what was to be done. How you got it done was how you got it done. And I thank you for it. This what Robert want?"

"Yes."

"That boy is a caution."

"And there's something else too."

"What you want now? Whole state conducted?"

I laughed. And then I said, "No. I want you to know that I am leaving. Harriet, I'm going home."

"Huh. Yes, I figured as much. Especially now that you done seen the power."

"It ain't that. And I still don't have it all."

"You have enough. Enough for me to tell you this. I want you to remember that I revealed this to you and only you. And I did this because you are the bearer, no one else. Don't forget that. Once you get that train on the track, and you will, there will be folks with all sorts of notions of how it should run. You know what I am saying. I love the Virginia station, for their hearts are truly pointed toward the Lord. But do not let them pull you into their schemings, Hiram. They will try and pull you into all type of capers, but remember there is a price, always a price. You seen it on me when we went down. You seen it even today. There is a reason we forget. And those of us who remember, well, it is hard on us. It exhausts us. Even today, I could only do this with the aid of my brothers.

"If you need to speak on it, if you ever not sure, write Kessiah a few lines. I am never far from her. If you need anything, if you find yourself under it, you talk to me before you try to handle it all on your lonesome. A man might be lost out there and no telling where the story might take you. Call on me, Hiram, understand?"

I nodded and sat back. We had some more small talk until she tired. Then Harriet went back upstairs. I fell asleep on the couch. The next day I awoke to a gleeful exchange. Rising, I walked into the dining room and found Otha, Raymond, and Kessiah at the table.

"Just brought these up," Otha said with glee. It was the most hopeful I'd seen him since Lydia's capture and Bland's death.

"What is it?" I asked

"It's Lydia and the kids, Hiram," Otha explained. "We think we got a way."

"How?" I asked.

"McKiernan," Raymond said. "He wants to sell. We have been in touch with him through an intermediary."

Kessiah then reached into a suitcase and pulled out a small book.

"It is not our way," she said. "But we must tell our stories."

She handed me the book and I read on the cover, *The Kidnapped and the Ransomed*. I flipped through the book and discovered it was the story of Otha White's escape to freedom.

"Ain't this something," I said, handing the book back to her. "So then, what's the plan?"

"Otha and a few others will make a tour of the North," Raymond said. "They will sell the book to abolitionist audiences and use the profits to purchase Lydia and the family."

"And McKiernan, he gon wait?" I asked. "After what we tried to pull on him?"

"You mean after what he pulled on us," Otha said. "Bland is dead. Truly in the coffin. We ain't giving up on Lydia and that man know it. Why, I hate paying a ransom for my own people, but this ain't the time for high standing, I guess."

"No," Kessiah said. "It's not. If you got a way to get them out, Otha, do it. Keep your end of the yard clean and leave the justice to the Lord."

"Indeed," I said. "On that count I have something that must be said . . ."

"Time to get back, huh?" Otha said.

"It is," I said. "I . . . I am not who I was."

I don't even know if they understood. Perhaps Kessiah did. But even if they did not understand, I wanted it said, I wanted them to know that I had been changed by Philadelphia, by Mars, by Otha, by Mary Bronson, by all of them. I wanted them to know that I understood. But all those years of holding my words, of listening and not talking, still bore on me so that all I could muster from this feeling was, "I am not him. I am not him."

"We know," Otha said, rising to embrace me.

Before I returned to the coffin, I had promises to keep. On a crisp November Sunday, I found myself walking with Kessiah toward the promenade along the Schuylkill. The wind rustled its way up Bainbridge, this lovely thoroughfare—lovely, yes, I had come to believe this, for where I once perceived chaos, I now saw a symphony in the city, in the low things in the alleys, in the abominable odor, in the great variance among the peoples, spilling out of their brick hovels, piling into the omnibus, heaving in the pewter shops, bickering in haberdasheries, haggling over groceries.

On we walked, counting the numbered streets until we were at the river, which we followed to the promenade, barely peopled that morning. Kessiah pulled her shawl tight around her shoulders and said, "We are not built for this, you know. We are a tropical people, that is what they say."

"My favorite season," I said. "World is so beautiful this time of year. There's a kinda peace that just falls on everything, even up here. It's like summer wear the world out, and by October everyone is just ready for a nap."

"I don't know," Kessiah said, shaking her head. She laughed lightly and pulled the shawl tighter. "This wind coming up off the river as it does? Give me spring. Give me green fields. Give me blossoms."

"Season of life, huh?" I said. "Naw, I prefer this season of loss, this season of dying, for I think it is the world at its most true."

We sat there quiet for a moment. Kessiah took my hand and held it, slid over until she was close, and then kissed me on the cheek.

"How are you, Hi?" she said.

"Lotta feelings," I said.

"Yes, indeed," she said. "Those comings and goings, my Lord, I feel it every time I leave my Elias back at the home-place, feel my heart ripped right out of me."

"And how bout him?"

"Elias? Well, I like to think my leaving don't please him too much. But I do not ask. And you must remember I was always a kind of woman who would be hard to tie. Very few men could cope with this. But my Elias was different. And I think it was mostly 'cause of Harriet. We are of the same understanding, so that when Elias fell to me, my manner was not so strange to him. Might well be the whole reason he fell to me as he did. I was what he knew. I was as a woman should be.

"We do need help on the home-place, though. Lot of work. And I am not really a part of it. He keep talking about getting a girl. I tell him he can do that if he wants, but he will lose one too."

We laughed at this for a moment, and then I said, "Maybe not, though."

"I assure you he will," she said. "Do not let that 'free love' Convention talk get to you."

"I am not speaking of free love. I am speaking of your mother."

Kessiah looked out to the river and said nothing.

"Ain't right," I said. "Ain't right what been done here."

"Ain't right for no one, Hi," Kessiah said. "You also aiming to go to war with Virginia?" she said.

"There were promises made," I said. "Promises before Bland died."

"Not for Thena."

"No. Not for Thena. I don't have it all figured. But I do believe I am owed something here. I am happy to be Underground, happy that it all happened. But I was not asked into this. I was drafted. I do not believe it too much to ask that Virginia let loose the woman who made it possible for me to survive all those years before."

"No, it is not. And up here, with just Raymond and Otha, or even with Harriet and Maryland, it'd be done. But Virginia . . . they are different."

"I know," I said. "I have been tangling with them in some manner for almost half my life. But I am telling you, I am determined to get Thena out. I can't tell you how. I can't tell you when. But I will get her out."

Kessiah sat back and looked out toward the river. A knot of sparrows then flew up from the trees. I watched as a harrier dipped and dived among them.

"Well, I can't say I would not love to have her," Kessiah said. "But you will forgive me if I do not get my blood up over such a thing. I said goodbye a long time ago, Hi, and it is a hard thing to say goodbye to your mother, do you know?"

"I do," I said.

"If you find your way to her and see her back up here, well . . . We have a place for her. Lovely farm west of here. Lancaster-way. It is truly a sight, I will say that. And it is waiting for her."

The very next morning I dressed myself in the style of tasking men I had observed up here, those who dressed well above their station—fine trousers, damask waistcoat, and a high stove-pipe hat. It was still early, just about sunrise, but when I came down, Raymond, Otha, and Kessiah were there. We sat together in pleasing conversation for a few minutes. Raymond had hired a private hack to take us all to Gray's Ferry Station, as this entire party insisted on seeing me off. The carriage arrived presently and we boarded and prepared for the trip down Bainbridge, but just as we did, I saw Mars running toward us, hollering, holding a bag in one hand and waving wildly with the other.

"Hey now!" he said as he approached us, and I greeted him with a smile and a doff of my hat.

"Heard you would be leaving us for a while," he said. "Wanted to give you a touch of something."

And at that he handed me the bag. I opened it and saw a bottle of rum and gingerbread wrapped in paper.

"Remember," he said. "Family."

"I remember," I said. "Goodbye, Mars."

When we arrived at the station, the train was there idling and the passengers were making last preparations to board. Scanning among the crowd, I saw my contact, a white agent who would second me should anything prove amiss. I turned to them all and said, "Well, this appears to be my train," and then embraced each of them. I walked down to join the milling crowds below and presented my ticket, boarded, and found my place in the car, one distant enough that I could no longer see this new family of mine, for I feared what might happen should I be forced to watch them fade from me. And I thought of Sophia then, and I thought of how much I would like to bring her here, to meet these people and hear their wild adventures, to eat gingerbread by the promenade, and watch white men wave from unicycles. And then I heard the conductor shout and the big cat roar, and my descent into the Southern maw began.

• • •

Long before we crossed the border, before Baltimore, before the sight of the conductor walking the aisle, inspecting every colored, before the mountains of western Maryland broke into Virginia, I felt the change. To task is to wear a mask, and what I now saw clearly was that I would miss Philadelphia because in that city of noxious fumes, I had been the truest version of myself, unbent by the desires and rituals of others, so that now the change I felt overtaking me—my chest tightening, my eyes lowering, my hands open and loose, my whole body slouching in its seat—was a kind of total self-denial, a complete lie. And when I stepped off the train, at that Clarksburg station, I could feel the shackles clamping down on my wrist, the vise tightening around my neck. Having lived as I had, having tasted my own freedom, having seen whole societies of colored but free, I felt it as a weight beyond anything I had ever known.

By the following evening, a Tuesday, I was back at Bryceton, installed in my old cabin. Corrine offered me a day to myself. I spent most of it walking in the woods, imagining myself walking in Philadelphia, as I'd so often done. I thought again of how much I wanted to take Sophia there, and thinking further, how much I wanted to take Thena there, and it occurred to me on that day that I was happy to have returned, for I never wanted to again breathe free air with those two in chains.

Bland had promised me he would convince Corrine to rescue Sophia. But Bland was dead. And so I must, on my own, somehow convince Corrine to liberate them both. There were obstacles to this beyond the death of Bland. Sophia was the property of Nathaniel Walker, personal property, so that any such rescue would raise his ire, and raise suspicions. Thena was of such an age that the Virginia Underground would likely oppose her rescue, for it was felt that a life of freedom should first be given to those able to make the most use of it. But I had told Kessiah we would have it, and I was determined to make it so.

I met Corrine and Hawkins early the next morning in the parlor of the main house, and walking through that doorway, memories of times past, and my first visit to Bryceton, and the unveiling of its incredible secrets, struck me. And I saw my old tutor, my Mr. Fields, my Micajah Bland, laughing as Hawkins related some story, and I saw him turn to me with the gravest look imaginable, and in his eyes I saw all the terrible knowledge that would soon be put upon me.

"Hiram," Corrine said, as we settled down in our chairs. "When you tumbled into the river with Maynard, you achieved two effects. The first of these was relief—you saved me from a union with such a man and all the horror you might imagine that entails. And for that I thank you."

"I took no pleasure in it," I said. "But at least it improved your lot."

"Two, boy," said Hawkins. "She said two."

"Unfortunately," said Corrine, "you also deprived this station of an entrée into the highest portions of Elm County society."

"There wasn't anything high about Maynard," I said.

"Yes, but you understand my meaning," she said. "Now I am condemned to spinsterhood and out of connection with the ladies of that country. Had the union with Maynard been achieved, that connection would have proven fruitful for the strength and intelligence of the Underground. I believe you can see how."

"I can."

"And so by Maynard's death we lost an investment. Months of planning were gone and we were forced to make do with what remained."

"She means you," said Hawkins ruefully. "Had to carry you off."

"And while you have not given to us in the way in which we believed Maynard would, you have given your share. We know what you did in Philadelphia and in Maryland. Have you made an acquaintance of the powers which, a year ago, you only dimly perceived?"

I said nothing. I did indeed have an acquaintance, but there was still something missing, something that would unlock the deep memory at will, and allow me to conduct the train, as I wished, along the track. And even if I had understood it all, I still remembered Harriet's warning, and I believed her when she said that the power was for me, not for them.

"We are not without gratitude or admiration, Hiram. And yet this hardly brings you to a settling of the account."

"I am here," I said. "As much as possible, of my own will. Tell me what you need. Ask me. I shall do."

"Good. Good," said Corrine. "You recall your father's servant, Roscoe?"

"Of course," I said. "Brought me up top."

"Well, Roscoe has passed. It was his time."

"I'm sorry to hear it," I said.

"As soon as Roscoe started going down," said Hawkins, "your old man Howell sent a letter to Corrine, here. He wants you back—in Roscoe's place."

"Recall now the intelligence we were to garner from the union between myself and Maynard," said Corrine. "Perhaps you would like to be the source of this intelligence. We desire a knowledge of your father's situation and the future of Lockless. Would you help us?"

"I would," I said. My suddenness shocked them, for I was pledging myself to return to the man who was my master, even if he was also my father. "But I need something from you."

"I would say you've gotten plenty," said Corrine.

"No more than I deserved," I said.

Corrine now smiled at me and nodded. "Indeed," she said. "What do you wish?"

"There are two still there—a woman and a girl," I said. "I want them out."

"The girl is, I assume, the one you ran with. Sophia," said Corrine. "And the woman would be your caretaker from your earliest days at the house, Thena."

"Yes, them," I said. "I want them conducted to Philadelphia through the Ninth Street station and Raymond White."

"Forget it," said Hawkins. "All you'll do is bring down Ryland, likely right on us. The girl who ran with you, gone again as soon as you get back? And then the woman who is like a mother to you? No, that don't work."

"And this Thena woman," said Corrine. "She is past the age when we can justify such a journey."

"I know the dangers and I know the problems," I said. "And it don't have to be now. But I want it on the books. I want you to promise me that when the time is right, that we will get them out. Listen, I am not the same man. I know what this war means, and I am with you in it. But I cannot rescue on a symbol. They are my family, all the family I have ever had. And I want them out. I cannot sleep until they are out."

Corrine appraised me for moment. She said, "I understand. We will do it. At the right time. But we will do it. For now, prepare yourself. You leave tomorrow. I've already informed your father to expect you."

And so early the next day, I awoke, washed, and donned my old clothes, clothes of the tasking man, and when their coarse threading chafed my skin I saw a black gate clanging shut before my eyes. So this was it. I truly was now back under. I felt an odd relief in this, for the chafing of my clothes put me in connection with all those who chafed under the Task. I knew that Corrine had set the slave deed, the deed to my soul, afire, but this had no meaning in a place where the whole society thought me a slave. And I recalled then Georgie Parks, whose specious freedom was pinned to the arrest of any other colored who should aspire to rise as he did. I was not Georgie. I could not truly torch the deed that held me until the Task itself was torched.

I met Hawkins at the stables and we brought the horses around to the main house. We waited there in silence for Corrine, and when she walked out with Amy, I truly understood the majesty of the Virginia station's endeavor. I had now seen two different versions of Corrine, so far from each other as to not even seem to be the same person. There was Corrine of the Virginia Underground and the New York Convention, with her hair tumbling down to her shoulders, with a wild and free laughter. And then there was this Corrine, prim, walking before us as though royalty, her face impeccably painted, with that rose-like glow about her that all women of Quality sought. But she was still in her mourning clothes and now the ensemble had grown more elaborate, a black bustle trailing behind her, a black veil so long that when it was lifted and thrown back, it fell down to her waist. She must have caught my surprise, and Corrine could not help but giggle. Then, with an assist from Amy, she pulled the mourning veil over her head and the game was afoot.

It was a funny thing, seeing the country again from this angle. To see the woods I had sometimes raced through, and all the geography I had navigated during the rigors of training. I could see all the birches, ironwoods, and red oaks alive in their beautiful fans of russet and gold. The mountains just beyond us, with their overhangs and clearings where the world opened up and you could see the bounty of this deathly season clear for miles. But in my heart I felt the fear of having returned to slave country and that this world now had eyes on me.

By late afternoon, we had arrived at Starfall, and I knew, almost instantly, that the decline that had been in motion when I left had now accelerated. Everything was too quiet. It was a Thursday, a day of business, but as we rode into town, our only greeting was the wind whipping leaves up Main Street. We passed the town square, which had been in another time a place of bountiful activity, and I saw that the wooden platform, where the highest men of

Quality would address the town, had splintered and rotted and been left in disrepair. Buildings that once advertised fur-traders, wheelwrights, and emporiums now stood empty. We drove past the racetrack, and I saw that the pine fencing from where I once watched the races had collapsed and the green field had begun to invade the turf.

I looked over to Hawkins, who was driving and seated beside me, and said, "Race-day?"

"Not this year," he said. "Maybe not ever again."

We stowed the horses at the stable, and then walked across the street to the inn. When we walked inside, this is what I saw: a large room filled with ten whites, Low by their appearance, seated throughout. None of them were in conversation with each other, preferring instead to be off to themselves nursing their lagers or their private thoughts. To the far right, cosseted in a small ante-room, there was a clerk, attending to his ledger. No one took note of our arrival. There was something odd at work, though I could not place what. I stayed behind Corrine and followed her over to the clerk, who never lifted his head.

Then she said, "How goes the Kentucky comet?"

Now the clerk looked up, paused a moment, and said, "Derailed this morning."

At that Corrine looked over at Hawkins and nodded. He moved quickly to the door and locked it. Two of the men sitting at the tables now looked up from their lagers, stood, and went to the windows, where they drew the Venetian blinds. And that was the second time, in one day, that I understood the genius of Corrine Quinn. I tell you, I was at a point in my life, and had seen so much, that I was prepared to believe that she herself had laid waste to the tobacco fields of Virginia, for what I now saw, looking around, was that the faces of these men, these low whites, were not unfamiliar at all, were in fact men I'd seen in training back at Bryceton, and in this manner I comprehended exactly what had happened—right there in the heart of once-storied Elm County, Corrine Quinn had opened a Starfall station.

Within the hour everyone was in meetings. I was excused from these, having my assignment, which would begin on the morrow. I walked out of the back of the inn and then circled around until I was on the street where we had entered. I turned up the collar of my coat to my cheeks, then pulled my hat low. A manic curiosity had taken hold of me only minutes earlier—What of Freetown? What of Edgar and Patience? What of Pap and Grease? Of Amber and the baby? I could have very easily asked Hawkins or Amy, but I think I knew what they would say, because deep in my heart, I was neither mystified nor confused as to what had come, for I well knew the price for what we put upon Georgie Parks.

What I found then was what I expected, there in the shadow of Ryland's Jail—which itself seemed to contain half the life left in Starfall. Freetown was in ruins, but not the kind that now afflicted the rest of Starfall. The shanties were nearly destroyed, and what remained were wooden planks black from burning, ashes, and among those structures still standing, doors torn off hinges, as though crashed in by some tremendous force. Such was the home of Georgie Parks. I walked in and saw that everything was smashed—the bed broken in two, a chest of drawers axed down the middle, the shards of pottery, a pair of spectacles. I stood there for a few moments taking in the fruit of my ways, the harvest of the Underground's terrible revenge, which had not merely vented itself on Georgie Parks but on the entirety of Freetown. And I felt a deep and pervading shame. That was when I saw it—in the corner, a small toy horse, which I had given to Georgie on the birth of his child. I bent down to pick up the horse, and then walked back outside. It was now early evening. Ryland's Jail stood a block away in a stony silence. The sun was falling over the trees in the distance. I felt a gray menace blowing up the abandoned street. I put the toy horse in my coat pocket and walked on.

III.

The negroes, in the meantime, who had gotten off, continued dancing among the waves, yelling with all their might, what seemed to me a song of triumph. . . .

ALEXANDER FALCONBRIDGE

· 28 ·

THE FOLLOWING AFTERNOON, I took the horse and chaise from the stables and out of Starfall, steering away from the stone bridge, Dumb Silk Road, and the Falling Creek turnpike, for the proper way back to Lockless. I was drowning in a bleed of feelings, and what bled most was not the proposed meeting with my father, was not shame at my last words for Thena, was not even the sight of Sophia. All of that was there, but reigning high above it all was a deep-seated and boyish hope that the decay that I could now see had overrun Elm County had somehow spared my Lockless.

Who knows why we love what we do? Why we are what we are? I tell you I was, by then, mortgaged to the Underground. All that I knew of true humanity, of allegiance and honor, I had learned in that last year. I believed in the world of Kessiah and Harriet and Raymond and Otha and Mars. Still, the boy in me had not died. I was what I was and could no more choose my family, even a family denied me, than I could choose a country that denies us all the same.

But when I turned off the West Road, into Lockless, I understood, almost immediately, that my wish would not be granted. Like the race-way, the main road had begun to submit to the growth of the forest. And then I rode farther, past the fields, and saw that the regular team had shrunk in number, and looking out at them, I recognized no one.

A hint of hope came from the apple orchards, closer to the main house, which seemed perfectly maintained, and did not smell of fruit left to rot on the ground. And better than even the apple orchards was the garden of late asters just before the main house. I pulled the chaise up at the stables, tied the horse, and noticed that there was now but one horse, save the one I'd just driven, in the stable. My horse was thirsty and panting. I carried the trough over to the spring, filled it with water, and set it down in the stable, and when I looked into the water it shimmered a bit, shimmered for me. Soon come, I thought. Then I began my walk to the white palace of Lockless.

I saw him before he saw me. I was standing at the end of the road, just before the main house. He was seated on the porch, behind the bug-blind, in his hunting clothes, with his rifle at one side, and his afternoon cordial in the other. I had in my hand a crate of gifts sent along by Corrine. It was almost evening. The autumn sun was just beginning to fall. I stood there and watched for a moment and then I called out, "Good afternoon, sir." I saw him awake, blink, and when he understood, his eyes were as wide as full moons. He did not so much run as he swam out into the road with bizarre abandon, his arms flailing the air like water. He pulled me close, right into an embrace, right there in the full open, and the old savage smell of him was all over me.

"My boy," he said. And then he stepped back to get a look at me, holding both shoulders, soft tears streaming down his face. "My boy," he said again, shaking his head.

I do not know what manner of reception I imagined on returning to my father's house. Memory was my power, not imagination. But then there was my father himself, and when he guided me up to the front porch, and we were seated, I was able to take the measure of him. He seemed to have become the town of Starfall in miniature. I had been gone but a year, and in that time he seemed to have aged ten. He was weaker. His severe features had softened and his whole body seemed to sag into his chair. There were coin-sacks under his eyes and his face was discolored and pocked. I felt his heart working for every beat.

But there was something else—a kind of joy in him at my return, a joy that I had glimpsed in him all those years ago when I'd caught the rotating coin in my hand while never breaking my gaze.

"By God," he said, looking me over. "We can dress you a sight better than that. Dignity, son. Remember Old Roscoe? Polished as a piano, God rest his sorrowful soul."

"Yes, sir," I said.

"Glad to see you, son. Been too much time, much too much time."

"Yes, sir."

"How you find Miss Corrine's place, boy?"

"Fine, sir."

"Not too fine, I'm hoping?"

"Sir?"

"Hasn't she told you, son? You are back here at Lockless. How's that strike you?"

"Strikes me very well."

"Good, good. Let's see what you've got there."

I helped him rummage through the gifts Corrine had sent—a collection of treats and candy, other odds and ends including a volume from Sir Walter Scott. The supper hour was now upon us and so I helped my father upstairs and then into his evening dining clothes.

"Very good. Very good," he said. "You are a natural at it. But get yourself changed. I think Old Roscoe was smaller than you. I am thinking you could outfit yourself in some of Maynard's old garments. That boy had more finery than he could put to use. Miss him though, I do. Damn, that boy was trouble."

"A good man, sir."

"Yes, he was. But no use in garments gone to seed. Make something distinguished of yourself up there, boy. You may take your brother's old quarters, in the house, not down in those tunnels below."

"Yes, sir."

"One thing, boy. So much has changed round here since you have gone. The old place cannot be what it was. We lost so many. But I have done as I could, and what I did otherwise could not have been helped. Son, I am old. But all I can think of now, in this time, is ensuring some kindly heir for the place and for our people. I want you to know that is a particular concern to me, do you understand?"

"Yes, sir."

"It was not right of me to let you go, boy. I was in grief and that girl Corrine, well, she talked me right out of your name. But since you been gone, I have been at her to bring you back to where I know you want to be. And by God, I have done it. You are here, boy. I know you will fill quite well for Old Roscoe, as you did for my Little May. But I need you to be more. Once you was hands, son. I got plenty of those. What I now need is your eyes. All got to stay in order. Can I count on you for that, boy?"

"Yes, sir," I said.

"Good. Good. I am a conflicted man, I cannot help it. Two mistakes I made in my life. First was letting go of your momma. Second was letting go of you. And it was all done in a horrible fit. No more. I am an old man, but I am, too, a new one."

So that evening, I found myself installed in my dead brother's room, and in my dead brother's clothes. And when it was time for supper, I went out to the kitchen, and did not recognize a one of them. There was a staff of two working there, down from five. And they were both elderly, which itself said something of the straits Lockless now navigated. Because they produced no children, nor many working years, elderly slaves were the cheapest to acquire. They had, by their own intelligence, heard of "that Ryland business," but they seemed oddly pleased that my father seemed so pleased with me, and spoke at length of my father's pride and regret, despite my having run. I think now they thought, perhaps prayed, that I would prove some manner of stabilizing force on the house.

I served supper—terrapin soup and chops—and cleaned up with the staff, then took my father to his study with an evening cordial. With that completed, it was now upon me to come face to face with my shame. I left my father sitting there, stripped down to his shirt-sleeves and tartan vest, lost in dreams of Lockless yore, and slid behind the wall of the study, until I was in the secret staircase that descended into the Warrens below. So many were now gone, and where there once had been life, I found an emptiness, a haunt, in all the abandoned quarters, with their doors left open, and various odds and ends—washbasins, marbles, spectacles—left behind. Walking in the Warrens, peering by the lantern-light, running my hand across the cobwebbed doorframes of the people I'd known, of Cassius, of Ella, of Pete, I felt a great rage, not simply because I knew that they had been taken but because I knew how they had been taken, how they had been parted from each other, how I was born and made by this great parting. Better than before, I understood the whole dimensions of this crime, the entirety of the theft, the small moments, the tenderness, the quarrels and corrections, all stolen, so that men such as my father might live as gods.

My old room was just as I left it, washbasin, jars, and bed. But I was not much in the mood to inspect any of that. For I could hear, just next door, a woman humming, and knowing the voice, I slowly walked out of my room, and then to the adjacent room, and pushing the door, which was slightly ajar, I saw Thena there humming to herself, with two pins between her teeth, and a garment in her lap that she was presently darning. I stood waiting there for some moments for her to acknowledge me, and when she did not, I walked over, pulled out a chair, and sat across from where she was seated on the bed.

"Thena," I said.

She kept humming but never looked up. I had by then learned the price of my silence, the cost of holding my words as a shield to my heart. I knew what it was to feel that someone you deeply loved was gone from you, and that you would never be able to tell them all that they had meant. But sitting with Thena, who I thought I'd lost, whose volume and character had only been amplified through my knowledge of Kessiah, I felt that I now had a second chance and I resolved not to waste it.

"I was wrong," I blurted out. I had no pretense. I did not know how else to be. The feelings of the past year were all so new, and I was still, in so many ways, a boy with no understanding of how such feelings should be borne. But I knew that too much had gone unsaid. And our time together could no longer be presumed.

"I came here to confess how badly I had spoken to you when I last saw you, how poorly I have treated you, who are all the family I have, more family than anyone who has ever lived in this house."

At this Thena looked up for a moment, then looked back down, still humming. And though there was no compassion in her eyes, indeed she was cold as ice, I took even her skeptical regard as a measure of progress.

"It is not easy for me to say. You have known me all my life. You know it is not easy. But I am sorry. And for so long I have feared that those words would be the last ones I had given to you. And to see you here, again . . . to see you . . . Listen to me. I was wrong. I am sorry."

She had stopped humming. And she looked up again and placed

the garment, which I now saw was a pair of trousers, down on the bed. Then she took my right hand in both of hers and she squeezed it tight, all the time looking away from me, and I heard her breathe in deep and then breathe out. Then she released my hand, picked up the garment, and said, "Hand me that patch of corduroy."

I walked over to the chest of drawers, picked up the patch, and passed it to her. As I did this, I felt something set right in me. My mother was lost to me. This was true. But before me now was one who had lost as I had, who had been joined to me out of that loss, out of that need, and had become my only unerring family at Lockless, just as she had told me. And where I feared she would hold my words against me, what I saw even in her most contrary gestures was a joy at my safe return. I did not need her to smile. I did not need her to laugh. I did not even need her to tell me how much she had loved me. I only needed her, as it happened, to take my hand.

"Well, I am upstairs now," I said. "Maynard's old room. Don't love it but it is what Master Howell say it be. Holler if you need me."

And her only answer to this new information was to pick up her humming again. But then as I walked out the doorway, I heard her say, "Missed supper."

I turned back and said, "Missed more than that."

I now returned to my old room and gathered a few of my effects—my water-jar, my books, my old clothes, and even my old trusty coin was there, undisturbed on the mantel. I stuffed these into my washbasin and walked up the secret backstairs into the study, where I saw my father quietly dozing. I carried my effects up to Maynard's old room and returned to the study. Then I escorted my father up to his room, my arm under his, helped him out of his clothes and under the covers, and bid him good night.

The next morning, I dressed, tended to my father again, and

then drove the chaise into Starfall to retrieve Corrine, Amy, and Hawkins. Corrine and my father lunched and walked the property alone. An hour later, they returned and we served tea. In the evening, after the visiting party had set off, I served my father supper, and then went down into the Warrens to see Thena.

In another time, the Warrens teemed with humanity, tasking hands moving amongst each other, singing their songs, trading their stories, and venting their complaints, so that they were almost a world unto themselves, and you could, if you tried, forget that you were held there. But now all the human warmth of the early years had drained from the place, and the Warrens were revealed for what they had always been—a dungeon beneath a castle, dank and gray, an effect augmented by the array of lanterns that had fallen into disrepair and now left long stretches of the Warrens in darkness.

When I arrived, Thena was not there. I decided to sit and wait. She arrived a few minutes later, looked at me, and said, "Evening."

"Evening," I said.

"You ate?"

"Naw."

We had greens, fatback, and ash-cake. We ate silently, as we had always done when I was a child. Then, after cleaning up, I bid Thena good night and returned to my room. We continued this routine for a week. And then one unseasonably warm evening, at my suggestion, we took our plates out to the end of the Warrens tunnel, where I had, all those years ago, entered with her. We sat there eating, watching the sun set over the country.

Thena said, "So you done seen Sophia?"

"Not yet," I said. "Figured she spent most of her time over at Nathaniel's now."

"Naw," said Thena. "She right down there on the Street. Nathaniel almost always in Tennessee now. So ain't too much reason for her to be over there. But he and Howell and Corrine got some sort of arrangement on her. Can't say I understand it, except that she is left there to her business."

"To her business?" I asked.

"Till they figure out what to do with her, I'm guessing. They don't make a habit of sharing such things with me, as you know."

"I should see her," I said.

"Only if you ready," Thena said. "Best not to rush such things. Lot done changed down this way."

The next day was a Sunday, my day. I held myself back until the afternoon. Then, realizing I must see her sometime anyway, and feeling I would never be ready, I took my walk down to the Street, down to the place of my birth. And much as I had expected, the Street too had fallen into disrepair. There were no chickens roaming about, and all the old gardens were overgrown. These were the last days of the section of the vast Southern Empire that held Virginia as its ancestral seat. And it has been said, the fact of this falling is the fault of its masters, that had the Quality adhered to the hollow virtues of old, perhaps this empire would have stretched forth for a thousand years. But the fall was always ordained, because slavery made men wasteful and profligate in sloth. Maynard was crude and this was his greatest crime. In fact, he mirrored so much of the Quality. He simply lacked the guile to hide it.

The first bite of winter air had blanketed over Elm County, so that I grew wistful of summer Sundays and that other time when all of my young friends would have been out playing our little games of marbles and tag. Thena told me that Sophia had taken up in that same far cabin at the end of the Street where Thena and I had lived in the days following my mother's departure. Looking down the bank of houses, I saw a woman emerge with a small child on her hip. The woman bounced the baby a few times, and then looked up and saw me. She gave me a look of puzzled interrogation, nodded an acknowledgment, and walked back inside. I stood there a second waiting, and then the woman stepped out of the cabin again, without the baby, and it was only then that it dawned on me that the woman was Sophia.

When Sophia stepped back out, she was different. She stood there, a few yards away, at the far end of the street, Sophia, my Sophia, unsmiling. I did not know what any of it meant. Was she angry with me for leading her to Ryland? Had I dreamt up that whole evening, of us out there, in union? Had it all been a childish flirtation between us? Did she now love another? And who was that baby?

"Gon stand down there all day?" she yelled down at me. Then she walked back inside. I followed until I was outside Thena's old cabin, and memories of myself, appearing before her with only my victuals, overran me. But there was not much time for such things. And looking in, I saw Sophia had the baby on her hip again, bouncing her just as she had outside, singing a song.

"Hello," I said.

"Well, hello, Hiram," Sophia said. She had a smug look about her and I could not decide if this was her usual teasing or if it was something deeper. She sat on a chair by the window and then invited me to take a seat myself on the bed. The baby was brown, about my complexion, and cooed quietly in Sophia's arms. It was only then that I began to do the math of it all. So much had changed. I must have given some sign of this awareness, perhaps an arched eyebrow, or a widening of the eyes, because Sophia sucked her teeth, rolled her eyes, and said, "Don't worry. She ain't yours."

"I am not worried," I said. "I am not worried about anything anymore."

And when I said this, I saw her relax just a bit, though she was trying to maintain that same cool distance she had offered up when I first arrived. She stood and walked to the window, all the time cradling the child.

"What is her name?" I asked.

"Caroline," she said, still looking out the window.

"It's a beautiful name."

"I call her Carrie."

"And that is beautiful too," I said.

Now she sat down across from me, but she did not meet my eyes. She focused on the child, but did so in such a way that I knew the child was a pretense for not looking my way.

"I did not think you would come back," she said. "Don't nobody ever come back here. I heard Corrine Quinn had gotten ahold of you. Somebody said you was up in the mountains somewhere. In the salt mines, they said."

"And who is 'they'?" I asked, laughing quietly.

"That ain't funny," she said. "I was worried for you, Hiram. I am telling you, I was terribly scared."

"Well, I wasn't nowhere near no mines. It's true I was in the mountains," I said. "Up at Bryceton. But wasn't no mines. Wasn't half-bad, in fact. Quite beautiful up there. You should go sometime."

And now Sophia laughed herself and said, "And you come back a joker, huh?"

"Gotta laugh, Sophia," I said. "I have learned that you gotta laugh in this life."

"Yeah, you do," she said. "Though I find it harder every day. Need to think of good things and better times. Do you know I talk about you, Hi?"

"Talk about me to who?"

"To my Carrie. Tell her everything."

"Huh," I said. "Ain't much else to talk about, it seem. Place so empty now."

"Yeah," said Sophia. "So many lost. So many gone. Natchez got 'em. Tuscaloosa. Cairo. Hauled 'em down into that big nothing. It get worse every day. Long Jerry from over at the MacEaster Place was by here only two weeks ago. I felt surely he was too old for them to take. He was here, right here, with a offering of yams, trout, and apples. Thena even came down. We fried it up and had a good supper together. Was just two weeks ago. And now he gone.

"It's been so many, Hi. So many. I don't know how they keeping this thing afloat. Was a girl named Milly come through here a few months back. Beautiful girl—which was her loss. She ain't last but a week. Natchez. Fancy trade."

"But you still here," I said.

"Indeed, indeed," she said. Now Caroline began to stir, wriggling in her mother's arms, until she could turn her head and get a good solid look at me. And the child held me there with a stare of the deepest of intentions, regarding me in the way infants do when brought before someone unknown. I never knew what to do with that look. It discomfits me. But there was more because that look, and all its intense study, was the inheritance of her mother. Perhaps it was all the moments I had spent conjuring the face, recreating the particulars. And there was something else now, more math. Caroline had the same sun-drop eyes as her mother, but the color—an uncommon green-gray—came from somewhere else. I knew this because my own eyes were the same color, and the color was a Walker inheritance, given not only to me but to my uncle, Nathaniel.

Again, my looks must have betrayed me, because Sophia sucked her teeth, pulled Caroline close, stood, and turned away.

"Already told you," Sophia said. "She ain't yours."

I know now what it is to feel things that you have no right to feel, I knew it even then though I did not know how to describe it. What I remember was one half of me wanted to get away from Sophia, to never speak to her again, to disappear into the Underground and cut away that girl who would not be *my* Sophia. And then another part, a part of me conceived in my mother's own strife, then reared on the Underground, the part that was dazzled by that "university" upstate, the part that found the wisdom to tell Robert that nothing is pure and thank God—was shocked to find such resentment still curdling in me.

I watched Sophia watch the baby for a moment, then shifted away and said, "So how many of us left?"

"Don't know," Sophia said. "Was never sure how many was here to begin with. And for the sake of my own heart, I stopped counting the departed. Surely these are the last days of Lockless. They are killing us, Hi. And not just here. Across Elm County. They are killing us all."

She sat back down with Caroline.

"But you did come back," she said. "And you look good for yourself. It has been a blessing of mine to see you return to us, to be reborn, twice in a lifetime—up out of the Goose, and now out of the jaws of Ryland. Must be some powerful meaning, for we are not in Natchez, but right here before each other. Some meaning in us, I think. Some powerful, powerful meaning."

But the discovery of that meaning would have to wait. I walked back that evening and tended to my father and his supper. Then I descended into the Warrens and joined Thena for supper. There was no ambient action outside the doors, nor in the house above. It felt like we were all alone on some far side of the world, and I understood some of how it must have been in the earliest days of Lockless, when it was only the progenitor and his team of tasking men, with nature closing in around them.

After we finished, we walked outside and sat at the edge of the tunnel to the Warrens.

Thena looked over at me and said, "So you went to see her."

I looked to the ground and shook my head.

Thena laughed to herself.

"You could have told me," I said.

"Like you could have told me?"

"Was different then," I said.

"Naw, the same. You judged it to be no business of mine. I did not agree. But I am struggling to see how telling you that girl was

333

a grass widow would make me anything more than a gossip. There are things between you two that do not concern me."

She was right. I thought back to that moment when I'd last seen her before running, and I recalled my harsh words and I knew that while I could apologize for the pain I had caused, the break was real. The child had left home. He could not return.

"I'm not even angry with her," I said. "Wasn't ever like she was mine."

"Nope."

Caroline was, by my estimation, perhaps four months old, which meant that when I ran with Sophia, she was already carrying the baby. And knowing her intellect and independence, and thinking on all our conversations, I understood that she was not simply with child when we ran, but likely ran with me because she was with child.

"Thena, I am feeling that she had reasons to run, reasons that she declined to share with me."

"Yup."

"And that has left me . . . with feelings. Like I laid myself bare before that girl. And when I ran, I did so giving all of my reasoning. Straight down the line."

"Straight down the line, huh?"

"Yup."

"Yeah, all right. Listen, I'm gon tell you—ain't nobody straight down no line, Hi. Least of all two young'uns like y'all two. Hot after each other as you was."

"I did not lie," I said.

"Huh. 'Straight down the line,'" Thena said, shaking her head. "You sure about that? You sure you telling everything? I gotta say, I know I don't feel like I done heard the whole of it. And I would bet my next week's victuals that Sophia ain't either."

· 29 ·

A UTUMN MOVED TO WINTER and our days grew gray and cool,
 our nights lonesome and blue. In those early days back, I
worked as Roscoe once had, though my duties were lighter on account of the diminished number of guests entertained. The old
days of Elm County royalty, of parasols and powdered faces, lady-
cake and card-games, the old days when I would amaze whole parties with the magic of memory, were gone. From time to time,
older friends, as ancient as my father, would call upon him. They
would spend hours denouncing the young Quality, dazzled by
tales of boundless land out west, who'd abandoned their Virginian
birthright. There was still my uncle, Nathaniel Walker, who held
Sophia and somehow maintained himself and all of his land. But
his tasking folks had, besides a small team for maintenance, all
gone west. Harlan was still there at Lockless, pushing the tasking
folks to extract all they could from the dying land. But his wife,
Desi, no longer ruled the house, because the house had so diminished that there was no need for her hand. My father's most constant companion was Corrine, who, no matter Maynard's death,

he still held as the daughter he'd never had. She would arrive in full grieving costume—driven by Hawkins. She comforted my father. She let him regale her with that other age before the yawning fallows, when tobacco ever-flowing endowed the estates.

Still, the duties of everyday companionship mostly fell to me. So every evening, after preparing supper for my father, and taking mine with Thena, I would tend the fire in the parlor, serve warm cider, and listen to the last true lord of Lockless unspool his regrets. We now fell into the oddest arrangement, one that had been my secret wish in my younger years. I tasked for him, but the nature of the relation so shifted that he would, on those blue evenings, with the Argand lamp casting its long shadows against the old family busts, ask that I sit with him and imbibe. And it seemed to me, in those moments, that the whole world had fallen away, fallen into the pit of Natchez, and I alone was left bearing witness. On such an evening as this, finding himself far into the cider, my father spoke of his greatest regret of all—Maynard Walker.

At first he seemed to be speaking almost aimlessly, but then his words focused and out of them came a mourning that was larger than Maynard himself.

"My father never loved me," he said. "It was another time, boy. Nothing like today where you see the young folks open and frolicking. My daddy's only concern was station. And all my actions had to honor my lineage. Of course, I married a lady, Lord rest her soul, handsome enough. But she was never the girl I burned for, and she knew that. So when Maynard came, I was set on never putting him in that situation.

"I wanted him to be what his own nature commanded. So I gave the boy wide berth—too wide as it happened. He had no handling. He was not built for society and I, never loving society myself, did nothing to encourage it. And when his mother passed, well . . . He was my boy."

He paused here. His head was now in his hands, and I sensed he was doing all he could to keep from breaking down and weeping.

He pulled his hands away, then stared into the fire for a few long moments.

He said, "I almost feel as though May was put out of his misery. I know I was put out of mine. It is a terrible thing to say it. But there was nothing for him here, you see? I had not built him for this life. I had barely been built for it myself. And the young ones are now all headed west. He would have got himself skinned by an Indian, or lost everything to swindle. I know it, the boy was not prepared, and that is the fault of me.

"I am not a good man, Hiram. You, among them all, know this. I have not forgotten what was done to you."

I remember how he was still looking into the fire when he said this. He was as close as he could come to an admission, an apology, for an act I knew but could not then remember. And even as we sat there, with our cider, as close as any Quality and Tasked in Virginia could be, still he could not look to me and speak with truth. He was as ill-prepared for repentance as Maynard was for mastery. His world—the world of Virginia—was built on a foundation of lies. To collapse them all right then and there, at his age, might well have killed him.

"The land, the management of Negroes, takes a special hand," he said. "It was always beyond me. And what is odd is I always felt that you were the one who had it. You were colder than all of us, colder than Maynard, colder than me, perhaps because of what was done to you. But you had the makings, and I do believe that in some other time our separate acres could be swapped and perhaps there I might be the colored and you might be the white."

I heard this the way an old man hears a young unrequited love attest to their true feelings from that bygone era—the mix of trivia and nostalgia, an ancient wound reawakened by the rain, the ghost of a feeling, once deeply held, but now only a stray memory from what seemed another lifetime.

In this lifetime, I looked over and saw my father now nodding into sleep. I took my glass, still half-filled with cider, and walked upstairs to his second-floor study. In the corner, I saw the ma-hogany highboy, the same one I repaired only a year ago. I took a drink of cider, set it on the windowsill, and then opened the draw-ers. Inside I found three thick bound ledgers. For the next hour I slowly pored over these ledgers, committing them to memory. Together they painted a picture, a grim picture, that would help fulfill my mission, according to Corrine, to ascertain the situation here at Lockless.

When I was done, I closed up the ledgers and returned them to the highboy. I thought of Maynard, when we were young, rifling through our father's things. I laughed to myself and then opened a second drawer. Within it, I saw a small but ornate wooden box. I thought to pull the box out and open it, but thinking again of Maynard, I remembered how shameful I felt when he pilfered from our father. So I shut the drawer and walked back downstairs. My father was snoring lightly. I roused him to take him up to bed.

He said, "I got plans for you, boy. Plans."

I nodded and moved to help him out of his chair. But he looked at me like a man condemned to death, as though he feared that if he slept he might never again awake.

"Tell me a story," he said. "Please, any story."

So I withdrew and sat in my own chair, leaned back, and I sud-denly felt myself grow old right there, because I saw before me the room come alive with the specters of Caulleys, Mackleys, and Beachams, and all the families of Quality who'd once bid of me a story, a song. No, I thought. Not far enough. And I, with my words, took my father's hands, back through the ages, back to the stone monument in the field, back to the Bowie knives, the cata-mounts and bears, the tasking men hauling stones and breaking creeks, back to the time of our progenitor.

The next day Hawkins drove Corrine over for one of her visits from Starfall, where she had installed herself for some time. Bryceton was mostly left to Amy and the few other agents who could keep up the cover. On these visits, I would confer with Hawkins and deliver any intelligence I had discerned. And so it happened on that day. We walked down to the Street, where the cabins were mostly abandoned, thinking this would provide us the privacy we needed. I maintained a hope of seeing Sophia, though I had begun to keep her at arm's length. I was divided against myself. The intense feelings of only a year ago had not dulled, indeed had grown, so that knowing she was right there at Lockless, but not with me, made me sick. And that sickness scared me, for I now knew that some part of my welfare was in the hands of someone who held her own secret motives and designs.

"So what you think?" Hawkins asked.

We were seated in one of the abandoned cabins closest to the main house, and farthest from Sophia's. We could see the tobacco fields, now mostly left to fallow.

"Not much," I said. "Not much at all."

"Yeah, I know," Hawkins said, looking over the fields. "Place look dead."

"The whole county feels dead. Nobody come to see him. No afternoon tea. No big dinners. No socials."

"Yeah, not sure how Corrine think this gon fit into anything. Maybe it's good she ain't marry that boy."

"I will tell you this, she would be marrying into a pile of debt." Hawkins looked over at me. "How much debt?" he asked.

"Well, there ain't been much intelligence to be gleaned from society on account of there being none," I said. "But I got a look at the ledgers last night. He's in over his head. There's an interest on almost every inch of this property. He's stalling. Hoping for some relief."

"Well, I'll be," said Hawkins. "Make sense, I guess. The soil was the wealth, and the soil done gone to dust. My pappy used to tell stories about the land, bout how red it was. But they done stripped the place for all the tobacco they could. It's a shame, I tell you.

They got as much out of this county as they could and now, having gotten it, the whole heap of 'em headed west."

"And the tasking hands with 'em," I said.

"Yup."

"How bout the man's brother? Nathaniel? He lending a hand?"

"By the looks of them books, he done lent several hands. Howell ain't paid him nothing back. Blood money after bad money, I guess."

"Huh," Hawkins said. "Nathaniel smart. Smart as any man can be in this business. He out Tennessee way, now. He moved while the moving was good. That's the whole game, you know? Eat up the land, then keep going. Someday they gonna run out of land, and I don't know what they'll do then."

We walked back up to the house to meet Corrine. Just before the main drive, Hawkins stopped.

"Something you said back there be turning over in my head," he said. "The man own brother done left him out there, huh?"

"Seems so."

"Stay on them books. Might be something in this."

But there were those who profited in this new arrangement, in the most unlikely ways. Thena now hired herself out, taking in laundry, not just at Lockless, but for a number of the neighboring old estates who'd sold away their own laundry women. And she had brokered a deal with my father, allowing her to split payments with him, and in that way, someday, purchase her own freedom.

"Where will you go?" I asked. I was walking with her to the stables, for I had been enlisted in this partnership now, as a driver.

"Farther than you," she said, smiling sardonically.

We loaded ourselves into one of the old chaises, sturdy but dating back to my father's youth, and headed down the drive. At the juncture with the main road of the estate, I saw Sophia standing, wrapped in a shawl from her head down. I could see the little head of Carrie looking out. Thena told me to pull over, which I did, then I stepped out of the cart.

"She coming?" I said to Thena.

"Don't be so joyful," Sophia said.

"Been coming," said Thena, taking Carrie from Sophia, who now, not waiting for any assist, climbed into the back. I got back into my seat, pulled on the reins to start up the horse, and asked, "How long y'all been doing this?"

"Quite a bit while you was out," said Sophia. "When I got back, I felt a need to make myself useful in some other way than before. Started giving Thena a hand with the washing, till Caroline prevailed upon me, and then I had no more hands to give."

"Got some things straight," Thena said. "Had our share of talks."

"About what?" I said.

"About you," Thena said.

I shook my head, and blew out a dismissive breath through my teeth, and then all was quiet for a while, until we turned onto Hookstown Road and old memories began to spring forth for Thena.

"I had family all up and down here," she said. "Uncles, aunts, cousins. Had to know who I could marry and who I could not. There was so many associations. The old folks kept the memory. Knew who was kin and who was not."

"That is what they there for," said Sophia. "To hold the stories. Keep the blood clean."

"But they all gone now," said Thena. "All the knowledged ones is gone, and we are reduced to our surmising upon a nose or eyebrow or a particular demeanor. Don't matter much, I guess. So few of us left, and another year like this, Elm will be dust."

We drove farther, stopping and picking up the washing from all the old mansions. The trees had all turned over and were now depositing themselves upon the floor of the woods in sheets of brown. The light of the season gave a ghostly glow to the old mansions, which had, only a year ago, heaved with their last energy and feeling. Most of them were like Lockless, stripped down to the barest of staffs, and I felt then that winter was not just marching on Virginia, but on Elm in particular, and would not be leaving.

In the back I heard Carrie grow restless. Thena told me to pull over and we watched as Sophia took Carrie in her arms bouncing and singing through a nearby field. Thena unwrapped some salt pork and shared it with me.

Sophia came back with Carrie, still bouncing and singing:

> *Who's been here since I been gone?*
> *A pretty little girl with a blue dress on.*

We drove on and Thena considered her reminiscence.

"This path right here, used to lead right up to Phinny's place," she said. "I had a whole passel of people here. Had a aunt who used to cook for the first Phinny himself. And in a time when y'all was but the smallest of peppers, they used to have the grandest kind of social down at the quarters here."

"I have heard," I said. "By my time, Phinny the Second was mostly known for being so evil. Story was he shot Pap Wallace, put him all to pieces because he would not submit to correction."

"Who you hear that from?" Thena asked.

"My uncle Creon," I said.

We were quiet for a while, riding along. It was late in the afternoon now, and we had one more pick-up at the Granson place before turning back to Lockless.

"That was your uncle?" Thena asked.

"Sure was," I said.

"He used to come down to the Street, at night. Would hang near your momma's place for whatever scraps she had. It was not his best days. I remember him well."

"I remember him too," I said. "But he is all I remember of those times. I can see him at the door, and everything else is fog."

"Might be good," Sophia said. "No notion of what's lurking behind that fog."

"Ain't nothing good about it," I said.

We stopped at the Granson place. Caroline was asleep now and Sophia wrapped her in her shawl and made a hollow for her among the washing, which was tied in bedding sheets. She reached for a bundle left on the ground to hoist onto the chaise.

"I got it," I said.

"Let me help," she said.

"You done helped plenty," I said, with more heat in my words than I intended. Sophia's eyes widened but she said nothing. She went back to the chaise and we kept loading laundry.

We got back with the sun still hanging just over the trees. She stepped down and said her goodbyes to Thena and then she turned to me. It was only now that I saw that something had gone wrong.

"So this is what it is, huh?" she said. She had Carrie wrapped on her back now, with her shawl.

"What?" I said, indignantly.

"This is who you are? This is how you come back?"

"I don't know nothing—"

"Don't you dare lie to me. Don't you dare, not after you done come back. Don't you dare. You was suppose to be better. I told you be better. I told you I wasn't trading no white man for a colored. And now look at you, stewing over what you don't own, over what no man should ever try to own. You was supposed to be better."

Then she was walking down the road, her anger made manifest in how she shook as she walked away.

When we got back to the house, I unloaded the washing while Thena started on supper. Then I went to the kitchen, picked up my father's meal, and began to walk it in to him. He wanted company for his supper. So I stood there and watched him eat as he interrogated me about the day. I fell back into myself, until my face was a servile mask. After, I walked out, down the secret staircase, to Thena's quarters. We sat at her table and ate silently as we always did. When we were done, she looked at me and said, "You punishing that girl."

"I—"

Thena cut me off. "You punishing her."

I came back up and saw my father in the library, flipping through a volume. I went to the dining room and cleared his setting. Then I heated his cider and brought it to him and retreated upstairs to my room. The old toy horse I had carved for Georgie's son was on the mantel. I picked it up and ran my fingers across it. I thought on Sophia's words, the command to *be better*. I walked out of my room, down through the library, past my already dozing father, into the Warrens, and out through the tunnel. I walked down the long path past the orchards into the woods until I was down on the Street. And I walked to the end, where I found Sophia, seated out on the steps, alone.

Sophia shot me the coldest eye imaginable, and then she walked inside. I came to the door and looked in. I saw that Carrie was asleep on the bed. Sophia was looking away from me. I sat down next to her.

"I am sorry," I said. "I am so terribly sorry. For everything I have put upon you, I am so very sorry."

I slipped my fingers between hers. All of my days spent dreaming of her, all of my hours spent wondering if she was lost out there, and all of my amazement at learning that she was down here, and all of my wondering again about what had become of her here, and about who she loved and who loved her, all of those hours of dreams and ghosts and blue whispers, all of it now was real, was right there, between my fingers.

"I want to be better," I said. "I am trying to be better."

And Sophia pulled my hand to her lips and kissed it and then turned to me and said, "You want me to be yours, I understand. I have always understood it. But what you must get is that for me to be yours, I must never be yours. Do you understand what I am saying? I must never be any man's."

Sophia, my Sophia—the notions I had, the lives I thought we might build, notions and lives all in my head, all built on my sole, lonely ambitions. I sat there looking into her big sun-drop eyes. She was so very beautiful, as beautiful as they said my mother was. And I knew, looking at her there, that those notions, those lives, had never considered Sophia, as she knew herself to be. Because *my Sophia* had not been a woman to me. She had been an emblem, an ornament, a sign of someone long ago lost, someone whom I now glimpsed only in the fog, someone whom I could not save. Oh, my dear dark mother. The screams. The voices. The water. You were lost to me, lost, and there was nothing I could do to save you.

But we must tell our stories, and not be ensnared by them. That is what I was thinking that evening, in that old cabin down on the Street. And that is why I reached into my pocket and pulled out the small toy horse I'd collected from Georgie's and put it in Sophia's hands.

"For Carrie," I said.

And now Sophia laughed quietly and said, "She a little young for this, Hi."

"I am trying," I said, smiling. "I am."

345

· 30 ·

I N THE END, WE—THENA, Sophia, young Carrie, and myself—
were all that was stable at Lockless. Powers of blood bound us.
Sophia was Nathaniel's chosen, and Carrie was her daughter. I was
my father's son, and as for Thena, well, to my father, she was the
symbol of a bygone era. He had sold her children, an act that, in
his mind, was a turn in the road that marked the end of the Virginia he knew. He never quite said this, but my father avoided
saying too much to Thena, and if he was walking the property and
saw her coming, he would turn the other way. I think now that
this was his ambition for her laundry runs, to somehow assuage
the guilt of selling a woman's children on the racetrack.

Guilt or not, it saved Thena, and together, in those gray days,
the four of us formed a kind of unit. We fell into a kind of routine.
We took our meals together. After, I would see to my father, and
then walk Sophia and Caroline back to their quarters down in the
Street. One night I was seeing them home and Sophia said, speaking of Thena, "You know she is getting old."

"She is," I said.

"It is a hard life, Hi, a hard life on a woman—the laundry, the hauling, the rendering, the lye. I help out as I can, but it is hard. I am glad you came back. She need a break. Tell her sit tight tomorrow. You and me, we can handle the washing. And we'll do the run on Monday too."

When I got back, I told Thena our plan. She looked at me and gave some manner of protest, relenting only after insisting on looking after Caroline while we worked. The next day was Sunday. Corrine was coming in to take my father off to church. With Hawkins attending them both, I could take up the extra labor. That night, I lay in bed thinking of Thena and her plans. She still held out the hope of laundry money buying the last of her days in freedom. I held not to her plan but to my own, the plan of the Underground. Winter was upon us, the nights growing longer. I thought of Kessiah and how her face would look when she found her mother was delivered, and I thought, even then, that I saw in that look not just the fulfillment of a promise, but the healing of some ancient wound in me.

The washing was not easy work. We met in the early morning, with the sky still black and illuminated by the pin-prick of stars and the sliver of moon. We spent the first hour drawing up water from the well and filling our cauldrons. Then, while I gathered wood and got the fires going, Sophia separated the garments and searched for small tears. Then she delivered those few to Thena, whom we were not wholly successful in keeping from work, for darning. With the fires going and the black cauldrons heating, we held up the garments and bedding and beat the soiling out of them. While Sophia finished the beating, I carried three large washing tubs out from the Warrens to the side of the house, where we were heating the water. The stars had now faded and I could see the pale sliver of moon dissolving into the dark blue of those last small hours. When the tubs were in place, together, with our work gloves on, we lifted the cauldrons and poured the hot water. And then for the next few hours we scrubbed, rinsed, and wrung, and then scrubbed, rinsed, and wrung twice more.

We finished long after sunset. After hanging all the clothes, we walked over to the gazebo, as we had done in what seemed to me a lifetime ago. Our arms and backs were sore. Our hands were raw. We sat there in the silence of things for twenty minutes. And then walked back to eat with Thena.

"Not so easy," she said, and our exhausted silence was the loudest affirmation imaginable. Afterward, I walked Sophia down to the Street, and lingered as she washed and dressed Caroline for bed. I stepped outside and knocked my knuckles around the gaps in the filled spaces between the cabin wood. A piece chipped away.

I came back in and said, "Daubing going to pieces here. Thinking I might could go over it one time."

Sophia was then swaddling the baby's bottom in cloth, singing softly. She stopped singing and said, "Is she a problem for you?"

I laughed nervously. "Takes some adjusting."

"So you gonna be adjusting or no?"

"It is my notion," I said.

I stepped in and sat down on the bed next to Sophia.

"Remember where your notions got us last time," she said.

"I have not forgot a single thing," I said. "But what I remember is not the hounds nor what came after. What I remember is you. What I remember is being tied to that fence, how I felt right ready to die, but when I looked over, I saw not an inch of dying in you—no matter what Georgie had done to us."

"Georgie," she said. At the mention of his name, I saw a look of rage. "He was gone when I got back here. Good for him he was, too. I cannot tell you of the vile and vengeful thoughts I put upon that man."

"Maybe for the best, then," I said.

"For him," she said. "For him."

We were quiet for a while. Sophia was holding Caroline over her shoulder now, gently rubbing her back.

"Hiram," she said. "Why did you go away?"

"Wasn't no 'go' about it. They up and carried me off," I said. "You seen it."

"Just like that, huh?" she said. "Carried you off?"

"You know how it happen," I said. "We were not the first. Hounds catch you out there. Carry you off."

"Well, I got this feeling that there was more to it. Things that maybe you cannot say, things that are not meant to be spoke about. Maybe it was you being Walker-kin. But that don't feel like all of it, for I know that men down here, men who believe in the Task like Howell Walker do, why, they will sell their kin in a second, if only to no longer have to gaze upon the fruit of their sinful ways."

"But I am Tasked," I said. "Sure as you are Tasked. Blood can't change that. It's just as simple as it look. Corrine had a need. Howell felt bad about Maynard dying and sent me for consolation. Fact that we had run made it even easier."

"Well, that is the other part. While you was gone, I seen my share of Corrine—more than I have seen of Nathaniel, even. She come down here every few weeks or so. And I do not know why she would have reason to see me. And I do not know why I myself wasn't sent Natchez-way. Why are we here, Hiram? Why do we remain?"

"Seem like a question for Nathaniel."

"Hi," she said, "I don't think he even know we ran. Times I have seen him since, and it has not been very often, he has not bothered a mention."

"I don't know. I ain't in nobody's heads."

"I ain't saying you are."

"Yeah. Well, you are always saying something."

She slapped me on the shoulder with her free hand and frowned. It was quiet between us for some long moments. I was thinking of

Corrine, and why she would feel a need to look in on Sophia. I was wondering about what I had been told. And then I looked over to Sophia, who now had Carrie on her lap and was singing to her something soft and soothing. Baby Caroline was batting at the air, fighting sleep, fighting her own eyes.

For a moment I was back in Philadelphia, back with Mars, and I remembered how he opened himself to me, how the whole White family opened themselves and what that meant for me, how Bland had opened himself to me, how his words had freed me from the guilt of Maynard's dying. And I felt now that I owed some of that to Sophia.

"I know a child ain't only a joyful thing. I seen it. But so often I have seen women who would not wish a child upon themselves, still and all, forming their whole life around it. And I see you have formed your life around this young'un, formed your life around her before she even came. You would run for her. You would kill for her. I see how you look at the girl now, and I remember. I remember what you told me. 'It's coming, Hiram,' you said. 'And I will watch as my daughter is taken in, as I was taken in.' None can say it was not said. And though I remember everything, I cannot say I always hear it. But I hear you now, and I hear much more.

"And I know that men put such terrible and wretched things upon a child brought to them who ain't they blood. Mayhaps I'd be one of them men. Mayhaps I'd be so far in my own regard, in my own wrath and hate, that I . . ." I shook my head. "I am saying that she ain't no problem, and you ain't no problem, I am the problem." And I paused here for a moment and Sophia squeezed my hand.

"I am saying that I knew who her daddy was, almost the moment I saw her. It was the rules. I come back and see you here with this baby Caroline, who is not blood . . ."

And I swear at this moment, it was as if baby Caroline could hear my words, for she looked over and reached a hand toward me. And I slipped my hand out from under Sophia's and reached toward the baby, who took my small finger in her grip.

"'Cept, she is my blood," I said. "High yella like me, with green-gray eyes like mine—but not only mine. These are Walker eyes and that is Walker hair. Goes back to the earliest one, for I have seen it noted in all descriptions of him in the local Elm County history.

"And it is the funniest thing. Because them green-gray eyes skipped Maynard. But they have arisen most prominently in Caroline, baby Caroline.

"And there is pain in that. Ain't clean. It's muck. I have told other men the same, even though I must now struggle to take my own medicine. I want you to know what I have seen, the men I have known since I have gone. The men who have had to decide what they love more, the everything, lovely and mean, right in front of them, or their own wrath and regard. And I choose the muck of this world, Sophia. I choose the everything."

There were tears now in her eyes.

"Can I hold her?" I asked.

And she laughed through her tears and said, "Careful. She might well carry you off."

Then she smiled and pulled baby Caroline up off her lap and, cupping her backside in one hand and shoulders in the other, presented her to me. And I saw baby Caroline look up with those green-grays and that same infant obsession. I reached out, trying to do my best imitation of Sophia, putting my hands directly under hers and then slipping them out. And I pulled the girl close to me until her head sat in the crook of my elbow. And when I felt her settle in, and she did not cry or wail, when I felt the warm muck of her in my arms, I thought of my father, and how he had never held me like this, not in symbol or in fact. And I remembered how I had, for all my youth, chased him, in search of this moment. And I thought of the woman who had given that moment to me, because that is what everyone told me, that my mother loved me more than anything, that she formed her life around me, until she was ripped away, my mother, whom I could not remember.

. . .

With Lockless hollowing itself out, with the Warrens all haunted and gray, and that dying season now folding into winter, Caroline was a light upon our world. It was Thena, with no one else there and willing, who had midwifed Carrie, and so, out of that feeling, Thena would at times care for the baby herself, to spell Sophia. That she did that following Sunday, when I was to repair the daubing on Sophia's cabin. I worked for about an hour and then stepped inside. Sophia had started a fire. She was all bundled up and sat in front of the fireplace holding her hands toward it.

She looked at me and said, "You ain't cold?"

"I am," I said. "Can't you tell?" And I put my hands on her cheeks and reached down to her neck. She laughed and shrieked, "Boy, stop!"

I chased her out of the cabin and into the Street for a few minutes until we collapsed in laughter onto the ground.

"All right, I really am cold now," I said.

"I'm trying to tell you," she said.

We went inside and sat by the fire. "Day like this," she said, "could sure use me a demijohn. My Carolina Mercury, I tell you, he used to keep his share." Then she looked at me and said, "Forgive me, Hi, I do not mean to speak of old things."

"To be mine, can't be mine," I said. "Besides, give me an idea. Just wait right here."

I walked back up to the house and into the Warrens. I stopped past Thena's room and saw the door cracked open, and looking in I saw that Caroline was asleep on Thena's bosom, much as Kessiah had told me she would be in days past. I walked into my room and took the bottle of rum that Mars had given me on my departure. When I got back, Sophia was sitting there with her hands underneath their opposite arms, and when I showed her the bottle she smiled and said, "I know there is something with you, something about the places you been."

I opened the bottle and she said, "You ain't the same man who left. You can try as you might to fool me, but you ain't the same, I can see it, Hi. Can't hide from me."

I passed her the bottle and she took it to her mouth and tilted her head back as if trying to catch rain in her face, and then drank. "Ooh," she said, wiping her mouth with her sleeve. "Yeah, you been some places."

"But I am here now," I said, and took a drink. "And besides, what about you?"

"What about me?" she said. "What you wanna know? I shall lay it out all before you."

I took another drink, then sat the bottle on the ground.

"What happened?" I asked. "What happened after that night they had us out there?"

"Huh," she said. "Well, they kept me pinned in that jail, much as I assume they pinned you. And I knew I was done, I tell you. Natchez calling, Natchez. And a girl like me, baby or no, I knew I would be put right out to fancy. I was right terrified, I tell you. I know I tried to be strong that night out there, Hi, and I was because I had you, and I felt I had you to worry for, and long as I had that, wasn't much time for thinking of my own worries.

"But that day the hounds pinned me in that jail, it all hit me, all the evil that was bout to come down on me. Wanted to cry, but I knew I had to be strong. I just talk to my Caroline, that whole time. Just talk to her, and I am telling you, she soothed me. Like I felt myself to no longer be so alone. It's like you say, I did not ask for her, but in that moment I was so happy to have her even though she was but a small thing blooming in me.

"And I think that was the moment when I became a mother to her. I was angry at what that man, Nathaniel, had done to me. What he had put upon me. And though I am thankful for her, I will never be thankful to him. Caroline belongs to me and my God. I named her for my lost home, for my Carolina, the land from which I was stripped by no doing of my own. And that is the whole of it—in that jail, with the knife of Natchez at my throat, Caroline—my home—she saved me."

I handed her the bottle and she took another drink, shivered, and said, "Mmmm." She wiped her mouth with her sleeve. And was silent for a moment and I just sat there watching her in this silence. When she turned back to pass the demijohn to me, I felt that she looked different, as though the very texture of her story had somehow been etched into her face.

"But that's not really the whole of it," she said. "Late that night, same night, I was drifting off to sleep, huddled in the corner of the jail, rats scurrying around, cold drafty air blowing in, and I look up and see a shadow looking in on me. And then the shadow walk away for a few, and I am wondering if this is some kind of dream. But then the shadow come back with one of the hounds, who opens the door to my jail and he say, 'Get on.'

"Ain't got to say it again, you know? So I get up and then I see that it ain't no shadow at all. It is Corrine Quinn in her mourning clothes. And when I walked outside, her chaise was there with her people. They sat me in the back with her and she told me she knew what I was headed for, what was coming, should Nathaniel hear of my run. But he really ain't need to hear nothing, she was sure of it. Nobody needed to know. I could go back to everything as it was before. Onliest thing she ask is, if she could stop down to the Street every now and again and speak to me."

"Speak to you about what?" I asked.

"Mostly things down here," Sophia said. "Like I tell you, she stop in now and again and ask about who still here and who gone Natchez-way. Always struck me as curious, you know. But after Caroline come, my only desire was to keep that baby safe. I ain't care about much else.

"But I did ask her about you," Sophia said. She put her arm around mine as she said this. "I asked her what they would do with you. She told me not to worry. You'd been gone a spell, but you would return. You would come back.

"Can't say I believed her, Hi. You know I have lost so much in my time, and I have found that what's gone is gone, and that is all there is.

"'Cept you. You came back," she said. And she was looking at me, looking through me, with dagger eyes. I felt the room spinning all around me. "I can hardly believe it, but you have come back. Come back to me."

I had now stopped thinking. I felt the beams and rafters and daubing of the cabin bend, and with them, the beams and rafters and daubing of the whole world encircle us, enclose us together. All of nature seemed in on it, so that when I tasted the rum of her mouth, it was the sugar of life.

And only then did I understand that I did not really remember everything, that there were things beyond my mother that I had chosen to forget—not pictures, but the feelings behind them. I had forgotten how much I dearly missed Sophia, how much I longed for her; had forgotten those days in Philadelphia, when all I wanted was for Raymond and Otha to leave me be, so that I could be alone with the memory of her, dancing by that large Holiday fire. And I had forgotten the low and deep sickness of longing pushing through the vessels of my body like a train pushing down the track. I had forgotten how I accepted this sickness, like a cough I could not shake, had forgotten the days when, alone, I drew my arms around my stomach and doubled over, feeling loneliness consume me. I loved her, and perhaps knowing, even then, the great danger of such a feeling under the Task, under slavery, and even in the Underground, I had forgotten as much of it as I could, though it had not forgotten me. And now it was here, with us, between us, and when she stroked her hand against my face, when she took my arm in her hands, she did not take it soft, but firm and wanting, and I knew then that all that I felt, all of the longing in me, all the bridled wanting of blind and violent youth, and the low need to vent it, was not solely my own.

• • •

Hours later, we were in the loft, staring upwards. Her arm was across my chest, her hand fingering my shoulder as if playing a piano.

"By God, it is you," she said. "Your hands. Your eyes. Your face."

It was now way past dark, so much so that I knew morning would soon be upon us, and then the rafters of the world would relax and we would be left in our regular places, and with our regular tasks at Lockless. But some things could not go back, and among them was a new knowledge that I felt upon me, and it was the same knowledge that compelled Otha White, the mania that took hold of him, how he could never truly sleep without Lydia. For the first time, I understood Conduction, understood it as a relay of feeling, assembled from moments so striking that they become real as stone and steel, real as an iron cat roaring down the tracks, chasing blackbirds from the awning.

As I dressed, while Sophia watched from the loft above, I looked at the mantel and saw the toy horse I had retrieved from the home of Georgie Parks, and I swear to you that it almost glowed. Sophia came back down from the loft now and stood behind me with her arms wrapped around my waist, her head on my back, as I studied the wooden horse in my hands.

"Go head," she said. "Take it. Told you it's a little soon for her to have such things."

"Yeah," I said. "Guess so."

I turned to Sophia then, with the small wooden horse still in my hand, and one last time, there in the dark, the world drew my lips to hers, and we held each other as if holding to the mast of a ship in a great storm.

"All right," I said. "Prolly should go."

"Prolly should," she said.

"All right," I said again, and when I walked outside into a different world, I did so backwards to preserve the look of her in those small blue hours, to hold it for as long as I might.

Everything would have been easier had I simply gone back up to the Warrens then and blacked my brogans and wiped myself clean. But this new understanding, this unlocking of old notions, prevailed on me. What I did instead was walk down a path that led me through the darkness to Dumb Silk Road. I now risked the hounds, which even then patrolled these roads for what had to be the last runaways out of a diminished Elm County. But as I walked, I fingered the wooden horse in my hands, and I knew that even if it had been the good years, the hounds could never truly threaten me.

Twenty minutes later, I was back there, back at the river Goose, which appeared not as a river but as a wide black mass stretching out across the land. I walked toward that mass until I could hear the river lapping gently up against its banks. It was cloudy out, so that there was no moon to illuminate anything. But there at the banks, I held up my hand, the same hand in which I held the wooden horse, and I saw the blue light of Conduction glowing out. And when I looked back at the river, I saw the now familiar mist rolling toward me.

No one had to teach me what came next. I did it almost by animal instinct—it was the simplest of motions, a firm squeeze that I now applied to the wooden horse—and having done this I saw the new mist over the river reach out, like the white tendrils of some mythical beast, and snatch me into its maw.

· 31 ·

THE SUMMONING OF A story, the water, and the object that
made memory real as brick: that was Conduction. What I
might do with such a power was not my immediate concern, so
much as making it through that day. The fatigue fell on me hard,
the same fatigue I'd felt before and the same that I had seen on
Harriet. Somehow I struggled through my duties, but when they
were over I slept through supper until the next day, when I awoke
to dress Howell, serve his morning meal, and assist him through
the light rigors of his day. And when supper came, there was a part
of me then that glowed bright as Conduction itself, for I knew
that I would see Sophia there. And when I did, that evening, I felt
myself walking in some other world. I wondered if I had dreamt
it all. But she was right there, with Thena, and with Caroline, and
when she saw me, she smiled and simply said, "You came back."

We spent the next few weeks happily together. At first, we tried
to hide the new developments from them. After supper, after Sophia made a show of leaving with Caroline, and after I had taken

my father his cider, sat with him, and put him to bed, I would walk down to the Street. Early in those smallest hours, I would make my way back up to my own bed, lie there for a half an hour or so, and then begin my labors. It was not as strange as it sounds. For many a tasking man at Lockless, with wife and children on other manses, this had long been the ritual. But my version was bizarre because it seemed to pin itself on the blindness of Thena. And she was not blind. So it should have been a surprise when she said, one evening, after supper, while holding Caroline, "I am happy for you." No more was said of it.

But there was not just Thena to worry after. Nathaniel Walker still held a known and particular title to Sophia and Caroline, and I well knew what happened to tasking folk found to have interfered with such claims. Corrine may have saved us once, but nothing would save either of us from his prideful wrath. It was a beautiful time, one of the best of my long life, but still it was built upon the shifting ground of the Task, and we knew that sooner or later the ground must shift again.

Early in December we heard of Nathaniel Walker's return and, a week later, of Sophia's inevitable summons. My father, still unwise to what was happening around him, told me to deliver Sophia. I cannot say that I found this pleasing. But I had now well absorbed the lesson—for Sophia to be mine, she must never be mine. And what was between us was not ownership, but a promise to be in the company of each other, by any means, for as long we could. And preserving the illusion was our means that wintery day when I drove her out to Nathaniel Walker's place.

We left early. Sophia slept for the first leg. We talked for the second.

"So what was the daily with Corrine?" she asked. "A clawfoot tub? Five white maids, each one naked as the day?"

We laughed.

"I do not hear you denying it."

"I don't deny nothing, Sophia."

"'Cept intelligence on your time away," she said. "Boy, what in God's name did they do to you?"

"Nothing really. I mean, ain't much to tell."

"It ain't you I'm interested in, Hi. I am interested in her interest in me. I still can't get, for the life of me, why she ain't leave me to Natchez."

"Don't know. Maybe she favor you."

"Whites favoring another man's slave? When you done heard of that?"

I said nothing.

"I hear she travel a bit. Hear she always filling your daddy's ear with stories of the scandalous sights she done seen up North. Guess she wouldn't never take no colored with her on that kind of jaunt."

"Maybe. I don't know."

"Sure you do, Hi. Either you been or you ain't."

I kept looking straight ahead at the road.

"Whatever. Don't try that on me. You ain't never been out of this here county, much less up North. If you had, I am sure I would never have caught a sight of you again."

"Why's that?"

"'Cause if you was up there with them free folks, you'd have to be as dumb as rocks to come back down here. I tell you, should I ever set my foot onto any grain of free soil, you will not hear any tell of me ever again."

"Huh. And that'd be the end of us, I guess."

"Now, you know you are not, in any way, built to run. Tried it once before. But you are tied to Lockless. The very fact of your return is the proof."

"Not my choosing. Not my choosing."

We reached Nathaniel Walker's place in late morning and drove off to the side road, where we waited for the courier who would greet us and then disappear with Sophia, and I must leave them to their private business. What did I feel out there? Surely there are higher callings than delivering a woman you love to another man. But I had years of practice having had to hide so much, and I knew whatever agony I felt being there must be doubled in Sophia. And I was older now. I understood things I could not even imagine months ago, so that I felt my greatest desire, in that moment, was to ease her. So when I noticed the edgy silence between us, and none of her usual jest, I spoke up and said, "How'd you get here while I was gone?"

"Walked," she said.

"You walked here?"

"I did. With my whole costume and effects. Thank God for Thena. She watched my Caroline that weekend. Only had to do it once, but I tell you, when I got that call, I was a mess. But I did it. Fit my face, my dress, and unmentionables right over there behind them bushes."

"My God . . ."

"Of all the things I done did, that was the one that left me feeling the most low. Had to strip down to what God gave me, in them bushes, afraid of who might walk by and what they might do. All I could do was sing to myself as I did, sing low and quiet, sing for courage."

Then Sophia breathed out long and heavy and said, "Don't ever doubt that I hate them. Don't you dare doubt it."

And as she said it, her face shifted into an executioner's mask. There was no furrowed or raised eyebrow. No spread of the mouth. No light in her brown eyes. Her face mirrored the truth of the hate she now spoke. She shook her head and said, "The things I would put on them, Hi. The things that I would be capable of. You see me here now, in this small body . . . Why, if my hands, my arms, were as those of men, what I would do with my energies. I have thought of it, you see. I thought of it even in this body, my God, what I would do while he slept, with a kitchen blade, or a tincture in his tea or white powder in his cake. . . . I thought of it very often, and, well, then I had my Caroline and that was that. And I am a good woman, Hi, I tell you I am. But what I would put on them, given my time, what I would put on them . . ."

She trailed off here into her own thoughts. After twenty minutes or so, a well-dressed tasking man emerged from the woody path. He walked over to the chaise and shot us a stern and disapproving look. "He cannot have you today. He will send word."

Then he turned away and walked back down the path.

"Did he say anything else?" Sophia called out. But the man did not turn back, and even if he heard Sophia it was clear he had no inclination to answer.

We sat there for a few moments, not quite sure what to do. Then Sophia turned to me with a wry smile and said, "You happy about this, ain't you?"

"I ain't unhappy," I said. "Besides, way you was just talking, I'd think you felt much the same."

"I do. I do," she said. "But it is odd. I have never had it happen this way before."

She was quiet for a moment, thinking to herself, turning over some recent theory.

"What?" I said.

"You probably did it," she said. "Some sort of way, I am betting that this is all your doing."

I laughed lightly, shook my head, and said, "It is amazing what you take me as, like I got powers over these white folks. Or I am some sort of conjure-man."

"You some sort of something, I will say that."

We laughed. I pulled the reins on the chaise and turned back around toward Lockless.

"I am sorry, Hiram," she said. "You know I don't want to be back there. I wanna be as far away as I can get. But if I got to do the work, I'd like to be done with it. Hate having this hanging over my head. I am a slave with him. But since you done come back, I feel myself to be as free as I have ever been. And though I know this is not the true article, it is something. And I want it."

Then she leaned over and kissed me lightly on the cheek. "I want as much of it as I can take."

Oh, to be back there, and be young again. To be seated in the dawning hours of my life, the sun of everything breaking over the horizon, and all the promises and tragedies ahead of me. To be there in that chaise, with a day-pass, and a girl I loved more than anything, in the last doleful days of old and desolate Virginia. Oh, to be there with time to spare, with time to dream of riding out as far as that Elm County road went until fortune abandoned us.

We rode on, speaking of the old days and all the Lost Ones of Elm County—Thurston, Lucille, Lem, Garrison. We talked of how they had gone, how Natchez had taken them. Some quiet. Some singing. Some laughing. Some swinging.

"What happened to Pete?" I asked.

"Sent over the bridge about a month before you come back," Sophia said.

"Thought Howell would never part with him," I said. "That man had such a hand for them orchards."

"All gone now," she said. "Natchez. As are all the rest. As are we all, soon enough. All gone. All done."

"Naw," I said. "I think we are survivors, you and I. If by devilish means, we are survivors. Maybe not much more than that. But we are, I do believe, survivors."

The winter had not yet given its full effect, and now we rode through a clear, crisp winter morning. We climbed high up on the road now, and I could see the Goose, and see across the shore over toward Starfall, and in the far distance I could see the bridge from which I had conducted myself into this other life.

"But what if we are not, Sophia?"

"What?"

"All gone. All done," I said. "What if there was some way by which we might make ourselves more than all the misery we have seen here?"

"This more of your dreams without facts? All sideways. You remember how that went, right?"

"I remember well. But we are connected, just as you say. We are older than our years. The place has made us that way, by all we have seen. We are out of time, you and I. What was glorious to them is crumbling before our eyes. But suppose we did not have to crumble with them? We know well that they are going down, Sophia. Suppose we did not have to go with them?"

She was now looking at me directly.

"I cannot, Hiram," she said. "Not like that. Not again. I know it's something about you. And when you are ready to tell me what that is, then I shall be with you. But I cannot go on just a word, not again. Ain't just me anymore, so if you have something, I have to know the all of it. I have said it. I would kill to be off of this, kill to save my daughter from it."

"Can't kill this one," I said.

"No," she said. "Can only run. But I must know how and I must know to what."

We did not speak much after that, as both our time was now much occupied with what had been said and the events of the day. But when we arrived back at Lockless, we found Thena seated at the edge of the tunnel with her head in her hand. There was a bandage wrapped around her head. She was in her work dress with no coat. Caroline was nowhere to be seen.

"Thena!" I said.

"Yeah?" she said.

"What happened?" Sophia said. "Where's Caroline?"

"Inside sleeping," Thena said.

Sophia darted into the tunnel. I squatted down and touched the side of Thena's temple where a spot of blood had pooled in the bandage.

"Thena, what happened?" I said.

"Don't know," she said. "I—I can't remember."

"Well, tell me what you do," I said.

She squinted her eyes. "I-I don't . . ."

"All right, all right," I said. "Come on, let's get in."

I put her arm over my neck and lifted, and as I did, I saw Sophia coming back out of the tunnel.

"She fine. Asleep, just like Thena said it," she said. "Look like Thena put her in your bed, and . . . I can see why." Then Sophia started to cry and said, "Hiram, they took it. I know what they was doing. They took it."

We walked a few steps and I felt Thena's feet begin to drag. So I picked her up in my arms and carried her. "Hold on," I said. We passed Thena's room first and what I saw was a half a chair on the ground and splinters everywhere. I walked past there to my old room, where I saw Caroline just beginning to stir. Sophia pulled the covers off and picked her up. I laid Thena down in her place and pulled the cover back over her.

I turned to Sophia. "The hell happened?"

She shook her head. She was still crying.

I walked back to Thena's room. It looked like someone had taken an axe to everything—the bed, the mantel, the one chair, it was all smashed. And then I looked over and saw the true aim— Thena's lockbox, which was splintered in two. Kneeling down, I saw some old souvenirs—beads, spectacles, a couple of playing cards. But what I did not see was the laundry money that Thena had so dutifully deposited every week, as her payment on freedom. I stood there for a moment trying to understand who would do such a thing. I had heard stories of old masters making such deals and then reneging, keeping all the money for themselves. But this made no sense with Thena—who was old, and willing to compensate Howell for her freedom and relieve him of her care. And the violence of it, the axing, spoke of someone who had no other means to compel Thena, and I knew, right then, that whoever had done it had to be Tasked.

You don't ever know how much you need your people until they are gone. By then Lockless was down to perhaps twenty-five souls. But it was not as it had been before, when, though there were more, we were all known to each other. Now I only knew a few of them on the Street and knew fewer still down in the Warrens. In the old days there were men, slave-doctors, who could have seen to Thena. But they were all gone, sent out, and we were left to ourselves. I thought of Philadelphia, and the warmth I felt knowing there was always someone, and I felt that a kind of lawlessness had now descended upon Lockless. Whom would I tell of the assault on Thena? My father? And what would be his answer then? To send more across the bridge? Could I even believe that the right perpetrator would be sent?

We made our share of changes over the next week. We moved, all of us, out of the Warrens and down to Thena's old cabin in the Street. It was where we felt our safest, and all it meant for me was that I would rise a bit earlier in the morning to get to my father in time for my duties. We did not leave Thena alone. Sophia took up the washing and I assisted as I could on Sundays, hauling up the water, gathering the wood, and wringing the laundry. Thena was mostly back to normal after a week. But the terror of that assault changed her, and for the first time in all my time of knowing her I saw true fear on her face, fear of what could happen remaining there at Lockless. And that was when I thought of Kessiah, and knew that the time of redeeming promises had come.

Thena was not my only concern. I learned later, through my father, that Nathaniel had never returned from Tennessee, despite his summons, and had been delayed by some urgent business. What that might be I could not know. But I thought that perhaps his intentions for Sophia might well go beyond what I had previously conceived. And I was not the only one thinking this.

Sophia said, "You ever think about me going that way?"

We were up in the loft, staring through the darkness up at the rafters. Caroline was asleep between us, while down below, on the ground floor, Thena snored softly.

"I do," I said. "Especially lately."

"You know what I hear?" she asked.

"What?"

"I hear things are different in Tennessee. Hear that it's far from this society and there are different customs, and there are white men there who take colored women like man and wife. And I been wondering bout Nathaniel and his particulars, for instance the desire that I make myself up like . . ."

She trailed off as though working her way through a thought, and then said, "Hiram, is that man grooming me for something? Is it his intention to get out of custom, and finally install me as his Tennessee wife?"

"Is that what you want? Tennessee?" I asked.

"Is that what the hell you think I want?" she asked. "Don't you know by now? What I want is the same thing I have always wanted, what I have always told you I wanted. I want my hands, my legs, my arms, my smile, all my precious parts to be mine and mine alone."

She turned toward me now, and though I was still looking at the ceiling I could feel her looking directly at me.

"And should I feel a need, should I desire to give all that to some other, then it must be my own need, my own desire to do as such. Do you understand, Hiram?"

"I do."

"You do not. You can't."

"Then why do you keep telling me?"

"I am not telling you, I am telling myself. I am remembering my promises to myself and to my Caroline."

We lay there in silence until we fell asleep. But I forgot none of the conversation. The time was so clearly now. I had performed my duties well, keeping Hawkins informed. And more, I had opened the secret of Conduction for myself. I felt it now time for Corrine Quinn to make good on her portion of the bargain.

Holiday came upon us. It was to be a lonely time. The Walker clan would not be returning that year, and with Maynard gone my father now faced the prospect of the blessed season all alone. But Corrine Quinn, having grown closer and closer to him, relieved his lonesome situation by coming to Lockless with her own retinue—this time much larger than merely Hawkins and Amy. They were trusted cooks, maids, and other caretakers. And too Corrine brought a collection of cousins and friends to entertain my father, who was now up in age. And this ensemble pleased him greatly, for there was a rapt audience before him eager to hear the tales of old Virginia.

It was a charade, of course. Every one of these cooks, caretakers, and cousins was an agent—some whom I'd known from my time training at Bryceton and others who'd worked out of the Starfall station. The plan was now clear to me. As Elm County declined and fell into obsolescence, and the Quality quit the country, in the crawl-space left behind, the Underground would ply its trade, expanding its war. Looking back now from the prospect of years, I confess myself filled with admiration. Corrine was daring, ruthless, ingenious, and while Virginia lived in fear of another Prophet Gabriel or Nat Turner, what they should have feared was right in their own home, in the garb of ladyhood, the model of fine breeding, porcelain elegance, and undying grace.

I could not see the genius of it, not at the time, for we were, even if united in our goal, too much committed to opposing routes. The tasking men were people to me, not weapons, nor cargo, but people with lives and stories and lineage, all of which I remembered, and the longer I served on the Underground, this sense did not diminish but increased. So it was that day, at the closing of the year, when I insisted on what must be done, that we stood at opposite ends.

We were down by the Street. Our story was simple—Corrine had desired a tour of the old quarters and I was her guide. So I had escorted her down from the main house and we made small, insignificant talk, until we cleared the gardens and the orchards and found ourselves on the winding path to the Street.

"When I came back to Howell's, it was on the promise that a family would be conducted north," I said. "The time for that conduction is now."

"And why now?" she asked.

"Something happened here a couple of weeks ago," I said. "Somebody got after Thena. Took an axe-handle to her head and then busted up her quarters. Took all the money she had been saving from the washing."

"My Lord," she said, and a look of real concern broke through the mask of ladyhood. "Did you find the villain?"

"No," I said. "She don't remember who it was. Besides, the way people are moved in and out of here these days . . . tough to tell. I know more of this crew you have brought with you than of the people who work here every day."

"Should we investigate?"

"No," I said. "We should get her out."

"But not just her, right? There is another—your Sophia."

"Not mine," I said. "Just Sophia."

"Well, I'll be," Corrine said with a faint smile. "How much have you grown in one year? It truly is a marvel. You really are one of us. Forgive me, it is a thing to behold."

She was regarding me in amazement, though I now think she was not so much regarding me in that moment as regarding the fruit of her own endeavor, so that it was not I who amazed Corrine so much as her own powers.

"Do you yet remember?" she asked.

"Remember?"

"Your mother," she said. "Have your remembrances of her returned yet?"

"No," I said. "But I have had other concerns."

"Of course, forgive me. Sophia."

"I am worried that Nathaniel Walker will call her title, call her down to Tennessee."

"Oh, you needn't worry about that," Corrine said.

"Why?"

"Because I made arrangements with him a year ago. In one week, her title will revert to me."

"I don't understand," I said.

Corrine gave me a look of bemused concern.

"Don't you?" she said. "She's had his child, hasn't she?"

"Yes," I said.

"Then you understand," she said. "You are, after all, a man yourself, a simple creature of severe but brief interests, subject to seasons of lust that wax and wane. As is your uncle, your man of Quality, Nathaniel Walker. And now that he is in Tennessee, he has an entire field for his passions. What would he need of Sophia?"

"But he called on her," I said. "It was not but two weeks ago that he called on her."

"I am sure he did," she said. "A souvenir, perhaps?"

Corrine Quinn was among the most fanatical agents I ever encountered on the Underground. All of these fanatics were white. They took slavery as a personal insult or affront, a stain upon their name. They had seen women carried off to fancy, or watched as a father was stripped and beaten in front of his child, or seen whole families pinned like hogs into rail-cars, steam-boats, and jails. Slavery humiliated them, because it offended a basic sense of goodness that they believed themselves to possess. And when their cousins perpetrated the base practice, it served to remind them how easily they might do the same. They scorned their barbaric brethren, but they were brethren all the same. So their opposition was a kind of vanity, a hatred of slavery that far outranked any love of the slave. Corrine was no different, and it was why, relentless as she was against slavery, she could so casually condemn me to the hole, condemn Georgie Parks to death, and mock an outrage put upon Sophia.

I had not put it together like this in that moment. What I had was not logic but anger, and not anger at the slandering of something I owned, but of someone who held me upright in the darkest night of my life. But I did not vent this anger. I had been practicing the mask long before I met Corrine. Instead, I simply said, "I want them out. Both of them."

"There's no need," said Corrine. "I have title to the girl, and so she is saved."

"And Thena?"

"It's not time, Hiram," she said. "There are a great many things in the works, and we must take care to not endanger them. The powers of Elm County are diminished and every day we grow stronger, but we must take care. And I have done much already that might arouse suspicion. There is the fact of what we have done at Starfall. There is the fact that both of you ran, that the girl ran. Did she tell you I looked after her?"

"She did."

"Then you must understand. There is too much to contend with at once. If we were ever figured out, so many would suffer." She had dropped her mocking tone and was now on the verge of pleading. "Hiram, listen to me," she said. "Your service to the Underground has been of great value. Your reports on your father have opened up possibilities we had not even considered. Even if you never master Conduction, you have proven yourself more than worth the risks we took in bringing you out. But we have much to balance and consider. What does it look like for me to take the title of Nathaniel Walker's consort, only for her to immediately disappear? And this woman Thena has made an enterprise out of the washing. Will people not wonder when she suddenly stops coming around? We have to be so very careful, Hiram."

"You made a promise," I said.

"Yes, I did," she said. "And it is my intention to keep it. But not just now. We will need time."

I locked on to Corrine with a hard gaze. It was the first time I had looked at her without the respect that Virginia demanded. She was not being unreasonable. In fact, she was correct. But I was hot over her mocking of Sophia and there were my own feelings and shame at having delivered Sophia into outrage all those times, at having left Thena to run, and then left her again to be assaulted, at my mother who was sold, who I could not protect, who I did not avenge. All of that roiled in me and it shot out in the look I now put upon Corrine.

"You cannot do it," Corrine said. "You will need us, and we will not consent. We will not put ourselves to the sword for your brief and small infatuations. You cannot do it."

And then a look of recognition bloomed across her face until it covered the whole of her visage in horror, and she understood.

"Or maybe you can," she said. "Hiram, you will bring hell upon us all. Think. Think beyond your emotions. Think beyond all your guilt. You have no right to endanger all who might be so rescued. Think, Hiram."

But I was thinking. I was thinking of Mary Bronson and her lost boys. I was thinking of Lambert under the Alabama ox and Otha presently tracking cross the country for the freedom of his Lydia. Lydia, who endured all outrage for the chance of family.

"Think, Hiram," she said.

"You told me freedom was a master," I said. "You said it was a driver. You said none can fly, that we are tied to the rail. 'I know,' you told me. 'And because I know, I must serve.'"

"You know I am not without sympathy," she said. "I know what happened to you."

"No, you don't," I said. "You can't."

"Hiram," she said, "promise me you will not doom us."

"I promise that I will not doom us," I said. But the word-play put no folly upon her, and the less said about our remaining interview the better, for I hold her, all these years later, in the highest respect. She was speaking in full faith and honesty. And so was I.

· 32 ·

I WAS OUT THERE ON my own now, and if Conduction was to be achieved, it must be done by my hand alone. And it seemed to me that there was no longer any avoiding the facts of my departure. I would have to tell them both—Sophia and Thena. I decided I would tell them each separately, for my confession to Thena involved matters far greater than the Underground. So I would start with what I thought was the simpler of confessions—Sophia.

Thena had begun to have nightmares, we thought from her attack. And so we got in the habit, on difficult nights, of leaving Caroline down below with her to sleep on her bosom and calm her. And it was such a night as this when I felt it was time.

"Sophia," I said, "I am ready to tell you for what and I am ready to tell you how."

She had been looking up into the gabled rafters, and now she rolled over, pulled the osnaburg blanket over herself, and turned to me.

"It's about where I been," I said. "About where I was and what happened when I was there."

"Wasn't Bryceton," she said.

"It was," I said. "But that was just the start of it."

Even in that darkness, I could see her eyes, and they were too much for me to take. I rolled over so that my back was to her. I breathed in deep, and then breathed back out.

And then I told her that I had, in the time I was gone, seen another country, taken in the easy Northern air, that I had awakened when I wanted and moved as I pleased, that I had trained in to Baltimore, walked through the carnival of Philadelphia, and driven through the uplands of New York, and that I had done this all through my affiliation with that agency of freedom known only to her in whispers and tales—the Underground.

And I told her how it had happened, how Corrine Quinn had found me, how they had trained me at Bryceton, how Hawkins and Amy were in on the ruse. I told her how Georgie Parks had been destroyed, and how I had been party to that destruction. I told her about the family White, how they had loved me, how they had saved Mary Bronson, how Micajah Bland had given up his life. I told her how I had met Moses, how Kessiah had survived the racetrack, how she remembered Thena, how I had promised to conduct Thena and how I now planned to conduct her too.

"I promised to get you out," I said. "And I mean to keep that promise."

I turned back over, and I found those eyes waiting for me. There was a kind of deadness in them now—no shock or surprise, no emotion betrayed.

"That why you come," she said. "To keep your promise."

"No," I said. "I come back because I was told to."

"And had you not been told to?" she asked.

"Sophia, I thought of you all the time up there," I said. I reached over and stroked her face with my hand. "I worried for you, worried for what they might have done to you . . ."

"But while you were worrying," she said, "I was down here. Not knowing what was coming. Not knowing what had happened to you. Not knowing anything of that woman Corrine's intentions."

"She got your title from Nathaniel," I said. "You ain't going to Tennessee."

She shook her head and said, "And what am I supposed to make of that? You come back with this tale, and I do believe it, I really do, but Hiram, I know you, I do not know them."

"But you *do* know me," I said. "And I am sorry for how it has come down, but I have heard you now, I have heard all of what you were saying from the start. And I understand that it is not just you, but Caroline. I am getting you out. Thena too."

"And what about you?" she said.

"I am here until told otherwise," I said. "I am part of this now. It is bigger than me and my desires."

"Bigger than me too," she said. "Bigger than this girl who you said was your blood."

There was a long silence and then Sophia rolled over again, so that she was staring at the rafters.

"And you still ain't said how," she said. "I told you I needed a how."

"How, huh?" I asked.

"Yeah, how," she said.

"Come on," I said.

"What?"

"You said you wanted to know how. Well, you wanna know or you don't?"

By then I was climbing down the ladder. At the door I put on my brogans and wrapped myself in my fear-no-man coat. Looking back, I saw Sophia gazing at Caroline, still snoring lightly on Thena's bosom.

"Come on," I said.

We walked along that route that had now become sacred to me. I had been practicing, experimenting as I could with the powers and reach of memory, so that when we arrived, minutes later, at the banks of the river Goose, I felt myself in control.

I turned to Sophia and said, "You ready?" To this she rolled her eyes and shook her head. I took her hand, and in the other hand I clutched the wooden horse.

And then I guided her down toward the banks, and as we walked I spoke of that night, that last Holiday when we were all there together, and more than spoke it, I felt it, made it real to me— Conway and Kat, Philipa and Brick, Thena all wrathy in front of the fire—"Land, niggers," she said. "Land." And I remembered, then, Georgie Parks, Amber, and their little boy. And I remembered the free ones—Edgar and Patience, Pap and Grease. And no sooner did I think of them than I felt Sophia jump with a start, and squeeze my hand, and I knew then that it had begun.

There was a bank of fog covering the river, and over top of it we saw them—phantoms flittering before us, in that ghostly blue, the entire range of them who had been there on that Holiday night. Georgie Parks was on his jaw-harp, Edgar at the banjo, Pap and Grease were hollering, and all the rest circled and danced around the fire. We could hear them, not in our ears, but somewhere deep beneath the skin. It seemed that the bank of fog was alive, for its wispy fingers seemed to move in time with the music, seemed to stretch toward us and, on beat, gently induce us to join.

It was a simple thing to accept the invitation—all that it required was a squeeze of that wooden horse. When I did this, those same fingers shot out, took hold of us, jerked us forward and released us. I felt Sophia stumbling, and grabbed ahold of her hand. When she'd recovered, she looked back at me stunned. And then when we looked out forward, we saw that the forest was in front of us, and the river, the bank of fog, and the phantoms were behind. Looking back across, we could see what happened—we'd been conducted across the river to the other side.

Looking down, we saw the blue tendrils of mist retreating off of us, and we heard the music picking up again, louder and louder—Georgie still on the jaw-harp, Edgar with his banjo, while the rest of them hollered and danced, and again we saw the fingers of fog reach for us, beckoning us with the beat. Now I pulled the wooden horse from my pocket and held it aloft—and it glowed blue in my hand. And I looked to Sophia and then I squeezed again, and the mists shot out, snatched us up, and pulled us to the other side of the river. When we were released, Sophia stumbled and fell. I helped her up and we turned again and heard the music rising and saw, again, the fingers of fog beckon.

"It's like dancing," I said.

And I squeezed again, but this time, Sophia leaned into the fog with all her weight, giving in to it, riding it, so that she landed firm on her feet. I squeezed again and we were again conducted. Squeezed again and were conducted. Squeezed again and were conducted. Then, thinking of my old home with Thena and all my days there, and what it had been to me through all those years, I squeezed again and the blue tendrils snatched us up, and this time, when they released us, we found ourselves right back there on the Street, and as the fog retreated, the last image we had was of a woman water dancing, a jar on her head, dancing away from us until, with the most incredible grace, she angled her head so that the jar slid down, and reaching up she caught the jar by the neck, laughed, drank from it, and offered it up to someone unseen as she faded away.

When we returned to the cabin, Sophia climbed up to the loft. I tried to follow but collapsed back in a heap and crash so loud that I woke Thena.

"Hell are y'all doing?" she yelled.

"Just out for some air," Sophia said.

"Air, huh?" Thena said skeptically.

Sophia reached down and helped me up the ladder, and when I got to the top I collapsed into a dreamless sleep. I awoke early the next morning and dragged myself through my tasks.

The night following, we were there laid out in the loft as usual, in our late-night conversations.

"Where'd you first see the water dance?" I asked.

"Don't even remember," Sophia said. "Where I'm from, everybody do it. Some better than others. But they start us on it young down there. It's tied to the place, you know?"

"I don't," I said. "Never knew where it came from."

"It's a story," she said. "Was a big king who come over from Africa on the slave ship with his people. But when they got close to shore, him and his folk took over, killed all the white folks, threw 'em overboard, and tried to sail back home. But the ship run aground, and when the king look out, he see that the white folks' army is coming for him with they guns and all. So the chief told his people to walk out into the water, to sing and dance as they walked, that the water-goddess brought 'em here, and the water-goddess would take 'em back home.

"And when we dance as we do, with the water balanced on our head, we are giving praise to them who danced on the waves. We have flipped it, you see? As we must do all things, make a way out of what is given. Ain't that what you done last night? Ain't that what you say you do? Flipped it. It's what Santi Bess done, ain't it? She all I could think about when we came back up out of it last night. That king. The water dance. Santi Bess. You.

" 'It's like dancing.' Ain't that what you said? It's what Santi Bess done. She ain't walk into no water. She danced, and she passed that dance on to you.

"And that's why they came for you, the Underground," she said.

"Yep," I said. "I had done it before, but not of my own deciding. And they had caught wind of me, and had been watching me. And then after Maynard, well . . ."

"That's how it happened, huh? That's how you come up out the Goose. That's how you taking us up out of Lockless."

"It is," I said. "But there is a problem, one I do not yet quite have figured. The thing works on memory, and the deeper the memory, the farther away it can carry you. My memory of that Holiday night is tied to Georgie, and it's tied to this horse that was my gift to him and his baby. But to conduct y'all that far, I need a deeper memory, and need another object tied to that memory to be my guide."

"How bout that coin you used to always carry?"

"Yeah, I done tried that. It can't carry me far enough. One thing to cross a river. Whole nother to cross a country. Gotta be deeper."

Sophia was quiet for a moment and then she said, "That's quite the power. Gotta be that you are a man of some importance to this Underground."

"That's what Corrine say."

"And this is why she won't let you loose."

"It's more than that," I said. "But that is the larger part of it."

"So then, Hiram," she said. "What is your intention toward me, toward my Caroline? What is our life to be?"

"I don't know," I said. "I figured I'd get you set up somewhere. And I could see y'all from time to time."

"No," she said.

"What?" I said.

"We not going," she said.

"Sophia, it's what we wanted. It's why we was running."

"'We,' Hiram," she said. "'We,' you understand?"

"I would like nothing more than to go with you, to leave it all back here. But you must see why I cannot. After all I have told you, after what I have shared of this war that we find upon us, you must see why I can't leave."

"I am not telling you to leave. I am saying that we, my Carrie and me, we are not leaving without you. I have lived here so long watching these families go to pieces. And here I have formed one, with you, with a man who is, as you have said yourself, blood of my Caroline. She is your kin, and I know it is a horrible thing to say, but I am telling you, you are her daddy, more of a daddy than that girl would ever have."

"You know what you saying?" I said. "Do you know what you are walking away from?"

"No," she said. "But one day I will and when I do, I will know it with you."

I felt in that moment something low and beautiful. Something born down here on the Street, and all the Streets of America. Something nurtured and birthed out of the Warrens. It was the warmth of the muck. It was the relief of the low-born. The facing of the facts, the flight from Quality, the gravity and excrement of the true world where we all live.

I turned away to sleep and felt Sophia pulling close to me and slipping her arm underneath mine, until her hand found the warm, soft part of me.

"You know you chaining yourself to something here."

And for a while the only answer was the soft warm breath on the back of my neck, and then she said, "Ain't a chain if it is my choosing."

The next day, Thena and I went out on our route, collecting the washing. And then we spent the next hauling up the water and tubs, beating the jackets and trousers and then hanging them in the drying room down in the Warrens. Sophia was not with us, pleading illness on behalf of Caroline. But there was no illness, it was part of our plan, one that was ill-thought, for now, at the end of the day, with our hands worn and our arms exhausted, Thena was ornery at her absence.

"What is wrong with her, Hi?" Thena said. We were walking slowly back down to the Street. The sun had faded long ago and we moved like shadows down the path, past the orchards and through the woods. "I wish you had chosen a girl with more back to her. That Sophia don't know nothing about work."

"She work just fine," I said. "She worked for you while I was gone."

"If that is what you must call it," Thena said. "Way I see it, she only start really doing it once you was here. How you gonna make a way with a woman like that, Hi? All that's put on a man's life, how you gonna get it done with a woman who only work for show? When I was young, I outworked every man on the home-place, every one, even mine. I was terror in the tobacco fields, and I kept house too. Of course I sometimes wonder what it all got me—cracked over the head and robbed of my little stack of free-dom. So maybe that girl know something I do not."

"I seen Kessiah," I said. All day I had tried to weave this an-nouncement, somehow, into our conversation. I had failed at dis-covering some decorous way to accomplish this, and knowing that it had to be done, I elected for the most direct route.

Thena stopped and turned to me. "Who?"

"Your daughter," I said. "Kessiah. I seen her."

"Is this you being mad for what I said about that girl?"

"I have seen her," I said, as firm as I could muster.

"Where?" said Thena.

"North," I said. "She lives just outside Philadelphia. Was taken to Maryland after she was stripped from you. From there, escaped north. She got a family. A husband who is good to her."

"Hiram . . ."

"She want you to join her," I said. "She want you up there with her. Thena, this ain't no joke. When I left her I told her I would get you back to her. I promised, and I now mean to honor that promise."

"Honor? How?"

And there in the forest, as I had done with Sophia, I explained what had happened to me, what I had become.

"So this the Underground?" she asked.

"It is," I said. "And it ain't."

"Well, which is it?"

"It's me," I said. "It's me. And I'm asking if you can hold to that."

"Kessiah?" she asked of no one in particular. "Last time I seen her she was such a small thing. Willful as hell. She loved her daddy, you know? And he was so very hard. We used to have camellias. It was another time, another time. She would go out back and pick in them until I . . ."

She paused here and her face took on a look of confusion.

"Kessiah . . ." she said softly. And then the tears came, slow and silent, and without a cry or wail. She said her daughter's name again and then she turned to me and asked, "Did you see any of the others?"

I shook my head and said, "I am sorry."

And that was when the wailing came, and it was low and deep and throaty, and she moaned to herself, "Oh Lord, oh Lord," and shook her head.

"Why you bring this back to me? Why you do this? You and your Underground? Hell I care. I have settled up with it. Why you bring this to me?"

"Thena, I—"

"Naw, you done spoke, let me speak. Do you know what I done? And you, you should have known. You who I took in, you bring this back to me! You do this to me.

"In this very house where I took you in, when you wasn't spit, and you come down here and do this to me? Do you know what it took for me to make peace with this?"

She was backing away from me now, backing her way out of the cabin.

"Thena . . ."

"No, you stay away from me. You and your girl, y'all stay away from me."

She ran out into the night and I chased after her, tried to take her arm. She shook me off, elbowing, punching, and wrenching her way loose.

"Stay away, I say!" she yelled. "Stay away! How dare you bring me back like this. Stay as far from me as you can, Hiram Walker! You are done to me!"

I should not have been surprised. I knew by then how much the past weighs upon us. I knew this more than anyone. I knew men who had held down their own wives to be flogged. I knew children who'd watched those men hold down their mothers. I knew children who rooted through slop with hogs. But worst of all I knew how the memory of such things altered us, how we could never escape it, how it became an awful part of us. And I must have known this in my young years. Why else that one memory, that memory of my mother, taken and shut up in a lockbox.

So who was I, in that moment, watching Thena disappear into the night, to begrudge her desire to forget? Oh, I understood it all. I walked back into that cabin and sat there silent for long hours, knowing how well I understood Thena's rage. And all night I turned this over, until lying there with Sophia, and young Caroline between us, I knew what must be done. Kessiah would always be a souvenir of what Thena had lost, of what was taken, so that to see her daughter again, Thena must remember. And I knew that I could in no way ask this of her if I were not prepared to do the same myself.

· 33 ·

EARLY THE NEXT MORNING, I rose, drew up water for the washing, and cleaned myself. Walking up to the white palace in those small hours, I thought of all the pieces that had been assembled before me, the bread-crumbs along the road. I thought of that old African king, who had flipped it, and danced into the waves, as my grandmother had done, and with the water-goddess's blessing danced his people back home. And what did it mean that I saw my mother there that night with Maynard, dancing on the bridge, patting juba, dancing over and under the water, flipping it?

Even if Thena came around and decided to go, it would take a powerful memory to move her. So that morning, after serving my father breakfast and taking him out for a survey of the property, while he rested in the parlor, I walked up into his study, where he kept his correspondences, and scrawled a few lines in care of the Philadelphia Underground. I had to be careful, of course. I made use of a local alias and directed my missive to one of our safe-houses on the southern docks of the Delaware, and by code and misdirection let it be known to Harriet what I would now be attempting. I do not know what I then expected. And more, I did not know, even with family in the balance, what side Harriet might take in the struggle. But she had said that should I find myself in need, I was to make it known. And I had done so.

With that done, I went and collected my father and went with him through his various correspondences—almost all of them now originating in the West. His eyes and hands had by then grown much too weak, so I read them aloud, took down his responses, and then prepared them all to be sent out. When that was done, we walked back to his room and I helped him change into a suitable set of work clothes. After this, I went down into the Warrens and changed into my overalls, and met him in the garden out behind the house and together with spade and fork we worked until the sun had just begun its descent. We walked inside, changed again, and then I served my father his afternoon cordial, and, as was his tradition, he soon fell fast asleep. It was now time.

I walked upstairs and then into my father's study, and looked at the mahogany highboy and thought back again with shame to Maynard's game of rummaging among things that were not his own. It was an absurd shame—nothing in this house, on this land, indeed on this earth, could be called the rightful property of Howell Walker. And yet, being Quality, being a pirate, this never stopped him from laying claim. It was only natural that Maynard do the same. Perhaps I should too.

When I pulled at the small bottom drawer and saw the ornate rosewood box, its silver clasps gleaming, I cannot say I knew what was inside. But when I rubbed my hands over the top of the box, I sensed that should I choose to open it, nothing could ever be the same again. And so it was.

What I saw was a necklace of shells, and in an instant I was sure that it was that same necklace that I had seen the night my brother died, shaking from the neck of the dancer, shaking from the neck of my mother. And what I did now was bring the necklace to me, reaching behind my own neck to put it on, and when the hook-and-eye clasp locked into place like a lost jigsaw, a wave rippled out through my fingers, through my wrists and arms, into the deepest part of me, so that I stumbled back. When I regained myself, I knew that the wave, which was only then subsiding, was the force of memory. The memory of my mother. And now, all that I had known as the words of others formed into portrait and pictures. The fog and smoke of my years blew away, so that I saw my mother in her full form, in all our short years together, and too, I saw her end, and I saw exactly how that end had come and I saw precisely who had brought it about.

I tell you, it took all of my restraint to not rush down those stairs and into the garden where the spade and fork were still planted in the cold ground, pull them out, and relieve my father of that brief splash of life that remained in his mortal vessel. And that I did not is only testament to what I felt then at stake, to those whom I loved, who I then knew were counting on me to remember, and to remember I had to live.

I closed the box and shoved it back into the highboy. Then I tucked the necklace of shells under my shirt. I walked back downstairs and saw that my father was now awake, and looking out the window I could see that evening was upon us. It occurred to me then that what felt like mere seconds had been much longer. I went out to the kitchen and saw that my father's meal was being prepared and remembered that he was not to be dining alone that evening. I walked up the first course—bread and terrapin soup—and found waiting there at the dinner table with my father Corrine Quinn. She never betrayed anything that evening, but at the end, as they repaired to the parlor for tea, she mentioned to me that she believed Hawkins wished a word with me.

I walked outside and down to the stables, well anticipating what he would have to say. Hawkins was tied to the Virginia Underground and thus to the word of Corrine Quinn. It was her figuring, no doubt, that if she could not stop me, perhaps someone who had once seen the world as I had would make me understand. It was now late. The air was crisp and cold. A bright moon hung high in the sky. I found Hawkins seated inside the chaise, puffing on a cigar. When he saw me, he smiled and held out his hand to offer me a seat.

"I know why you here," I said. "Ain't nothing you can say to change what's coming."

"Huh," he said. Then he reached into his pocket and said, "My only notion was to offer you a cigar."

"That ain't your only notion," I said.

"Naw, it's not."

He handed me the cigar.

"My feeling is that I have been hard with you," he said. "It is by virtue of my position, but it is also by cause of what I have seen and how I come to the position. You understand that me and my Amy, we were pulled out by Corrine, yes?"

"I do."

"And you know that we was at Bryceton before she came."

I nodded.

"Then I guess all I want you to know is how much hell passed on that place. It was not the normal, small stepper. It was not just the Task. Edmund Quinn was the meanest white man this world has known, I am convinced of it. And you see how it is now? You see how Bryceton put on a face whenever the Quality is about? Look like Virginia of old, don't it? And then when they are gone we are back to our business.

"Bryceton always been that way—two-faced—but Edmund Quinn's business was different. Many years I watched him pose as a man of God and honor, toasting at the socials, sending his money to the alms-house, money made off our backs. Forgive me, Hiram, but I cannot speak of what he did. What I will say is that it was such that I would have done anything to be out from under him, to save me and mine from that man's wrath. And that chance only came from Corrine Quinn.

"I am thankful for Corrine. I truly am—thankful for what she done for my sister and me, and for all and every soul that come through the Virginia Underground. Ain't too much I would not do in her service, for it was her plotting that rid us of that demon and, more, put us upon this new task of ridding the greater Demon he served."

Hawkins leaned back and puffed on his cigar so that the tip glowed orange against the dark and wisps of white smoke flowed out.

"So when she come to me and say that one of our own, who was brought out of the Task, as so many have been brought out, was now planning to go against her, to go against us, and she ask me to speak to him and prevail upon him with truth and wisdom, I could only oblige."

"Ain't no point," I said. "You don't know what I seen."

But he kept talking as though I had not spoken.

"I seen a lot of folks come through that Virginia station, and man, do they ever and always bring they troubles right along. Nothing ever go as it should on rescue. You seen it yourself. Bland into Alabama. That fellow who brought his girl with him last year. You know what I mean. It never play out like you draw and figure it. And when you out here in the field, it can be hard on you when folks do not act as you need them.

"Take you, for instance. What we heard was that you would be the one. You would open the door. You would snap your finger or twitch your nose and whole plantations would vanish." Hawkins laughed to himself. "Ain't quite work out as such."

"I have tried," I said. "I have done—" But once again he talked through me.

"But I think this is the lesson in it all. We forget sometimes—it is freedom we are serving, it is the Task that we are against. And freedom mean the right of a man to do as he please, not as we suppose. And if you have not been as we supposed, you have been as you were supposed to be."

Now Hawkins was silent for a moment and we sat there and smoked, the cool crisp wind blowing through us.

"I don't know what you done seen, Hiram. I don't know what happened to them folks you bent on bringing out. And I would like to tell you, very much, that what you are doing is not what I would do. But I cannot speak as such in any righteous way, for who can say what I would have done to bring myself out, to bring out my Amy? You are free and must act according to your own sense. Can't be according to mine. Can't be according to Corrine."

"Don't matter none," I said. "Look like they don't want out anyway."

Hawkins laughed quietly.

"Yes they do," he said. "Everybody do. Ain't a matter of if they want out. All want out of this. It's just a matter of how."

That following Sunday, I met Thena early that morning to deliver the washing, which was folded and boxed in crates. We did the rounds in silence, and when I returned the chaise and tied up the horse, she walked off without a word. I followed her up into the tunnel and found her in her old room, where she'd been living for the past week.

"Well?" she asked sardonically, looking up at me.

"So that's it, is it?" I said.

"Seem like it."

"All right," I said, and walked down to the Street. But the next day when I came up for my dealings with my father, she was waiting there just before the secret staircase that led out of the Warrens into the upper house. I could see by the lantern-light that she had been crying. When she saw me, she shook her head and wiped her cheeks.

"It is a lot to put on anyone, Hi. It is a weight. A whole other Task."

"I know," I said. "I have seen it all now, remember it all now, and I know."

"Do you?" she said. "Because I do not think you do. I think you know your end of it, which is the end of the child stripped from the bosom. But do you know the other side of things? Do you know how hard it was for me to love you as I did, Hiram? To be in that space again, after what had been done to my Silas, my Claire, my Aram, my Alice, and my Kessiah. It was so very hard. But I seen you up in that loft, looking down, and I knew that mines was never coming back, and yours was never coming back, and if we had nothing between us, at least we had that.

"And I did love you, Hi. I did go back into that room. And when you left me there, when you run off with your girl, I cried myself to sleep every night for a month. I was so very afraid for what they would do to you. I could hardly believe it. I had lost another one—but not even to the Task. And so it must be me. Something in me that push everything I love away. It tore me up, something awful. Then you come back, except you do not come back alone. You come back with stories, stories from that room where I was violated and trespassed upon. And now you are telling me that I have to go back.

"What will I say to her, Hi? What will I be? What will I do when I look at her and all I can see are my lost ones?"

Her head was in her hand and she was weeping softly and quietly. I pulled her to me and put her head in my chest and we held each other there, and so began the countdown of our last hours at Lockless.

We could have in no way remained, not at Lockless as it was, nor at Lockless as we believed it to be becoming. Sophia had protections now, the protections of Corrine, who for whatever her demerits had always been true to her word. But for Thena, the advance of age and the assault upon her propelled matters forward in my mind. My father was by then so much in the dealing and trading of his people, doing all that he could imagine to stay afloat and dodge the debtors that seemed to swarm all around him. He could not continue as such, and he would not, though I did not know that then. But even if I had, there was a promise I had made to Kessiah and I was determined then to make it good.

I waited two weeks for some reply from Harriet. But receiving none, I deduced that I could expect no assistance, a fact to which I could muster no rage nor disquiet. I had been with the Underground only a year, and knowing the intensity of the work, I understood the need to preserve allegiances. I was on my own then, an Underground station all to myself. I had done it in the smallest way on the banks of the Goose, but to conduct as the old African king, as Santi Bess, as Moses, seemed fantastic. I had my memories, though. All of them. And I had the object by which I hoped to focus the energies of those lost-found years.

Our last night all together was the coldest of that season. It was a Saturday, so picked because it would give a day for me to recover myself and be back at my duties on Monday, arousing no suspicion. We gathered together what we would then have considered a feast—ash-cake, fish, salt pork, and collards. We ate quietly together and then sat in the cabin, where Thena had returned. And now Thena amused Sophia with stories of her own youth, and much laughter passed on this account. And then the hour came upon us. There was a hurried goodbye. I told Sophia to wait for me back at the quarters, and were I not back by dawn for her to look for me down by the riverbanks.

Outside the cabin, I looked up into the night, which was big and clear, the moon bright as a goddess, the stars all her progeny, all her fates and dryads and nymphs, spread out across the cosmos. Then I held Thena's hand and walked with her out from the cabin, through back-paths of the woods, the earth snapping and crunching beneath us, until we were at the banks of the river Goose. I had not told Thena what to expect. I did not know how I could. All she knew was that I had found the route of Santi Bess and that Sophia had testified to its truth. So it was understandable that right here Thena, holding tight to my hand, stopped in her tracks, and when I turned to her, I saw that she was looking up, and when I followed her stunned gaze, I saw that the night sky that had, moments before, been so big and bright, was now obscured by clouds. Wisps of white fog were now coming up off the river, which was only evidenced by the sound it made gently washing up against the shore. The necklace of shells was warm against me.

And on we walked, taking a southern route along the banks, until the wisps rising gently off the river began to congeal into a stew of fog, and over top of it all, we saw, looming in the darkness, the bridge that had carried so many of us Natchez-way. We had gone the back way to avoid Ryland, which, even in its diminished and infiltrated capacity, still haunted the county. Now we circled around, until we were at the bridge's approach, and looking out, I saw that the fog had thickened so that it seemed the clouds had fallen and enveloped everything. But not everything, for in the distance rising up from where the water must have been, or where the water used to be, I could see the blue glow of halos all around, ringing out like memory, and I now felt the necklace burning underneath my shirt, burning bright as the North Star. I pulled the thing out so that it was over my shirt.

It was time.

"For my mother," I said. "For all the so many mothers taken over this bridge from which there can be no return."

And then I looked at Thena, and I saw now she was softly illuminated in blue light emanating from the necklace of shells.

"For all the mothers who have remained," I said, with one hand clasping hers and the other on her cheek. "Who carry on in the name of those who do not return."

I turned back to the bridge now and began to walk, and as I did saw the tendrils of fog lapping over the bridge and the blue lights dancing softly in the distance on what would have been the far end, though I knew that night that no such end would be our destination.

"Thena," I said. "My dear Thena. I have told you much about me, but I have never revealed the essence of all that has guided me, for all of it has been for so long tucked away, hidden in a fog as thick as what surrounds us. It had to be as such, for I was too young to bear what happened, too young to survive with the memory.

"You know that my mother is Rose. And my father is Howell Walker. I was the product of their outrageous union. I was not alone. My brother, Maynard, was born two years before me, to the lady of Lockless, and it was believed that his blood carried all that was good and noble of the old place and he should someday make for a wise and careful heir, for the blood was magic, science, and destiny. But I defied the blood, and so defied destiny, and I think now, knowing all I know, that it was my lost mother who made it so.

"For so long I could not see, could not remember, but I see it all now. Her bright joyous eyes, her smile, her dark-red skin. And I remember her stories of the world that was, stories brought across from water, stories she would share only at night, before bed, if I had been a good boy that day. I remember how the stories glowed in my mind, how they filled our nights with colors. I remember Cuffee, who tucked the drum into his bones. And Mami Wata, who lived in that paradise under the sea, where we would all arrive, after our Task, and find our reward."

And now the fog gathered around us, and I felt the bridge disappear under my feet. Thena still had my hand, and I could feel the heat pushing out from the shell necklace all around me, and the waves that once marked the river were quiet and low.

"But Cuffee, with the drum tucked into his bones, was in the now time, in the midst of the Task. And my mother had the drum beating in each and every one of her bones. There were stories when she danced, maybe more true than stories in her words. I remember her patting juba with her sister Emma, how the shell necklace would shake, how the jar of water stayed fixed upon her head. And those were the good years, good years, under the Task. But the Task is the Task, and I do believe my mother, my aunt Emma, danced as they did because they knew what good there was could not last."

And at this, they came, the phantoms that I had seen flittering about that fateful evening. They were all around us, and I could see that it was Holiday, a Holiday I remembered, when I was five, and it was still the high times of Elm County, and Howell Walker had sent demijohns down to the Street. And down near the bonfire, I saw them, my mother and my aunt Emma, trading dances back and forth. I stopped here and watched, for though the moment was conjured up by me, I wanted to savor it, but when I tried, I saw them begin to fade from me, fade like mortal life and mortal memory, and I knew that I must keep telling the story.

"The world changed. Tobacco fell. I remember the strange men with their worried faces. I remember the soil now hard and the old manses along the Goose left to possums and field-rats. And I remember that there were fewer uncles about; that cousins were off on long jaunts that did not end. And I remember how we were conducted over the bridge, off to Natchez. And I remember because I was there."

And now, where the phantoms had once danced before us, we saw that these same men and women were walking before us, and where they had once worn looks of great joy, there was now sorrow, and a longing in their eyes deep as the river itself, and where their arms and their legs had once been dancing, I saw now that from ankle to wrist they were chained.

"I remember my mother kneeling at my bedside, waking me, and carrying me off into the night. And for three days and nights we lived out in the forests among the animals, sleeping by day and running by night. And all she would say to me was that we must go, 'fore we end up like Aunt Emma, and though I was young then, I understood that my aunt Emma had been sold. If we could get to the swamps, that was her aim, to get us there to get us away, for she could not run across the water like her mother.

"But they ran us down, Ryland did. Caught us and brought us back. And we were held in their jail in Starfall. I was there with my mother, and I could not wholly understand. And so lost was I that when my father came, I truly believed he had come bringing salvation. He was so soft, Thena. He held his hand on my cheek, and when he looked at my mother, he was pained.

"'Why did you, go?' he asked. 'What have I ever done to push you so?'

"But there was only silence in my mother's regard, and when he asked her again, still she would not speak. And I saw then that his pained look twisted into a rage, and what I then knew was that my father's pain was not for my mother, nor for me, but for himself. For my mother had seen him, had seen through all the noble facade, and she knew what he was—this was what her flight meant—that she understood, that he would sell her, as sure as he would sell her sister, as sure as he would sell his own son.

"My father walked away and my mother understood. She took the necklace of shells from her neck and handed it to me and she said to me, 'No matter what shall happen, you are remembered to me now. Forget nothing of what you have seen. I am soon a ghost to you. I have tried, best I could, to be as a mother should. But our time has now come.'

"And then my father came back with the hounds and they pulled me away from her, yelling, crying, pulled me from my mother and left her there to be sold off, while I was to be taken back to Lockless."

And now, for the first time in our journey, I experienced Thena as a weight upon my arm. It was the oddest thing—as though some force were trying to pull her from my arm and drag her back into the hole. The words I spoke were a power. We did not so much walk as float across the fog. I felt the heat in my chest and the blue shine of light pushing out. I could not let go.

"We returned to Lockless with a horse, for that is what he traded Rose for. He had taken my mother from me. But it was not enough. He took my memory of her too, for when we left, my father in more rage than I had ever seen in him, he took the shell necklace from me. And I ran from him. And the next morning I ran down to the stables, where I saw the same horse my mother had been traded for, and there by the trough of water, I felt my first inclination of what I give to you now—Conduction.

"I sat there in the stables crying. An ache filled me until my skin tore apart, my bones popped from their sockets, and my small muscles ripped at the tendons. I clinched to hold myself in. But a wave roiled through me, carried me out the stables, past the orchard, past the field, back to my cabin.

"The pain of memory, my memory so sharp and clear, was more than I could bear, so that this one time, I forgot, though I forgot nothing else. I forgot my mother's name, forgot my mother's justice, forgot the power of Santi Bess, of Mami Wata, and turned my eyes to the great house of Lockless."

Now a ripping feeling overtook my body, and Thena was such a weight that I felt as though my arm would be torn away, and all around me was fog and blue light.

"So many . . . so many gave me the word . . . but they could not give memory. They could not give story . . ."

My words were halting before me now. And I felt us sinking back . . . sinking into something, into the fog.

"But I shall remain . . . and Sophia shall remain . . . And the child, Caroline, shall know the North Star, which . . ."

And then I had no words. The heat in my chest stamped them out and I felt as though we had been hurled from a cliff. And as I fell a sheaf of memories fell around me like leaves in yellow September. I am eating ginger snaps under the willow. Sophia is passing me the demijohn. Georgie Parks is telling me not to go. I am falling down.

Then a voice came from out of the fog, for as the light dimmed in me, I could see another—green and bright—call out from the distance.

". . . which holds that no man shall spread his net in the sight of birds, which we are, Hi, though we were taken from our aerie and installed in the valley of chains."

Then I was floating, again. Thena had my hand.

"What is this?" she yelled into the fog.

The green light came closer and answered, "It is Conduction, friend. It is the old ways, which shall and do remain."

I looked into light and saw her there, Harriet clutching her walking stick, and holding her other hand was, my God, Kessiah.

"I am sorry for the late hour, Hiram Walker," said Harriet. "But it took some doing."

I could not speak. I felt her words were a rope from which I now dangled. I looked to the way where Harriet had come. I saw, amidst the fog, the Delaware docks.

"It's all right, baby boy," Kessiah said. "Go back. We have her now. It's all gonna be all right."

There was more, I assure you. But I cannot describe the fatigue and pain that was then upon me. I would like to give you some final notion, some look upon Thena's face at the reunion with her daughter, recovered from among the lost. But I was then falling again, tumbling, amidst all the memory of my life, tumbling back through years, through Micajah Blands and Mary Bronsons, tumbling through my many lives, through free lovers and factory slaves, tumbling past Brothers White, tumbling back into the world.

· 34 ·

I AWOKE IN A STRANGER's bed, and like the morning a year ago when I had been conducted into the river with Maynard, all my muscles felt weighted. I looked over and saw sunlight peeking through the drawn blinds. I was in that rattled and confused state that one so often finds oneself in having just awakened, but slowly the memories of that night came back to me. Thena was gone.

I stood and, wanting to know the hour, walked gingerly over to the blinds, pulled at the rod, and brought in the sun. It was a blaring and bright January morning. When I turned to walk away, I fell to the floor, and likely would have lain there had Hawkins not then come through the door.

"Carried her off, did you?" he said. He was reaching down to help me back to the bed. I managed to sit and I felt life returning to my legs. "Carried her right off," he said again.

I rubbed my eyes, then craned my neck toward Hawkins and said, "How?"

"Likely you know better than me," he said.

"No, how?" I said again. "How did I get here?"

"Your girl called on us," he said. "Your Sophia. Say she found you, just outside her cabin yesterday morning, shivering on the cold ground, fevered and mumbling. She sent for us in Starfall. We knew. Talked to Howell. Said you should be brought into town for treatment, of course."

"Of course."

"You know we had no angle on what you might say in your condition, who you might speak to and who it might come to. So we thought to keep you here. Which was a good thought, because this Thena is gone and though Howell is not precisely aware of all events, he will take note. And it is the oddest thing how her vanishing do match up well with your fevers. But we know nothing of it, do we? Not even here. Because ain't no way you had anything to do with that. No way you would countermand Corrine. No way you would endanger the Virginia Underground."

"No way," I said.

"Just what I thought. Soon as you feel fit, you may dress yourself and tell Corrine that directly."

By evening I felt somewhere close to myself. I dressed and walked down to the common room of the Starfall Inn. At a far table there were three men, agents, enjoying an ale. At the far end of the common room a barkeep stood in conversation with Corrine, who was just then laughing at some joke or story. She was in her lady clothes—face-paint, balloon dress, and purse. I stood at the edge of the room, just by the staircase, watching her for a moment, wondering why her, what was it in Virginia, or in the North, that had so awakened the spirit of revolution? And what was it that would make this woman, this lady, who had it all, risk it all? I looked out on the common room, marveling at what Corrine had managed right there in the heart of Starfall, taking root right there in the heart of slavery.

Presently, she looked over and saw me, and the mirthful look faded. She nodded toward a table by the fire. We walked over and as we were sitting down she said, "So you have done it."

I did not answer.

"You need not reply. We knew what you were, and the possibility of such a thing has long been told since the stories of your grandmother. Hawkins knew."

"I did not," I said. "And it ain't work quite how I wanted it."

"But she is gone."

"She's gone," I said.

"I don't like it," said Corrine. "It is a problem. I must be able to depend on my agents. I have to know their minds."

I shook my head and laughed. "Do you ever hear yourself?"

She was silent for a moment and then smiled.

"I do," she said. "I do. But I need reminding every now and again."

"I don't doubt you," I said. "But my grandmother, Santi Bess, she was before all of this, and this Conduction, it belongs to something older than the Underground. And as sure as I must be loyal to you, I have got to be loyal to that."

"And the other girl, this Sophia? Will you conduct her too?"

"I will be loyal to her," I said. "That is what I can say. Loyal to what she has done for me. This the second time she saved me. I cannot forget what I am working for, and there can be no distance between what I am working for and who I am working for."

The barkeep brought over two warm ciders. The agents were still in their chatter. I drank from mine and said, "These people are not cargo to me. They are salvation. They saved me and should I be presented with any instance where I feel I must save them, I will do it."

"Well then, we'll just have to make sure no such instance arises," Corrine said.

"And how will you do that?" I asked. "We are here in the heart of it, in the maw of the beast. Even with you having her title. What more could possibly be done?"

Now it was Corrine's turn to be silent, and this she did, drinking from her cider and staring out on the common room, marveling at her own work.

It took another year to understand what Corrine's cryptic meaning was, but I think now I should have seen the outlines of it all the time. My father died that following fall, and at his inquest the facts of his last days became clear. He had driven Lockless completely into debt—but had been rescued by Corrine Quinn under the stipulation that the entire manse and all who remained within its borders become her property.

And so the month after he died, we began a transformation of the property so that it resembled in form and function Bryceton, which is to say, on its face, an estate of old Virginia, but on its interior, a station on the Underground. We arranged to have the few remaining Tasked quietly dispersed into the country of upstate New York, New England, and some areas of the Northwest where Underground men had their share of land.

And with each of these sent out, we replaced them with agents, who continued their work throughout the state and even farther into those states that bordered. To the outside world it was Corrine's property. But the stewardship of the estate fell to me. It is not how I imagined. But there I was, putative lord of the manor, agent for the Lockless station.

Two days after Thena's departure, Hawkins drove me back up to Lockless. It was evening when we arrived, and my father was being served his supper. I looked in on him and he smiled.

"All better now, are you?" he said.

I leaned down low next to him, so that the cowrie shell necklace, which I still wore, shook a little and fell out from under my shirt.

"Better," I said to my father. I did not bother to look at him as I said this. I was not interested in his response. But I wanted him to know that I now knew all that he knew, that to forgive was irrelevant, but to forget was death.

Then I walked down to the far end of the Street. I found Sophia in the cabin, over the fire, preparing supper. Carrie was on the bed, pulling gently at the cover and calling out various infant nothings. When Sophia saw me, she smiled, walked over, and kissed me softly. Then, while she finished dinner, I played with Carrie. We ate together in the far corner, the same corner where I once ate with Thena. I held Carrie on my lap, and pulled off small bits of ash-cake for her. Sophia just sat there watching us for a moment, smiling, and then she ate.

We all slept up in the loft that night, for even though Thena was gone, it felt somehow proper to respect, and observe, her place in the house. Halfway through the night, we were still awake. Sophia was looking up at the gabled ceiling, with Carrie asleep on her bosom. I had my fingers in Sophia's thick hair, gently twisting the strands into nothing in particular.

"So what about us?" I asked. "What are we now?"

Sophia shifted Carrie off her bosom, so that the baby lay between the two of us, and turned on her side until she was facing me.

"We are what we always were," she said. "Underground."

AUTHOR'S NOTE

THE STORY OF THE White family takes the real-life saga of William and Peter Still and their family as its inspiration. You can read more about their story—and the stories they collected from the formerly enslaved—in a new edition of William Still's *The Underground Railroad Records*, edited by Quincy Mills.

TA-NEHISI COATES

WE WERE EIGHT YEARS IN POWER

Obama's presidency was a watershed moment in American history. From 2008–2016, the leader of the free world was a black man. In those eight years, Obama transformed the conversation around race, gender, class and wealth – inspiring hope but also attracting criticism and breeding discontent.

In this unflinching book, Ta-Nehisi Coates takes stock of Obama's eight years in power, through such iconic, unmissable essays as 'Fear of a Black President' and 'The Case for Reparations'. His account traverses the intersections of the political, the ideological and the cultural, presenting an America in radical flux and yet still in the grip of racial injustice, class warfare and institutional conspiracy. And it reflects on the author's own journey through these eight years, charting the public through the private in passages of startling intimate and piercingly relevant memoir.

'The pre-eminent black public intellectual of his generation'
The New York Times

'A wake up call . . . More compelling than almost any other public voice about the state we're in' *Observer*

'I've been wondering who might fill the intellectual void that plagued me after James Baldwin died. Clearly it is Ta-Nehisi Coates' Toni Morrison